Robert Ludlum is one of the world's bestselling authors and there are more than 300 million copies of his books in print. He is published in 32 languages and 50 countries. As well as blending sophisticated plotting and extreme pace, Robert Ludlum's novels are meticulously researched and include accurate technical, geographical and biological details. In addition to the popular titles in the Covert-One series, Robert Ludlum's best-known books include *The Scarlatti Inheritance*, *The Chancellor Manuscript* and the Jason Bourne series – *The Bourne Identity, The Bourne Supremacy* and *The Bourne Ultimatum* – among others. Visit Robert Ludlum's website at www.orionbooks.co.uk/Ludlum.

Kyle Mills is a *New York Times* bestselling author of over 10 novels including *Rising Phoenix* and *Lords of Corruption*. He lives with his wife in Jackson Hole, Wyoming where they spend their off-hours skiing, rock climbing and mountain biking.

Also available

Also by Kyle Mills

Robert Ludlum's™
THE ARES DECISION

A **Covert-One** Novel

Series created by **Robert Ludlum**

Written by **Kyle Mills**

An Orion paperback

First published in Great Britain in 2011
by Orion
This paperback edition published in 2012
by Orion Books Ltd,
Orion House, 5 Upper St Martin's Lane,
London WC2H 9EA

An Hachette UK company

1 3 5 7 9 10 8 6 4 2

A CIP catalogue record for this book
is available from the British Library.

ISBN 978-0-7528-8380-9

Printed and bound in Great Britain
by Clays Ltd, St Ives plc

The Orion Publishing Group's policy is to use papers
that are natural, renewable and recyclable products and
made from wood grown in sustainable forests. The logging
and manufacturing processes are expected to conform to
the environmental regulations of the country of origin.

www.orionbooks.co.uk

THE ARES
DECISION

CHAPTER ONE

Above Northern Uganda
November 12—0203 Hours GMT+3

The roar in Craig Rivera's ears combined with the darkness to make everything he knew—everything real—disappear. He wondered if astronauts felt the same sense of emptiness, if they wondered like he did whether God was just at the edge of their vision.

He looked at a dial glowing faint green on his wrist. The letters were Cyrillic, but the numbers tracking his altitude and coordinates were the same as the government-issue unit he trained with.

Rivera tilted his body slightly, angling north as he fell through fifteen thousand feet. A hint of warmth and humidity began to thaw the skin around his oxygen mask, and below the blackness was now punctured by widely scattered, barely perceptible points of light.

Campfires.

When his GPS confirmed that he was directly over the drop zone, he rolled onto his back for a moment, staring up at a sky full of stars and searching futilely for the outline of the plane he'd jumped from.

They were alone. That, if anything, had been made perfectly clear.

He knew little about the country he was falling into at 125 miles an hour and even less about the man they'd been sent to find. Caleb Bahame was a terrorist and a murderer so cruel that it was difficult to know if the intelligence on him was accurate or just a bizarre tapestry of legends

1

created by a terrified populace. Some of the stories, though, were undeniable. The fact that he demanded his men heat the machetes they used to hack the limbs from infants, for instance, had considerable photo evidence. As did the suffering of the children as they slowly died from their cauterized wounds.

The existence of men like this made Rivera wonder if God wasn't perfect—if even he made mistakes. And if so, perhaps his hand was directly involved in this mission.

Not that those kinds of philosophical questions really mattered. While Bahame wasn't good for much, he would probably be just fine at stopping bullets—a hypothesis that Rivera was looking forward to testing. Preferably with multiple clips.

He glanced at his altimeter again and rolled back over, squinting through his goggles at the jungle canopy rushing toward him in the starlight. After a few more seconds, the glowing numbers turned red and he pulled his chute, sending himself into a fast spiral toward a clearing that he couldn't yet see but that the intel geeks swore was there.

He was just over a hundred feet from the ground when he spotted his LZ and aimed for it, beginning a sharp descent that sent him crashing to earth with a well-practiced roll. After gathering up his canopy, he ran for the cover of the jungle, dropping his pack and retrieving his night-vision goggles and rifle.

The well-worn AK-47 felt a little strange in his hands as he swept it along the tree line and listened to his team touch down at thirty-second intervals. When he counted four, he activated his throat mike.

"Sound off. Everyone okay?"

These kinds of jumps were impossible to fully control and he felt a little of the tension in his stomach ease when all his men checked in uninjured.

Rivera moved silently through the jungle, the roar of the wind now replaced by the buzz of insects and the screech of tropical birds. They'd picked this area because the brutal terrain discouraged people from settling it. About twenty miles into the hike out, he imagined he'd be cursing the choice, but right now the fact that no one was chasing them with red-hot machetes was a big check in the plus column.

His team coalesced into an optimally spaced line as they moved north. Rivera fell in behind a short, wiry man wearing a black sweatshirt with cutoff sleeves revealing arms streaked with green paint. The Israeli machine gun in his hands swept smoothly from left to right as he glided over terrain that would have left a normal man stumbling hopelessly from one tree to another. But he wasn't a normal man. None of them were.

Their equipment and clothing were a patchwork collected from around the world. None of them had any tattoos or other identifying marks—even their dental work had been altered to make its country of origin indeterminate. If they were captured or killed, there would be no fanfare or place in history. No heroic stories for relatives and friends to take comfort in. Just a tiny headstone over an empty grave.

"Approaching rendezvous point," the man on point said, his voice slightly distorted by Rivera's over-the-counter earpiece. "Approximately ten meters."

The neat line of men dissolved into the jungle again, surrounding a small patch of land that had been recently burned by a lightning strike. Rivera peered through the foliage at the blackened trees, finally spotting a tall Ugandan standing alone in the ash. He was completely motionless except for his head, which jerked back and forth at every sound, as though the earth was jolting him with leftover electricity.

"Move in," Rivera said into his throat mike.

He'd seen it a hundred times in training, but watching his men melt from the jungle always made him feel a twinge of pride. On neutral ground, he'd put them up against anyone in the world, be they the SAS, Shayetet 13, or hell's own army.

The man in the clearing let out a quiet yelp at the ghosts materializing around him and then threw an arm over his face. "Take off your night-vision equipment," he said in heavily accented English. "It was our agreement."

3

"Why?" Rivera said, peeling his goggles off and signaling for his men to do the same. It had been a bizarre precondition, but it was indeed part of the deal.

"You must not look at my face," the man replied. "Bahame can see through your eyes. He can read minds."

"Then you know him?" Rivera said.

The Ugandan was only a shadowy outline, but he sagged visibly as he answered. "He took me as a child. I fought for many years in his army. I did things that cannot be spoken of."

"But you escaped."

"Yes. I chased a family that ran into the jungle when we attacked their village. I didn't harm them, though. I just ran. I ran for days."

"You told our people that you know how to find him."

When he didn't respond, Rivera dug a sack full of euros from his pack and held it out. The Ugandan accepted it but still didn't speak. He just stared down at the nylon bag in his hands.

"I have six children. One—my son—is very sick."

"Well, you should be able to get him help with that money."

"Yes."

He held out a piece of paper and Rivera took it, sliding his night-vision goggles in front of his eyes for a moment to examine the hand-drawn map. The level of detail was impressive, and it seemed to more or less match the satellite photos of the area.

"I have done my part," the Ugandan said.

Rivera nodded and turned back toward the trees, but the man grabbed his shoulder.

"Run," he said. "Tell the men who hired you that you could not find him."

"Why would I do that?"

"He leads an army of demons. They cannot be frightened. They cannot be killed. Some even say they can fly."

Rivera shrugged off the man's hand and slipped back into the jungle.

Hell's own army.

4

CHAPTER TWO

Off the Eastern Coast of Africa
November 12—0412 Hours GMT+3

You must understand, Admiral, that it is precisely the destructive reign of Idi Amin that makes Uganda such a shining example. We have made tremendous strides—economically, politically, in the control of disease. But the world doesn't see this. It doesn't see how far my country has come. And because of that, donors are pulling back. Problems that were so close to being eradicated are reemerging."

Smoke from one of Admiral Jamison Kaye's personal stash of Arturo Fuentes flowed from Charles Sembutu's mouth as he continued to pontificate about the world's moral obligation to the country he led.

Kaye kept his expression impassive, exercising his well-practiced gift for hiding his distaste for politicians. He himself had grown up dirt-poor on a farm in Kentucky, and no matter how bad it got, his family had never gone looking for a handout. His father always said that no one had the power to pick you up. Either you did it yourself or you stayed the hell down.

"So you can see the importance of what we're doing here, Admiral. You can understand the magnitude of the threat."

"Yes, sir, Mr. President."

His wife constantly admonished him for judging politicians too harshly, and she was usually right. Not this time, though. Sembutu had taken over Uganda in a bloody coup that had ended in the deaths of the former president, his family, and no less than a thousand of his supporters.

There was a quiet knock on the door, and the admiral watched gratefully as his captain entered.

"The feeds are up and running, gentlemen. If you could please follow me."

The control center for this operation was buried in the depths of the carrier—a cramped space designated for monitoring events that weren't ever going to hit the papers.

The two women manning the room's sophisticated electronics leapt to their feet when the admiral and his guest entered, but a dismissive wave sent them immediately back to their seats.

"These are pictures from your soldiers?" Sembutu asked, pointing to five live monitors. Each cast a greenish glow, depicting a hazy view of the jungle as it slid slowly past.

"Each man has a camera on his uniform that transmits to us via satellite," Kaye said.

Sembutu moved forward, reading the names of the individuals scrawled beneath their respective monitors while Kaye dialed a number into a secure phone.

He was feeling distinctly queasy as it rang. As far as he was concerned, fighting was the natural state of Africa—war didn't occasionally break out there; peace did. Sending his boys into a situation that they didn't fully understand and, in his opinion, was none of America's business had too many shades of Somalia. But there was absolutely nothing he could do about it. This wasn't some harebrained operation dreamed up in a forgotten corner of the Pentagon. Not by a long shot.

The phone clicked and the unmistakable voice of Sam Adams Castilla came on.

"Yes, Admiral?"

"They've made contact and are on the move."

"Anyone hurt in the jump?"

"No, Mr. President. So far, everything's by the numbers."

CHAPTER THREE

Northern Uganda
November 12—0609 Hours GMT+3

The light of dawn was beginning to penetrate the jungle canopy, dispelling the darkness that had become so comfortable. Lt. Craig Rivera slipped past the man in front of him, wanting to take point personally until the confusing twilight finally gave way to day.

The condensation on the leaves was already starting to heat up, turning into mist that weighed down his clothes and felt thick in his lungs. He eased up a steep, rocky slope, dropping into a prone position at its crest. More than a minute passed as he scanned the tangle of leaves and branches for a human outline. Nothing. Just the endless shimmer of wet leaves.

He started to move again but froze when a voice crackled over his earpiece. "Keep your eyes on the sky."

Rivera pressed himself against the broad trunk of a tree and looked up, putting a hand to his throat mike. "What have you got?"

"Bahame could swoop down on us at any minute shooting fireballs from his ass."

The quiet snickers of the men closest to him were audible in the silence, and he started forward again, trying to decide how to respond. "Radio discipline. Let's not forget what happened to the other guys."

An African Union team had gotten a tip on Bahame's location and come after him about six months ago. All that was left of them was an audio recording.

He'd never admit it to his men, but Rivera could still hear it in his head—the calm chatter and controlled fire devolving into panicked shouts and wild bursts on full automatic, the screams of attackers who sounded more animal than human. And finally the crash of body against body, the grunts of hand-to-hand combat, the bloody gurgles of death.

After he and his team had listened to it, they'd blown it off with the expected bravado. African Union forces? Hadn't they gotten taken down by a Girl Scout troop in Cameroon? Weren't they the guys whose mascot was a toy poodle?

As team leader, though, Rivera had seen the dead soldiers' files. They weren't reassigned meter maids from Congo as one of his men had suggested after polishing off the better part of a twelve-pack. They were solid operators working in their own backyard.

Rivera threw up a fist and crouched, aiming his AK through the trees at a flash of tan in the sea of emerald. Behind him, he could hear nothing but knew his men were fanning out into defensive positions.

He eased onto his stomach and slithered forward, controlling his breathing and being careful not to cause the bushes above him to sway with his movement. It took more than five minutes to cover twenty yards, but finally the jungle thinned and he found himself at the edge of a small village.

The woven straw wall of the hut in front of him was about the only thing that hadn't been burned—and that included the residents. It was hard to determine precisely how many blackened bodies were piled next to what may have once been a soccer goal, but forty was a reasonable guess. It seemed that their intel was good. This was Bahame country.

Behind him, he heard a quiet grunt and something that sounded like a body hitting the ground. Swearing under his breath, he headed back toward the noise, finger hooked lightly around the trigger of his gun.

"Sorry, boss. Nothin' I could do. She came right up on me."

The woman was cowering against a tree, holding her hands in front of her in frozen panic. Her eyes darted back and forth as his men materialized from the foliage and surrounded her.

"Who you figure she is?" one of them said quietly.

"There's a village up there," Rivera responded. "Or at least there was. Bahame got to it. She must have given him the slip. Probably been living on her own out here for the past few days."

There was an infected gash in her arm and her ankle was grotesquely twisted to the right, bones pushing at the skin but not quite breaking through. Rivera tried to determine her age, but there were too many contradictions—skin the color and texture of an old tire, strong, wiry arms, straight white teeth. The truth was he didn't know anything about her and he never would.

"What are we going to do with her?" one of his men asked.

"Do you speak English?" Rivera said, enunciating carefully.

She started to talk in her native language, the volume of her voice startling in the silence. He clamped a hand over her mouth and held a finger to his lips. "*Do you speak any English?*"

When he pulled his hand away, she spoke more quietly, but still in the local dialect.

"What do you think, boss?"

Rivera took a step back, a trickle of salty sweat running over his lips and into his mouth. He didn't know what he thought. He wanted to call back to command, but he knew what Admiral Kaye would say—that he wasn't there on the ground. That it wasn't his call.

"She's no friend of Bahame's based on what he did to her village."

"Yeah," one of his men agreed. "But people are afraid of him and don't want to piss him off. They think he's magic."

"So what are you saying?" Rivera said.

"If we let her go, how do we know she won't talk? Hell, we can't even tell her not to."

He was right. What was it their contact had said? That

Bahame could see through people's eyes? Legends had roots in reality. Maybe people were so terrified of the man that even the ones who hated him told him everything they knew in hopes of working their way into his good graces.

"We could tie her to the tree and gag her," another of his men said.

This was stupid. They were exposed and wasting time.

"Boss?"

"We can't tie her to a tree. She'd die of thirst or an animal would get her."

The man standing behind her silently unsheathed his knife. "She's not going to last out here on her own anyway. We'd be doing her a favor."

Rivera stood frozen for what he knew must have seemed like far too long to his men. Indecisiveness was not a particularly attractive quality in his profession.

The knee-jerk reaction was always to fall back on his training, but this kind of situation had never been dealt with in a way that meant anything when actually faced with contemplating ending the life of an innocent woman.

"We're moving out," he said, turning and starting in a direction that skirted the burned-out village. There would already be a lot of explaining to do in the unlikely event that he ever laid eyes on the Pearly Gates. Murdering helpless women wasn't something he wanted to add to his list.

CHAPTER FOUR

Southern Namibia
November 12—1358 Hours GMT+2

Dr. Sarie van Keuren threw a hand out, grimacing as her fingers closed over a branch covered in thorns. There had been no rain for weeks, and the dirt on the embankment she was scaling could barely hold her fifty-four kilos.

She ignored the blood running down her sweaty palm and hauled herself forward, fighting her way to the tripod-mounted video camera set up on the ridge.

She blew the dust from the lens and peered into the leafy bush it was trained on. Even under the glare of the African sun, it took her a few moments to find what she was looking for among the berries—an ant from a nearby colony.

Normally, members of this species were slim black ground dwellers. But this individual had been transformed by the invasion of a tiny parasite. Its abdomen had swollen and now gleamed bright red, perfectly mimicking the surrounding berries. Even worse, the parasite had infected the ant's brain, compelling it to climb into the bush, clamp its jaws around a stalk, and stick its colorful abdomen in the air.

At first, it had fought to get free, six legs pulling mightily against the grip of its jaws. But now all its appendages appeared to be paralyzed—probably because its clever little invader was chewing through the nerves.

She glanced into the washed-out blue of the sky, looking for the birds the parasite was trying to attract. This particular nematode could breed only in avian guts and had no

11

means of transportation of its own. A match made in heaven. Unless, of course, you were an ant.

Van Keuren sat, wrapping her arms around her knees in an effort to get as much of herself as possible into the shade of her oversized hat. Below, the dry landscape stretched endlessly in every direction. The only way she could be sure that the modern world even existed was her Land Cruiser, broken down at the base of the slope.

She tried to calculate how many species she'd discovered over the years but soon found her mind drifting back to the first. It had been twenty-five years ago this week that her father had come home with a slightly dented VCR and a box of tapes—an unheard-of luxury in the Namibian farming community where she grew up. She'd been barely eight at the time and was absolutely mesmerized by the children's videos, sitting for hours examining every nuance, memorizing every line. After a while, though, they'd started to get boring and she'd dug into the box again, finding a worn copy of *Alien* beneath a flap at the bottom. Her father had insisted that it would give her nightmares, but she'd watched it anyway, transfixed by the creature that grabbed people's faces and gestated inside them.

Who would have thought that a horror movie hiding in the bottom of a box would spark an obsession that would define her life? Thank God it hadn't been a copy of *Rocky*. She'd probably be getting beat up in some ring right now.

The angle of the sun continued to dip, but that did nothing to diminish the temperature she guessed was creeping up on forty-five Celsius. Time to retreat back to the shade of her truck.

Down was easier, the loose dirt allowing for a semi-controlled standing slide to the bottom. Once back on solid ground, she dabbed a little water on a rag, looking in the side-view mirror as she unstuck the blond hair from her cheeks and wiped the dust and salt from around her mouth.

Her hat was large enough to border on sombrero but wasn't enough to keep her skin from turning deep red and her nose from looking like it was molting. Despite her family tracing its history in Namibia back for generations, she was cursed with the smooth, fair skin her mother had taken such pride in.

Deciding it was hopeless, she reached into a cooler full of melted ice and pulled out the makings of a gin and tonic. A couple of prospectors had driven by six days ago and assured her that they'd tell the Toyota people in Windhoek that she was out there, but now she regretted refusing their offer of a ride out. Sometimes her single-mindedness could be a virtue, but mostly it just got her into trouble.

Sarie pressed her back against the vehicle and slid down the hot metal, settling in against the slightly cooler rear tire. She had no more than a day's water left in her primary container, but there was a spring a few kilometers away. Her food stores were a bit better, but it didn't really matter—she could live off the land pretty much indefinitely if she had to. The real problem was the gin. There were only a few centimeters left, and that was just unacceptable.

She frowned and sighed quietly. When the sun went down, she'd have to start walking out. It was probably two days to the road and another day of waiting around for someone to drive by. What had happened to the note she'd written herself to buy a satellite phone? Probably in the glove box with all the other unread reminders.

Halfway into her third drink, a distant shape began to form in the heat distortion. At first she just thought it was the alcohol, but soon it coalesced into an outline that was distinctly human. She reached back through the truck's open door and pulled out her rifle, sighting through the scope at the approaching figure.

It was a boy of about sixteen with skin turned almost obsidian by a life spent outdoors. He was shoeless, wearing only a pair of khaki shorts and carrying a canvas sack over his bare shoulder.

She poured the last of her gin in celebration, sipping happily at the hot liquid as he drew nearer.

"Howzit!" she said when he came within earshot. "If you have an alternator in that sack, bru, then you're my hero."

He stopped in front of her, a look of confused concentration on his face. She tried Afrikaans with no more success and finally succeeded with the now very rusty Ndonga she'd learned from the people who had worked her family's farm.

"Yes," the boy responded, nodding wearily. "The car men in Windhoek gave it to my father and he told me to bring it here."

She dug a Coke and some food from her sweltering cooler, handing it to him before crawling into the back of the vehicle for her tools. "Rest in the shade. With a little luck, we'll be driving before dark."

CHAPTER FIVE

Northern Uganda
November 12—1739 Hours GMT+3

Lt. Craig Rivera dropped to one knee and reviewed the hand-drawn map again before scanning the jungle ahead. The foliage had thinned somewhat, with trees spread out at about ten-foot intervals in a sea of knee-high bushes. Easier to punch through, but not much in the way of cover.

He glanced back, managing to pick out the man closest to him—low to the ground and stone still. The rest of the team was completely invisible, even to his practiced eye.

"We're getting close," Rivera said into his throat mike. "Anybody have any problems?"

All negatives.

They'd been hiking almost nonstop for fifteen hours, and he thanked God for the grueling training they'd undergone in Florida. His CO's philosophy was "Train twice as long, twice as hard, and ten degrees hotter than you'd ever have to face in the real world." It was ops like these that made all the suffering worth it.

"Everybody stay sharp. We're moving."

According to the map, the camp they were looking for would be fairly spread out, with equipment under camouflage netting and most of Bahame's soldiers sleeping on the bare ground. The outer ring would be children armed with light assault rifles—cannon fodder to warn Bahame of incoming danger. The next ring would be more-seasoned adult troops, and then the guerrilla leader's personal guard.

Assuming they actually found the camp, the plan was

to quietly penetrate its outer defenses under the cover of darkness, dig in, and wait for Bahame to wander into range of their sniper rifles. Unfortunately, that plan left a lot to chance. Would they be able to find positions that allowed them to stay hidden but still offered a decent line of sight? And even more important, would they have a clear path for an extremely hasty retreat after they put a bullet in a guy whose troops thought he was God-made-flesh?

All were questions that had been left up to his discretion. There just wasn't enough solid intel to do anything but show up and get creative.

Ahead, the trees became even more sparse and Rivera spotted a stump that had the mark of human tools. He signaled for his men to stop and dropped to his belly again, crawling forward to investigate.

The winding, grassy track that he finally stopped at the edge of was a good fifteen feet wide but seemed to have been created specifically to be difficult to spot from the air. He slid fully beneath the bush next to him and looked down the path to the south, seeing nothing but a lone cow grazing on a small patch of flowers.

"I found the road," he said quietly into his throat mike. "We'll parallel it heading…Wait. Stand by. I've got activity."

A young girl appeared around the corner, naked except for a three-foot-long chain hanging from her neck. Her breathless wailing was shockingly loud as she ran, and Rivera tried unsuccessfully to make sense of the words she got out between sobs.

The cow broke from its daze as she passed, but instead of watching her, it looked back the way she'd come. Dust billowed from its back as it stamped and bucked nervously, seemingly uncertain what to do.

Rivera remained completely motionless, wanting the girl to be well out of sight before he broke cover. Instead of passing by, though, she crashed into the jungle less than ten feet from him and began desperately pulling back the edges of bushes as though she was searching for something.

A moment later, what she had been fleeing became visible around the bend in the road about a hundred yards to the south.

It looked like the entire population of one of the tiny local villages, each person sprinting so desperately that they could barely stay upright. Blood coated their faces, mixing with sweat and fanning out across their clothing and skin. Adult men and women were in front, with children and the elderly lagging a bit—physically slower, but apparently just as motivated.

"Hostiles coming from the south," Rivera said quietly into his radio.

The leaves above him parted and he grabbed the girl, pulling her to the ground and clamping a hand over her mouth. She squirmed beneath him, but her size and exhaustion made her easy to control.

Using his free hand, he touched his mike again. "Thirty-five, maybe forty total. No weapons visible. Pull back. We're going to try to walk away from this fight."

He began sliding from beneath the bush but then froze when he saw the cow bolt for the jungle. At least five of the people coming up the road changed their trajectory and hit the frightened animal broadside, knocking it off its feet. Rivera barely noticed when the girl squirmed from beneath him and started pulling on his sleeve, trying to get him to run.

The cow struggled to get back to its feet, but the weight of the people on top of it kept it pinned on its side. They screamed in rage and frustration as they tore into the helpless beast with fists, feet, and teeth. A man wearing nothing but camo shorts got kicked powerfully in the face and Rivera assumed he was dead when he collapsed in the dirt. A moment later, though, he was crawling unsteadily back toward the weakening animal.

Rivera leapt to his feet, grabbing the girl and starting to run back the way he'd come. They hadn't made it more than ten yards when he heard the unmistakable crash of people entering the jungle behind.

A muzzle flashed in front of him and then another and another. The reassuring crack of gunfire drowned out the otherworldly screeching of his pursuers and he felt the hint of panic that had overtaken him dissipate.

His boys never missed. Never.

Finding a defensible position between two large trees, he stopped and turned, taking in the entire scene through the sights of his AK.

No one was chasing him anymore—they had been distracted by the more obvious fixed positions of his men and were going down left and right as they ran into withering fire. Their compatriots didn't seem to notice, running past—and sometimes over—the fallen, focused only on the men shooting at them. In some cases, the people who had been hit didn't seem to understand what had happened. They tried repeatedly to get up before finally succumbing to a wound that should have dropped them like a sack of potatoes.

His second in command had four people bearing down on him from fifteen yards away. One was a child no more than six years old and another a woman with what appeared to be a badly broken arm. Rivera ignored them and trained his gun on one of the two uninjured adult men in front, taking a gulp of air and holding it before pulling the trigger. The target went down but the other three got through, colliding with his old friend in an impact that reverberated through the trees.

Rivera tried to get another clear shot, but it was impossible—all he could see was a jumble of flesh, the flash of a knife, the color of blood. There was nothing he could do. His friend—a man he'd fought and trained with for more than five years—was never going to leave this place.

"Retreat!" he said into his throat mike.

His men broke cover and he tried as best he could to slow their pursuers.

Donny Praman was running hard for the relative safety of a ditch with a plump woman in the bloody tatters of traditional dress angling in on him. Rivera initially dismissed her

18

but then blinked hard, thinking his eyes were playing tricks. She was overtaking him.

He fired a round, but his heavy breathing and confusion caused him to go wide, taking a chunk out of a tree next to her shoulder.

Gunfire was becoming more uncontrolled and the shouts of his men more desperate as he lined up for another shot. She was nearly in his crosshairs when she leapt on Praman's back and they went rolling down a steep embankment together.

The girl behind him was crying and babbling again, but he barely heard, stunned by the image of a fat woman taking down the best soldier he'd ever worked with. Maybe the best alive.

She finally jumped in front of his gun and pointed. When he followed her finger he saw that his shooting had attracted the attention of no fewer than five Africans, who were now bearing down on them. Fast.

Rivera fired into them, knocking the lead man down and causing two others to trip over him. They didn't look down as they fell, seeming unconcerned by any rocks or branches that could injure them, instead staying locked on him and the girl.

He lined his sights up again, but it was hopeless. The two who had fallen were already back on their feet, and there were another three coming in from the east.

He grabbed the girl's arm and ran, trying to ignore the intermittent fire and shouts of his friends going silent.

CHAPTER SIX

South Dakota, USA
November 12—0830 Hours GMT–7

Dr. Jonathan Smith shuffled slowly through a stack of charts as the nurse gave him a rundown of the changes in his patients' conditions. He glanced up at her every few seconds—mostly so she knew he was paying attention but also to admire the red hair flowing over her shoulders and ivory skin unblemished by so much as a freckle.

"Jon Boy!"

Dr. Derek Canter appeared at the end of the hallway and began hurrying toward him, huffing audibly. The gray halo of hair ringing his bald head bounced in rhythm with his belly and, combined with the outsized wingtips slapping the floor, made him look a bit like an off-duty clown. It was one of many reasons the kids in the ward loved him.

"Derek. Just the man I wanted to see," Smith said. "I was at the grocery store yesterday and they still won't let me pay."

"I talked to them, JB, but the fact is, your money's no good here. Hell, I'm actually looking *forward* to writing a check to the tax man this year."

Smith scowled. This was getting out of hand. The owner of the old cowboy motel he was staying in brought him home-cooked dinners every night, and yesterday, when he'd flagrantly run the stop sign in front of the police station, the sheriff had just smiled and given him the thumbs-up.

Canter pointed at the nurse hovering over Smith's shoulder. "So how are things looking, Stace?"

20

"I think we're out of the woods."

"Even Tina?"

"Visibly improved since last night."

Canter clapped his hands together loudly and then darted off, his voice echoing through the building. "I wonder if there's a line for tips on the 1040. Somebody call my accountant!"

Smith went back to his chart, shaking his head and laughing quietly.

"It's starting to snow," Stacy said. The nervousness in her voice was obvious enough to make him look through the window at the widely spaced flakes. Not a storm that should concern a girl born and bred in this little South Dakota town.

"Dangerous driving for people not used to it," she continued. "I could give you a ride back to the hotel tonight ..."

He tossed the chart on the counter between them and searched her face for even a hint of a wrinkle. Coming up empty, he silently calculated her age at about twenty-five—nineteen years his junior.

"Oh, and you know, Jon, my brother owns the best restaurant in town. We could maybe stop off and grab a bite on the way."

It was likely that she took him to be significantly younger than he actually was. His shoulders were still broad and his waist trim, but she would be blissfully unaware of the ever-increasing effort it took to keep them that way. His short black hair was still thick, complementing naturally dark skin that had so far proved impervious to the brutal conditions he regularly subjected it to.

Smith's initial reflex was to say no—the lifestyle he'd chosen didn't really lend itself to personal entanglements. On the other hand, dinner with a smart, beautiful woman looked pretty good when compared to another night watching reruns on the one channel the hotel got.

"Do they have steak?"

She smiled broadly, though it wasn't enough to conjure even a small crease in the corners of her eyes. "Like you've never had."

He started toward the makeshift quarantine unit they'd set up in back of the facility. "Then you've got a deal."

At the end of the hallway, Smith slipped through a duct-tape-and-plastic curtain, then through a set of double doors.

"All right, how is everyone feeling?"

There were eight children in beds lined up neatly against the walls—some playing video games and looking about ready to go home while others struggled a bit to sit up.

"Good morning, Colonel Smith," they said in a practiced chorus.

He sat on a low stool and kicked off, gliding gracefully to the bed of a young girl who had just entered the fifth grade. "I hear you're kicking butt, Tina."

She coughed, clearly trying to make it sound better than it was. "I'm feeling way better than yesterday."

"Well, I'm very glad to hear it," he said, slipping on a pair of gloves and checking her lymph nodes.

Growing up in a small, close-knit community could be wonderful, but, like everything, it had its downsides. This town happened to have a very charismatic woman who was convinced that vaccinations caused her son's autism and had gone on a devastatingly successful campaign to get her neighbors to skip or delay vaccinating their children.

The first case of measles had sprung up about a month ago in a six-year-old boy living on a ranch to the north and had been passed to his classmates in the town's only school. The speed with which the disease spread surprised everyone, its transmission bolstered by the fact that the vaccination rate had dropped below what was necessary for herd immunity.

When a young girl died of complications, the over-whelmed medical staff started making desperate calls to the government and Centers for Disease Control. Eventually, word had made it to Fort Detrick, where Smith was an army infectious disease specialist. It had been too long since he'd actually sat down with a patient, and he immediately volunteered.

"How's my neck feel?" Tina said, looking up at him hopefully.

22

"Feels great. You're officially on the mend."

"Really?"

"Swear to God."

His cell phone rang and he reached into his pocket to check the number, frowning when it came up all dashes and a tiny encryption symbol appeared.

"Who is it?" Tina asked.

"My mom," Smith lied smoothly—a skill he'd picked up during his time with Military Intelligence. "And you know you can't blow off your mom, right?"

CHAPTER SEVEN

Northern Uganda
November 12—1853 Hours GMT+3

Lt. Craig Rivera dropped his empty rifle and yanked a pistol from the holster on his hip, concentrating on not letting his pace slow even a fraction. A jumble of loose rock beneath the carpet of vines nearly tripped him, and he dared a quick glance over his shoulder as he regained his balance. There were still four of them and they were gaining fast. The young girl next to him had been keeping up out of sheer terror but was now starting to fall behind, fatigue finally trumping adrenaline.

He put a round into the chest of a man in a blood-soaked Manchester United shirt and scooped up the exhausted girl, trying to coax a little more speed from his cramping legs.

The incomprehensible truth, though, was that the people chasing him were faster than he was on his best day. And with the added weight of the girl, it was now a matter of seconds before they ran him down. Rivera angled right into a stand of bushes with leaves the size of elephant ears, hoping to confuse his pursuers as they plummeted in after him.

The wet vegetation slapped painfully at his face, obscuring his vision and throwing off his equilibrium as the girl began to squeal and squirm. They were no more than a few paces behind. He wasn't going to make it.

Rivera felt a hand claw the back of his neck, and then the gloom of the rain forest suddenly gave way to blinding sunlight. The sound of his footfalls and those of the people behind him went silent, and he was tumbling through the

24

air, his mind trying to make sense of a spinning universe—the red and brown of the people falling with him, the green of the jungle, the blue of the sky.

The pain of the impact surprised him. Based on the length of the fall, he'd expected to die instantly. Muddy water swirled around him as he fought to keep hold of the girl and figure out which way was up.

The burning in his lungs started quickly, but he ignored it as long as he dared, waiting until he was in danger of losing consciousness before surfacing. Only one of his pursuers was visible, thrashing wildly, unable to keep his head above the churning river. The others seemed to have already gone down for the last time.

Rivera looked up at the sixty-foot cliff he'd fallen from, focusing on the people standing at its edge. Their eyes were locked on him, but they seemed unsure what to do.

He turned to face the direction the water was taking him, adjusting his grip on the motionless girl to get a more solid hold. When her head hit his chest, though, he saw the unnatural angle of her neck beneath the chain still secured there, and he reluctantly let her body drift away.

Above, the Africans were beginning to track him, following along the top of the cliff, trying to find a way down. He swam for the opposite shore, but the current was too strong, funneling him and all the other debris to the river's center.

A submerged tree trunk hit him hard from behind, flipping him forward and pulling him under. He tried to kick away from it but found that his right leg was useless. Water filled his mouth and forced itself into his lungs as he struggled to get back to the surface.

He could see the light of the sun, he could imagine its warmth, but the more he fought the more distant it seemed to become. He remembered the lake that he and his family used to go to when he was young, and suddenly he was there swimming with his brothers. He was so tired. Wasn't it time to rest yet?

*

25

Charles Sembutu watched impassively as Admiral Kaye barked orders at the women manning the computer stations. Three of the video feeds had gone black, and another was permanently fixed on the sky. The fifth showed a motionless Caucasian hand holding a knife buried in the throat of a young boy.

"Can we get anything on Rivera?" Kaye said, though the answer was obvious.

"Radio's dead, sir. Along with the video feed."

He leaned over one of the women's chairs. "Replay the last thing we have from his camera. Slow it down this time."

She brought the monitor assigned to Rivera back to life and they watched leaves colliding with the lens, a flash of the people chasing him, and then the fall.

"Sir, that looks like water at the bottom of the ravine, and our satellite photos confirm that there's a river cutting east to west close to where the skirmish started. He could still be alive. Can I give the extraction team his last known coordinates?"

Kaye glanced back and Sembutu met his eye, making sure to hide his anger. Normally, when someone failed him, that person's life became very short and very unpleasant. No such remedies were available when the Americans were involved.

It had been a perfect scenario for him—let the foreigners get rid of a man the world had come to despise and then take credit for it. In one brief moment he would neutralize the growing threat to his own power and make himself a hero to the rural population taking the brunt of Bahame's attacks.

But the Americans had botched the operation as he had suspected they would. For all their skill, first world soldiers were too mired in tradition and meaningless moral codes to operate effectively in Africa.

He now had no choice but to accept the partnership the Iranians had offered. It was a dangerous gamble, but he was quickly running out of options. Bahame's army continued to creep south, trying to get into a position that would allow a full-scale assault on Uganda's capital. Something had to be done.

But it had to be done with the utmost care. If the Americans discovered the Iranians' plot and his involvement in it, there was little doubt that their retaliation would decimate his country and leave him dead or on the run.

Kaye took a hesitant step back, demonstrating his weakness through his concern for a single, inconsequential soldier.

"No," the admiral said. "Tell the extraction team to stand by at the rendezvous point."

"But, sir, the fall. He's probably—"

"You heard me, Lieutenant. We'll wait seventy-two hours. After that, we're pulling the plug."

CHAPTER EIGHT

Washington, DC, USA
November 12—0900 Hours GMT–5

President Sam Adams Castilla put his feet up on a heavy pine coffee table he'd brought with him from the governor's mansion in Santa Fe. The décor in the Oval Office had evolved since he'd first moved in, objects from home being slowly replaced with things he'd received on his official travels. A reminder of the magnitude and scope of his responsibilities.

"Any questions, sir?"

Lawrence Drake, the director of the CIA, was sitting across from him in a wingback chair that had been a gift from the French—a people that would immediately declare war if they ever saw the native American blanket it had been reupholstered with.

"About North Korea?"

"Yes, sir."

Castilla frowned thoughtfully. It seemed like these intelligence briefings got more complicated and more depressing every time he sat down to one. China, Russia, Israel, the Middle East—impossibly complex individual pieces intertwined into an utterly unfathomable whole.

"No, let's move on, Larry. What's next?"

"Iran."

Castilla's frown deepened. There was only one thing he wanted to talk about that day, and it seemed they were never going to get around to it. He waved the DCI on impatiently.

"Thank you, sir. The antigovernment demonstration last

week in Tehran numbered at least ten thousand—"

"Were there casualties?"

"Our information is a little shaky, but we're estimating a little over a hundred injured. Two confirmed dead—one person was trampled after tear gas was thrown by government forces, and one died in the hospital from injuries sustained in an attack by riot police."

"I saw the video on CNN," Castilla said. "A lot of chaos for a country that likes order."

Drake nodded gravely. "Iran's destabilizing faster than anyone anticipated, sir. Ayatollah Khamenei is getting more and more hard-line in the face of the opposition. We have reports of the secret police going after dissidents' families all the way out to cousins. And there are rumors of an upcoming purge of government workers who've been deemed too liberal. We've seen this a thousand times throughout history. When the paranoia hits this pitch, collapse can't be far behind."

"Time frame?"

"Hard to say. There are a lot of variables and we're fairly blind in that country. Having said that, I wouldn't be surprised if we saw it happen within the next eighteen months."

Castilla drew in a long breath and let it out slowly. "Can't say that I'll be sad to see them go."

The edges of Drake's mouth tightened perceptibly.

"What?"

"Sir?"

"I know that look, Larry. What?"

"The enemy of our enemy is not necessarily our friend."

"Farrokh."

Drake didn't bother to hide his distaste at the utterance of the Iranian resistance leader's name. "The sanctions we put in place have been somewhat effective, but much more important is the fact that the government just doesn't have the support of young people or intellectuals. And let's face it, building a nuke without those two groups can be pretty time-consuming."

"But Farrokh *does* have the support of the youth and intellectuals."

"Yes, sir. We still don't know much about him, but we know he's a wizard with technology—particularly cell phones and the Internet. The way he uses music from alternative Middle Eastern artists and historical video to drum up support would put most Western campaign consultants to shame. What we have to focus on, though, is that his message isn't pro-West. He wants change, but at his core, he's a nationalist."

"Come on, Larry. You can't be suggesting that having a progressive democracy in there could be worse than what we have now."

Drake didn't answer immediately, and Castilla waited. He'd made it clear from his first day in office that everyone was free—in fact obligated—to speak their mind inside the walls of the Oval Office. The best way to lose your job in his administration was to hand out politically sanitized information that caused him to get caught out in front of a camera.

"Sir, fundamentalists tend to be backward-thinking people who can be played off each other, isolated, and bribed. Farrokh is different. Under someone like him, Iran could very easily get over the technical barriers keeping it from becoming a nuclear power. But that's not all. So far, Khamenei's success in using the region's instability to increase Iran's influence has been fairly limited. People are suspicious of the Iranians, and the Sunnis aren't anxious to see an increase in Shia power. Farrokh is seen as being much less divisive by the people trying to shake up the status quo—and I'm not just talking about liberals and progressives. There's a very real danger that, under someone like him, we could see the Middle East unify into something resembling the Soviet bloc. Only with a much more convenient and effective weapon ..."

"Oil."

"Yes, sir."

Castilla leaned back and sank a little deeper into the leather sofa.

Farrokh was a ghost. In fact, many people in the intelligence community didn't even believe he existed, hypothesizing that he was just an avatar for the people pulling the strings of the Iranian resistance. As a career politician, though, Castilla knew better. Composites couldn't take the reins of power—that was something reserved for individuals. And whoever this Farrokh was, he wanted his hands on those reins something awful.

The truth was that as unstable as the region looked, it was actually worse. The Iranians were financing any group sympathetic to them or antagonistic to the United States, the Israelis had their fingers hovering over the button, and the few remaining stable Muslim governments were using back channels to urge U.S. military action. Of course, if America did move against Iran, those same governments would provide little more than a quiet thank-you while publicly declaring jihad on the Christian invaders.

"The devil you know, right?" Castilla said finally.

"I think we need to consider that a takeover by Farrokh might actually turn out to be detrimental to our interests. And in light of that, I think we should act on—"

Castilla held up a hand. "We've been over this before, Larry. I'm not going to keep an entire country in the Dark Ages over a bunch of 'maybes' and 'coulds'. Change can be dangerous as hell, but it can also provide opportunities. Giving up the possibility of a decent relationship with a democratic Iran in favor of perpetuating the current disaster is too defeatist for my blood."

"Is it defeatism, Mr. President? Or realism?"

Castilla folded his hands over a belly that seemed to expand and contract with his stress level. "I figure that when you have no idea what you're doing, you're better off not doing anything. Now, let's move on."

"But, sir—"

"We're moving on, Larry."

As usual, Drake's face was an impenetrable mask—something that had always made Castilla uncomfortable. He relied on his gift for seeing through people and it made him nervous when he couldn't.

"The only thing we have left on the agenda is the matter in Uganda."

Castilla's feet slid to the floor and he leaned forward, focusing his full attention on the DCI. "Have we figured out what happened?"

"Apparently, the same thing that happened to the force the AU sent to track down Bahame. We believe our entire team was wiped out, though it's possible that the team leader survived. We have people waiting for him, but honestly, I think we're wasting our time—"

"Like hell we are!" Castilla said, his voice rising to something just below a shout. "No one saw that man die, and we're not going to abandon him."

"I wasn't suggesting we should, sir."

The president stared down at the carpet for a moment. He'd sent those soldiers in against everyone's recommendation. As much as it horrified him to get into bed with Charles Sembutu, the atrocities being perpetrated by Caleb Bahame had become too grotesque to ignore.

"I'm sorry," Castilla said when he finally looked up again. "I know that's not what you were saying, Larry. And I know you were against this from the start."

Drake watched Castilla settle back into the sofa again. Politicians liked action without consequence—to create a show that would please their constituents but not actually cause anything to happen that would be tangible enough to garner criticism. And while Castilla was more impressive than most, he was no different. Sometimes you rolled the dice and lost. Sometimes you sent men to die.

"Did you watch the video?" the president said finally.

Drake didn't allow himself to react but felt the anger well up inside him. Kaye. That overambitious navy hack had made an end run around him and sent the raw feeds from the soldiers' cameras directly to the White House.

"Yes, sir. I reviewed it this morning."

"Have you ever seen anything like that? What the hell was

going on out there? Have your people been able to come up with an explanation?"

Drake considered his answer carefully. The information he'd been feeding the White House on Uganda was carefully massaged to include only the bare minimum necessary to keep the CIA from looking like it was withholding—and even that had been enough to get them into this pointless and extremely inconvenient skirmish. Did Castilla know more than what was included in the agency briefings? Did he have other sources?

"I'm sorry, sir. An explanation?"

Castilla's exasperation was obvious and expected. "Our top special ops team was wiped out by a bunch of unarmed Africans, some who looked like women and children to me. You don't think that demands some sort of explanation?"

There was nothing in the president's demeanor that suggested he was suspicious, and Drake had no choice but to move forward based on that very dangerous assumption.

"No, sir, I don't. Bahame was tipped off that they were coming and he sent some of his soldiers to intercept them."

"Soldiers? Those weren't soldiers, Larry."

"I respectfully disagree. That was a typical representation of the army Bahame's put together by raiding villages and giving the people living in them the choice of dying or fighting for him. In the context of Africa, this isn't new."

Castilla was clearly shaken, as anyone who saw that video would be, and Drake decided to take advantage of the president's momentary weakness.

"Sir, Bahame is as bad as they come, and you tried to help. I feel for the Ugandans, but this is an African problem. What can we do? Send a battalion? Neither the AU or Sembutu are going to go for that, and even if we could convince them, where would we get the troops? We've been down this road before, sir, and it doesn't lead anywhere."

"So you're telling me that you don't think there's anything on that tape that's unusual?"

"I'm sorry, sir, but I don't. Our men were outnumbered eight to one by a bunch of people brainwashed into thinking

Bahame is some kind of god. To some extent, a small team's survival in this kind of a tactical situation hinges on generating fear—if you shoot enough people, the others will break and run. That didn't work in this case."

"Your recommendation?"

"We bury our dead and walk away."

Castilla nodded slowly but didn't speak.

"Is that all, sir?"

"Yeah. That's all. Thanks, Larry."

Alone again, President Castilla walked to the windows behind his desk and looked out at the clouds boiling over DC. He didn't turn when the side door to his office opened. "You heard?"

"I did."

"Thoughts?"

"I gave you that video because I knew you'd want to see it, Sam. But in this case, I have to agree with Larry."

Castilla turned and watched Fred Klein settle into a chair. He looked a lot older than he did a few years ago—his hair had receded another inch and he'd lost so much weight that his suit seem to swallow him. Being the president's most trusted friend wasn't an easy job.

"I sent them there, Fred. And now everyone just wants to forget about them."

"No one wants to forget. It's just that this is a fight you're never going to win."

"You've spent most of your life in intel, Fred. Tell me you've seen something like that video before."

Klein took off his glasses and wiped them on his tie. "I can't say that I have."

"Something isn't right here," Castilla said, taking a seat on the sofa across from him. "I want you to use your resources to look into this for me. I need to know what happened, Fred. I need to be able to sleep at night."

A nearly imperceptible smile flickered across Klein's lips as he continued to polish his lenses.

Castilla's eyes narrowed. "God, I hate being predictable."

CHAPTER NINE

Western Cape, South Africa
November 12—1701 Hours GMT+2

The town of Paarl, South Africa, and the granite domes that framed it, were just visible in the afternoon light. Grape-vines radiated in every direction, the neat rows eventually disappearing into rolling hills.

Sarie van Keuren swung her Land Cruiser onto an empty rural road and squinted into the sun. She should have stopped for the night in Springbok but hadn't been able to bring herself to do it. Twenty-one hours, thirteen cups of coffee, and an embarrassingly large bag of farm-stall saus-ages later, home was less than a kilometer away.

She slowed and veered onto a gravel track, skidding to a stop in front of the century-old wall she'd spent two years restoring. At the press of a button, the flower-covered gate began to swing open and she eased through, stopping in front of a meticulously whitewashed Cape Dutch farmhouse.

None of her friends understood why she lived alone in what they referred to as the "hinterlands", and sometimes she wasn't sure either. Every six months or so she got to thinking about moving into Cape Town and leaving behind the forty-five-minute commute to the university where she worked, but when it came to actually calling an estate agent, she could never bring herself to do it.

Two of the many reasons for her reluctance came barrel-ing around the house as she turned off the ignition. They jumped up on the car door, adding to the deep gouges their claws had made over the years and fighting to get their faces through the open window. Sarie pulled away, but she was a fraction too slow to avoid getting a wet tongue in her ear. "Halla! Ingwe! Down!"

They ignored her, barking joyously as she stuck a foot against the door and shoved it open against the weight of the two Rhodesian ridge-backs. A rack of specimen jars with ants still clinging to the stalks inside were resting on the passenger seat, and she held them over her head as she fought her way to the front door.

She set the jars next to the mail her caretaker had piled on an old sideboard and knelt, rubbing the dogs' heads and trying to keep out of slobbering range.

"Did Mandisa feed you today?" she said in Afrikaans. "No? Okay, let's get you two troublemakers something to eat."

Maybe her friends were only half right, she mused as she lugged a heavy bag of dog food from the pantry. It could be that living in the country wasn't the problem. Maybe the problem was the alone part. It was so easy for her to bury herself in work, to shut everything else out. But where would that leave her in the end?

Dembe Kaikara peered over the lip of the irrigation ditch at the gate across the road. Through the bars, he saw the woman begin unloading her truck, teetering back and forth beneath armloads of cameras, camping gear, and scientific equipment.

When he was told she was a college professor, he'd pictured a sagging old woman with gray hair and thick glasses—the stern, disapproving face of the Belgian nun who had come to his village so many years ago to teach reading and the white man's religion.

Sarie van Keuren was none of those things. Even from this distance, he could see the well-defined muscles in her arms and the athletic grace of her movement. Her hair, like the Land Cruiser, was covered with a layer of dust, but when it was cleaned it would once again be the sun-bleached blond he found so exotic.

36

She would fight. He could almost feel her beneath him, trying to use the strength that she was so confident in until she finally understood that she was nothing and succumbed to his power. Maybe when she was no longer of use, she would be presented to him as a reward for his loyalty.

Kaikara retreated back into the ditch and pulled a phone from his pocket, dialing a number from memory.

"Yes."

"She is here."

"And the road?"

"There is no traffic and no other houses for more than a kilometer. It will be easy."

"Nothing is easy!"

The sudden anger in the voice caused a jolt of adrenaline to course through him. "She is just a woman. I've never failed you before. And I never will."

"Wait until night when she's asleep."

The voice was calm again, and Kaikara let out a silent, grateful breath. "I understand."

"The code to her gate is four-three-nine-six. Do you understand?"

He pulled out a pistol and used the barrel to draw the numbers into the dirt just like the Belgian woman had taught him. "Yes, I have it."

CHAPTER TEN

Prince George's County, Maryland, USA
November 13—1112 Hours GMT–5

Jon Smith leaned over the wheel of his 1968 Triumph, bringing his face close enough to the windshield that a bank of well-hidden cameras could ID him. A moment later a gate designed to look much less formidable than it really was swung inward, allowing him to idle onto the lush grounds of what the sign said was the Anacostia Seagoing Yacht Club.

He weaved through the utilitarian buildings, finally turning to parallel a lengthy dock full of what appeared to be well-maintained boats. In truth, they were unused boats—brought in and out at intervals designed to make things look credible to the other marinas in the area.

It was hard for him to get used to the fact that Covert-One had grown to the point that it rated an honest-to-God headquarters. When the president had first authorized it, they'd been nothing but a loose collection of independent operators with complementary areas of expertise and a convenient lack of personal entanglements. Funding had been—and still was—completely black, consisting of tax dollars quietly diverted from much more mundane government projects and agencies.

Covert-One was partially a victim of its own success and partially a victim of the failures of the traditional intel agencies. The creation of Homeland Security, which was supposed to streamline communication between critical branches of government, had instead created a battleship of a bureaucracy paralyzed with turf wars, politics, and ass covering.

C1's unique ability to move quickly and decisively, unfettered by the normal approval process and administrative battles, made it a formidable, if entirely illegal, weapon in the president's arsenal.

"Jon," Fred Klein said, standing and extending a hand over his simple desk. "I'm sorry to take you away from those kids."

"No problem. They're all out of the woods, and a friend of mine at the CDC agreed to keep an eye on things for me. So what's up?"

Klein looked strangely uncertain as he sat, pulling a pipe from his drawer and lighting it. An overhead fan started automatically, drawing the smoke upward.

"I'm honestly not sure we should be getting involved in this at all, Jon. As you know, I spend a lot of time finding ways *not* to use Covert-One."

Smith nodded. The secrecy surrounding the organization was both ridiculously oppressive and entirely necessary. Every time Klein unleashed his people, he risked exposure—something that would be a disaster for both the administration and the country as a whole.

"I take it the president wouldn't agree to keep us out of it?"

"He has his teeth into this thing and we've been friends long enough for me to know when I'm not going to be able to change his mind. My hope is that this will turn into a very quick and very quiet wild-goose chase." He paused for a moment. "Have you ever heard the name Caleb Bahame?"

"Guerrilla leader with delusions of godhood," Smith responded. "He's got a force of mostly child soldiers that he's using to create a lot of chaos in northern Uganda."

"I'm impressed. What you don't know is that we recently sent a special ops team after him."

"Good," Smith said. "That guy's a nasty piece of work. Did they get him?"

Klein took a deep drag on his pipe and let the smoke

roll slowly from his mouth. "The team was wiped out over the course of a few minutes. Their leader, a SEAL named Rivera, managed to escape and spent two days crawling through jungle to get to an extraction point."

"I hadn't heard that."

"Neither has anyone else. The president is exposed politically on this. People are getting tired of watching our boys die in fighting that never seems to get us anywhere. And as hopeless as the Middle East is, sub-Saharan Africa is seen as being ten times worse."

"If it's so unpopular, what were we doing there?"

"Bahame's become more effective lately. His forces are overrunning villages almost daily—completely wiping them out. There's a panic starting that could destabilize not only Uganda but Kenya and the DRC. We're talking about a humanitarian nightmare that's hard to imagine, and the president felt we had a moral obligation to step in."

"I can't say I disagree with him," Smith said. "But how does Covert-One fit in? This seems more like a UN or AU issue."

Klein tapped a few keys on his laptop and then turned it so Smith could see the five separate videos starting to play.

He watched intently until they all went dark and then slid his chair back, feeling the need for a little distance between himself and the screen. He'd spent half his life getting into situations that he didn't have much chance of getting out of, but in all those years, he'd never seen anything like what those soldiers had come up against.

"Jesus," he muttered finally.

"Thoughts?"

"I'm still processing."

Klein nodded knowingly. "I've probably watched it twenty times and I can tell you it doesn't get any easier. My initial thought was mass hypnosis. By all reports, Bahame makes Charles Manson look like an amateur. I figured some kind of ritual sacrifice to get everyone riled up; then he paints them with blood and turns them loose. Now I'm not so sure."

"Why not?"

"I put our research people on it and they came across some chatter in Iran about Bahame. Something about a new weapon."

"Is it solid?" Smith asked.

"No. High-level, but brief and ambiguous. We dug deeper and found another comment from a less reliable Iranian source—it mentioned Bahame and the possibility of some kind of compensation or negotiation."

"Does the CIA or NSA have anything?"

"No indication that they're aware of the connection. Or, if they are, it's not something they're pursuing."

Smith looked past Klein at an antique globe positioned to display the continent of Africa. The strange reality of the intelligence business wasn't that there was too little data; it was that there was too much. Limited manpower forced you to prioritize, and it was easy to see how a few quick mentions of an African guerrilla leader could get shoved to the bottom of the pile. Something crazy was always happening in Africa.

"Have any experts looked at that video?" Smith asked.

"Just you."

"I'm a microbiologist, Fred, not a psychologist. What I don't know about mass hysteria is a lot."

"But based on what little you *do* know, do you think it could be a credible explanation?"

Smith shrugged. "Occam's razor—the simplest explanation is usually the correct one. It doesn't take a very hard look at history to realize just what human beings are capable of. It's why you and I have jobs."

"Okay, but I want you to do a little digging," Klein said. "Hopefully, you'll just confirm the psychological hypothesis and that will be the end of it."

"Can I get a copy of the video?"

"I'll have Maggie get you one before you leave for the airport."

"Airport?"

"The surviving SEAL is in the hospital at Camp Lejeune. I assumed you'd want to talk to him."

"My CO's expecting me back at Fort Detrick, Fred.

People are aware that I left South Dakota, and you know how the army is about people showing up for work."

Klein's expression turned a little bored, and he leaned far enough right to see through the open door to his office. "Maggie!"

Maggie Templeton, his longtime assistant and the only other person who understood the entire scope of Covert-One, appeared a moment later carrying a large manila envelope.

"Here you go, Jon. An indefinite leave of absence signed by General Stapleton, plane tickets, and information on the contact who will be picking you up from the terminal in Wilmington. Also, hotel reservations, and a flash drive with the raw video footage you wanted. Oh, I almost forgot ..." She hurried out the door and reappeared a moment later holding an army uniform that still had the dry cleaner's plastic on it.

"Maggie, you are truly a force of nature."

She smiled. "Chop-chop. Your plane awaits."

CHAPTER ELEVEN

Western Cape, South Africa
November 14—0102 Hours GMT+2

Sarie van Keuren could see her father—the broad shoulders supporting his overalls, the tattered cowboy hat he'd bought on a trip to America, the pale blue eyes that seemed to see and understand everything.

He was standing in front of their barn holding a sharp-edged farm tool that she couldn't identify. Curious, she started running toward him but couldn't get traction. It was as if gravity had suddenly lost its power to hold her to the ground and her feet just skidded uselessly over the fertile soil.

He approached and she reached for him, but he stopped a few meters away, leaving her to stare down at her tiny hands, confused by the smooth skin unblemished by years working in the African wilderness.

He hefted the enormous blade, raising it high above his head. The sun glinted off it for a moment, and then it came down, arcing toward her neck as she raised her arms and screamed.

Sarie jerked upright in bed, unable to breathe until she recognized the room floating around her in the glow of her alarm clock. She lifted a shaking hand and wiped the sweat from her forehead, trying to will her heart to slow.

She hadn't had the dream in years, and it had never ended like that before. He always just turned and faded away while she called out and struggled to reach him—not something it took a genius to analyze. What the hell had this been all about?

Certain that she wouldn't be getting back to sleep

anytime soon, Sarie grabbed a pair of sweatpants and padded to the kitchen for a quick tour of the refrigerator. A few gulps of orange juice that had gone off a bit helped calm her down but failed to pull her fully back to the present.

She closed her eyes, trying to blank her mind like she'd been taught, but it didn't work. Sometimes the past refused to rest.

She remembered her father trying desperately to unlock the gun cabinet and the cruel laughter of the men who had broken into their home. She remembered being slammed to the floor so hard that she couldn't even scream as the clothes were ripped from her young body.

Her father tried to get to her, but a thick club cracked into the back of his head, sending him careening to the floor. They'd beaten him for what seemed like hours, and when he finally went still she'd turned numb. Her mother reached out for her as they were repeatedly raped, but as it had in the dream, gravity conspired against her.

Eventually, the men had gone, stealing everything they could carry and leaving them for dead. Sarie hadn't regained consciousness until the heat of the sun found her through the windows. She'd looked over at her parents and saw them staring back at her, the morning light reflecting off their dead eyes.

She'd wanted to die, too. To be with them in the heaven they taught her about every Sunday. But her twelve-year-old heart just wouldn't stop beating.

She'd finally dragged herself out of the house, naked and bleeding, unable to stand because of a shattered pelvis and dislocated knee. When the farmhands coming to work spotted her, they'd sprinted through the fields, men shouting furiously and women shrieking in despair.

Their farm in Namibia had been sold shortly thereafter, and she'd been shipped to her aunt in Cape Town for a proper upbringing and education. But now even that kind, wonderful woman was gone.

As a sense of loneliness that she wasn't usually susceptible to started to take hold, Sarie became aware of the silence.

Where were the dogs? They never failed to make a noisy fuss when she got up at night.

"Halla? Ingwe?" she called, walking to the back door and pushing it open. "I've got some *boerewors* left over. Come in and get a treat."

Something moved in the darkness and she sank to her knees, arms outstretched. Sometimes a good face-licking was the only answer to your problems.

The force of the impact sent her sprawling back into the house, but it wasn't from the dogs. The outline of a man appeared in the doorway and she rolled to the side, using her momentum to carry herself toward the living room.

He dove but came up short and landed hard on the ancient wood floor, cursing as she scrambled to her feet.

The sofa was only a few meters away, and she went for it, pitching forward when the man managed to swat one of her feet. She didn't bother to try to maintain her balance, hitting the floor and sliding forward with a hand outstretched.

The holster screwed to the bottom of the frame held one of many guns stashed throughout the house. She wouldn't make the same mistake her father had.

Her fingers grazed the cold metal, but before she could unsnap the strap securing it, a powerful hand clamped around her ankle.

Sarie rolled immediately onto her back and kicked hard for the man's groin. Miraculously, her bare foot connected and he released her, again cursing loudly in a tribal dialect she couldn't place.

Her heart was hammering in her chest as she went for a tiny side table that contained an even tinier .22 pistol. Not her first choice, but still stout enough to make an impression if the bullet happened to hit you in the face.

Again, she was a fraction too slow, and this time the hand clamped around the back of her leg. A moment later, she was being lifted into the air. The ceiling fan was still running, and she clipped it with her shoulder as she sailed over the sofa, landing across an old armchair that flipped backward with the sound of cracking wood.

The man, just a ghost in the darkness of the room, was almost on her but slipped on the old floorboards, polished by more than a century of foot traffic.

Cut off from the rest of the house, Sarie sprinted toward the island that dominated her kitchen, grabbing a knife from the block on it. She spun just as he came up behind her, thrusting the knife out and feeling it penetrate flesh just before his thick forearm came across her throat and slammed the back of her head into the tile countertop. She slid to the ground, fighting to stay conscious as he stumbled backward, staring down at the knife protruding from his side. She watched as he pulled it out and gritted her teeth at the pain flaring in her head. A paring knife. In her panic, she'd grabbed the smallest thing in the block.

He rushed her, and she tried to stand but didn't have the strength even to bring a hand up to deflect the bloody knife coming at her.

He shouted, spittle hitting her in the face as he shook her and pressed the blade to her neck.

"Why don't you just shut up and do it," she said, her voice sounding strangely distant.

He backed away, his rage clearly growing to the point that he was having a hard time putting together coherent thoughts. He dropped the knife and picked up a floor lamp, holding it above his head just like her father had in the dream. But instead of crushing her skull with it, he hesitated and let it fall to the ground.

A moment later she was being dragged through her front door by the hair, her hands clawing weakly at the man's forearm.

The sight of her dead dogs lying in the driveway robbed her of what little strength she had left, and she didn't resist when she was dragged onto the asphalt and rolled onto her stomach. Consciousness came and went with her only vaguely aware of the sound of tape being pulled from a roll and the sensation of it being wound around her wrists.

Maybe she wasn't supposed to have survived all those years ago. Maybe fate had finally come back for her.

CHAPTER TWELVE

Camp Lejeune, North Carolina, USA
November 13—1826 Hours GMT–5

Dr. Ronald Blankenship pushed through the metal door, and Jon Smith followed him into an empty stairwell at the Camp Lejeune Naval Hospital.

"So what's Fort Detrick's interest in a beat-up SEAL?"

When he didn't get an answer, Blankenship stopped and leaned against the railing. "I mean, I reviewed the kid's chart, and beyond looking like he spent a few hours in a washing machine with his bowling ball collection, he couldn't be healthier. Not so much as a sniffle to get one of you virus hunters excited."

Smith just smiled amiably.

"Don't even give me that look, Jon. Am I helping you out here or what?"

They'd known each other for years, having done part of their residency together and serving in MASH units all over the world. Smith had called him from the airport and asked him to make sure his discussion with the injured sailor was kept quiet. Or better yet, dead silent.

Ironically, it wasn't his association with Covert-One that was the problem this time; it was his day job at USAMRIID, the army's infectious disease research group. While details of the SEAL's operation were classified beyond top secret, it was impossible to keep the fact that he'd been in Africa from the medical team treating him. The sudden appearance of an army microbiologist charged with tracking deadly diseases and bioweapons was bound to raise eyebrows.

"Yeah. You're helping me out," Smith said. "But there isn't much to tell. My guess is that all this is nothing but a waste of perfectly good tax dollars."

Blankenship frowned and started up the stairs again. "You're back in intelligence, aren't you?"

"No."

"Come on, Jon. I went from MASH units to three kids and a pool that leaks no matter how much I spend to fix it. Do you know what the most exciting thing that happened to me in the last month was? My wife told me she wants to quit her job and become a full-time artist. And that's not exciting in a good way, you know? So throw me a bone, here. Tell me how the other half lives."

Smith enunciated carefully. "I swear to you that I am not working for Military Intelligence."

"And this guy isn't carrying some supersecret bug we should know about."

"I think you're moving into tinfoil-hat territory now, Ron."

Blankenship slammed the bar handle of a door leading to an empty hallway. "You win, Jon. Just like always. Go down there and take a left. It's the second door on the right."

"I owe you one, Ron."

They shook hands and Blankenship clapped him on the shoulder. "Next time you're in town let's have a drink. Since you don't like the subject of current events, we'll get hammered and relive the glory days."

"Sounds good. Maybe even take a dip in your pool if it has water in it."

His old friend grimaced and ducked back into the stairwell as Smith made his way down the hall. He found the door and paused with his hand on the knob, mentally running through the list of questions he'd put together and wondering again about the best way to handle them.

When he finally entered, the young sailor struggled to his feet.

"At ease, Lieutenant."

Rivera ignored him and, teetering on his casted leg, gave

a sharp salute. "Good evening, Colonel."

Smith returned the salute. "Good evening. Please. Sit."

He did, and Smith took the only other chair, placing Rivera's personnel folder on the table between them. Blankenship's description of a washing machine and bowling balls was right on—in addition to the leg, the young man's face was bruised and stitched, and his left shoulder was in a harness.

Despite that, though, he was in a dress uniform meticulously altered to work with his injuries and complete with gleaming sidearm. A soldier's soldier.

"I appreciate you agreeing to see me on such short notice," Smith said. "I know how difficult this has been for you."

"Yes, sir."

"I've read your report, but I'd like you to tell me what happened in your own words."

"My entire team was wiped out," he said, the bitterness clearly audible in his voice. "Except me. I understand they made a movie about it. You should try to catch it sometime."

Smith kept his expression impassive and didn't respond. Eventually, the silence went on long enough that Rivera felt compelled to fill it.

"A kid came running up the road with people chasing her. She seemed to know we were there. She wanted us to help her. To save her."

"The people behind her weren't normal soldiers, though."

"Not the way we think of soldiers, sir. It just looked like random people from a village or a market or something."

"Were any of them armed?"

Rivera shook his head in shame. "A few may have had sticks. I'm not sure. Some of them didn't even have clothes. They were covered in something that looked like blood ..." His voice trailed off and his expression turned blank.

"You fired into them," Smith prompted.

"Didn't really want to kill them, sir. Just get them to back off so we could disappear. But they didn't back off. It was like they didn't care. Like they didn't even notice." He paused for a moment. "They tell me you know who we are. Who we were ..."

"The very best of all our special forces combined into one elite team."

"That's right. And the best of us was a guy named Donny Praman. He was a high school football player from Ohio, and even by my standards, the guy wasn't human. He never got scared, he never got tired, he never got hurt or sick. And I watched a fat woman chase him down like he was nothing. How does that happen, Colonel? Can you tell me that?"

"I'm afraid I can't. But I'm going to find out. What happened next? After Praman went down?"

"I don't know," he said, his bitterness becoming more and more intense. "I was too busy running."

Smith looked down at his pen, rolling it back and forth across the tabletop with his index finger. "Could you have saved them, son?"

He could feel Rivera's eyes lock on him but didn't look up.

"It doesn't matter if I could save them or not, sir."

"I disagree. If you couldn't, then it was your job to survive and report back."

"Report back? Report what? That I let my team get killed by a bunch of unarmed women and children? That I walked into an ambush?"

"Calm down, Lieutenant."

"You look like a pretty hard man, Colonel. But with all due respect, you're just a doctor. You have no idea what we're talking about right now."

Smith let out a quiet breath. In fact, he knew *exactly* what they were talking about. He'd watched friends die when he'd managed to walk away. He'd spent endless nights playing and replaying what had happened—what he could have done differently. But the operations that he'd been involved in were so classified that, technically, even *he* wasn't cleared to know about them.

"I should have killed the woman," Rivera said, now fixated on an empty wall, talking to himself. "She must have gotten word to Bahame that we were there. The safety of my men was my responsibility, and I copped out."

"Killing an injured woman that you have no reason to believe is connected with your target is a serious decision, son. In your position, I wouldn't have done it."

"It doesn't matter what you would have done!" Rivera shouted. "I was in command! The bitch was probably going to die anyway. And so she could live a few more hours, I watched my men get butchered. And then I ran—not to come back and report. Not to try to flank the people tearing them apart. I ran because I *saw* those people. I looked into their eyes and I panicked!"

"Enough!" Smith said, slamming his hands down on the table.

Rivera was breathing hard, and one of the wounds on his forehead had started to seep, creating a thin red line along the bridge of his nose.

Smith's phone rang, and he looked down at it. Klein.

"I don't have time for all this navel gazing," he said, standing. "I'm going to take this call, and while I'm gone you're going to think about what details you left out of your report that could help me figure out what happened to you and your men. Are we clear, Lieutenant?"

51

CHAPTER THIRTEEN

Western Cape, South Africa
November 14—0157 Hours GMT+2

The Land Cruiser's speedometer was showing 150 kilo-meters per hour when the sharp left turn appeared in the headlights. Dembe Kaikara slammed on the brakes and twisted the wheel, listening to the scream of the tires strug-gling to maintain traction.

The bitch had cut him!

He had a hand clamped over the deep slice across his side and could feel the blood oozing around his fingers. It wasn't a serious wound, but the pain radiated from it, stoking his anger.

The road straightened and he took his hand off the wheel, balling a fist and slamming it repeatedly into the dashboard. His orders were to take her to the meeting place unharmed. And, as always, it was very clear that failure to carry out those orders would be severely punished.

But she owed him for what she had done. Surely Bahame would agree that he had a right to take his payment. She would still be alive for whatever he wanted her for.

A car appeared in front of him, and he slowed as it passed, looking behind him at the helpless woman bound in the backseat. She had regained consciousness and stared defi-antly back at him.

It wouldn't last, though. Soon her anger would turn to terror. She would use that beautiful mouth to beg him to stop, to offer him whatever he wanted. After a time, they all did.

He faced forward again, easing back some more on the accelerator. The road had gone black again, and he scanned the edge for a place he could pull over far enough to be invisible to the occasional passing car. Somewhere they wouldn't be disturbed.

Sarie gave up pulling against the duct tape binding her hands. Her head had cleared enough to know she was accomplishing nothing but peeling the skin from her wrists.

What did this man want? Violent break-ins certainly weren't uncommon in Africa, but theft clearly wasn't his goal. He hadn't taken anything but the Land Cruiser—and that just seemed to be a convenient mode of hostage transport.

Of course, sexual assault was also rampant in South Africa, but why be so elaborate? Her house was totally isolated, and he'd sure as hell had the upper hand.

No. There was more to it than that. How did he get through the gate and beat her alarm system? Tears began to well up at the thought of her dogs, but she fought them back. There was no time for that now. She had no idea what this man wanted, but whatever it was, she doubted she would survive it. If she'd ever focused in her life, this was the time.

The African leaned out the open window and jabbed at the brake, jerking the vehicle enough to give her an excuse to roll to the floor behind his seat.

He reacted immediately, twisting around and grabbing her hair with a bloody hand. The anger dissipated a bit from his voice as he shouted at her, and while she couldn't understand his words, the reason for his improving mood was clear. He had won. And he was ready to take his reward.

The sound of gravel beneath the tires forced him to return his attention to the road, and he kept talking as they drove, occasionally slowing and leaning out the open window as though he was looking for something.

His attention occupied, Sarie pressed her back against his seat and worked her hands beneath it. The lessons of her father's death didn't end at the walls of her house.

She could just barely touch the gun she'd hidden there, but the holster was positioned with the assumption that she'd be driving when she reached for it. And that her hands wouldn't be taped behind her back.

Using her knees for leverage, she gritted her teeth and crammed her arms a few centimeters farther. Her shoulders felt like they were being pulled from their sockets, but it still wasn't quite far enough.

The African whooped joyously and jammed on the brakes again, throwing her weight toward the front of the vehicle. One of her elbows felt like it was going to snap beneath the edge of the seat, but the sudden deceleration allowed her to get a hand around the gun and turn the holster. He threw the Land Cruiser into reverse as she yanked the pistol free, but the front sight got caught on the springs.

She tried to push it forward again but realized that she'd reached the limit of what she could do without breaking an arm. A wave of despair washed over her and she beat it back, bracing her knees in front of her. One hard push. That's all it would take. It wouldn't be the first time she'd broken an arm, and it would almost definitely be preferable to what the man in the driver's seat had in mind.

On three, she told herself. One … two …

The wheels fell into a deep rut as the African backed the car off the pavement, the sudden jerk followed closely by the crack of the pistol and the acrid scent of gunpowder.

From her contorted position, there was no way to know where the gun had been aimed when it had gone off, and she assumed that the bullet had passed harmlessly through the seat until a wail loud enough to overcome the ringing in her ears filled the cramped vehicle.

He'd been hit, which was good. But he wasn't dead, which was bad. Maybe very bad. In any event, there was no reason to wait around and find out.

Using a toe to get the door open was easier than she anticipated, but getting out from under the seat wasn't. She squirmed wildly, feeling the cool breeze running over her as she inched toward what she prayed was freedom.

In the driver's seat, pain had turned to fury and the Land Cruiser rocked with the force of the driver's door being thrown open. Just as her foot touched dirt, Sarie heard the handle of the door behind her head being pulled and a frustrated howl when the man discovered it was locked.

It didn't seem to occur to him to reach through the open front door, and instead he shattered the glass with his elbow while she desperately tried to pull herself out with heels hooked over the running board.

But it was too late. His hand was in her hair again, and a moment later the jagged glass clinging to the window frame was cutting across her back. There was no way to stop it, so she decided to do the opposite, kicking off one of the seats and sending him staggering backward into the road.

She hit the ground hard, but not so hard that she couldn't roll to her feet. In the moonlight, the right leg of his jeans had turned a glossy black, already completely saturated with blood.

Whether the bullet had hit him in the leg or the ass was impossible to know, but either way he was going to be a hell of a lot slower than he'd been at the house.

He'd obviously come to the same conclusion and reached behind him for something that Sarie wasn't interested in waiting around to see. She ran past a flowering rose bush at the head of a row of vines, struggling to stay upright with her hands still bound and her shoes still back at the house.

The first shot tore through the plants to her right, and she ducked, veering left. The second shot came close enough for her to hear the hiss of it as it passed, but as she penetrated deeper into the vines, his aim became more erratic.

She finally fell to the ground in a narrow trough, breathing hard and listening to him empty the gun in her general direction.

She stayed completely still, waiting for the sound of him wading in after her, but instead she heard distant voices shouting in Afrikaans. A moment later, the Land Cruiser roared away, skidding wildly across the asphalt as a group of farmers approached from the east, loudly listing the types of rifles they were carrying for anyone who might doubt their resolve.

What was left of Sarie's strength faded and her forehead came to rest in the damp earth. She'd done it again. She'd survived.

CHAPTER FOURTEEN

Camp Lejeune, North Carolina, USA
November 13—1932 Hours GMT–5

Jon Smith walked down the empty hallway, peeking into unused rooms as he talked on his cell phone.

"Have you gotten anything interesting?" Fred Klein asked.

"The interview started a little rocky. The kid's pretty torn up emotionally."

"Understandable."

He turned the corner and spotted a break room equipped with a refrigerator. "How about you? Have your people been able to dig anything up?"

"Not much. Apparently they found a mention of similar attacks from a Jewish doctor who ran to Africa during World War II."

"Is he still alive?"

"I doubt it, but we're trying to get confirmation and track down his last known location in Uganda."

"Any speculation from him that there was something behind the behavior beyond the obvious? A biological or chemical agent?"

"Not yet, but our people just found this thread. They'll keep pulling on it. If there's anything there, they'll find it."

Smith slipped into the break room and opened the fridge, reaching for a couple of Cokes before spotting a six-pack of beer at the back.

"Call me when you finish the debriefing," Klein continued.

"Don't worry about how late it is. I want to be kept in the loop."

"I'll catch you on my way back to the airport."

The line went dead and he exchanged two beers for a ten-dollar bill from his wallet. Just what the doctor ordered.

A bottle opener was a tougher find, but he managed to pry the caps off with the edge of the counter before heading back down the hall. He needed to do better—to get Rivera to focus. The question was how.

Smith was older and supposedly wiser, but he wasn't sure he'd react any differently if their positions were reversed. He'd watched people die of their wounds while he tried desperately to save them; he'd stood helplessly by as the woman he loved succumbed to a virus created by a madman. And he'd knowingly sent men and women into fights that seemed unwinnable.

You never really learned to deal with it. The best you could do was push it away every night so that you could get a few hours of sleep free of the ghosts.

He opened the door to the conference room, holding the beers up in front of him like the prize they were. "I found—"

He fell silent when Rivera looked up from the sidearm lying on the table in front of him.

Smith let go of the bottles and was already sliding across the table when they shattered on the floor. His reaction was faster than most men half his age could ever hope to match. But Rivera wasn't most men.

The SEAL snatched up the gun and shoved it beneath his chin, squeezing the trigger just as Smith reached him.

The bullet tore the top of his skull off and they both went crashing to the floor in a spray of blood and brain matter.

Smith's immediate reaction was to check for a pulse, but there was clearly no point. Instead, he fell back against the wall and began slamming his head repeatedly into it.

He'd completely blown it. He'd been so focused on what he was doing, so mired in his own preconceptions, he'd ignored the signals that seemed so obvious now.

The young man's blood continued to flow, running along

the floor until it began to pool around Smith's foot. There was always something you remembered from situations like this—something that, no matter how many years went by, you could never shake. This time he knew it would be the smell of that damn beer.

CHAPTER FIFTEEN

Langley, Virginia, USA
November 14—0901 Hours GMT–5

When Drake entered, Brandon Gazenga was already there shuffling nervously through the papers on his lap.

"Good morning, sir."

Drake nodded and sat, breaking the seal on a folder stamped *DCI's Eyes Only* and flipping through the contents. "Is it completely done?"

"Yes, sir. I consider that a final draft. It's just waiting for you and Dave to sign off."

Gazenga's parents had come over on the boat from Congo when he was only six, immediately becoming a shining example of the American dream. His father had gone into the restaurant business, starting as a dishwasher and ending up the owner of a café chain serving cuisine from his home continent.

Despite their commitment to their new home, Brandon's parents had never let him forget where he came from. He spoke Kituba fluently and while growing up had spent at least a month a year with his cousins in Kinshasa.

That, combined with a degree in international studies from Yale, had made him an obvious target for recruitment by the CIA. And since that recruitment, he had performed admirably—becoming one of the agency's top central African analysts despite his relative youth.

Those qualifications alone, though, wouldn't have been enough for Drake to include him in the off-the-books operation he'd undertaken. In the end, it was Gazenga's personality profile that made him so perfect.

The young man still had one foot in an extremely hierarchical culture and had spent his life serving a powerful father whose recent death left him adrift. Even better, his time in poverty-stricken Kinshasa had given him a deep gratitude toward America for the opportunities it had provided. All these things combined to make him extremely susceptible to manipulation by authority figures.

"So you're confident that it's going to satisfy the president and his people?"

Gazenga made a subtle swipe at the sweat forming along his hairline. "I think I've put the best possible arguments forward, sir. Beyond the video, all anyone has regarding Bahame's raids is legend and unreliable reports from survivors. I covered that in the first few paragraphs, highlighting the level of superstition and the discrepancies in eyewitness reports. The rest is mainly the opinions of psychologists and descriptions of similar phenomena throughout history with a focus on Pol Pot's ability to brainwash children into perpetrating genocide in Cambodia. I sum up with a description of pertinent rituals known in Africa, including ritualized cutting and the painting of warriors with cow's blood before going into battle."

"What about the Iranians?"

"That's obviously not included in the report we're going to deliver, but I put the information at the back of your copy in the format of a Q&A. I've gone through every piece of information the intelligence community has connecting the Iranians to Bahame and recommended responses in the event the president is aware of the association and asks questions. Frankly, it wasn't too difficult. The intel is pretty tenuous at this point."

Drake skimmed the Iranian section for a moment and then tossed the file on his desk. "Another excellent job, Brandon. It's what I've come to expect from you."

Gazenga's smile had a slightly queasy edge to it, and he took another swipe at his forehead. "Thank you, sir."

Drake looked over his reading glasses and scowled,

mindful of the importance of maintaining his role as a replacement for the father who had been lost. "Is there a problem?"

Fear flashed briefly in the young man's eyes. "No, sir. Why would there be?"

"Because this is a tough assignment. About as tough as they get. But that's the job we're stuck with. Castilla is a damn fine man, but he's a politician. I'd already been working in intelligence for fifteen years when he decided to leave his law firm and run for local office. We're the experts, and to some extent we have to protect the country from the revolving door of Congress and the White House."

"Yes, sir, I understand." His voice had a comforting force to it, but there was still something audible in the background. Doubt.

"You've seen the same things I have, Brandon: the military and intelligence communities getting more and more politicized and bureaucratic. Constant grandstanding and posturing by the people who are supposed to be leading us. A deficit that's pushing us into another collapse. This country is on life support, and as much as I hate to admit it, the energy coming out of the Middle East is our blood supply. Without it, this country dies."

"I completely agree, sir," Gazenga said, but Drake was unconvinced and decided to press his point home.

"Can you imagine what will happen if we let Iran modernize and go nuclear? There won't be any way for us to combat their influence in the Middle East—we'll end up in a groveling contest with the rest of the world to see who gets the opportunity to spend the rest of their lives kissing Persian ass. We have a window of opportunity here, Brandon, and it's closing fast. We need to make the politicians understand that the American military's failure as a nation-building organization doesn't mean that it's not the greatest instrument of punishment ever created."

Gazenga nodded, seemingly regaining the resolve he'd let slip. But for how long? Drake was starting to see the limits of his influence over the young man, and it worried the hell out of him.

"All right. That's all, Brandon. I'll go through your report in detail tonight and let you know if I find any problems."

Gazenga seemed relieved to be dismissed and hurried from the office. A moment later a side door opened and Dave Collen strode in.

"Have you had a chance to go through this yet?" Drake said, tapping the folder on his desk.

"Yeah, Brandon sent it to me this morning. His normal thorough job. Hell, he almost had *me* convinced."

Drake nodded slowly, fixing his gaze on a blank section of wall across from him.

"This has the potential to put our problems with Castilla to bed," Collen said. "Why don't you look happy?"

"It's Brandon. I'm starting to see cracks."

"Are they wide enough that you want to do something about it?"

"No. Not yet. But I think we have to start considering the possibility that he's going to become a liability sooner than we'd planned."

CHAPTER SIXTEEN

Near Bloemfontein, South Africa
November 14—1620 Hours GMT+2

Dembe Kaikara grimaced as the ancient Volkswagen bounced through a deep rut, causing the bullet lodged in his thigh to grind against bone. The bleeding in his side had stopped on its own, but the wound in his leg was far worse. The scarf tied around the entry wound was so tight, he could no longer feel the accelerator beneath his foot, and yet the seat was still soaked through.

The narrow dirt track cut through an informal settlement consisting of buildings clapped together from old signs, discarded lumber, and wire. People sat in the shade, glancing briefly at him as he passed and then just as quickly turning away. It was a place where those who didn't quickly learn to mind their own business didn't survive to adulthood.

His head was becoming increasingly fuzzy from blood loss, and he struggled to recall the directions that had been so thoroughly drilled into him before leaving Uganda. A toppled water tower became visible to his right, and he turned hesitantly toward it, forcing the low-slung car off the road and onto the dry, cracked earth it had been carved from.

He had considered running, but where would he go? He was in South Africa illegally, and a hospital would report his gunshot wound. Van Keuren certainly had called the police by now, and they would be looking for him.

Not that he really feared things like deportation and prison—he had faced far worse from the time he was a small child. No, the only thing he feared in this world was Caleb Bahame. There was no way to run from him. He would see. And he would send the demons.

Kaikara finally rolled to a stop in front of a group of men sitting on the hoods of a line of polished luxury cars that looked hopelessly out of place in the surrounding poverty. He recognized only the thin, scarred face of Haidaar—one of Bahame's most trusted disciples. The others were Nigerian drug dealers who controlled the surrounding settlements and understood how to get things done without attracting the attention of the South African police. Guns of various types and a few stained machetes leaned against their bumpers, never far from reach.

His vision blurred and he nearly fell trying to get out of the car, leaving himself leaning heavily on the door with blood rolling down his leg. The laughter of the Nigerians wasn't quite loud enough to cover Haidaar's footfalls, and Kaikara tried to find the strength to meet his eye.

"What happened to you?"

"The woman had a gun. She shot me."

More laughter from the Nigerians. They seemed to think his misfortune should be commemorated with a drink and began passing a bottle of liquor.

"I've been bleeding for a long time," Kaikara said, his voice sounding as weak as a woman's, even to him. "Is there someone here who can stop it?"

Haidaar gave him a disgusted sneer and pulled the car's rear door open. When he threw back the blanket spread across the seat, he took a hesitant step backward.

"What is this?"

Kaikara looked down at the bodies of the young couple he'd car-jacked. "The van Keuren woman escaped. I had to get rid of her car ..."

Haidaar stood in stunned silence for a moment, fear flashing across his face before being replaced by anger. He grabbed Kaikara by the back of the neck, pulling him away from the car and throwing him to the garbage-strewn ground.

"You lost her?" he screamed. "You let a woman do this to you and then you let her get away?"

Kaikara tried to get to his feet, but he was too weak. All he could manage to do was hold his hands up in a pathetic attempt to protect himself. "She had a gun. She ran. I—"

Haidaar kicked him hard in the side, flipping him onto his stomach and then grinding a foot down on the bullet wound in the back of his leg. "Not far from your ass, is it, Kaikara? It looks like *you* were the one running."

The Nigerians had taken notice and were surrounding them, weapons in hand. One with a machete moved in, and Kaikara's words came out in a panicked flood. "No! I was driving! The bitch must have had the gun under the seat. She—"

The machete came up and Kaikara tried to crawl away, but pain and blood loss made his progress almost comically slow.

"Stop!" he heard Haidaar shout. "Find him a doctor."

"What?" one of the Nigerians said. "Why would you want this worthless piece of shit to live even one more minute?"

"Because I'm not going to be the one to tell Bahame that we don't have the woman."

Kaikara suddenly understood the enormity of his mistake. "No! It wasn't my fault. I've never failed Bahame before."

"Shut up!" Haidaar yelled, kicking him again, but not as hard this time. His own survival was now in serious doubt, but if he didn't return with someone to focus Bahame's rage, death would be certain.

"Go!" Haidaar said. "Get a doctor!"

Kaikara tried again to escape, crawling painfully toward an open sewer as the Nigerians began to argue. If he could make it, he might be able to drown himself. Or find a piece of glass to plunge into his heart. He couldn't allow himself to be taken back to Uganda. To Bahame.

"We transport things and people over borders," one of the Nigerians said. "We're not a hospital."

"Fine," Haidaar said. "I'll call Caleb and tell him that you can't help him. That he's paid you for nothing."

There was a brief silence before an argument that Kaikara couldn't understand broke out between the Nigerians. His hand fell on the sharp edge of a section of barbed wire, but there was no pain, only elation. He pulled it free from the rotting stake it was wound around and brought it to his jugular. One deep gash and no one would be able to save him. He would be free.

The rusted steel had barely touched his skin when the wire was wrenched from his hand and he felt himself being dragged back toward the line of vehicles.

CHAPTER SEVENTEEN

Prince George's County, Maryland, USA
November 16—1448 Hours GMT–5

"What in God's name is going on in here?" Fred Klein said, coming to an abrupt halt in the doorway. Covert-One's massive bank of computers and the cinema-like screens built into the walls were all dark, their power cut off at the supply.

Jon Smith finished winding tape around a garbage bag covering the security camera above him and jumped from the chair he was standing on. "Marty's the best computer guy on the planet. But he also has an overdeveloped sense of curiosity. You don't want him in your system."

"It's just a videoconference, Jon. Our system is completely compartmentalized and our security is state-of-the-art. I've been assured it's unhackable."

"Trust me, that's like waving a red flag in front of a bull to this guy. The only way to be sure he doesn't learn about you and Covert-One is to go low-tech."

Klein shrugged and entered the room, examining Smith's face with a strange intensity. "How are you doing, Jon? What happened to Rivera was horrible. But you understand it wasn't your fault, right?"

Smith smiled weakly. In truth, he wasn't so sure. Maybe he shouldn't have taken Klein's call. Maybe they should have given the young SEAL more time before running in there with a bunch of questions. Maybe he could have been a split second faster.

"Yeah, I'm fine, Fred. Thanks for asking."

"Okay. Are we ready, then?"

"Just about."

Smith sat at a small table and opened a brand-new laptop, covering the built-in camera with a piece of tape and connecting it to one of the room's oversized displays. He slapped a 3G stick in the side to get an Internet connection independent of the one Covert-One used and pressed the power button.

The login screen that he expected didn't appear, replaced by a full-screen image of the evil clown from the Stephen King movie *It*.

"Where've you been, Jon?" It said. "I've been waiting around for, like, a year, now."

Smith frowned as the image morphed into the puffy, disembodied face of Marty Zellerbach. How did he do this stuff?

"Sorry, buddy. I had a few things I needed to take care of."

"What? Cleaning your oven? Are you kidding me? Have you *seen* this video? It's crazy, man! And I know crazy."

He and Zellerbach had known each other since grammar school, when the sickly boy had first displayed both his stunning intellect and the mental instability he continued to struggle with. They'd formed an unlikely friendship, and ironically Smith's early training in hand-to-hand combat came from defending the helpless genius from jocks who mistook his mania for disrespect.

"Hey, I can't see you, Jon. What's up with your camera?"

"Must be on the fritz."

The face on the screen turned perplexed. "I'm showing everything working, but I'm just getting a blank screen. Hold on. Let me fix it."

"It's not important, Marty. You know what I look like."

"But there shouldn't be anything wrong," he whined. "I can figure it out. I'm not going to be beaten by some crappy webcam. Not now. Not ever."

"Marty! Focus, okay? We'll fix the camera later. How'd you do on the video?"

"The video. Yes! The video. Horrifying! Fascinating!

Like nothing that's ever been recorded before! Can you imagine—"

"Did you *learn* anything?"

"What are you talking about? Of course I did. So are you living in Prince George's County now?"

Klein's eyebrows rose and he glanced nervously at the bags covering the security cameras. Smith pointed to the 3G stick and mouthed "cell tower".

"No, I'm just here for the afternoon. We were talking about the video?"

"Right." Zellerbach's head faded and was replaced by a stream depicting a blood-soaked woman running down one of Rivera's men. The images had been significantly sharpened and were even more horrifying than they were before. Smith had to fight the urge to turn away as the woman began beating and tearing at the struggling soldier.

"Did you see how fast she overtakes him?" Zellerbach said. "It's like Praman was moving in slow motion."

Klein shot him a stern look and Jon shrugged helplessly. He hadn't told Zellerbach who the men in the video were or anything else beyond a broad idea of what he wanted analyzed. The drawback to hiring the best information guy in the business was that you had to live with the fact that he was going to figure out things you'd rather he didn't.

"Yeah, Marty. It's hard to miss. I figured he was maybe injured or just really tired from the hike in."

"*Au contraire, mon frère.* That guy was *screaming* fast. Did you know he was one of the best high school wide receivers in the country? Could have gone to any college he wanted to and probably ended up in the pros. Cheerleaders. Supermodels. Lamborghinis. But for some unfathomable reason, he wanted to be a soldier."

"Lord only knows why anyone would be stupid enough to join the army," Smith said wearily.

"I'm not even sure the Lord's figured *that* one out. The bottom line is that woman's going too fast."

"What do you mean 'too fast'?"

"I mean I ran simulations, and her speed just didn't make sense."

"Hard to accurately simulate the real world."

"Completely untrue, but I knew you'd say that, so I created a three-D map and handed it over to some contractors. They reconstructed it as an obstacle course on a piece of land I own in West Virginia."

"You did what?"

"I had that piece of jungle built."

"You've only had the video for three days."

"It's like they say in car racing. Speed costs money. How fast do you want to go? By the way. Where do I send my bill? Directly to you?"

"Sure, Marty. That'd be fine."

"Okay. So then I hired WVU's top sprinter to run the course. I gave him as many practice runs as he wanted, then had his best effort recorded."

"And?"

A grid of green lines overlaid the video, and it restarted, the sprinter being represented by a stick figure. He was slightly faster than Praman but noticeably slower than the woman.

"Can't be right, Marty."

"I agree. It can't be. But it is. That rather corpulent woman, running on uneven ground, seems to have just set the fifty-meter world record."

Smith chewed his thumbnail for a moment. This wasn't what he'd wanted to hear. "What about the blood?"

"It's not painted on, if that's what you mean." The screen faded to black for a moment and an image of a shirtless African man running directly at the camera came on.

"Look how the blood is laid out on this guy—starting at the head, flowing uniformly down the torso, and collecting around the waistband of his pants. I turned up the heat in my living room and ran a humidifier, mimicking the reported conditions for that day in what I'm fairly certain is Uganda, then covered myself with blood and ran around."

Smith's brow furrowed as he pictured a half-naked Marty

71

Zellerbach wringing a prime rib over his head and then prancing around with his inhaler. It was a surprisingly disturbing image.

"You know, this physical experimentation thing is really exhilarating, Jon. I thought you microbiologists eschewed computer models because, as a group, you're not the sharpest tools in the shed. But now I'm starting to see the appeal."

"I'm so happy to hear it. What did you learn?"

"That when you start to sweat, the blood just thins out and then it's gone. I'm certain now that they're bleeding from their hair."

"Maybe cuts on their heads? Some kind of ceremony?"

"Sorry, Jon—no way to know. I cleaned up the video as much as I could, but we're at nowhere near the resolution we'd need to see little self-inflicted wounds. Call me before you do something like this again and I'll build you some decent cameras."

"Okay. Anything else?"

"Just one more thing," Zellerbach said as another video started running in slow motion on the screen. "Look in the back—the tall guy with the sunglasses falling on his face."

Smith watched the man drop to the ground and skid to a stop, lying motionless in the dirt.

"Was he shot?"

"Nope—no impact. Now look at these stills and the time codes." A collage of the man lying on the ground came up, spanning almost the entire time of the attack.

"I compared all these down to the millimeter, and that guy doesn't budge. I'm pretty sure he's dead. And what's interesting is that this is just the best video we have of this phenomenon. I counted three separate occurrences."

"If not a bullet, then what?"

"Nothing, as near as I can tell. That's what's so weird. They just dropped dead."

Smith drummed his fingers quietly on the table. The mind automatically inhibited extraordinary physical feats to prevent catastrophic injury and exhaustion. That safety valve could be bypassed, but it was rare— women pulling cars off their children, people under the influence of certain narcotics, extreme fear.

"Okay, thanks, Marty."

"No problem at all. If you ever get anything like this again, send it to me right away. I'll drop everything. Unbelievable. Crazy—"

"I will. Now I want you to delete the video and your analysis."

"No problem."

"I don't just mean delete it; I mean write zeros to it. I want it completely unrecoverable from your system."

Zellerbach sounded a little put out. "Fine."

The screen went blank and Smith powered the laptop down.

"What do you—," Klein started but then paused when Smith made a cutting motion across his throat.

"The computer's turned off, Jon."

Smith picked it up and slammed it repeatedly into the edge of the desk, leaving the floor strewn with parts. "Never underestimate Marty Zellerbach."

CHAPTER EIGHTEEN

"So you've got nothing, Barry?"

Jon Smith cradled the phone against his shoulder and looked around the office Klein had set him up in. Beyond a chair, a desk, and a pad of paper, it was completely empty—reflecting the utilitarian nature of the man who ran Covert-One.

"I dunno, Jon. Bleeding from hair follicles is pretty unusual. Scurvy is the only thing that comes to mind, but it wouldn't create the kind of flow you're talking about. Are there any related symptoms?"

"Not that I know of," Smith said, irritated that he had to lie. Science was about the free exchange of ideas, and keeping the big picture from one of Harvard Medical School's top people wasn't the way to get answers.

"Then I don't know what to tell you."

"Thanks anyway. If anything comes to mind, you know my number."

He hung up and marked the man off the long list of scribbled-through names representing luminaries in every field from toxicology to infectious disease to psychology. And what did he have to show for it? A bunch of guesses. Incredibly educated guesses, but guesses nonetheless.

There was a quiet knock on his doorjamb and he glanced up from the pad. "Tell me you're here with good news, Star."

Her training was as a librarian but her look leaned more

74

toward outlaw biker. It drove Klein crazy, but there was nothing he could do—she was to paper what Marty Zeller-bach was to the cloud.

"I think I may have found *everything*," she said, sounding strangely despondent.

"Thank God. I knew you'd come through."

"Yeah … The problem is that when I say 'everything', I mean this." She held up what looked depressingly like two sheets of paper.

"That's it?"

"Sorry, Jon." She slid one of the pages onto the desk. "Did Mr. Klein tell you about the German doctor who mentioned attacks like this sixty years ago?"

"Yeah, but he didn't give me any details."

She tapped the document in front of him. "This is a note from a Stanford professor who spent a few months working with the late Dr. Duernberg on a project in Uganda. Skip to the highlighted part—the rest is just a bunch of yada yada yada."

The passage was only a few lines long and discussed a possible parasitic infection that caused insanity in humans. It went on to say that the transplanted Jewish doctor was looking into the phenomenon. And that was it.

"If Duernberg's dead, what about the good professor?"

"'Fraid not. Shark attack."

"Seriously?"

"Swear to God."

Smith leaned back in his chair. A parasite. Interesting, but improbable. He pointed to the sheet still in her hand. "What's that?"

A smile spread slowly across her face. "The pièce de résistance. You ready to be impressed?"

"Always."

She laid the black-and-white photocopy on his desk with a flourish and Smith leaned over it, reading an elegant long-hand description of a tribe of fierce warriors who fought covered in blood and didn't use weapons. Local villagers believed them to be possessed by demons.

"Flip it over," Star said.

He did and found a fuzzy photo of a dead African male in traditional dress. His hair was thick with dried blood and his torso was streaked black.

"Where did you get this?" Smith asked excitedly.

"The *National Geographic* archive."

"Can we get in touch with the guy who wrote it?"

Her expression turned a bit pained. "You didn't read as far as the date, did you?"

He ran a finger quickly down the page, stopping at the bottom. October 3, 1899. Great. The trail of dead scientists and explorers continued to lengthen.

"Any progress?"

Fred Klein had taken a position in the doorway, his arms crossed tightly in front of a tie that had seen better days.

Star immediately turned nervous. "I'll just take off and let you two talk."

She went for the door but Klein didn't move, instead pointing to the gold ring in her nose. "New?"

"No, sir. But I only wear it on Fridays."

To his credit, Klein managed to not grit his teeth when he responded. "Very becoming."

She flashed him a broad smile and ducked past, escaping to the relative safety of the hallway.

He frowned at her retreating figure for a moment and then closed the door behind him. "Thoughts?"

"No intelligent ones," Smith said. "Star found a brief mention of a possible parasite that causes insanity, but no details. And there's this hundred-year-old picture of a warrior who appears to be in a similar condition to the people who attacked our ops team. Doesn't prove anything, though. It could just be a forgotten ritual that Bahame brought back to life."

"People dropping dead for no reason? Women setting land-speed records? It's starting to look like more than a ritual to me."

Smith nodded. "Incredibly strange, I agree. But not completely unprecedented. Think of the berserkers, for instance."

"The what?"

"They were the most feared of the Vikings. There are a lot of theories about where they came from, but it seems likely that they were carefully selected for their personality traits—maybe including mental illness—and that was combined with elaborate rituals and alcohol or drugs. The bottom line is that they displayed very similar characteristics to the people in Uganda: superhuman strength and speed, imperviousness to pain, fearlessness, and so on."

"So you're saying Bahame's just filling them full of cocaine and religious imagery, then setting them loose?"

"It's not the only explanation, but it's sure as hell the most straightforward."

"What about the parasite angle?"

Smith shrugged. "I'm not ready to rule it out. You could have a carrier that doesn't present symptoms and lives somewhere humans don't go very often. Then, every hundred years or so, someone gets bit or eats some undercooked bush meat and they contract the infection."

"So maybe it cropped up again recently—Bahame's men tend to hide out in remote, unpopulated areas. He saw it, and now he's figured out how to use it as a weapon."

Smith opened a drawer and pulled out a file containing everything they had on Caleb Bahame. He was unusually intelligent and, despite being born in a tiny, out-of-the-way village, had spent two years at Makerere University in Kampala. He had been academically eligible for a scholarship to study in London but became prone to ecstatic vision and increasingly violent. Eventually, he'd been expelled.

After that, he'd spent some time as a drug trafficker, switching sides a number of times during his two-year stint in the business. Then he'd fallen off the face of the earth, reappearing five years later as the brutal terrorist and cult leader that he was today.

Smith dug through the pages and turned up Bahame's college transcript. "He started out as a biology major, but he only got through a few basic classes before he started focusing on religion. Straight As, though ..."

"Would it be enough?"

"Bahame's psychotic, but he's not stupid. I don't doubt that he'd know what he was looking at if some kind of biological agent cropped up in his own backyard. But it's just as likely that he found some natural hallucinogenic in the jungle—particularly in light of his background in the drug trade. In the end, though, I'm just speculating. The behaviors we're talking about are pretty sophisticated."

"Sophisticated?" Klein said incredulously. "They acted like a bunch of animals."

"Maybe, but they were all violent animals going in the same direction and not attacking each other. Think about the chaotic behavior you'd expect from a group with rabies or who had been dosed with LSD. By comparison, these people's behavior was incredibly well organized and predictable. If I had to bet the farm, I'd say mass religious hysteria enhanced with some locally produced narcotics."

Klein tossed him the folder he'd been holding. "You'll be happy to know that the agency analysts agree with you. This is a copy of what Larry Drake gave the White House."

Smith set aside the information on Bahame and opened the CIA report, paging through a detailed analysis that ranged from African rituals to Pol Pot to Nazi Germany.

"I can't say that there's a lot in here I disagree with, Fred. Did the president ask about the possible Iranian connection?"

"Yup."

"And?"

"Larry was aware of it and gave him perfectly reasonable explanations for the chatter we picked up. Castilla's satisfied and he left a message calling us off."

"That's good news, right? It's what you wanted?"

"Before I heard your friend's analysis of the video, yes. Now I'm not so sure. If there's even a one-in-a-million chance that this is something the Iranians could get their hands on and use, I feel like we're obligated to take a look."

"And the president?"

"I'm meeting with him later this afternoon to go over

Zellerbach's conclusions and I'm going to ask him to give us a little leeway."

Smith closed the report and looked up at his boss. "Then I guess I'm about to take an all-expenses-paid trip to Africa. But I'm going to warn you, Fred: what I know about parasites would fit on a postcard. I'm going to have to bring in help."

"When you get a name, give it to Maggie to check out."

"And I want to take Peter."

Klein grimaced. "We have people in Africa I can set you up with."

"I know, and I'm sure they're very talented. But Peter's got something they don't."

"What?"

"A perfect track record of keeping me alive."

CHAPTER NINETEEN

Tehran, Iran
November 17—1303 Hours GMT+3:30

Mehrak Omidi sat silently in the back of the van, fixated on a small bank of monitors depicting the mob occupying Tehran's heart.

The demonstration was much larger than their intelligence had predicted, and now it clogged not only Azadi Square but the surrounding streets, effectively shutting down travel through the city center. It was impossible to know if his people's failure to foresee the scope of this treasonous action was a problem with their intelligence gathering or if the protest had been joined by passersby who had not originally planned on getting involved. The meticulous organization of it, unfortunately, suggested the former.

On the west side of the square, where security forces were weakest, the crowd grew progressively more bold. A rock sailed through the air and bounced off a Plexiglas shield. When there was no reaction, a bottle flew.

International press had been banned, but with cell phones and video, everyone was a reporter. As the director of the Ministry of Intelligence, Omidi had tried everything to create a national communications system that could be selectively shut down, but the technology was too complex and diffuse for any government to control anymore. And, in truth, it was a medium that his staff didn't intuitively grasp like the resistance did. Iran's youth—and youth everywhere—seemed to be able to fully exploit every new advance the moment it came online.

The mob lurched toward the police line, and he watched the silent contrails of tear gas arcing through the air. Impact points were quickly abandoned, but the demonstration didn't dissolve into chaos, as it would have only a few months ago. A group of men carried an injured woman wearing a chador over their heads as their compatriots cleared a path. There was something different in these protests, something that had been building: a calm efficiency that suggested training.

It had been first noted a year ago when small groups within the crowds began holding fast, influencing the people around them, neutralizing the fear that the hopelessly out-numbered police counted on. Now those groups made up more than half the protesters, and with their increase in numbers came a command structure—an invisible hand that led these common criminals as though they were soldiers.

But now that hand was no longer invisible—it was the hand of Farrokh. And, with the help of almighty God, it was about to be severed.

The crowd surged again, directing itself with unlikely precision against the weakest part of the line. Omidi's finger hovered over a button that would authorize the police to use deadly force as they dropped their batons and replaced them with submachine guns. The crowd closed in, chanting for freedom and democracy but being very careful not to offer any further physical provocation.

As expected, the phone in his breast pocket rang and he took a deep breath before picking up.

"Yes, Excellency?"

The voice of Iran's supreme leader, Ayatollah Amjad Khamenei, contained a hint of panic that caused Omidi's stomach to burn with anger. Khamenei was a great man, a man chosen by God to lead the Islamic Republic. And yet, these people—these children—spit on him.

"Why don't you act, Mehrak? This mob has attacked our men; they've broken through our line. It is your responsibility to stop them."

"Yes, Excellency. I understand. But our po—"

"They are trying to destroy us—to replace the republic

with a government based on Western sin and corruption—and you just sit by. We have to show these people that the faithful will fight to the death to contain their blasphemy."

Discontent had been growing since the last presidential reelection. He himself had strongly opposed the way the government handled the voting but had been overruled. In his mind, the results needed to be close enough to appear legitimate, but Khamenei disagreed. He was unwilling to allow any indication that there was anything but overwhelming support for his regime.

The entirely avoidable chaos that ensued had given birth to Farrokh—a young, technologically sophisticated devil with a gift for corrupting youth and spreading his subversive ideas.

To date, every attempt to find him had been thwarted. In fact, until recently, they hadn't even been sure he existed. A month ago, though, their futile attempts to find Farrokh had been reborn. A chance interception of an unencrypted e-mail allowed them to capture a member of Farrokh's inner circle—a woman who had actually been face-to-face with him and who had intimate knowledge of his network.

It had taken some persuading, during which a number of her family members had been put to death in front of her, but eventually she had told them everything.

"Give the order to fire on the crowd," Khamenei insisted.

"Nothing would make me happier than to see these cowards die," Omidi said honestly. "Their defiance is an affront to God. But an escalation at this point would be counterproductive."

"Why? Are you going to tell me it's because the world is watching? What world? America? The Jews? You'll do as I say."

Omidi sighed quietly. He had explained this over and over, but the aging holy man simply couldn't understand that they were using this riot to trace Farrokh's communications back to him. Dispersing the crowd would send the rat back into the foul hole he lived in.

"Excellency, please—"

The van's rear doors were suddenly thrown open and his most trusted lieutenant stood backlit by the afternoon sun. Omidi smiled and said a silent prayer of thanks. "We have him, Excellency."

Mehrak Omidi examined the massive house perched on the side of a forested hill, focusing his binoculars on a satellite dish growing from its roof and then dropping his gaze to the arches and pillars that so gracefully combined French architecture with Persian.

He was hidden in the trees a few feet from the edge of the road, listening through his earpiece to the chatter of the men taking positions around the building. He had hoped that Farrokh would be in the city center, making it easier to bring assault forces in unnoticed, but while this was a more complex operation to set up, it also offered their quarry fewer opportunities to escape. Every road was blocked, helicopters were in the air, and traffic was being diverted. In Tehran, Farrokh could potentially disappear into the constant bustle. Here he would be alone and exposed.

When all thirty men involved in the elaborate trap signaled their readiness, Omidi started up the hill, running hard and using branches to help propel himself forward. He could hear the much younger men behind him breathing heavily as they tried to keep up. At their age, he had been in an elite unit attached to the Revolutionary Guard and he lived his life as though he still were, meticulously maintaining his body and mind to serve God and his representative on earth, Ayatollah Amjad Khamenei.

When he arrived at the edge of the meticulously tended lawn surrounding the mansion, Omidi stopped and brought a radio to his mouth. "Now!"

The roar of a car engine became audible as it raced up the long driveway, and Omidi leapt out onto the lawn just as it skidded to a stop a few meters from the front entrance. He reached for his pistol and held it in both hands as he ran up behind the men pulling a battering ram from the vehicle.

The ornate double doors flew open with the first impact and Omidi followed his men inside.

Normally, he'd be directing the operation from his control van, making sure there were no gaps that could be exploited by the enemy and coordinating on-the-fly tactical changes. But not this time. This time he wanted to be part of it. He wanted to be there when Farrokh was finally brought to his knees.

A woman in immodest Western dress appeared at the end of the marble entry, letting out a startled scream and then demanding to know who they were. She was quickly silenced by a rifle butt, and Omidi stepped over her motionless body as he passed through the archway at the back. Two young children appeared ten meters down the hallway but then immediately darted through a doorway.

He went after them, abandoning caution as he sprinted down the ornate passageway. More than a year of his life spent trying to find a ghost was coming to an end. Farrokh was there. He could feel it.

Omidi came to the end of the hall and signaled the men behind to cover him as he leapt into the adjacent room, scanning it over the sights of his pistol.

"Who are you?" a young man demanded, trying to free himself from the children clutching at his legs. "What are you doing here?"

He was in his early thirties, plump and dressed in clothes calculated to project wealth more than fashion. His round face was unremarkable and the fear was visible there despite his attempt to hide it. The great Farrokh seemed almost impossibly small when stripped of the electronic illusions he liked so much to hide behind.

"Don't move!" Omidi shouted.

"Who are you?" he demanded again. "Do you—"

"Silence!"

Omidi moved closer, reaching out for one of the bawling children while keeping his gun aimed at the man's face.

"So when the great Farrokh can't cower behind a computer screen, he hides behind children?" Omidi said as his men circled behind the godless terrorist.

"Farrokh? Are you crazy? I'm—"

The Taser hit him in the center of the back and he collapsed, convulsing satisfyingly on the floor.

Omidi shoved the pleading children away and knelt, grabbing the man by the hair and lifting his head. "I know exactly who you are. And so does God!"

CHAPTER TWENTY

Near Yosemite National Park, USA
November 17—1517 Hours GMT–8

Jon Smith felt the rented snowmobile loft into the air and was forced to throttle back a fraction when it landed. The heavy powder billowed over him, filling his open mouth and sticking to the stubble on his chin. Tall ponderosa pine were becoming more plentiful, and he slowed a bit more, picking his way through them as his eyes struggled to adjust to the transition from blinding sunlight to deep shadow.

He adjusted his trajectory slightly, using the thirteen-thousand-foot peak of Mount Dana to keep his bearings as he navigated the wilderness at the edge of California's Yosemite National Park.

A herd of deer watched him burst from the trees and head for a distant column of smoke bisecting the horizon. He'd never been to the Sierras when there was snow on the ground and regretted not making the trip sooner. The scenery was as spectacular as anything he'd seen in his extensive travels—massive granite walls, frozen waterfalls, untouched forest.

On the other hand, to say it was hard to get to would be a wild understatement. The nearest cup of coffee was a day's travel in good weather. In bad weather, you'd more likely just end up a permanent part of a snowdrift.

The tiny log cabin that was the source of the smoke came into view at the very limit of his vision, and Smith pulled off his hood and sunglasses to make sure he was easily recognizable to the man he knew was watching.

When he got within five hundred yards, he shut down the snowmobile and continued on foot, wading through the deep snow and keeping an eye out for the deep ravine he remembered blocking frontal access to the property.

It didn't take long to come to the edge of the precipice, and he traversed west until he spotted a narrow footbridge. There were no human footprints on it, but mountain lion tracks were clearly visible. Peter Howell had struck up an odd friendship with the cat a few years back—two dangerous creatures interested in occasional companionship as long as it was on their own terms.

Smith passed a pile of snow in the vague shape of Howell's pickup and crossed the slippery bridge, noting that a single misstep would end with a fall long enough for his life to flash by his eyes at least twice.

The area had recently been hit by one of the worst early winter storms in recorded history, and the snow had slid from the cabin's roof, burying its entire north side. Poking out from that minor avalanche were the mangled remains of a satellite dish—explaining his lack of success in reaching his old friend by conventional means.

"Why, if it isn't the elusive Jon Smith," came an English-accented voice to his left. "You do get around, don't you?"

Smith turned in time to see a thin, weathered man in his early fifties appear from behind a tree. He seemed impervious to the cold, wearing only a pair of jeans, a white T-shirt, and an old cowboy hat. In one hand he held a rifle upright, its butt resting on his hip.

It was hard not to feel as though he'd suddenly been transported a hundred years back in time, and Smith supposed that was appropriate. In many ways, Peter Howell would have been better off in the last century. He'd spent much of his life in the British SAS, fighting in nearly every hot spot on the planet before retiring to what he euphemistically called a consulting career. Smith knew for a fact that one of his clients was MI6 because his work for that organization had brought them together in the past. Beyond the British Secret Service, though, Howell's client list was murky—

various foreign governments and probably some private industry work. Smith didn't ask questions, and in turn, Howell accepted the fiction that he was just another army doctor.

"It's been awhile, Peter. You look good."

"Flattery. Now I really *am* worried. I've got a fire going inside. Why don't you come in and we'll have a little chat."

Entering the cabin was always a bit disorienting. An enormous flagstone fireplace was the only thing that hinted of the exterior or American West. The furniture was English country and the logs that made up the walls were almost completely obscured by regimental flags, antique weapons, and mementos from various skirmishes across the globe.

Howell pointed to a leather chair lit by the glow of flames and Smith stripped off his jumpsuit before sinking into it and holding his palms out to the heat.

"Can I assume this isn't a social call?" Howell said, handing him a glass and filling it from a bottle of Wyoming Whiskey.

"A guy can't come and spend the day with an old friend?"

"I seem to remember that the last time we spent the day together I was shot at numerous times and we were very nearly involved in a helicopter crash."

"You can't hold me responsible for the chopper. You were the one flying it."

"Of course, you're right."

Smith leaned back in the chair, kicking off his boots and feeling the blood start to flow to his toes again. "There's a little matter in Africa that I need to look into. Thought you might be interested in getting out of the snow for a couple weeks."

"A little sun and sand?" the Brit said with a hint of sarcasm. "What could possibly go wrong?"

Smith grinned and picked his jacket up off the floor, pulling a flash drive from one of the pockets and holding it out. "The password is 'Ares'."

The retired soldier inserted it into a laptop and played the Uganda video, staring intently at it while Smith sipped his whiskey.

"The god of war indeed," he said when it was over, sounding a bit stunned. "SEALs?"

"A black ops team pulled from a number of different units."

"Any survivors?"

Smith considered telling him about the team leader's suicide but then decided against it. "No."

Howell shook his head solemnly. "Africa."

There was a fatalism to his voice that Smith had never heard before—an undertone of something that sounded almost like defeat.

"Most likely this is nothing more than a charismatic cult leader whipping a bunch of terrified, superstitious people into a frenzy. On the other hand, there's some shaky evidence that there could be more to it—possibly a biological agent. The army thinks it's worth looking into."

"The army," Howell said, frowning at the game they were forced to play. "And yet they can't supply a single American soldier to accompany you."

"I'm sure they could, but you know how I enjoy your company."

The Brit didn't look up, focusing on the flames as though he was searching for something in them. "You can fight there until the end of your days, Jon. You can try to understand why Africa is the way it is. You can try to protect the weak from the strong. But it's never going to work. Take my advice. Walk away from this one."

"I hear what you're saying, but the guy behind this— Caleb Bahame—is a whole other level."

Howell twisted in the seat, looking directly at him for the first time in their conversation. "Bahame?"

"You've heard of him?"

The Brit returned his attention to the fire. "I've read a few things."

"Well, I can tell you that the stuff you read doesn't come

close to capturing what's really happening over there. Have you ever been to Uganda?"

Howell didn't seem inclined to answer, so Smith filled in the silence. "My guess is that we'll go over there, chase our tails a bit, and you'll walk away with the easiest fifty grand you ever made."

"I assume we're denominating in British pounds."

Smith grinned. "You drive a hard bargain."

Howell ran a hand through his shaggy gray hair and then just went to work on his whiskey.

CHAPTER TWENTY-ONE

Tehran, Iran
November 18—1500 Hours GMT+3:30

Mehrak Omidi paused in front of the closed door, a trickle of adrenaline making him vaguely nauseous. Only Ayatollah Amjad Khamenei had the power to make him feel this way.

They had known each other since Omidi was a young man serving in the Revolutionary Guard and Khamenei was an imam living in the remote northeastern part of the country. The holy man had seen Omidi's potential and taken him under his wing, counseling him spiritually, watching over his career—even paying for him to study abroad.

When Khamenei became supreme leader, Omidi had gone with him, starting as his personal assistant and then moving to various other posts before being put in charge of the Ministry of Intelligence. Despite his undeniable success and the respect he commanded throughout Iran, he had never felt worthy. But those feelings were changing. They had to.

Khamenei was getting old and nostalgic. His vision was perfectly clear when looking backward but increasingly hazy when trying to see into the future. Omidi considered the man more of a father than his biological one and found himself in the uncomfortable role reversal that all sons eventually suffered. Over the coming years, he would have to become his teacher's guide to a world that was quickly closing in on them.

He knocked gently and entered when he heard a muffled call welcoming him. There was no furniture or decoration

91

in the office, only tapestry-covered cushions strewn across the floor.

"Excellency," Omidi said, bowing deeply.

When they'd first met, Khamenei's long beard had been deep black and his eyes almost magical in their intensity. Now he'd gone completely gray beneath his turban and wore a pair of glasses thick enough to distort his regal features.

The man sitting on a cushion next to him started to leap to his feet, hatred etched deeply into his face, but sank obediently back to the floor when the aging cleric touched him on the arm.

"Mehrak. It is good to see you. Please come sit next to me."

Omidi did as he was told, bowing his head contritely to avoid acknowledging the furious stare of the clean-shaven man across from him.

His name was Rahim Nikahd and he was a powerful moderate voice in parliament, a cunning and ambitious man straddling the fence between what Iran was and what the mob wanted it to become.

It was infuriating that a man as great as Amjad Khamenei had to grovel at the feet of an insect like Nikahd, but those were the complex realities of politics. No leader was great or powerful enough to forget from where their power truly flowed.

"Why is this man here?" Nikahd said finally. "Why does he still have a place of authority in this government? I—"

"Shh." Khamenei touched the man's arm again. "Calm yourself, my old friend."

Unfortunately, beyond being a member of parliament, Nikahd was also the father of the young man Omidi had arrested the day before.

"Mehrak has been given a great weight of responsibility," Khamenei continued. "And it was his belief that your son was Farrokh."

"Farrokh? But this is idiocy!" the man protested. "How could he make such a stupid mistake?"

Omidi stayed respectfully silent despite his anger at being discussed—and insulted—as though he weren't there.

"It is my understanding that Farrokh used his vast technical knowledge to route his communications through your son's home. Clearly he planned for this to happen and believed that it would turn you away from me. Turn you away from God."

"My son's wife—the mother of my grandchildren—is in a coma from being hit with a rifle butt. This is competence? He couldn't make a phone call and check whose house he was attacking?"

"There was no time, Rahim. Farrokh has slipped through our fingers too many times. And to answer your question, Mehrak is here because he insisted on coming personally to beg your forgiveness."

It wasn't exactly true—in fact, it wasn't true at all—but Omidi dipped his head even farther, taking a posture of complete subservience.

"I'm asking you a personal favor," Khamenei said. "I'm asking you to forgive both of us for our hand in what happened to your family."

Omidi kept his eyes on the floor, grateful that the fury in them would be invisible to the fat parliamentarian sitting across from him. In the world of politics, there were always strings attached. One day Khamenei would have to repay the debt that Omidi had created. He'd let Farrokh outsmart him. Just as he had so many times in the past.

Nikahd didn't answer immediately, undoubtedly considering his position. He had to be very careful not to move so far left as to put himself in danger from the establishment but also not to move so far right that he wouldn't be embraced by the youth movement should it prevail.

"For you, Excellency, of course."

Khamenei put out a hand and Nikahd kissed it. "I'm grateful to have men like you around me, Rahim. Men still loyal to Islam."

Knowing he had been dismissed, Nikahd stood, but not before giving Omidi a glare that spoke volumes. If he should come out on top in this prolonged power struggle, he would see to it that Omidi and his family disappeared.

They watched him go, and Khamenei waited until the door was fully closed before he spoke again.

"That was very difficult, Mehrak. He is a powerful man, and make no mistake: I've made an enemy of him today."

"Yes, Excellency."

"You defied my orders and failed to fire on the crowd—emboldening them, making them think we're weak and afraid. And then this ..."

"I will step down immediately."

Khamenei smiled thinly. "A hollow offer, Mehrak. You know there's no one else I trust implicitly. Not any longer."

Mehrak acknowledged the compliment with a nod. "I serve at your pleasure, Excellency."

Khamenei recognized that enemies of the revolution were everywhere, but he didn't fully comprehend the extent to which the cancer had taken hold—Western fashion and video games, the Internet. Every day the tide grew stronger and the guardians of the faith grew older.

Support for the government was crumbling. The popularity of the nuclear program that was so broad a year ago had succumbed to the pressure of the outside world. Iran's youth would rather have portable music players and political freedom than strength and faith.

"I've known you since you were a child, Mehrak. You have more to say."

He pondered his words for a moment before speaking. "I am beaten, Excellency."

"What? I don't understand."

"Farrokh and his people have an inherent understanding of technology that I can't replicate."

"I don't expect you to personally understand everything, Mehrak— that's for God alone. What I expect you to do is build a team who can defeat him."

"How, Excellency? The people with that kind of expertise in our own country are sympathetic to the resistance. I could bring in consultants from outside, but how can I trust them?

With the rest of the world and America lined up against us, how can I give someone that kind of access without knowing if they're being paid by the CIA? No, we can't outplay him at his own game. There is no barrier I can erect that can stop Western ideas and values from flooding us."

"But you can stem the tide."

"Today, yes. Somewhat. Tomorrow? No."

The confusion on Khamenei's face was painful to watch. But this had to be done.

"What are you saying to me, Mehrak? That we should give up? That God is powerless against America's seduction? You should have fired into the crowd. You should have shown the resolve of our faith."

"Shooting into the crowd was impossible, Excellency."

"Impossible? Why?"

"Because I can't guarantee the loyalty of the police and military."

"If you suspect traitors, find them and arrest them."

"It's not as simple as traitors. These men love their country, but many of them come from a new generation—they don't remember the shah; they weren't alive during the revolution. They don't understand what the Islamic Republic represents. What they see is thirty percent inflation, isolation from the rest of the world, and double-digit unemployment. If some of them were to join the protesters, we could be firing the first shots in a civil war."

"It is Farrokh. If we—"

"It's not Farrokh," Omidi said, daring to allow the volume of his voice to rise. "He's important, but ultimately he's just a figurehead. Even if we capture him—and I have no confidence that we will—he will have people who can carry on in his name."

The old man's confusion deepened, and Omidi once again cast his gaze down. It was hard to see him this way.

"Farrokh is an agent of America, of the CIA. We just have to make people understand that—"

"No one believes it anymore, Excellency. President Castilla has been very clever in his policy of noninterference.

The West is responsible—but only through its existence and attractiveness to our youth. There is no direct intervention. And even if there were, it wouldn't matter. Farrokh portrays himself as a nationalist with no great love for America."

"You're telling me I am powerless in my own country, Mehrak."

"No, Excellency. Not powerless."

"And what weapon have you left me?"

Omidi once again focused on the cleric. "Caleb Bahame."

They'd spoken of it before, but Khamenei had been non-committal.

"The Ugandan."

Omidi nodded, pulling an envelope from his pocket and arranging the photos it contained on the floor. "The dead white men were killed by Bahame's people near his camp. The other photos are from an American newspaper article about a training accident that recently killed a group of special forces operatives."

Khamenei squinted through his glasses. "They're the same men."

"Yes, Excellency. The Americans sent them to assassinate or capture Bahame, and when they failed, they lied about the circumstances of their deaths."

"Then they know something. What?"

"We're not certain. I don't believe they understand the potential of Bahame's discovery, but they soon will. We have to act now or face the possibility of losing our ability—"

"To bring down the Americans and Jews," Khamenei said, finishing his thought.

"Not just to bring them down, Excellency. To unleash hell on them for all the world to see. To make people remember the terrible power of God."

The holy man sank into thought a moment. "I want you to go personally."

"Of course," Omidi said, hiding his elation at Khamenei's change of heart and attributing it to the hand of God. As with all great things, this path had significant risks. The rewards, though, were nearly infinite. Nineteen seventy-nine had been nothing. The *real* revolution—the one that would re-create the earth in God's image—had finally begun.

CHAPTER TWENTY-TWO

Cape Town, South Africa
November 20—1612 Hours GMT+2

Jon Smith jogged to the top of the stone stairs and turned toward the pillared building that dominated the University of Cape Town's lush campus. The craggy mountain that framed the nearly two-hundred-year-old college seemed almost too perfect to be real—a patchwork of gray and green beneath an unbroken blue sky.

The temperature had climbed into the mid-eighties, but a cool breeze coming off Table Bay rippled across the thin cotton of his shirt as he threaded his way through backpack-toting students in search of Dr. Sarie van Keuren.

After a few wrong turns, he found the door he was looking for and entered, scanning the lab for the meticulously groomed Betty Crocker look-alike depicted on the school's website.

He'd almost decided that she wasn't there when a bulky young man in a rugby shirt wandered off and revealed the woman behind him.

Granted, all faculty photos had a certain staged quality to them, but they'd taken it to another level with her. In real life, the wavy blond hair was well on its way to winning its fight with the tie trying to contain it. Her face was a slightly sunburned tan that faded into a yellow bruise on her left cheek. The nose that had seemed so regal from the angle the photo was taken hinted at an old injury and was just crooked enough to keep her face from devolving into generic California surfer girl.

She looked up from the clipboard in her hand and he immediately started toward her, hoping she hadn't noticed him staring.

"Can I help you?" she said in a pleasant African drawl.

"Dr. van Keuren? I'm Jon Smith."

"Colonel Smith! I was starting to think you'd gotten lost somewhere over the ocean."

"We spent some time sitting on the tarmac in London and got in a couple hours late."

He offered his hand and she pumped it energetically, the athletic outline of her body hinted at beneath the flow of her lab coat.

"Well, let me be the first to welcome you to our beautiful country, then."

"Thanks. And thanks for agreeing to meet with me on such short notice. Every time I ask someone about parasites, your name seems to come up."

She ignored the compliment. "Never a good idea to refuse a request from the most powerful military in history. USAMRIID, right? A virus hunter from Maryland. I've only been to New York and Chicago. I want to go to Montana, though."

"Being African, you might find it a little cold right now."

"But it's wild, isn't it? Big sky country. I love that phrase." She used her hands like a symphony conductor when she repeated it. "Big sky country. It explains so much."

She had an engaging way of talking just a little too fast, as though there wasn't enough time in life to say everything on her mind.

"I never thought about it. I guess it does."

"But you're not here to listen to me babble. You want to talk about parasites. Do you have an interesting one for me?"

He looked around him, confirming that none of the students were within earshot. "That's the problem. I'm not really sure. It's not my area of expertise."

"Of course. Viruses … How awful for you."

"Sorry?"

A pained expression spread across her face. "Well, I mean, they're just little bags of DNA, really."

"I take it you're not a fan."

"Oh, I don't mean to be insulting, but they're technically not even alive, for God's sake."

"They may be small, but they pack a big punch," he said, feeling a sudden inexplicable urge to defend his life's work.

"Oh, please. What's the best you've got? Smallpox? Malaria—now, there's a nasty little parasite that's killed more people than all other diseases combined. In fact, you can make a lucid argument that it's killed half the people who ever died."

She grabbed his arm and tugged him toward an enormous glass tank against the lab's far wall. "Let me show you something."

Her size belied her strength, and he allowed himself to be dragged along.

"This is Laurel," she said pointing to a foot-long fish swimming around the tank. "She's a spotted rose snapper from California. Tap the glass. Go ahead. Get her attention."

Smith did as he was told and Laurel swam toward him, opening her mouth as she approached.

He barely managed not to take a step backward when he saw something that looked like a small lobster staring out at him from the fish's maw. "What the hell is that?"

"Hardy," she said, grinning broadly. "*Cymotho*a *exigua*. When he was young and tiny, he swam through Laurel's gills and attached himself to her tongue to feed off the blood from the artery underneath. Eventually, the tongue rotted away and Hardy replaced it. Doesn't harm the fish at all. They'll live together like that for their entire lives."

"You win," Smith admitted. "That's truly disgusting."

"Isn't it brilliant?" she said, snatching a worm from a dirt-filled box and dangling it over the tank.

As Smith watched her feed the unfortunate fish, he couldn't help thinking of his fiancée, Sophia. They had worked together at Fort Detrick and she'd had the same endless fascination for her field as Sarie did. In the end, though, it had killed her.

"Colonel Smith? Are you all right? I'm sorry. Did Hardy upset you? He has that effect on some people."

His smile returned and he concentrated on making sure it didn't look forced. "No, Hardy's fine. In fact, if you have somewhere we can talk privately, I may be able to one-up you."

Her tiny office was crammed with books that looked like they'd spent most of their lives in the field, but most were completely obscured by her fetish for sticky notes. There was hardly a square inch available anywhere that didn't have a reminder of some type attached to it. He paused in the doorway to read one demanding—with multiple exclamation marks—that she not forget a faculty meeting held just over two years ago.

Sarie cleared a spot on her desk and pointed to the courier bag slung over Smith's shoulder. "Is your specimen in there? Is it from Maryland?"

"No and no."

Smith's attention was drawn to a picture of her and a very old man standing over a dead antelope of some kind. She was holding a rifle and grinning out from beneath a broad straw hat.

"Eland?"

"Kudu. Terrific eating if you get a chance while you're here." She pointed to the case again. "Now, did you mention something about a new parasite? Something no one's ever seen before?"

He chewed his lower lip. "What I have in here is very secret and—"

"*Ja, ja,*" she drawled. "You told me that over the phone, Colonel. Or do you prefer Doctor?"

"Jon."

"Jon. Secrets are so corrosive to the soul. Why don't you just show me? I'm certain it will make you feel better."

"I need to impress on you that this is something my

101

government would consider at the very least top secret."

"You're *killing* me, Jon. I am absolutely sweating with anticipation." Her tone turned playful. "I understand that if I talk, you'll have to kill me."

"I'm not sure that's the case, but it's an option that would get discussion."

She started to laugh but then seemed uncertain that he was joking. There was a brief pause before she nodded. "Fine. I swear on my father's grave. Now, give it here."

She seemed a bit perplexed when he pulled out a laptop and set it on the desk, but lowered the shades behind her and leaned over the computer to watch the video that was starting.

Smith cleared a chair of books and dropped into it, a cloud of dust rising around him as he watched her turn increasingly pale.

"Hectic," she mumbled when it was over. A few moments passed before she could get anything else out. "Who were the people that died?"

"It's not important."

"I'll bet it is to them."

He didn't respond.

"Where was the video taken? Somewhere in central Africa?"

"Uganda. The men you saw were there to try to capture Caleb Bahame."

"Bahame?" she said, the hatred audible in her voice. "I'm sorry they didn't find him. Find him and kill him."

He held out a redacted copy of the CIA's report and the information Star had come up with on the parasite angle.

"Eighteen ninety-nine?" she said, leafing through it. "I see you like to keep your research current."

He actually managed a half smile. "So what do you think, Doctor?"

"Sarie."

"Sarie. Could a parasite cause that kind of behavior?"

"It's certainly possible. Making people violent isn't all that difficult."

"But the behavior is more sophisticated than that."

"You're referring to the fact that they don't attack each other?"

He was impressed. She was as quick as her reputation suggested. "Exactly. That's why we're leaning toward the cause being a combination of narcotics and charisma. But we want to be sure."

"What do you know about the blood?"

"It's not painted on, if that's what you mean. But they could have cut their scalps for some kind of ceremonial purpose."

"I doubt it. Ceremonial cutting, sure, but why hide it under your hair? Why not a big, intimidating slash across your chest? And as far as them not attacking each other goes, it wouldn't surprise me. If a parasite *is* affecting their brains, what mutation could possibly be more beneficial than one causing them to recognize other infected people and leave them alone? It would be a huge evolutionary advantage over similar parasites that cause their victims to end up in some kind of free-for-all. From the parasite's standpoint, that's suicide."

"Still," Smith said skeptically. "The kinds of specific changes that would have to be made to the human brain in order to make all this work seem far-fetched."

"Oh, no, I disagree. Take *Toxoplasma gondii*, for instance. It's a protozoan normally parasitic to cats but it can infect a number of other species, including humans. The one we're interested in for the sake of this example is rats. Now, rats are terrified by the smell of cat urine—a not-so-surprising survival adaptation. However, rats infected with *Toxoplasma* are not only unafraid of cat urine; they're actually *attracted* to it. Not great for the rat, but just lovely for the *Toxoplasma*, which gets to return to its preferred host when the rat gets eaten."

"So you're saying—," Smith started, but she kept talking—whether to him or to herself he wasn't sure.

"And what about *Hymenoepimecis argyraphaga*? It's a parasitic wasp that attacks a certain Costa Rican spider. Its egg hatches on the spider's abdomen and sucks its blood. Eventually it releases a chemical that causes the spider to spin a complex web designed to protect the wasp instead of catching food. Then there's a different parasite that breeds underwater but infects grasshoppers. The only way it can procreate is to cause the grasshopper to commit suicide by drowning itself."

She began pacing back and forth across the crowded office, occasionally pausing to look at a particularly interesting note stuck to the walls or furniture. "So what we potentially have here is a parasite that's spread through blood—thus the bleeding from the hair."

"And the violence," Smith said.

"Exactly. You've got to get the blood into your victim, and what better way than to attack them, open cuts, and then bleed into them. It's similar to your viruses. They cause you to sneeze or cough or have diarrhea. All simple strategies to move from one host to another."

"So what do you think? Bottom line."

"I think there's a very good chance you're dealing with some kind of pathogen. Based on the documents you brought and the complexity of the behavior, I'd say a parasite is your best bet. It's really quite incredible! We've never seen anything like this in humans. I mean, *Toxoplasma* is fairly common in our species, but the only significant psychological effect we can find is that it makes us lousy drivers."

"Did you say 'drivers'?"

She nodded. "Might have something to do with appetite for risk. Not really sure. So are you going to Uganda?"

"Based on what you're telling me, I don't suppose I have much of a choice."

"Is there time for us to swing by my house?"

"Excuse me?"

"I just need to grab some gear before we leave."

Smith opened his mouth to protest but then caught himself. She had extensive field experience in Africa, was the world's foremost parasitologist, and based on the photo on the wall, could handle a rifle. No point in being hasty.

Jim Clayborn sat in the grass on the University of Cape Town campus, keeping an eye on an Iranian exchange student who had taken an intense, and extremely suspicious, interest in Dr. Sarie van Keuren.

In his peripheral vision, he watched the young man casually retrieve his cell phone as van Keuren appeared with a tall, fit-looking man who according to his rental car agreement was Colonel Jon Smith of the U.S. Army. The Iranian snapped a few shots of van Keuren being introduced to an older man who stank to high heaven of British special forces.

Clayborn tapped a brief text into his own phone, then ran it through a state-of-the-art encryption algorithm before sending it off to Langley. They weren't going to be happy. Things looked like they were about to get complicated.

CHAPTER TWENTY-THREE

Langley, Virginia, USA
November 20—1035 Hours GMT–5

The gloom was dispelled by a slide projecting an elegant line of stone buildings against a mountain backdrop. Brandon Gazenga zoomed in on three people standing at the top of a set of stairs.

"Starting at the far right, we have Lt. Colonel Jon Smith, a medical doctor and microbiologist attached to USAMRIID. He—"

"Brandon," Lawrence Drake said, not bothering to hide his impatience. "Dave and I have a meeting in ten minutes. What's so important about this that it couldn't wait?"

"Yes, sir, I understand. But we have reports that a week before this photo was taken, Dr. Smith was at Camp Lejeune talking to the surviving SEAL from the Uganda operation. Apparently, he was there when he committed suicide."

Drake leaned forward, feeling the muscles around his stomach tighten. "Okay, Brandon. You have my attention. Who's the woman?"

"Sarie van Keuren, a name I think you're familiar with."

"The parasitologist. Are the Iranians still watching her?"

"Yes, sir. They have roughly the same photo you're looking at."

"And the man she's shaking hands with?"

"That wasn't as easy to figure out—he's traveling on an Argentine passport under the name Peter Jourgan. His real name, though, is Peter Howell. Former SAS, former MI6, now retired and living in California."

"If he's retired," Dave Collen said, "what the hell is he doing in Cape Town talking to van Keuren?"

"I should have said *semi*retired. He still does some consulting work, but the details aren't clear."

"I assume you've accessed the army's records," Drake said. "What are Smith's orders?"

"He doesn't have any. He's officially on a leave of absence."

"Bull. Is he military intelligence?"

"He's been attached to Military Intelligence in the past," Gazenga responded. "But there's no evidence that he's associated with them now."

"And if he *was* still working for them, he wouldn't be over there with a British freelancer," Collen added.

"I agree," Gazenga said. "You probably remember that Smith was involved in the Hades disaster through his job at USAMRIID. After that, though, he starts turning up in a lot of places that can't be as easily explained."

"Someone recruited him after he brought down Tremont," Drake said.

"I think it's a safe assumption, sir."

"Who?"

"I can't find anything that would even indicate a direction to look. If he is working off the books for someone, they're incredibly good at staying in the shadows."

Drake settled back in his chair and examined the stark blue of Smith's eyes. Who had the juice to recruit and operate an asset like Smith? And who had an undue interest in Caleb Bahame? The answer to those questions had the potential to lead in a very dangerous direction.

"Where are they now?"

"On their way to Uganda."

Collen turned his chair toward his boss and spoke under his breath. "Jesus, Larry ..."

Drake nodded silently. "I want them followed, Brandon. I want to know everywhere they go, everyone they talk to, and everything they learn. And I want to know it in real time. Do you understand?"

"Yes, sir."

"I also want to know who the hell they're working for."

Gazenga nodded obediently but seemed increasingly uncomfortable.

"Do you have something else to say, Brandon?"

"No, sir."

"Yes, you do. Speak up."

He hesitated, shifting back and forth in the glare of the projector. "Sir, what we've done so far is ..."

"Legal?"

"All due respect, I was going to say *plausible*. Everything we've said about Bahame's methods and the Iranians' interest has been completely reasonable and defensible from an analysis standpoint."

"But?"

"While we don't know specifically who Smith's working for, it stands to reason that it's someone on our side ..."

"Are you making a recommendation or just stating the obvious?" Drake said.

Brandon stood a little straighter for the first time in their relationship. Defiance?

"In a way, this could have a silver lining for us, sir. The Iranians have been cautious up until now. An American virus hunter poking around could force their hand and give us corroboration of what Khamenei is doing."

"So you think we should throw a year of meticulous planning out the window and rely on two foreign nationals and an army doctor with no apparent orders?"

Brandon didn't back down. "I think we have to consider op—"

"The Iranians continue their nuclear weapons program," Drake said, cutting him off, "and we slap them on the wrist. Now their country is destabilizing and could very easily fall into the hands of Farrokh, who has the confidence of the Iranian scientific community. What do we do? We stand by. And that's what we'll still be doing when they have nuclear warheads that can reach our shores and OPEC is controlled from Tehran."

Gazenga's resolve began to waver and he moved out of the beam of the projector in an obvious attempt to hide the fact. "If we—"

"That'll be all, Brandon," Dave Collen said.

"But ... Yes, sir. Thank you."

Drake reflected on how quickly and violently the world was changing as the young man hustled through the door. Russia and China were more easily controlled than people suspected—both countries had large, sophisticated bureaucracies, populations with predictable long-term goals, and an arsenal of economic and military weapons that remained inferior to America's. Iran was different.

In direct opposition to Castilla's policy of noninterference, Drake had been waging a silent war against the Iranians. The two nuclear scientists recently killed by car bombs and the Stuxnet computer worm that had damaged their centrifuges were all off-the-books agency operations. But he was just delaying the inevitable. The threat posed by the Islamic Republic needed to be made clear and, more important, the American military's ability to deal with that threat had to be demonstrated. This time there would be no endless street skirmishes, no corrupt local politicians, no buried IEDs. Iran would be quickly and completely obliterated from the air.

The Muslim world had begun to mistake America's obsession with preventing civilian casualties for weakness. It was a misconception that would be quickly dispelled as the world stood by and watched Iran's few survivors scramble to eke out an existence in a land literally returned to the Stone Age.

Worldwide order would be restored and a clear message would be sent to the Pakistanis, the Afghans, and all the others: If you keep your fundamentalists under control, America will stay on the sidelines. But if you let them become a threat, you will be next.

All he needed was a catalyst, and Caleb Bahame's parasite was perfect. Even by biological weapon standards, it was so visceral and terrifying that virtually every government on the planet would turn their backs on a country that used it.

If he allowed Smith and his team to confirm the parasite's existence and learn of the Iranians' interest as Gazenga was suggesting, their plan would be stillborn. The politicians would move in, rattling empty sabers while Iran issued denial after denial. Castilla and the UN would debate, demand more evidence, make pointless resolutions. And the war-weary, financially strapped American people would resist a call to arms over yet another unseen and unproven WMD program.

No, in order for the United States to regain the determination to retaliate with overwhelming force, the threat couldn't exist solely in the mouths of newscasters and government spokesmen. The Iranians would have to be allowed to *use* Bahame's parasite. The soft and increasingly self-absorbed American people would have to *experience* the consequences of their apathy.

"Larry?" Collen said, breaking the silence in the still, shadowy office. "What are we going to do? We didn't anticipate any of these complications. And Brandon's starting to waver."

Drake let out a long breath as he forced himself back into the present. Gazenga's knowledge of central Africa had been critical to their operation thus far, but it had always been understood that he'd eventually have to be dealt with—that he wouldn't have the courage to go as far as was necessary. Losing him now, though, would be a minor disaster.

"I take it you've been learning fast, Dave?"

"Everything I can. But my level of expertise is nowhere near his. And neither are my contacts on the ground."

Drake nodded his understanding. "We're going to have to move up the timetable and go to full surveillance on him. I want it in place by tonight. Maybe he'll show more backbone than we expect."

"And Smith?"

"For now, we'll just track him—see if he tips his hand as to how much he knows and who he's working for. The moment it looks like they're going to come up with anything useful, though, they're going to have to disappear."

Brandon Gazenga smiled blankly at the people moving through the hallway, trying to keep his gait natural as he slipped into his office and closed the door behind him.

How the hell had he gotten himself into this?

It was a depressingly easy question to answer. Drake had come to him personally and he'd swooned at the personal attention from the DCI. Given a chance to advance his career and play with the big boys, he'd just closed his eyes and jumped.

A world that seemed so black-and-white in college turned hopelessly gray inside the walls of CIA headquarters. A little spin here, a little data selection there, and you could make a report say anything you wanted. But now things had been turned completely upside down. There was no doubt in his mind that Drake was going to eventually want Smith and his people dead. Of course the CIA's involvement would be as indirect as it always was—a quick cash payment to an intermediary, a passing along of information to bandits in the area, maybe a word to one of Bahame's people. It was a cardinal rule that he had learned well over the past year: deniability must always be maintained.

But *he* would know the truth. The fact that the blood didn't splash directly on him didn't absolve him of responsibility.

The entire operation was an incredibly delicate balancing act—let the Iranians go far enough for the evidence to be irrefutable, but not so far that they would be in a position to actually deploy the parasite.

As his vision cleared, though, Gazenga began to see just how subjective that balance point was. How far were Drake and Collen willing to allow Iran to run? How much risk were they willing to take that this could spin out of control?

"Welcome to the big leagues," he said to the empty office.

It was funny how different the reality was from the fantasy. Who would have ever thought he'd want nothing more than to join his brothers running the family restaurant chain? That standing elbow-deep in spiced beef and dishwater would be something he dreamed about?

Gazenga walked unsteadily to his desk and sat in the leather chair his father had presented him as a graduation gift. This was getting way too big for him to handle. He needed to talk to someone who knew what the hell they were doing. Someone he could trust.

CHAPTER TWENTY-FOUR

Entebbe, Uganda
November 21—1517 Hours GMT+3

Sarie van Keuren tossed a bungee cord over the crate of field equipment and Smith caught it, securing the hook to a hole rusted in the top of the cab.

"I think that'll get us to Kampala," he said, and the driver leaned through the open window, head bobbing in an energetic nod.

"No problem."

Those seemed to be his only two words of English, but with the right inflection and expression, they could communicate just about any point.

Smith climbed into the front passenger's seat, pulling his pack onto his lap before repeatedly slamming the tiny car's door in an effort to get it to stay closed. "Peter! Let's roll."

Howell was standing on the sidewalk staring up at Uganda's Entebbe Airport, hands jammed in the pockets of his faded jeans despite the heat and humidity. The original terminal building was gone now, but the airport was still something of a shrine for the men who served in the world's special forces.

In 1976, Palestinian terrorists hijacked a plane ferrying 250 passengers from Tel Aviv to Paris, forcing the pilot to land in Idi Amin–controlled Uganda. After releasing some of the passengers, they'd threatened to kill their remaining hostages if a number of their imprisoned compatriots weren't set free.

When it became clear that peaceful negotiations were

going nowhere—due in no small part to Amin's support of the hijackers—the Israelis began planning a rescue mission.

Operation Thunderbolt was carried out by one hundred elite commandos and took only an hour and a half to complete. When the dust settled, all but three of the hostages had been rescued and all the hijackers, as well as forty-five Ugandan troops, were dead.

It had been a very public demonstration of what a well-trained force could accomplish and had made that little airport a household name all over the world.

"Peter!" Sarie called, wrestling her pack into the backseat and then squeezing in next to it. "What are you looking at? Meter's running!"

Her voice snapped him out of his trance and he slipped in next to her.

"You okay?" she asked.

"Of course I am, my dear. Why wouldn't I be?"

Smith shot a quick glance back but then just settled into the vinyl-and-duct-tape seat as the cab shot into traffic. He watched the verdant hills dotted with houses pass by for a few minutes but found it more and more difficult to keep his eyes open. The drive to their hotel in the capital city wouldn't take much more than a half hour, but he might as well put the time to good use. Unless he missed his guess, opportunities for sleep were going to be scarce over the next couple of weeks.

Sarie's phone rang and he half monitored her circumspect questioning of the German parasitologist she'd left a message for earlier that day. When the inevitable disappointment became audible in her voice, he shifted his attention back to the monotonous drone of the engine. It seemed that Star had once again been right—whatever this phenomenon turned out to be, the two lousy pages she turned up were the entire body of knowledge on it.

Despite his exhaustion, Smith's mind refused to shut down, instead churning through an ever-lengthening list of problems and unknowns.

Dealing with deadly diseases in the field was dangerous

enough when you had iron-fisted control over every variable. Normally, he'd know more or less what pathogen he was dealing with, his patients would be grateful for his presence, and he would be leading a large team of highly trained specialists wielding multimillion-dollar equipment.

To say that his current situation wasn't optimal would be the understatement of the century. His protective equipment consisted of some surgical gloves and masks raided from Sarie's basement. He had virtually no knowledge of the pathogen they were after or, frankly, if it even existed. He had only guesses as to how it spread and no clue how it attacked its victims. And his patients, far from offering their thanks with donations of farm animals like they had last time he'd worked in Africa, were likely to try to tear him apart.

Then there was Caleb Bahame—a man who had brought the technological innovation of the jeep to the old tradition of drawing and quartering. A man who wasn't going to be happy about three white people wandering around in his backyard asking questions ...

The sudden blast of a car horn caused Smith to jerk upright in his seat. He squinted into the powerful sun, confused for a moment as to where he was. Ahead, tall concrete buildings broke up the outline of green hills, creating a vaguely Soviet skyline that overpowered the red roofs and whitewashed walls of colonial-era structures.

Kampala was a tidy and surprisingly attractive city at odds with its history of political turmoil, military dictatorships, and now Caleb Bahame. It was a deeply unfair but common story in this part of the world: just when the populace was about to get out from under—just when hope began to dispel fear and desperation—someone rose with a ragtag force and some murky motivation for destroying it all.

"Take your next left," Howell said, reaching up between the seats and tapping their driver on the shoulder.

The Ugandan seemed confused and pointed through the cracked windshield at the approaching city. "No problem. Hotel."

"Not the bloody hotel," Howell said more forcefully. "Do it. Turn there."

"No! Problem! Bad place."

Smith twisted around in his seat but was grateful when Sarie spoke first. "What's going on, Peter? I thought you'd never been to Uganda."

Her naïve openness was not only engaging but useful. Smith really couldn't ask questions—particularly in light of the fact that he had Howell on a mission for an organization the Brit didn't even know existed.

"I said here!" Howell said, pulling himself between the seats and grabbing the wheel. The taxi careened onto a dirt side road violently enough to slam Smith into the poorly latched door. He grabbed for the dash and barely managed to keep from falling out.

"What the hell, Peter?" he said, starting the process of trying to get the door closed again.

"I thought we'd take in the sights."

Howell passed three one-hundred-dollar bills to the driver, who didn't seem to know whether to be more afraid of the man in the backseat or what lay ahead. The cash broke the tie.

Smith managed to get the door latched again and twisted around to the degree the pack on his lap would allow. The fact that Howell hadn't told him about his history in Uganda didn't particularly bother him—their entire relationship was built on secrets. What did bother him, though, was that the normally squared-away SAS man had turned erratic and moody.

He'd never had reason to question Howell's judgment before and he wasn't anxious to start, but there was something wrong here. How much rope should he give his old friend before he yanked back?

As they approached a ramshackle township, the driver began talking irritably in his native language, obviously trying to convince himself of something. They'd closed to within about two hundred yards of the first building, a leaning shack built from corrugated tin and wire, when the African slammed on the brakes. "We go no more!"

Howell stepped calmly from the car and yanked the driver's door open, pulling the frightened man out into the road.

"Back in a jif," he said, sliding behind the wheel and launching the car forward again.

"Peter," Sarie said as they wound through the dense shacks, eliciting perplexed stares from the pedestrians hurrying out of the way. "I'm from this part of the world and I'm telling you we shouldn't be here. We aren't welcome."

He didn't respond, and Smith felt her hand light on his shoulder, a clear signal that she wanted him to intervene. But for one of the first times in his life, he wasn't sure what to do. He'd be dead five times over if it weren't for Peter Howell.

The farther they penetrated, the more the township changed in character. Women and children evident at the outer edges were gone now, replaced by increasingly well-armed men. A pickup with a mounted machine gun crossed in front of them and the shirtless man standing in the bed swung the gun in their direction but didn't have time to decide whether or not to pull the trigger before he disappeared around a corner.

"Okay, that's far enough, Peter," Smith said, grabbing the shifter and pulling it into neutral. "Either you tell us what we're doing, or we turn around and get the hell out of here."

The Brit just thumbed into the backseat, where Sarie was on her knees watching the crowd close in behind them. Unlike the machine gunner, they'd had time to think about the strangers in their midst and were well on their way to a decision that wasn't going to go well for anyone.

CHAPTER TWENTY-FIVE

Langley, Virginia, USA
November 21—1015 Hours GMT–5

There she was.

Brandon examined the woman waiting for the elevator and, when he was satisfied that she wasn't on speaking terms with any of the people around her, moved in.

As his discomfort with the Uganda operation had grown, he'd begun quietly researching people he could go to if he decided he was in over his head. His work with Drake allowed him access to the CIA's database well beyond his pay grade and he'd managed to come up with a short list of tough operatives with extensive experience and reputations for unshakable integrity.

Despite looking like she was still in her midthirties, the woman in front of him was a minor legend at the agency. He'd initially disregarded her because she was posted in Afghanistan but then heard she was back stateside sitting out the backlash over the death of a Taliban leader she'd tracked into the Hindu Kush. Maybe his luck was finally changing.

The elevator door opened and he shuffled in, staying close enough to her that he could smell the shampoo in her short blond hair. The athletic body, full lips, and tanned skin were undoubtedly significant assets in her work but a clear liability to him. The surreptitious glances of the men in the elevator weren't going to make what he'd come to do any easier.

Gazenga fought for a position beside her in the crowded space, watching in his peripheral vision as she fixed her dark eyes on the floor numbers counting down.

The elevator stopped with a jerk and he used it as an excuse to bump into her, slipping a note into the pocket of her jacket as he did so.

She turned slightly, black eyes wandering along the side of his face and giving him a sudden overwhelming sense of claustrophobia. At the last moment, he pushed through the people in front of him and out the closing doors. The hallway was nearly empty and he concentrated on controlling his breathing as a duct overhead blew cool air across his sweaty skin.

He hadn't lost his nerve. He'd done it. But for some reason the sense of relief he'd anticipated didn't materialize. If anything, the sensation of being trapped continued to tighten around his chest.

With that note, he'd irretrievably stepped off the diving board. All he could do now was hope the pool had water in it.

CHAPTER TWENTY-SIX

Outside Kampala, Uganda
November 21—1626 Hours GMT+3

Peter Howell smiled casually at a group of comically over-armed men staring dumbfounded at them as they cruised by. Ahead, an elaborate archway led through the stone wall they'd been paralleling for the last few minutes. By the time they stopped in front of it, there were at least three mounted machine guns and no fewer than thirty small arms trained on the aging taxi. A man in fatigues came cautiously toward them, looking over the sights of an Israeli-made Tavor assault rifle and screaming unintelligible instructions.

They were forced from the vehicle, and Smith grabbed Sarie's arm to keep her from being dragged away, trying to position himself so that she was shielded between him and the car.

"Is there a plan here?" Smith shouted over the hood, not sure if he was more angry with Howell or himself. "Or did you just pick today to commit suicide?"

"A bit of shopping," came the Brit's enigmatic answer.

A young man in a tattered Smurfs T-shirt gave Smith a hard shove and he pushed back, sending the man to the ground. "Back the hell off!"

The African jumped to his feet, clawing for the machine gun hanging across his chest, and Smith lunged for him. Someone to his left threw an elbow and he ducked around it, keeping his eyes locked on the compact Heckler & Koch lining up on him.

Then it all stopped. There was a brief shout from the

direction of the archway and the young man backed away, careful to keep his hands well away from his weapon.

The crowd began to disperse and the guards lost interest in them, going back to surveying the people moving back and forth in the dusty road.

"Peter! My good friend," came a heavily accented voice. What remained of the mob scurried out of the way of a tall African striding toward Howell.

"It warms my heart to see you again," he said, pumping the Brit's hand. "I never dreamed I would."

"Good to see you, too, Janani. I'd like to introduce you to my friends Sarie and Jon."

The African motioned toward them. "Come. We must get out of this horrible sun."

Smith looked over at Sarie and shrugged, taking her arm before following the two chatting men through the arch.

"You've gotten fat," Howell said.

"And you've gotten old, my brother. I live a good life. I have many wives and children. How many sons do you have?"

"None."

Janani shook his head sympathetically as they turned down a narrow alley lined with storefronts dedicated to merchandise built around the theme "Things that can kill you." There were numerous gun dealers, specialists in various types of explosives, and a shop with a canary-yellow awning advertising Africa's best selection of handheld SAMs.

Janani led them through an unmarked door that opened into a surprisingly large and well-equipped machine shop.

"Janani makes custom guns," Howell explained, waving a hand around him but not looking back. "The best in the world."

"You flatter me, Peter. Do you still have the pistol I made you so many years ago?"

"I'm afraid I lost it."

"But not before it killed many men."

Howell nodded, his voice suddenly sounding a bit distant. "Many men."

They passed through an open door at the back and came out onto a covered patio containing a dizzying assortment of guns lined up in racks. A lush butte started about twenty-five yards beyond, sloping gently upward, with targets spaced at measured intervals.

"Jon," Janani said, spinning to face him. "What do you normally carry?"

"A Sig Sauer. Sometimes a Beretta."

An unimpressed frown crossed the African's face and he pulled a pistol from a neat foam display.

Smith accepted it but barely had his hand around it before Janani snatched it back with a disgusted scowl.

"Completely wrong," he muttered, selecting one with a slightly thicker grip. "Tell me how this one feels."

He had to admit that it felt good—the same confidence-inspiring solidness of the Sig Sauer without the weight.

"Do you mind?" Smith said, pointing to the range.

"Please."

He fired a round at the fifty-meter target, putting it dead center in the human silhouette.

"It seems to agree with you," Janani said, a craftsman's pride audible in his voice.

"Fits good, shoots nice. But will it stop anything? The recoil feels light."

"You're firing a 170-grain ten-millimeter round with a thirteen-hundred-foot-per-second muzzle velocity."

"Come on ... Really?"

The African dipped his head respectfully.

"So what's the verdict, mate?" Howell said.

"If it's reliable, it's the best thing I ever shot."

"Of course it's reliable!" Janani whined. "Certainly more so than anything the *Italians* are involved in."

"All right," Howell said. "We'll take it and another one like it for me. Then I'll need a couple assault rifles. Something maneuverable along the lines of a SCAR-L, but I'll leave the final decision to you. No point in traveling light, so say a thousand rounds for the rifles and a hundred each for the handguns. Three spare clips apiece."

"Of course. We can have them ready by morning. Can I interest you in anything else? Perhaps a portable rocket launcher? I have a prototype that I think you'd find very compelling."

"Tempting, but we're trying to keep a low profile. You wouldn't happen to know anybody in the car business, would yo—"

"Excuse me!"

They all turned toward Sarie, who was waving a hand irritably. "Are we forgetting someone?"

The African was clearly confused. "I'm sorry. Are you making a joke?"

"I think she's serious," Smith said.

Janani shook his head miserably. "Women have become so ... What is the word you use? Uppity. It's this new feminism."

He walked over to a chest of drawers and pulled out a minuscule chrome .32. "This looks very nice with a handbag."

Even Howell managed a laugh, less at Janani's joke than at Sarie's deadly expression.

"I was thinking of something more like this," she said, walking up to a row of scoped semiautomatic rifles. She grabbed one and pulled the bolt back, confirming that it was loaded before starting for a table piled with sandbags.

"That's not a toy," Janani said as she laid the gun down and knelt behind it.

When she didn't acknowledge his warning, he turned back to Howell and Smith. "My first wife behaves like this. I blame Oprah. We get—"

All three of them ducked in unison as an explosion rattled the rickety thatched roof above them. There were shouts from inside the building and a number of armed men ran out, only to find Sarie joyfully clapping her hands. "You put dynamite behind them? I love that!"

The African frowned, looking at what was left of his plywood target cartwheeling through a distant cloud of dirt and shattered rock. "Only the ones at eight hundred meters."

"Do you mind if I shoot another?"

Janani walked over and snatched away the rifle. "Out of the question, madam. This weapon is far too heavy for you and the stock is all wrong. I'll have something more suitable when you and your friends return."

CHAPTER TWENTY-SEVEN

Kampala, Uganda
November 21—1741 Hours GMT+3

"No problem. Hotel."

Sarie chuckled quietly in the backseat as Jon Smith's head sank into his hands. They'd found their driver a few miles from the arms market hoofing it back to Kampala. He'd seemed a little shocked to see them alive but gratefully climbed back behind the wheel after checking his rust bucket of a cab for damage.

"No," Smith said for the fifth time. "*Hospital*. We want to go to the *hospital* first."

Howell's detour, while admittedly productive, left them no time to stop at the hotel before their appointment with the director of Kampala's main medical facility.

"No problem. Hotel."

Smith groaned and fell back into his seat.

"I think he's missing the subtlety between the words 'hospital' and 'hotel'," Sarie offered. "What's it actually called?"

He must have been more tired than he thought not to come up with that himself. Sixty hours of travel took a hell of a lot more out of him than it had when he was thirty.

"Mulago," he said, enunciating carefully. "Not hotel. Mulago Hospital."

The driver's eyes widened with understanding. "Mulago? You sick?"

"Yes! You've got it! I'm sick. Very, very sick."

"Mulago. No problem."

Fifteen minutes later they pulled up to an enormous crate of a building surrounded by a railing painted an unfortunate baby blue.

"Mulago!" the driver announced as Smith threw open the door and slid out from beneath his pack.

He crouched and leaned back in to look at Howell. After his hour of normality at the arms market, he'd turned melancholy again—something worryingly at odds with his personality. "Can you stay with the car, Peter? We won't be long."

The Brit leaned his head back and stared up at the mildewed headliner. "I don't have anything else on my calendar."

"Hello, I'm Dr. Jon Smith and this is Dr. Sarie van Keuren. We have an appointment with Dr. Lwanga."

The woman stood with surprising nimbleness from behind a desk about half her size. The stern expression she'd worn when they approached transformed into a toothy smile. "Of course," she said in lightly accented English. "I have your appointment right here. If you will just follow me, please."

She led them less than ten feet to an open office door and then stepped ceremoniously aside so they could enter.

"Dr. Lwanga?" Smith said, approaching a bespectacled man standing at an odd angle that suggested childhood polio. He closed the book in his hand with a snap and limped toward them. "Drs. Smith and van Keuren. It is a great honor."

"Likewise," Sarie said. "You have a beautiful facility here."

"There isn't much money," he responded. "But one does what one can."

"We know you're busy, Doctor, and we don't want to take up too much of your valuable time ...," Smith started.

"Of course. What is it I can do for you?"

Smith fell silent, letting Sarie take the lead as they had agreed. She was a minor celebrity across the continent for her work on malaria and knew better what questions to ask. He'd just stand by and make sure she didn't get overexcited and reveal too much.

"Jon and I are heading north on a brief expedition to find a parasitic worm that affects ants. But while we were doing our research, we found a mention of another parasite that caught our attention."

"I'm afraid this isn't really my area," Lwanga said apologetically.

"We came to you because there are reports that it may victimize humans, causing rabies-like symptoms and possibly bleeding from the hair follicles. Also, it seems to affect only the North, which is where you grew up, isn't it?"

Lwanga's expression seemed strangely frozen as Sarie continued.

"We couldn't find any information on what animals might host the parasite or really any corroboration that it even exists. Does it ring a bell by any chance?"

The African suddenly came back to life. "I'm afraid not. I've never heard of anything like what you're describing."

"Would you know someone we could talk to—maybe a doctor working in the rural areas to the north? Someone who could help us ask the right people the right questions?"

"It's been a long time since I left my village and I've been very remiss about staying in touch." He stuck out a hand in what was clearly a dismissal. "I'm sorry I couldn't be of more help. Now, you'll have to excuse me. I have rounds."

"That was a very strange meeting," Sarie said as they came back out into the heat of the afternoon sun. "I don't want to seem negative, but I'm not sure that he was being completely honest with us."

It was obvious that she was having a hard time coming right out and calling the aging physician a liar, but Smith had no such qualms. In the world of professional liars he lived in, Lwanga was a rank amateur.

"He knew exactly what you were talking about, Sarie. Did you see the tea service next to his desk?"

"*Ja.*"

"How many cups were on it?"

"How many cups? I don't know."

"Ah," Smith said. "You see, but you do not observe."

"Sherlock Holmes," she said with a grin. "Does that mean I get to be Watson?"

"Not yet. But I see potential. There were *three* cups and steam coming from the pot's spout. You know better than me that Africans are nothing if not polite."

She nodded slowly. "He intended for us to stay on a bit."

"Until you brought up crazy people bleeding from the hair."

"The stuff about him losing touch with his village is nonsense, too, Jon. African politeness is nothing compared to African devotion to family."

They crossed onto the sidewalk and Smith reached for their taxi's door. "And so the plot thickens."

Dr. Oume Lwanga stood at the edge of the window, peering down into the street below. The phone in his hand was slick with sweat, and he had to grip it tightly to keep the smooth plastic from sliding through his fingers.

"They said that *specifically*," President Charles Sembutu's voice on the other end said.

"Yes, sir. They didn't give details of which rabies symptoms, though madness seemed implied. They did distinctly say bleeding from the hair."

"That's all?"

"They were interested in a possible animal host but said their main objective was a worm affecting ants—that this other parasite was just something that came up in their research. They didn't seem certain it even existed."

"Where are they now?"

"Getting into a brown taxi with a box on the roof."

"Is there anyone else in it besides the driver?"

"I think there's someone in the backseat. From my

position it's hard to tell. Do you want me to—"

The connection went dead and Lwanga watched the cab pull away from the curb, feeling a pang of guilt. Their fate was in God's hands now.

CHAPTER TWENTY-EIGHT

Northern Uganda
November 21—1833 Hours GMT+3

Mehrak Omidi slowed when the young man in front of him broke into an elaborate karate pantomime, kicking at bushes and the humid air, spinning unsteadily, and making noises like a strangled bird. He nearly fell over a rotting log and shouted angrily at it before grabbing one of a number of beers stuffed into the pockets of his fatigues.

Omidi had landed in Uganda nine hours ago and immediately driven to the remote rendezvous point dictated by Caleb Bahame. He'd expected to be picked up by the man himself and taken to camp, but instead spent three hours riding blindfolded in the back of a rickety military vehicle. And now this.

They'd been walking through the wet, insect-infested jungle for long enough that he began to question whether the men around him had any idea where they were going. Most were drunk, and no fewer than three fights had broken out—one of which he'd been forced to break up when knives materialized.

"How much longer?"

The man in front squinted back at him and said something in his native language before forging on.

Omidi followed, keeping up easily despite the unfamiliar humidity and terrain. He hated sub-Saharan Africa and everything in it—the air, the disease, the worthless inhabitants. It would have given him great satisfaction to have sent one of his men in his place, but it was impossible. No one else could be trusted with a task so vast and historically important.

When he actually allowed himself to consider what, with God's blessing, he would accomplish, it made the breath catch in his chest. Centuries of dominance by America and the West would come to an end. Their arrogant citizens would finally understand that everything they thought they had was an illusion. They would watch in horror as the power and money they had so greedily amassed failed to protect them. And when it was finally over, they would shrink away like beaten dogs.

The sun touched the horizon, stoking his anger and frustration. Soon, they would have to stop. While his guides were well equipped with alcohol and pornography, none seemed to have thought to bring a flashlight or night-vision equipment.

He quickened his pace and reached for the man in front of him again but then heard a distant voice reverberating through the jungle. The men around him heard it, too, whooping in excitement and pumping their rusting assault rifles in the air.

Bahame.

As they closed on the amplified voice, the scent of human habitation assaulted him—open latrines, garbage, and the distinctive rot of death. They passed crated weapons and food, as well as a few light military vehicles that may or may not have been in operating condition. All were piled with tree limbs and vines so as to be invisible from the air.

They broke out into a clearing and Omidi spotted a man pacing across a makeshift stage speaking into a megaphone. He was dressed in worn fatigues accented by a large amulet made of what appeared to be human teeth and bones.

No fewer than a hundred people were packed into the clearing, transfixed by the graying figure looking down on them. Most were teens or younger, clad in tattered civilian clothing and holding weapons as sophisticated as AK-47s and as primitive as feather-adorned spears. At least a quarter were girls, some unashamedly shirtless, displaying budding breasts wet with perspiration. A disgusting display by a disgusting race.

The man on the log-and-stone podium spotted him and pointed, speaking unintelligibly as his audience parted.

Close up, Caleb Bahame was almost regal, with strong features and skin unblemished by his years of living in camps like these. His movements were strangely exaggerated, choreographed to give his every word its own sense of gravity. Seeing Bahame standing there, feeling the oppressiveness of his presence, explained a great deal about how the African had gained so much power so quickly.

Bahame had started bringing his clapped-together religion to the tiny villages of northern Uganda almost a quarter century ago. Not long after, he armed a group of disciples large enough to begin converting the region's farmers, whether they were persuaded by his dogma or not. He burned and raped and kidnapped, learning to manipulate the pliable minds of children and turning them into a fighting force unbounded by any moral or religious sensibility that didn't flow directly from him.

As time went on, the religion he'd created became more political and more about him. He had portrayed himself as everything from Muhammad to Jesus to the reincarnation of Karl Marx—fanning the flames of tribal animosity and promising a utopian society of milk and honey without work or effort. Now, thousands of followers later, Bahame no longer knew where he stopped and God started.

Omidi climbed onto the podium and Bahame threw down the megaphone to greet him. When their hands clasped, a loud cheer rose up.

"Mehrak, my good friend," Bahame said in English better than his own. "God told me you would be delivered safely to me."

"May his name be praised."

Bahame smiled and turned, using a claw hammer to break open a crate of whiskey. The exaltation of his congregation grew in volume as he tossed the bottles out to them, reserving one for himself.

"My magic has given us many victories and has made them love me," he said, breaking the neck off the bottle. His eyes were clear, but it was impossible to know what they saw. Unquestionably, a man to be very carefully handled.

"You're a great leader."

"Yes, but Uganda is a large country, full of evil. It will require more than magic to take it. Even my magic."

Omidi nodded gravely. "All great generals—all great men—face the same problem. You cannot do everything yourself. And to rely on others is ... unpredictable."

"What you say is true, Mehrak."

"I'd like to see your magic. To see if you can teach us to wield it without your power."

He seemed pleased by that and took a long pull on the bottle before holding it out to Omidi.

"My God doesn't permit it," the Iranian said.

"He gives you his permission."

Omidi smiled politely, making sure his eyes portrayed only serenity. Was Bahame saying that he had spoken to God on his behalf ? Or that he *was* God?

A murmur went through Bahame's people, and Omidi used it as an excuse to turn and see what had distracted them from fighting over the liquor.

A group similar to the one that had brought him there burst into the clearing dragging a badly injured African man along with them. Behind, a Caucasian in his late sixties appeared, terrified and exhausted.

Bahame jumped to the ground and Omidi followed at a distance that would allow him to be an observer of what was going to happen without risking becoming a participant.

"Where is the woman?" Bahame demanded.

One of the men pushed their injured comrade to the ground at his feet. "Dembe let her escape."

The prone man's right pant leg had been cut away and there was a bloody bandage wound around his thigh. He tried to crawl away but was stopped by the impenetrable ring of armed children that had formed around them.

Bahame pointed to the white man. "Who is he?"

133

"A doctor we found to keep this pig alive so he could face you."

The cult leader's eyes widened to the point of bulging, and his stare fixed on the man begging pathetically at his feet.

He dropped the bottle in his hand and picked up a rock the size of an apple, falling to his knees and bringing it down with horrifying force between the man's shoulder blades. An anguished scream erupted from him, though it was quickly drowned out by the laughter of the crowd.

"No, stop!" the doctor shouted. He made a lunge to protect his patient but was slammed to the ground before he could reach him.

Bahame continued to work with the rock, studiously avoiding the man's head and neck—attacking his arms, his torso, his legs. Sweat dripped from him and his breathing turned ragged as the dull thud of rock on flesh was joined by the sound of snapping bones and blood gurgling in his victim's throat.

The skill of it was admirable—turning a man's body into a broken bag of parts while keeping him not only alive, but conscious.

Eventually, Bahame began to tire, and he stood, still refusing to deliver the man into death. He picked up the whiskey he'd dropped, now spattered with blood, and drank from it before holding it out.

Omidi hesitated for a moment, looking down at the man twitching in the damp soil. Finally, he approached and accepted it, using the bottle to salute his host before bringing it to his lips.

CHAPTER TWENTY-NINE

Kampala, Uganda
November 21—2112 Hours GMT+3

Jon Smith put his face directly into the lukewarm water, letting the shower wash away the sweat and dust. The hotel had turned out to be perfect—quiet, mostly empty, and out of the way enough that they would attract minimal attention.

More important, though, the water pressure was good, the bed looked comfortable, and the restaurant served alcohol. It might be awhile before he got to enjoy those particular luxuries again, and he intended to take full advantage while they were at hand.

He stood there until the water turned cold, then toweled off and walked out into the main part of the room, where he'd left the glass doors open to a private deck. The moon was visible through the gauzy curtains, and he dressed in its light before grabbing a beer from a trash can he'd filled with ice and heading out into the night air.

From his vantage point, he could look down on a bar strung with Christmas lights and the sparsely populated area by the pool. Howell and Sarie were sitting at a dim table near the hedge bordering the property, both with drinks that rated multiple paper umbrellas. Some of Howell's strange malaise seemed to have lifted, and he smiled as Sarie lifted her hands to mimic the horns of an animal she was telling an extremely animated story about.

Smith was going to start down immediately but then thought better of it. The breeze was perfect, his beer was

135

frosty, and the distant lights of Kampala twinkled through the humidity. The calm before the storm.

"Mind if I join you?"

"Jon!" Sarie said. "Look at you. You clean up so nice!"

"I was about to say the same about you."

She was wearing a loose-fitting floral skirt and a sleeveless top that hugged her athletic torso. The hair he'd only seen tied back was now free to dance across her shoulders.

The bartender came up as he grabbed a seat, sliding some concoction in a coconut shell onto the table along with a place setting that included a knife large enough to field dress a rhino.

"Did we order?"

"Sarie took the liberty," Howell said. "You're having … Was it the zebra roulade?"

"*Ja*. Don't worry. You'll love it."

"I was just thinking how long it's been since I've had a nice piece of zebra," he joked, scanning the tables around them. It was nearly ten p.m. and most of the guests had drifted off to their rooms. A few people were left at the bar, and there was a young Scandinavian couple drinking beers with their legs dangling in the pool, but no one was within earshot.

"What's the plan for tomorrow morning?" Sarie said.

"We slink out of town and try to get out from under the neon sign we've got flashing over our heads."

"What do you mean?"

"I mean our detour to see Peter's old friend and our meeting with Dr. Lwanga weren't exactly the most anonymous way to start the trip."

She leaned toward him over the table. "I have to say all this cloak-and-dagger is kind of exciting. I feel almost like a secret agent."

Howell let out a snort that almost caused him to spit out the drink he'd raised to his lips.

"What?" Sarie said.

Smith continued before the Brit could conjure up a

response. "We'll pick up our gear first thing and then head out to the farm of the doctor who was looking into this back in the fifties. Maybe his family is still there."

Sarie nodded. "If not, we'll visit the villages in the area and ask the elders if they'd ever heard of anything like this before that bastard Bahame showed up. If this is a parasitic infection, it's possible that it's been popping up and disappearing for thousands of years."

"Why not just deal with the problem directly and go after Bahame?" Howell interjected.

"No one goes after Caleb Bahame," Sarie said. "He goes after you. He's a psychopath and a murderer."

"We'll try to steer clear of him for now," Smith said. "We don't even know what we're dealing with here—all we have is a few sketchy reports. If it *is* a biological agent, though, we need to get as much information as we can on its pathology and try to find out where it's hiding."

"Maybe look for an area that people have only recently started traveling in," Sarie said. "Contact with unusual animals. Things like that."

A figure appeared on the walkway next to the pool, and Jon watched him as Sarie began gleefully speculating on the selective pressures that could create a parasite like the one they were looking for.

The man moved casually, not focused on anything in particular, but stood out just the same. He was probably six foot three, with the look of an aging weight lifter whose muscle had started to migrate downward and whose fair skin had spent a lifetime being brutalized by the African sun.

His path to a table partially shadowed by flowering vines took him right by them, and as he passed behind Howell, his trajectory suddenly changed. Before Smith could react, he had dropped into the empty chair between him and Sarie.

At first, Smith thought he might be the hotel's manager, but then he saw the glint of a pistol as it disappeared beneath the table.

"Peter," the man said in a thick Dutch accent. "Here you

137

are in town and you didn't even call. I thought you Brits were supposed to be polite."

Howell's expression was placid, but Sarie's most definitely wasn't. It was impossible to know if she'd seen the pistol or if she just knew men like this from her travels. Up close, he had the distinct look of a mercenary—one of many who had cut their teeth on the war in Angola and then spent the rest of their lives fighting bloody skirmishes all over the continent.

"You'll have to accept my apologies, Sabastiaan. I'm afraid I thought you were dead."

"I'll bet you did. I was bleeding pretty bad when you left me. But I managed to get out."

"I'm terribly embarrassed. I could have sworn I hit an artery."

Sabastiaan smiled cruelly and reached for Sarie's drink, draining it in less than a second. "Aren't you going to introduce me to your friends?"

"Of course. Drs. van Keuren and Smith. I'm taking them into the field to find specimens."

Howell was obviously calculating, but there wasn't much he could do. The guy was a pro, and he was smart enough to be extremely cautious around the former SAS man.

"You hired this British son of a bitch? How much are you paying? You could do better."

Smith feigned the fear that would be expected of an American academic in this situation. "What's this all about? We ... we don't want any trouble."

His acting skills must have been more impressive than he thought. Sabastiaan dismissed him as trivial. A significant error on the mercenary's part. Perhaps a fatal one.

"And what about you, sweetheart?"

Sarie responded in Afrikaans, the distaste audible in her voice. Whatever she said obviously wasn't complimentary, and Sabastiaan responded angrily in the same language. His eyes locked on her in an attempt to get her to back down. Another mistake.

In one smooth motion, Smith picked up his steak knife

and swung it up beneath the man's chin. Sabastiaan was startled for a moment, but then a thin smile spread across his face. "The professor has spirit."

Smith leaned forward a bit, confirming in his peripheral vision that the people at the bar still had their backs to them. "Look closely, Sabastiaan. Do you really think I'm a professor?"

The mercenary's smile faltered. Being able to accurately size up your opponent was one of the most important qualities a man in his position could possess, and he was beginning to understand the extent of his miscalculation.

"I have a gun on your friend," he said hesitantly. "All I have to do is pull the trigger."

"That would be inconvenient. I'd have to find another guide, and since I plan to shove this knife so far that it breaks off in the top of your skull, you won't be available."

Smith heard the door leading to the hotel burst open but didn't dare take his eyes off Sabastiaan even when the clack of running boots sounded behind him.

"Put down the knife!" an accented voice demanded.

"He has a gun," Smith said. "He—"

"Put it down now!"

"Do it," Sarie said. "But do it slowly."

Howell nodded his agreement and Smith eased the knife to the table. A moment later, he was yanked from his chair and the table was surrounded by armed soldiers.

"Give me a second to explain," Smith said as his arms were wrenched behind him and secured with a zip tie. "We're—"

"Shut up!" someone behind him said and then hit him in the back of the head hard enough to blur his view of everyone else at the table being similarly bound.

They were led out to the street and separated from Sabastiaan before being shoved into the back of a black SUV. Smith struggled into a sitting position as they sped away, finally managing to prop himself up far enough to see out the windows.

In the dim street behind, the old merc was trying to protect himself from the clubs raining down on him. At the rate he was taking punishment, he'd be dead in less than a minute. The question was, would he turn out to be the lucky one?

CHAPTER THIRTY

"What's so important that it couldn't wait?"

Dave Collen closed the door behind him, giving it a solid push to make sure it was sealed. "We have a problem with Brandon, Larry."

"What kind of a problem?"

Collen slid his laptop onto Drake's desk and brought up a security video depicting an elevator full of people. "Watch him."

Drake leaned into the screen, squinting as the doors opened and five more people crammed themselves into the already crowded space. One of those people was Gazenga, and he wrestled his way to the back, taking a position next to a beautiful blonde.

The elevator descended three floors and Gazenga pushed his way back to the front. After he exited, the video ended.

"So, he doesn't like taking stairs?" Drake said. "I don't see that as a life-or-death issue."

"Watch more carefully," Collen said, restarting the video. He paused it at the point where Gazenga settled in next to the woman and proceeded frame by frame. "Look at his right arm."

Everything below the elbow was obscured, but Drake saw Gazenga's shoulder come up a bit and then drop back down when the elevator stopped. The woman glanced up at him and then watched incuriously as he got off.

"The elevator jerked, he bumped the woman next to him,

and then he left. What are you driving at, Dave?"

"He put something in her pocket. Watch it again."

Drake frowned skeptically as it rolled for a third time. It was possible to interpret the movement of his arm as lifting his hand level with the pocket in her jacket, but it was a hell of a lot easier to interpret it as nothing.

"I appreciate your thoroughness, Dave, and I think a little paranoia is probably warranted at this point, but—"

"Do you know who she is?"

"No."

"Randi Russell."

Drake knew the name—everyone with sufficient clearance did—but they'd never met personally. "Last I heard she was chasing some Taliban explosives expert through the Hindu Kush."

"Yeah. Apparently he met with an accident."

"What kind of accident?"

"He got in the way of one of Randi's bullets and then fell off a six-hundred-foot cliff. She's back at headquarters for a couple months while things in Afghanistan cool off."

"Okay, but she and Brandon would have no way of knowing each other, and as far as I can remember, she's worked on every continent on the planet *except* Africa. If you're right and he's getting cold feet, why would he go to her?"

Collen fell into one of the chairs facing Drake's desk. "Smith had a fiancée awhile back—she died from being infected by the Hades virus."

"So?"

"Her name was Sophia Russell."

Drake felt the knot that had been tied in his stomach since he'd started this operation tighten. "They're related?"

"Sisters. And to the degree that Russell and Smith are close to anyone, they're close to each other."

Drake stared down at the frozen image on the laptop for a moment. "Still, it could be a coincidence."

"There's more security footage of what Brandon did *after* he got off the elevator. He had no business on that floor and just went straight for the stairs and back to his office."

The tightness in Drake's stomach began to spread to his chest. "Have we checked her out?"

"As soon as I got this, I had her called into a meeting. We turned the heat up and she took off her jacket. When they broke for coffee I checked her pocket. Nothing."

"Then either there was nothing there to begin with ..."

"Or she got the message."

Drake opened a drawer and pulled out two Excedrins, downing them without a drink to stave off the headache he knew was coming. "If he did pass her something, it could have been anything—an invitation to a private chat room or to an e-mail account with a damn treatise on everything we've done."

"I've gone through all his computer usage," Collen said. "He's a clever little bastard, but I found the footprints of his search for someone to contact. I'm pretty confident that we have a handle on everything he's done electronically."

"Then a time and place. A meeting."

Collen nodded.

"If you're wrong and she has something on us ..."

"The minute I saw the video I put heavy surveillance on her. If she knows something, we'll eventually find out about it."

"Eventually isn't good enough, Dave. Randi Russell is the last person we need getting her teeth into this thing. If she ..." Drake's voice lost its strength for a moment, fading under the weight of the disaster scenarios playing out in his mind. He stood and paced across his expansive office for a few moments before stopping on a rug that bore the CIA seal. "Are we prepared to move against Gazenga?"

"We've been ready since the day we brought him in. Should we go?"

"Can we afford to?"

"The short answer is no," Collen said. "We think Omidi is in Uganda, and Brandon's using his contacts to try to confirm—contacts I don't have a relationship with. On the other hand, can we afford not to?"

"Damn Castilla and his ops team! This should have never

143

gotten this complicated. Do it. Get rid of him. And I expect you to pick up the slack, Dave. No excuses."

"What about Russell?"

"It's the same story, isn't it? Killing her is dangerous. But leaving her alive is potentially suicidal."

"Then we're considering dealing with her?"

Drake gave a short nod.

"I'll start laying the groundwork, but it's going to take time. When it comes to walking away when she should be dead, Randi Russell is a witch. This has to be planned to the very last detail."

"We don't have time to play around, Dave. I want to see a summary of possible options by tomorrow afternoon."

CHAPTER THIRTY-ONE

Outside Kampala, Uganda
November 22—0653 Hours GMT+3

Any hope that their arrest had been a simple matter of the army's coincidentally showing up at the worst possible moment could now be safely discarded. The situation they found themselves in exceeded even the worst-case scenarios Smith had come up with on the ride there. And he was a man whose life could pretty much be summed up as one worst-case scenario after another.

There had been no calls to the embassy, no lawyers, and no questions asked or answered. The windowless room they were in was made entirely of crumbling concrete, with a rusty steel door that looked like it had been salvaged from a battleship. The air was hot and increasingly unsuitable for breathing as the carbon dioxide from their breath slowly built up.

Furniture consisted of three chairs, each bolted down and each equipped with sturdy leather straps on the arms and legs. Much worse, though, were the streams of dried blood leading from beneath them to a drain in the floor.

Sarie was feeling around the jamb, slipping her shaking fingers into the gaps and pulling futilely when she managed to get a grip. Howell had nodded off on the floor shortly after he'd satisfied himself that there was no way they were getting through the door, past the guards posted outside, and out of the dilapidated military base beyond. Saving energy and air to fight another day.

Smith crossed the room and put a hand on Sarie's shoulder.

They'd been trapped there for eight hours, and probably half of that she'd spent pacing like a trapped animal.

"Why don't you take a piece of floor next to Peter and get some rest. Let me work on the door for a while."

She looked back at him, obviously trying to control her fear but still looking a little wild-eyed. "We have to get out of here, Jon. This isn't America. The government can do whatever it wants to you. They can—"

A quiet grinding became audible, and he grabbed her arm, pulling her behind him as he backed away. Howell was immediately on his feet and skirting the wall to take a position in a corner to the side of the door that was now slowly opening.

Five heavily armed soldiers poured in, taking up positions that made any thought of escape impossible. Howell folded his arms casually in front of his chest with no fewer than three guns lined up on him.

The next man who entered was easily recognizable. He was well over six feet, with spindly legs that didn't look sturdy enough to support his bulky torso or the countless medals splashed across his uniform.

Charles Sembutu. The president of Uganda.

He'd enjoyed iron-fisted control over the country for years now, but that control was slipping. It was widely believed that he'd tolerated Bahame's rise, using the man's brutality to drum up fear that allowed him to consolidate ever-more power in order to "fight terrorism". But he'd gotten greedy and given Bahame too long a leash, leaving Kampala in danger of being overrun from the north.

A leather-backed chair and a desk with the presidential seal laid into it were rolled in, and Sembutu sat, spreading their passports out on the blotter. "Dr. van Keuren's reputation precedes her," he said, appraising Smith coolly. "And despite his fake passport, I'm sorry to say that Mr. Howell's does as well. But you ... You are a mystery."

"My name is Dr. Jon Smith. I'm a microbiologist with—"

"The American army," Sembutu said, finishing his sentence. "With a fairly varied background, yes? Special forces,

Military Intelligence. And I'm told you're quite capable with a knife."

"That was—"

"You'll speak only when I ask you a direct question," Sembutu said, slapping a massive hand down on the desktop. "What are you doing in my country?"

"I'm on a leave of absence from the army. I'm a virologist by training, but I've been spending some time on parasites lately. I had an opportunity to come on this expedition with Sarie and I took it."

"And you brought along a former SAS man?"

"It seemed wise, Mr. President. I have some military training, but in the end I'm just a medical doctor—"

"You think my country is unsafe? That I cannot control it?"

This was probably a good time to dust off the little he knew about diplomacy. The purpose of the room was very clear, and spending the next few days strapped into one of those chairs freshening the stains on the floor wasn't how he wanted to end his life.

"Not at all, sir. I'm fully aware of the strides Uganda has made since you became president. But I also know how hard it is to implement reforms in remote rural areas, so I decided to err on the side of caution."

A humorless smile spread across Sembutu's face. "I am not a simpleton, Doctor. I think you'll find I'm not so easily handled."

"It wasn't my intention, sir. I—"

"Why were you at the hospital?"

Smith had spent much of the time they'd been imprisoned there considering every reason they could have been arrested, but their visit to the hospital had run a distant second to their side trip to see Peter's arms dealer.

"We found some research on a parasite that infects humans and wanted to ask Dr. Lwanga if he was familiar with it. We—"

"And then you described something very much like Caleb Bahame's attacks on villages in the North."

Smith let his expression go blank. "Caleb Bahame? The terrorist? I don't understand, sir. This is a parasite that causes insanity and blood loss. What would that have to do with Bahame?"

Sembutu examined him carefully, but it was impossible to discern if he was buying the completely plausible lie. Americans tended not to pay much attention to the various skirmishes going on in Africa. Why would an army doctor know the details of Bahame's attacks?

"It doesn't matter if you understand what this has to do with Bahame, Colonel. He is a psychotic who fills children with methamphetamines, paints them with blood, and convinces them to kill their own families. The uneducated people in the rural areas believe it is magic, and this is how he spreads misery in my country. If it becomes public that there is an American army doctor taking an interest in him, it will only serve to strengthen his legend and people's belief in his power."

"But we didn't intend—"

"I don't care what you did or did not intend!" Sembutu shouted. "If Bahame succeeds, he will kill every living thing in Uganda and then move on to other countries. America cares little about this, but I have a responsibility to the people of my country. To my subjects."

"Mr. President," Sarie cut in, her voice displaying a calm Smith knew she didn't feel. "We're not experts on politics or war. We're just scientists ..."

Sembutu glanced in her direction for a moment and then back to Howell and Smith. "All evidence to the contrary."

"Our main objective is a parasite that affects ants," she continued. "This was just something interesting that came up when we were doing research. We'd already discarded the idea of looking for it because we concluded that if Dr. Lwanga hasn't heard of it, it probably doesn't exist."

"An ant ...," Sembutu said skeptically.

"Yes, sir. I do a lot of work with ants."

The room went silent for a few moments before Sembutu spoke again. "I have to tell you that if it weren't for Dr.

van Keuren, you may well have found yourselves residents of one of our prisons. But her work with malaria has been a great help to people throughout Africa and I am indeed aware of her work with insects."

He held their passports out across the desk. "I've included a card with my personal phone number. If you encounter any problems, you have my permission to use it. And as military men, if you should come across any information on Bahame and his army, I would very much appreciate you passing it on to me. I understand that your government and many others question my legitimacy and methods. But I believe that you are realistic men who understand the way the world works. And as such, you understand that, while I may not be perfect in the eyes of the West, I am the lesser of the evils in this situation."

Smith didn't immediately move, a bit stunned by the sudden, almost schizophrenic turnaround. Was Sembutu saying they were free to go in return for the remote possibility of them passing him some minor intelligence?

"That's very gracious of you, Mr. President," Sarie said, snatching up the passports before the man changed his mind.

Sembutu nodded. "We are most grateful for your work, Doctor, and wish you continued success. Good day."

Charles Sembutu watched the three whites being escorted out of the room and sat alone as their footsteps faded. Despite the fact that they were lying, they would be taken back to their hotel, and when they checked out they would find their bill taken care of by the Ugandan government.

Smith worked at Fort Detrick and had been involved with stopping the Hades virus that killed so many in the West. Only an idiot would believe that one of America's foremost bioweapons experts would take a leave of absence to study Ugandan insects. And Sembutu hadn't become one of the most powerful men in Africa by being an idiot.

It was an impossibly dangerous situation that seemed to get more out of control every day. The Americans could normally be counted on to take a hands-off approach in all things African as long as their own interests weren't threatened. If they were, though, that apathy could turn. The lion must not be awakened.

His phone began to ring and he immediately picked up. "I am here."

"What did you learn?"

Mehrak Omidi's voice was low, as though he was trying to hide his conversation from those around him—something that was almost certainly the case.

"Smith says he's on a leave of absence, studying a parasite that affects ants in the North."

"Ants," Omidi replied in disgust. "Do they have so little respect for you that they would expect you to believe such a story?"

Sembutu bristled. Dealing with the Iranians was even more unpleasant than dealing with the Americans. For all their talk of Western arrogance, the Iranians' unshakable belief that they were God's chosen people was both insufferable and dangerous. Right now, though, they were in a position to give him what he desperately needed. The Americans were not.

"I want them dealt with," Omidi continued.

"And what does this mean—dealt with?"

"I think you understand me perfectly, Mr. President. I want them questioned and then I want them killed."

"Killing American and British military men wasn't part of our agreement."

"The Ugandan north country is a very remote and very dangerous place, Mr. President. People disappear here every day."

CHAPTER THIRTY-TWO

Annandale, Virginia, USA
November 22—0026 Hours GMT–5

Brandon Gazenga pulled into his garage and closed the door, sealing out the cold wind that had descended on the Washington area. A poorly placed bag of garbage nearly trapped him in the car, and he had to push with his shoulder to open a gap large enough to slip out. Another month and he was going to have to start parking in the driveway.

He'd said it before, but now he really meant it: this weekend he was going to rent a truck and haul all this crap to the dump. And then he was going to hire one of those organization consultants—preferably a dour old British lady with a riding crop. The time had come to take back control of his life.

The house wasn't in much better condition, but at least it was warm. He flicked on the lights and looked around before committing to the short trip to the kitchen. The Uganda operation had been burning a hole in his stomach for months, but now it was starting to kill him. Smith and his team had been arrested and the initial report that it was because of a fight by the hotel pool went out the window when he received confirmation that they'd been taken to a high-security military base.

And then there were the tentative reports that Mehrak Omidi was personally on the ground in northern Uganda. Finally, and perhaps worst of all, there was Randi Russell and the note he'd put in her pocket.

Had she found it yet? What would she think of an

anonymous request for a meeting? Would she report it?

The truth was that there was absolutely no way for him to know. He was just an analyst with delusions of grandeur. Most of what he knew about clandestine meetings he'd learned from James Bond movies just like everyone else.

But this wasn't a cheesy action flick and he wasn't Sean Connery. Drake and Collen had put their careers—maybe even their lives—on the line for this operation, and they wouldn't be happy to find out that some nobody from Langley's basement was working behind their backs. Not happy at all.

He made his way to the refrigerator and pawed through a mishmash of aging takeout containers until he found something that looked like it was still edible.

He left the living room dark, falling into a leather chair and stabbing into the box of General Tso's chicken with a dirty fork. The romantic fantasies he'd had about moving into operations were long gone now. There were no Panama hats and ceiling fans. No supermodels or fast cars. Just the constant nagging feeling that you'd made a fatal mistake somewhere and someone was slinking up behind you to make you pay for it.

Going back now, though, wasn't an option. Randi Russell had his note, and if he didn't show up to the rendezvous, it was unlikely she would just let it go. Her reputation for tenacity was one of the many reasons he'd picked her.

He crammed another forkful of chicken into his mouth, not hungry but also aware that if he lost any more weight he'd have to buy all new suits.

Things would be better soon. Russell was going to come through like she always did. She'd know what to do, who to talk to. But mostly, he wouldn't be alone anymore.

Gazenga put the empty food container on his cluttered coffee table and headed for the bedroom, locking the door behind him and positioning an empty beer bottle so it would tip if anyone tried to get in. He stripped to his boxers and crawled beneath a traditional African blanket his mother had given him. The lump in the pillow made by the Colt beneath it was even more comforting than it had been the day before, and he caressed the grip for a few moments before rolling onto his back and staring up at the dark ceiling.

Things were going to get better. Soon.

Gazenga awoke in a sweat, his stomach cramping and a numbness spreading through his chest. At first he thought it was just a dream and gave his head a weak shake to wake himself, but that just brought on a wave of nausea.

The clock glowed four a.m. as he pushed himself into a sitting position and struggled to get in a full breath. Because of his frequent travel in Africa, he'd had more than the normal complement of illnesses in his life, including bouts of malaria and river blindness. Enough to know when something was seriously wrong.

His cell phone was still in his pants and he was sliding awkwardly off the bed when he froze. The blackout shades he'd recently bought in an attempt to help him sleep were fully drawn but the light from the clock was enough to pick out an unfamiliar outline near the door. A chair? Had he put it there for extra security? No, he'd used a beer bottle. The chair should have been—

"How are you feeling, Brandon?"

A surge of adrenaline shot through him and he reached beneath his pillow. Nothing. The gun was gone.

"Sorry, I had to take that. Wouldn't want you to hurt yourself."

The voice was familiar, but it still took him a few moments to identify it in the absence of its normal context.

"Dave? What are you doing here?" Gazenga said, his initial shock turning to a deep sense of dread. It was Russell. It had to be. They'd somehow found out. "Has … has something gone wrong in Uganda?"

"In a manner of speaking."

Gazenga reached for the light next to him, but his arm didn't respond normally and he just ended up pawing weakly at the shade.

"You know why I'm here," Collen said. "Tell me what you gave Randi Russell."

"Russell?" Gazenga said, feigning surprise as he tried to calculate his options with a mind clouded by fear and lack of oxygen. "What are you talking about?"

He slid the rest of the way from the bed, discovering that his legs would no longer support him and collapsing to the dirty carpet.

"We have video of you sliding something into her pocket on the elevator, Brandon. You're wasting time. And you don't have much left."

"What have you done to me?"

The shadow grew as Collen stood and took a step forward. "I poisoned you at our meeting this afternoon. That last cup of coffee, remember? It's an interesting compound based on botulism that causes paralysis and respiratory distress. The official cause of death will be the half-rotted food in your refrigerator. That is, unless you tell me what I want to know."

"I don't know what you're talking about," Gazenga said, struggling to focus. The past and present were becoming muddled as his brain was slowly starved.

"I'm not going to ask again," Collen said, anger beginning to take shape in his voice.

"I've never even *met* Randi Russell. She's stationed in Afghanistan or Iraq or something."

Collen looked through the dim light at the prone figure of his colleague, examining the unnatural position of his mostly paralyzed limbs and the impenetrable shadow hiding his face. It was a frustrating and extremely unfortunate situation. The fact that the loss of Gazenga could put the operation in jeopardy was bad enough, but the lack of anything but the threat of death to extract information was potentially disastrous. There was no choice, though. Other techniques, while more reliable, were slow and left obvious marks—something that they couldn't afford. The young man's demise had to be above even the slightest suspicion.

"I have the antidote with me, Brandon. We're not angry. You got scared and you made a mistake. It happens to everybody. Just tell me what I want to know and we can fix this."

Gazenga gulped at the air like a dying fish, panic clearly starting to set in. "I didn't tell her anything. Just a … just a time and a place to meet."

Collen knelt and pulled a bottle containing two large pills from his pocket, shaking it so the young man could hear their seductive rattle. Of course, they were nothing but an over-the-counter pain reliever, but desperation had a way of making true believers out of even the most ardent skeptics.

"That's good, Brandon. Very good. Now, just tell me where and when and we can put this behind us."

CHAPTER THIRTY-THREE

Outside Kampala, Uganda
November 22—1046 Hours GMT+3

This time the crowd parted easily as their cab approached the elaborate archway. Of course, they still got a lot of stares, but by and large, weapons remained shouldered.

"Here is fine," Peter Howell said, reaching over the seat and holding out the two hundred euros they'd negotiated. "We won't need a ride back."

The three of them piled out of the vehicle and dumped their packs on the dusty road before removing Sarie's scientific equipment from the roof. A few of Janani's men came out to help carry it inside, where their boss was sitting on a low stool drinking tea.

"Peter!" he said, rising and shaking the Brit's hand. "You have once again returned safely to me."

"Barely. Did you know that Sabastiaan was in town?"

"I heard rumors. But now it is my understanding that he is no longer alive. No great loss to the world, in my humble opinion."

They followed Janani back to the outdoor range, where a table had been laid out with two custom handguns and two Belgian-made assault rifles that looked stock but probably weren't.

Smith picked up the pistol with a tag bearing his name and sighted along it. The grip felt like it had been molded to his fingers and the balance was dead-on.

"Will it be adequate?" Janani said.

"It's a work of art, my friend."

The African smiled and turned to Sarie. "You think I forgot you, but like all beautiful women, you jump to conclusions."

He put a hand on her back and escorted her to another table, where a scaled-down bolt-action rifle rested in an aluminum case. It was another beautiful specimen, with a Swarovski scope and gleaming black barrel. Those qualities, though, were overshadowed by a stock painted with colorful flowering vines. The artistry was undeniable, but a little out of place.

Janani offered the weapon to Sarie with both hands, frowning as he looked down at the pink and yellow blossoms. "I told my youngest wife about you, and she insisted that I allow her to do these decorations. She's only sixteen, and I am embarrassed to say that I find it impossible to deny her anything. Of course, I can have one of my men replace the stock before you leave."

Sarie accepted the gun, examining the lifelike images winding around the smooth wood. "Absolutely not. Tell her it's beautiful."

The African smiled broadly, obviously pleased that he wasn't the only one who appreciated his wife's work. "So everyone is happy, then? Our transaction is on the path to being a good one?"

"Didn't we also talk about a vehicle?" Smith said.

"Of course! How could I forget?"

They followed him into a small warehouse, threading through an extensive inventory of steel and exotic hardwoods on their way to a Toyota Land Cruiser parked at the back. It was a deep maroon with oversized tires and a crowded light bar across the top.

Smith stopped a few feet away, appraising his reflection in the chrome bumper. "I don't suppose you'd have anything that would blend in a bit better?"

"Blend in?" Janani said, sounding a little insulted. "If you want a twenty-five-year-old pickup that drags on the ground, go to a used-car dealer. I trade only in top-of-the line merchandise."

Sarie dropped to her knees next to the vehicle and flipped onto her back, wriggling under it for a look. A moment later a low whistle escaped her. "The frame's been reinforced, it's got protective plating that looks like it would take a direct hit from an atomic bomb, aftermarket shocks, locking differential ..."

She scooted out and reached through the open driver's-side window to pop the hood, which she promptly disappeared beneath. Her legs left the ground for a few moments, dangling over the brush guard while she fished around in the engine bay. "Chevy small block with a snorkel: simple, classic, easy to repair and get parts for. Exactly what you want."

Janani leaned in close to Smith. "What an extraordinarily useful woman. Would you consider parting with her?"

"Excuse me?"

"I was thinking that I could probably be persuaded to make an even trade. The car and the weapons for her."

"I don't think so."

"Of course not. I apologize. I've insulted you. The car, the weapons, and fifty thousand euros."

Smith grinned. "A generous offer, Janani. The problem is, she's not mine."

"Pity."

Sarie jumped into the driver's seat and started pressing buttons on the dash.

"So what do you think?" Smith called. "Should we take it?"

"Are you kidding? It's got leather and a place to plug in your iPod!"

CHAPTER THIRTY-FOUR

Near Lancaster, Pennsylvania, USA
November 23—2331 Hours GMT–5

Randi Russell emerged from the woods and stopped at the edge of a thirty-foot cliff. Below, the Susquehanna River ran black in the moonlight and patches of snow glowed on the abandoned railroad track running parallel.

There was no way down and she turned east, moving silently along the tree line. It had taken her two hours to get there, most of that time spent on the maze of rural roads that cut through Pennsylvania's farm country. With the exception of three cars and an Amish horse and buggy, she'd seen no one. It was approaching eleven p.m., and this part of the world obviously still adhered to the adage "Early to bed, early to rise."

She had studiously avoided the obvious entrance to the railroad cut, instead parking at the edge of a poorly defined dirt road and bushwhacking toward the river. Her preference was to have these types of rendezvous in crowded areas, and the whole midnight thing seemed a little melodramatic, but once her curiosity was piqued she had a hard time letting go.

A gulley appeared to her left and Randi appraised it, calculating the difficulty of the climb down and searching for icy spots. The satellite images had underplayed the steepness of the rock, but there wasn't much she could do about that now. The clock was ticking.

She dangled her legs over the edge, then flipped over and eased herself onto a narrow ledge below. Her hands were getting numb from the cold, and that, combined with the darkness, made the descent much more treacherous than it should have been. The smart thing would be to take it slow, but even with black pants and parka, she wasn't comfortable being exposed against the cliff.

The rock became more featured as she continued down, providing better cover and allowing her to move more efficiently. She let go when she was still almost ten feet from the ground, dropping into the gravel and then going completely still for a few seconds to scan for movement.

Satisfied that no one was bearing down on her, she leapt over the old tracks, wincing at the unavoidable crunch of her footfalls. Once back in the trees, she stopped again to listen. Still nothing. The night was completely windless and the animals that normally prowled the area all had the good sense to dig in and get out of the cold.

She started east again, moving deliberately and occasionally looking to her iPhone for an update of her position. The note she'd found in her jacket had been brief—only a set of GPS coordinates, a date, a time, and a very intriguing name: Colonel Jon Smith.

Undoubtedly the man she was there to meet would be disappointed to know that he wasn't as anonymous as he thought. A life spent in unstable countries full of petty criminals and pickpockets had given Randi an awareness of her surroundings that didn't shut down just because she was in Langley. And while Brandon Gazenga's technique wasn't bad for an Ivy Leaguer, he was no Iraqi street urchin.

The question was, what was a young Africa-division analyst with an impressive, if unspectacular, record doing passing her notes in elevators? And even more interesting, why was the name of an army virus hunter scrawled across the bottom?

Her phone indicated that she was within twenty feet of the coordinates she'd been given and she slid a Glock from beneath her coat. The direction arrow pointed left to a spot that looked to be dead on top of the tracks.

She went right, finding a boulder large enough to protect

her flank, and positioned so she could see anyone coming up the railroad cut.

Jon Smith.

There was nothing Gazenga could have put in his note that would grab her attention more. She'd spent a long time blaming Smith for her sister's death. As unfair as it was, he had provided something she needed—a target for her anger, despair, and helplessness. Strange that she would end up as close to him as to anyone in the world.

Despite that relationship, though, there was a great deal she didn't know about the man. He insisted that he was just a medical researcher, but then had a way of popping up in places that had nothing to do with his job at Fort Detrick.

The first time they'd run into each other in the field, she'd completely fallen for his beautifully delivered "simple country doctor" line. And she wasn't *too* bothered by the second time their lives collided—coincidences happened. Occasionally.

After that, though, things just got stupid. He was clearly an operator and he wasn't working for one of the normal acronyms.

Usually, this kind of thing would raise the hairs on the back of her neck, but with Jon it was different. As much as she hated to admit it, he was one of the few people in the world whose motivations and integrity she didn't question. If the word didn't always get stuck in her throat when she tried to utter it, she might even say she trusted him.

A quick glance at her phone suggested that her contact was late. Five minutes and counting.

The cold was starting to seep into her—something she had become sensitive to since an operation had gone badly wrong on an island near the Arctic Circle. An island that would now be home to her frozen body if it hadn't been for Smith.

She stood, wrapping her arms around herself but remaining still enough to blend into the trees around her.

It was possible that Gazenga was playing the same waiting

game, but there was no way she was going to go stand out in the open with nothing but a note from someone she'd never met. She'd collected far too many enemies over the years to offer up that easy a target.

Randi Russell slipped behind the wheel of her borrowed car, turning the heater on full blast and confirming the road was completely dark before pulling out.

Her thumb hovered over her phone's number pad for a moment, and then she thought better of it and dug an untraceable satellite phone from the glove box. No point in taking chances.

She dialed and listened to it ring for a while, immediately hitting redial when it flipped to voice mail. The third time was a charm.

"Yeah?" a groggy voice said. "Hello?"

"Trip, it's Randi."

"Randi? What … Do you know what time it is in the States?"

She wasn't in the habit of broadcasting her whereabouts and didn't see any reason to correct her friend's assumption. "Two p.m., right?"

"No, it's two *a.m.* As in two in the *morning*."

She'd known Jeff Tripper for more than five years—ever since they'd teamed up to track down an Afghan terrorist who'd managed to slip over the Mexican border. Since then, his career at the FBI had been in overdrive and he'd recently been made the head of the Baltimore field office.

"A.m.?" she said innocently. "Sorry, bud. It's a subtle difference, you know?"

"Not from where I'm sitting," he said, now awake enough to be suspicious. "Is it safe for me to assume this isn't a social call?"

"I'm insulted."

"And I'm tired."

"Okay, I'll admit it's not *entirely* social. How are your contacts with the Virginia cops?"

"Good. Why?"

162

"I need you to have them send a black-and-white to a guy named Brandon Gazenga's house."

"Why?"

"I don't care. Say a neighbor was complaining that he was playing his stereo too loud."

"I mean, what are we after?"

"I just want to make sure he's okay."

"Do you need to know now or would nine o'clock work for you?"

"Are you going to make me remind you that you owe me?"

Tripper swore under his breath. "I'll call you back."

Randi had just crossed into Maryland when her sat phone began to ring. She put in an earpiece and picked up.

"What's the word?"

"I'm not a happy man, Randi."

"Have you considered meditation?"

"Brandon Gazenga's body was found late this morning."

Randi glanced reflexively in the rearview mirror, cataloging three sets of headlights behind her and estimating their distance. "How?"

"A coworker went to his house when he didn't show up for work and found him on the floor of his bedroom. They're thinking food poisoning."

"Food poisoning? You've got to be kidding me."

"Do I sound like I'm kidding? According to the cops, it's not as uncommon as you'd think."

"Was there anything suspicious about the circumstances?"

"Beyond getting a call from a CIA operative at two in the morning, you mean?"

"But you never got a call from a CIA operative at two in the morning, right?"

"Right. Look, I talked to the investigating officer—who really appreciated being called in the middle of the night, by the way—and he said the guy's house was a complete pigsty and his fridge was crammed with moldy takeout. He said it's a miracle Gazenga survived as long as he did."

A new set of headlights appeared behind her, and they were coming up fast. Randi waited until the last possible moment before swerving onto an off ramp. The car stayed on course, passing harmlessly by.

"Okay. Thanks, Trip."

"Now hold on a minute. That cop also told me that Gazenga worked for a certain government agency you'd be familiar with. What are we talking about here?"

"We're not talking at all, remember?"

"That's fine and good, but consider the position you've put me in, Randi. I just made a very suspicious call about a CIA agent whose body isn't quite cold yet."

"I have complete confidence that you'll figure out a way to explain that."

There was silence over the phone for a few seconds. "Hey, Randi?"

"Yeah?"

"About that favor you did me. We're even."

The line went dead and she immediately began dialing a number from memory. There was no choice at this point.

It rang twice before transferring to voice mail.

"You've reached Jon Smith. I can't take your call right now, but leave me a message and I'll get back to you as soon as I can."

"Hi, Jon, it's Randi. You know, it's getting close to Sophia's birthday and I'm feeling a little blue. Just wanted to talk. Give me a call when you get a chance."

She disconnected the call and tossed the phone into the passenger seat. No one hearing that message would think much of it. Even if they were thorough enough to check, they'd find that her dead sister's birthday was indeed at the end of the week. But Jon would know better. She had never been one for melancholy reflection, and her call would set his alarm bells ringing.

CHAPTER THIRTY-FIVE

Northern Uganda
November 24—0904 Hours GMT+3

Mehrak Omidi gripped the dashboard as the open jeep bounced through a series of muddy ruts. The humidity was just starting to ease, and despite the fact that Bahame was piloting the doorless vehicle like the maniac he had proven himself to be, Omidi reveled in the sensation of air flowing across his skin.

The cult leader made a great show of sleeping with his troops and insisted that his guests bed down in a similar manner, exposing them to the biting insects and sudden downpours that plagued this forsaken part of the world. Beyond nodding off for a few moments here and there, Omidi spent his nights swatting malarial mosquitoes and listening to the drunken fights and sexual activity of those around him.

God willing, it wouldn't be much longer. If all went according to plan, he would soon leave this place to collapse beneath the weight of its own decadence. And with the help of the Almighty, he would never have any cause to return.

Bahame drifted the jeep around a blind curve and then slammed on the brakes, skidding to a stop behind an eighteen-wheeler making a U-turn on a rare piece of open land.

The trailer was jerking back and forth—not with the contours of the land but seemingly with a will of its own. Holes about thirty centimeters square had been cut from the steel, and desperate arms were shoved through, tearing on the sharp edges and sending fresh blood rolling down old stains.

Hands grabbed futilely at the air as frustrated, animal-like screams overpowered the sounds of the jungle.

The truck came to a stop and a group of armed men climbed out of the cab, dragging a terrified young boy along with them. Their faces were painted with something that looked like white chalk, and all wore elaborate amulets that Bahame had promised would protect them from the demons they were hauling. Interestingly, though, he had also equipped them with goggles and surgical gloves. Obviously, the medicine man had a practical side.

Despite their protective gear, the three men looked only slightly less frightened than the child they were pulling along behind. They gave the trailer a wide berth, keeping at least five meters between them and the bleeding arms reaching so frantically in their direction.

"Come," Bahame said, jumping from the jeep.

He passed much closer to the trailer than his soldiers had, though he still kept well out of range as the rocking increased to the point that, for a moment, Omidi thought it might tip.

He followed the African to the rear, where a long chain leading from the bolt in the door was being secured around the struggling boy's neck. The trailer's locking mechanism seemed far too complex for this part of the world, but Omidi was unwilling to get close enough to inspect it.

The boy immediately began trying to get free, his bawling rising above the inhuman sounds coming from inside the truck until he saw Bahame approaching and fell silent.

The cult leader knelt and spoke a quiet prayer, dipping his thumb into a can of reddish powder and streaking the child's cheeks with it. The soldiers watched transfixed as their leader called to gods and demons, blessed the boy, and demanded victory. The man's charisma was almost as astounding as his lack of shame in wielding it.

When the ceremony was finished, he motioned for his men and Omidi to follow him into the jungle. They took a position that provided both excellent cover and a view of the boy, who was opening cuts on his hands and throat as he pulled helplessly against the rusty chain.

They were crouched there for almost five minutes before Omidi pointed to the radio control in Bahame's hand. "Are you going to release them?"

"In time. First, we must leave their minds."

Bahame had carried out similar operations many times and obviously had learned a great deal about how to use this weapon without it destroying himself along with his enemies. Some of the people in the trailer would have seen them go into the woods, and they would be a significant danger if they remembered that when they were freed. Omidi wondered idly how many young soldiers had died during the early attempts to use the parasite.

Another ten minutes passed before Bahame flipped the protective cover off the remote in his hand and held it out. "It's your honor."

Omidi hesitated for a moment and then pressed the exposed button. There was no sound, but from his position he could make out the simple electric actuator on the trailer beginning to pull back the bolt. The chain holding the boy dropped and he ran, dragging it behind him as he headed for his village a short distance down the road. The infected wailed inconsolably as they watched their quarry escape.

The bolt kept moving, though. After another forty-five seconds, there was a loud crack and the doors flew open, spilling a tangle of writhing bodies to the ground. The tone of their screeches went from frustrated to excited as they gained their footing and took off after the boy.

It was a primitive system, but one that seemed to work. Without the child to focus on, the infected would just disperse randomly, becoming disoriented and eventually dying in the jungle. With him, though, they would be led directly to the village Bahame had targeted.

CHAPTER THIRTY-SIX

Central Uganda
November 24—0930 Hours GMT+3

"You see it?" Peter Howell said.

They were on the crest of a tall butte, lying in the middle of the dirt road that they'd spent the last hour switchbacking up. Smith adjusted the focus on his binoculars, sweeping across verdant valley until he found the cause of the dust plume.

"Yeah. Open personnel carrier. Two men in front, another six in back. All armed."

"And since that's the only motorized vehicle we've seen for going on fourteen hours, I reckon it's safe to say they're following us."

"President Sembutu told us to call him if we had any problems," Sarie said. "Maybe he sent those men to make sure we don't get in any trouble."

They both looked back at her.

"Just a thought."

"I agree that they're probably Sembutu's men," Smith conceded. "But I'm not sure their intentions are so benign."

"Well, one thing I can tell you for certain is that someone in his office has been calling ahead," she said. "We've driven through three military checkpoints without so much as anyone even looking in the car. I'm guessing that's a first in this part of Africa."

Smith rolled onto his back and looked up into the unbroken blue of the sky. "I think you're right about Sembutu greasing the skids for us ..."

"The question is, why?" Howell said, finishing his thought.

Sarie pulled her new rifle from the backseat and sighted through the scope at the approaching truck. "I don't think there's much we can do at this point. There aren't a lot of intersections and we're leaving a pretty obvious trail."

"Maybe I'm just being paranoid," Smith said, putting a hand out and letting Howell pull him to his feet. "He might think we'll find something he can use. And how does it hurt him if we find out that Bahame is using a biological weapon? I don't think he'd object too much if the U.S. unloaded a few B-52s on Bahame's camp."

"Or maybe he believed the ant story," Sarie said.

Smith shrugged. "Anything's possible. And there's no telling when you might need a little extra firepower."

"Depending on who it's aimed at," Howell said, sliding back behind the wheel of their vehicle and slamming the door behind him.

"He doesn't seem all that happy," Sarie said, shouldering her rifle.

"No, he doesn't, does he?"

"Something happened to him here," Sarie said. "Something horrible."

It was a reasonable hypothesis that he himself had considered. But it left the question of what exactly that thing was. He knew Howell and men like him—hell, he *was* a man like him. After everything the Brit had seen over the course of his career with the SAS and MI6, what could affect him like this?

"You should ask him about it," Smith suggested.

"Me?" she said, lowering her voice to a harsh whisper. "Are you kidding? I mean, he's an interesting guy to have dinner with, but have you noticed that he always looks like he's about thirty seconds from killing you with a pocket-knife?"

"I think that's an exaggeration."

"Yeah? Then why don't *yo*u ask him? You've known him for years, right?"

169

"Yeah, a long time," Smith admitted. "But our relationship is ... Well, it's complicated."

Sarie tilted her head a bit and concentrated on his face. "Why is it I get the impression that all your relationships are complicated?"

Howell started the engine and revved it loudly, giving Smith cover for a strategic retreat. "I have no idea. I'm just a simple country doctor."

"Okay, we're looking for a turn," Smith said, running a finger along the fuzzy satellite photo Star had printed for him. She'd marked distances on both axes, which was a testament to her thoroughness but completely useless in the real world of African roads. "I assume it will be an obvious left in the next twenty clicks or so, but it's hard to be any more precise than that."

They entered a small village and Smith waved through the open window at the children running alongside them. It was impossible not to be taken by the ease of their laughter in the midst of poverty unimaginable to most Americans.

"It's incredible, isn't it?" Sarie said from the backseat. "These people have nothing of value to anyone—no running water, no electricity, no money. But even that's too much for people like Bahame. He can't just leave them alone to enjoy the simple life they can carve out for themselves."

She leaned through the window, briefly clasping the hand of the most persistent kid as they rolled out of the village.

"Any one of those children could end up being forced into Bahame's army," she continued. "Or worse, they could end up like the people who attacked those soldiers in the video you showed me. If we're right and this is a parasite, Bahame's eventually going to lose control of it. The more he uses it, the harder it's going to be to contain."

The apparent contradiction broke Howell from his trance. "It seems that the more practiced he becomes at using it, the less likely he is to lose control, no?"

Sarie stretched out on the seat, laying her rifle next to her and using her hat to block the sun streaming through the window. "Not exactly. What I'm worried about is that by using it like he is, he's going to weaken it."

Howell pondered that for a moment. "I'm still not following. Weaker is better."

"The word 'weak' doesn't mean what you're thinking," Smith said. "Right now the parasite—assuming it even exists—is fairly unsophisticated. Call it poorly evolved where humans are concerned. It infects people every few decades, those people infect a few others, and they all die within a time frame short enough that it never spreads very widely."

Sarie picked up his thought. "But these types of infections can become more effective by getting weaker. Killing your host quick is a bad survival strategy—particularly when the population concentrations are well separated."

"Exactly. The longer the host lives, the more copies the parasite can make of itself—both in the original victim and because it has more opportunity to jump to a new host."

"And that's only part of it," Sarie said. "Other mutations could be beneficial too. If this infection was ever widespread enough for natural selection to really start working on it, you could see less-violent behavior."

"Definitely," Smith agreed. "All the parasite wants its host to do is open a few cuts in an uninfected person so it can find a new home. Better to attack and injure instead of attack and kill. A dead body is no good to it."

"I'd also expect to see the onset of symptoms slow down," Sarie said. "Which would allow the parasite to travel farther to find a new host. Right now, I'd hypothesize that fast onset is beneficial because a lot of the victims are so badly injured in the process of transmission, they don't have much time left. Their strength and speed actually might not even be an adaptation to help them infect new victims—in a way it makes them too dangerous. That might just be a by-product of the parasite trying to animate a person who, under normal circumstances, would be too badly hurt to do much more than lie there."

"Interesting. I hadn't thought of that," Smith said. "But what if—"

171

"You people spend a lot of time on mental masturbation, don't you?" Howell interrupted.

"It's more productive than the other kind," Sarie said with a quiet chuckle.

"So what you're telling me is that if we just sit back and do nothing, the parasite might eventually become harmless."

"It's not unprecedented," Smith said. "There are some formerly nasty bugs out there that aren't much worse than a cold now. The problem is the millions of people who would die while we sat around waiting for Mother Nature to help us out."

CHAPTER THIRTY-SEVEN

Northern Uganda
November 24—1001 Hours GMT+3

Mehrak Omidi ran alongside Bahame, trying to stay close but occasionally having to dodge around trees and other obstacles. They and the armed guards surrounding them were moving as quickly as they could without making undue noise, paralleling the road at a distance that provided an intermittent view of it.

Most of the infected had outpaced them, but two stragglers remained visible through the leaves. One was a child of no more than four—too young to understand his own rage and how to exercise it. The other was even more disturbing: an old man with a severe compound fracture of the lower leg that he didn't seem to be aware of. He repeatedly stood, lurched forward a few meters, and then collapsed with a spurt of arterial blood. Omidi slowed a bit, transfixed by the man's struggle as he finally became resigned to dragging himself forward with his elbows.

It took another five minutes to reach the village, and Bahame grabbed his arm, pulling him to a place that provided sufficient cover but still afforded a partially blocked view of what was happening.

Again, Omidi found himself stunned. The village men were fighting desperately—with sticks, with machetes, with farm implements. One man had an old rifle but was taken down while he was still trying to get it to his shoulder. The infected were everywhere—their speed and strength making them seem like a much larger force than they actually were.

173

A fleeing woman crashed into the trees directly in front of them, causing Bahame to pull Omidi beneath the bush they were crouched behind. She barely made it ten meters before a young boy drenched in blood chased her down and dove onto her back. It took only a few moments before she succumbed to the brutal beating, but he didn't stop. The dull thud of his fists mixed with the screams and panicked shouts coming from the village until he finally collapsed. Whether he was unconscious or dead was impossible to determine.

One of the huts was on fire now, and Omidi glanced at Bahame, seeing the flames reflected in eyes glazed with power. It was at that moment he realized the African wasn't playing a role or pandering to his followers. He truly believed in his own godhood.

The wails of an infant began to emanate from the burning hut, and an infected man ran in like a savior. A moment later the child went silent.

When he reappeared, the long, bloodstained robe he wore was burning. Despite the increasing intensity of the flames, he rejoined the fray, sprinting toward a woman trying to find refuge in a corral full of panicked goats. He fell just short of reaching her, collapsing with his hands on the rickety fence as he was consumed.

Omidi slipped from beneath the bush as the remaining villagers were run down. He no longer saw rural Uganda, though. He saw New York, Chicago, Los Angeles. And it was magnificent.

CHAPTER THIRTY-EIGHT

Northern Uganda
November 24—1906 Hours GMT+3

Caleb Bahame slowed the jeep, increasing the distance between it and the lumbering truck turning twenty meters ahead. The terrified faces of the villagers they'd captured peered at Omidi through the holes cut in the trailer, fighting for air and trying to understand what had happened to them and their families.

All were injured, but only superficially. The seriously wounded villagers had been executed where they lay and their bodies burned. The few who had managed to avoid contact with the infected had been allowed to escape in order to spread word of Bahame's sorcery and power.

It was the slightly injured villagers who were the unlucky ones. They had been herded into the truck to replace the infected who had disappeared into the jungle and would eventually die there, lost and bleeding.

Bahame had calculated the time to death after infection took hold and the range of one of his demons on foot—making sure to attack only villages remote enough to not allow a chain of infection.

Details, however, were not of great concern to the African. Could animals spread the parasite? Was there variation in the way it attacked the brain? Could it mutate? What if one of the infected came upon and attacked a herdsman or traveler who then returned to their village?

All these important questions were answered the same way: with assurances that his network of spies would recognize and kill anyone infected by the parasite who managed to escape his makeshift quarantine.

It was a system that would work for a time in Africa but that would be completely unscalable. No, to use the parasite in Europe or America, a good deal more sophistication was needed.

It took another half hour to reach camp, and when they finally pulled in, it was to the deafening cheers of Bahame's soldiers. They surrounded the jeep, falling silent only when their shaman stood on his seat and raised his arms. He recounted his tale of victory, the rich baritone of his voice rising over the buzz of the jungle and the pleas of the people packed into the sweltering truck.

Omidi slipped out of the jeep and weaved through Bahame's mesmerized troops. A quick glance behind him confirmed that it wasn't only the ragged children who were captivated—Bahame himself seemed completely lost in his own delusions. A perfect time to exercise a bit of curiosity.

The Iranian made his way to a cave glowing with electric lights. There were two guards at its entrance, one no older than twelve and the other looking a bit queasy from the cloud of diesel fumes spewing from the generator next to him.

Omidi carefully ignored them as he approached and scowled dismissively when they started speaking to him in their native language. Both had undoubtedly noted his favored position with Bahame, leaving them wide-eyed and unsure whether to try to stop him.

The benefit of being a psychotic messianic leader was that your terrified followers were desperate to succumb to your will. The drawback was that they sometimes couldn't be sure what exactly your will was. If they challenged Bahame's honored guest in error, they would almost certainly be slowly and horribly put to death. On the other hand, if this wasn't an authorized visit and they didn't intervene, their deaths were equally assured and would be equally unpleasant.

In the end, they were swayed by his calculated confidence

and let him pass into a natural corridor narrow enough that he had to occasionally turn sideways to get through. Bare bulbs hung from cables secured to the cave's low roof, and he followed them, ignoring branches leading into the darkness. The temperature and humidity diminished as he penetrated deeper, but the stench of blood, excrement, and sweat became increasingly oppressive. Finally, the passageway opened into a broad chamber and Omidi stopped a few meters short, examining it unnoticed.

He recognized the elderly white man as the one who had arrived with the man Bahame beat to death. He was wearing a stained canvas apron and goggles as he leaned over a partially dissected corpse. At the back of the chamber was a wall of blood-spattered plastic set up in front of a hollowed-out section of stone fitted with steel bars. Inside, an infected man lay on the dirt floor, panting like an animal and watching an outwardly healthy woman sobbing in a similar cage some three meters away.

When Omidi finally stepped into the chamber, the infected man let out a high-pitched scream and rammed an arm through the bars with enough force that the sound of crunching bone was clearly audible.

The old man looked up and took a few hesitant steps back, holding the scalpel he'd been using out in front of him.

"Be calm," Omidi said in English. "I'm a friend."

"A friend?" the man stammered. "My name is Thomas De Vries. I was kidnapped from my home in Cape Town. I was taken—"

The Iranian held up a hand for silence as he scanned the equipment around him. It was in poor condition and a bit haphazard, but most seemed functional—including a modern microscope and small refrigerator. "What have you learned?"

"Learned? I'm not a biologist. I'm a retired general practitioner. You—"

"Be silent!" Omidi said. There wasn't much time. Bahame's speeches were characterized not only by their intensity, but also by their brevity.

"Help me and I'll take you with me when I leave this place." He pointed to the corpse the elderly physician had been hovering over when he arrived. "You must know something."

"Yes," De Vries said, looking around him nervously. "It's a parasitic infection similar in some ways to malaria, but after it gets into the bloodstream it concentrates in the head—bursting the capillaries around the hair follicles and attacking the brain."

"Is that how it spreads?" Omidi said. "Through the bleeding?"

"Yes ... Yes, I think so. There are high concentrations in the blood and it enters through breaks in the skin and possibly the eyes; I'm not sure."

"How long?"

"What?"

"How long until it takes effect?"

"Will you take me back to Cape Town? Back to my home?"

"I will put you on a commercial flight at Entebbe," Omidi said, straining to hide his disdain for this descendant of the Christian conquerors who had subjugated Africa and the world.

De Vries nodded. "It's a difficult question to answer. The only victim I've had an opportunity to observe began to experience agitation and confusion at around ten hours. My understanding is that there is significant variation, though. I would guess a range of seven to fifteen hours to the beginning of identifiable disorientation. After that, the disease appears to be very fast and consistent. Growing agitation until bleeding starts around three hours after initial symptoms and violent behavior follows almost immediately."

"Death?"

"About forty-eight hours after full symptoms, though I'm told that most die of injuries or what is probably heart failure."

The healthy woman in the cage sprang suddenly to her

feet and started talking, wrapping her hands around the bars, unashamed by her own nakedness.

The doctor looked back at her, compassion visible in his expression despite the fact that his situation wasn't much better. "Bahame always keeps one infected person imprisoned in here so that there's no chance of the parasite dying out. When that one looks like he's going to die, the woman will be infected to carry on the line."

Omidi nodded. Again, workable in Africa but not practical for a large-scale attack on a modern country. He looked behind him to confirm they were alone and then pointed to the refrigerator. "Can a sample be frozen for transport?"

"No. It can't live outside the body for more than a few minutes and is extremely temperature sensitive—every sample I've tried to refrigerate dies almost immediately."

Footsteps became audible in the corridor, and they both fell silent. A moment later Bahame appeared at the entrance to the chamber.

Omidi tensed, uncertain how to act. Should he try to explain or just remain silent? There was no telling from one minute to the next what would cause the African to explode.

Fortunately, Bahame made the decision for him. "Get out."

Omidi nodded respectfully and ducked back into the narrow passage, keeping an even gait as the cries of the doctor and the crash of toppling equipment echoed around him. Hopefully, Bahame would kill the old man. It was more likely that he would create unwanted complications than additional useful information.

Let him rot.

CHAPTER THIRTY-NINE

Langley, Virginia, USA
November 24—1205 Hours GMT–5

"Brandon wouldn't have wanted all this fuss, but as his friend I'm really happy to see it," the man said, shifting uncomfortably behind the lectern.

Dave Collen tuned him out, unable to remember his name and completely uninterested in what he had to say.

The small auditorium was jammed with people, and he scanned the faces, wondering how many had actually known Brandon Gazenga and how many had come out of curiosity and the promise of free pastries. There were a few expressions of real emotion, but most of the people just looked on with grave detachment.

"I'm sure everyone here knows what a talented analyst Brandon was, but with the way the agency works, a lot of people never had the time to find out what a great guy he was," the man continued, his throat constricting with sadness. "I had the privilege of working closely with him for the past few years …"

Collen continued surveying the crowd, still not finding what he was looking for.

The ramifications of having to kill Gazenga so soon were still evolving, but *how* he had died made matters even worse. Who would have thought he'd wait until he was suffocating on his filthy carpet to grow a backbone? After admitting to contacting Russell, he'd finally fessed up to the time and place of their meeting, and Collen had lived up to his end of the bargain, holding out the phony antidote.

He'd expected Gazenga to snatch the bottle and shake the useless pills desperately into his mouth. Instead, he accepted them calmly, slowly swallowing them and then letting his head settle to the floor. Collen hadn't left until the analyst's gaze became fixed and unseeing.

They'd sent their team to the rendezvous point, but it quickly became clear that Gazenga had known he was a dead man and lied. The tracker they'd put on Russell's car showed her heading into Pennsylvania—something they discovered too late to set up another ambush.

Collen perked up when the door at the rear of the room opened and Randi Russell slipped through. He nudged Larry Drake and gave a nearly imperceptible nod. It wasn't proof that she'd known Gazenga was the one who slipped her a note, but it was a strong indication. She was hardly the type to show up to a memorial—particularly one for a person she didn't know.

"When am I going to see a final?" the DCI whispered, referring to the revised plan for Russell's elimination.

"Soon. We have a few more details to work out. She's living alone in a friend's cabin while she's stateside. It couldn't be more perfect for us— no security system, no neighbors for miles, and only one lightly traveled rural road in."

"Then why isn't it done?"

"The contractor I want to use is difficult to contact in a way that doesn't leave a trail."

"No mistakes, Dave. Do you understand me? We can't afford any more."

Collen nodded, wondering if it was an overly optimistic assessment of the situation. He'd completed an exhaustive survey of Gazenga's computer use, uncovering his carefully hidden search for someone to help him, but otherwise coming up empty. Russell appeared to be similarly clean.

Just because he hadn't found anything, though, didn't mean there was nothing to find. Most likely, Gazenga had been telling the truth when he said that he'd given Russell only a time and place. But it was far from certain.

Finally, the loss of their eyes in Uganda had been a

disaster. They were left tracking Smith with marginal satellite images and a single unreliable man on the ground. As of an hour ago, they could pinpoint the team's location with only a thirty-mile margin of error.

The fact that they couldn't afford another mistake was certain. The question was whether they'd already made too many.

Randi Russell slid along the wall, joining in on the subdued laughter as the speaker told a story about a rafting trip he'd taken with Gazenga. She finally stopped at a table and lifted the tinfoil on one of the plates lined up on it.

Doughnuts.

She pulled one out and began gnawing at its edge as she made her way to an unoccupied corner of the room. The size of the crowd made her wonder how many people would show up on the day her own luck inevitably ran out. Living a life doing things that couldn't be talked about in countries most people couldn't find on a map hadn't left her with a particularly large circle of friends. And the few she did have tended to be a little skittish about showing their faces or admitting they knew her.

No, there would be no brightly lit, pastry-fueled eulogies celebrating her life and service. She'd have to settle for a few toasts by anonymous men and women sitting in dusty third world bars scattered across the globe. And truthfully, she'd have it no other way.

The speaker wrapped up his story and indicated to his right. "Director Drake had the privilege of knowing Brandon personally and wanted to say a few words, so I'll shut up now. Are you ready, sir?"

Randi watched Drake stride to the lectern amid respectful applause. This seemed to confirm the rumor that Gazenga was working on something high-level. What it was, though, she still had no idea. His focus was on central Africa, and there was nothing she could find going on there that couldn't be explained by the continent's normal state of barely controlled chaos.

Of course, the digging she'd done had been fairly superficial thus far. The fact that he'd died of a perfectly credible accident so soon after passing her that note suggested two possibilities. One, he should clean out his fridge more often. Or, two, someone very slick and very powerful had wanted him dead. Assuming the latter was true, it had made sense to be as discrete as possible.

Unfortunately, there was only so much you could learn from the shadows. There was still no response to the message she'd left Jon, and all she'd been able to determine was that he was on leave from his job at Fort Detrick. Why he'd requested the leave or what he was doing with it was still a mystery.

She had a friend at TSA checking into whether or not he'd taken a commercial flight anywhere, but the answer was taking longer than she felt comfortable with. If Jon was in trouble, she needed to find him and bail his stupid ass out.

So there she was, making an appearance at Brandon Gazenga's wake. It'd be interesting to see who noticed.

CHAPTER FORTY

Northern Uganda
November 24—2242 Hours GMT+3

Flying insects looked like smoke in the headlights as Peter Howell eased the vehicle into a muddy ditch and then gunned it out again. Beyond the tiny circle of illumination, the darkness was as complete and unbroken as the bottom of the ocean.

Smith glanced into the backseat, where Sarie was stretched out with a limp hand resting on her rifle. She reminded him of Sophia in so many ways—the unrelenting enthusiasm for her work, the easy smile and sense of adventure.

What would his life have been like if she hadn't died? Where would he be at that moment? Mowing the lawn? Carting their kids around in a minivan? Neither image was particularly easy to conjure.

When he faced forward again the bugs had relented enough to allow him to roll down the window and let in the warm, wet air.

"Ever wonder what you'll do after all this, Peter?"

"After all what?"

"You know ... When we're too old to chase things through the jungle."

Howell, visible in the light from the gauges, shook his head. "People like us don't get to retire, Jon. One day we're not as quick as we once were or we make a mistake, and that's the end."

Smith let out a long breath and sank deeper into the leather seat. "That's a cheerful thought."

Howell reached over and slapped his leg, a rare smile playing at his lips. "We're not there yet, mate. I reckon we've got a few good fights left in us."

Just ahead, an old fence constructed from local trees appeared and Smith pointed. "Could that be it?"

"Are we there?" Sarie said groggily, sitting upright and leaning forward between the seats.

"I'm not sure yet."

Howell paralleled the fence, finally pulling up in front of a gate. Sarie jumped out before the car was completely stopped, stretching her cramped back before letting them through. There was no protest from either the latch or the hinges, and the road leading onto the property wasn't overgrown. Maybe their luck was taking a turn for the better.

It was another ten minutes before a house appeared—an old, sprawling building with blooming flowers climbing faded walls. Sarie pulled the handle on her door, but Smith threw a hand back and stopped her. "Movement right."

"I see it," Howell responded, eyes darting to the rearview mirror. "Behind us, too. At least three. One machete, two rifles. Neither are automatic."

"What? What's going on?" Sarie said.

"Wait in the car," Smith said as he eased his door open and got out. A security light on the porch came on, and he slowly raised an arm to shade his eyes. A moment later, a barefoot Caucasian man wearing jeans and a T-shirt came cautiously through the front door holding a shotgun.

"Who are you?" he demanded.

"I'm Dr. Jon Smith, from the United States."

"And your friends?"

Smith glanced behind him, spotting the Africans Howell had seen in the glow of their taillights. Added to the ones hiding at the edges of the house, there were at least five guns on them. Howell and Sarie might survive if things went their way, but Smith knew he wouldn't.

"My friend Peter Howell and Dr. Sarie van Keuren from the University of Cape Town."

The man considered what he'd heard for a moment and

then leaned his gun against one of the pillars supporting the porch.

"I'm sorry for the reception," he said, extending a hand as he came down the stairs. "We don't get many surprise visitors, and this part of Africa isn't as peaceful as it used to be. I'm Noah Duernberg."

"Good to meet you," Smith said as the vehicle's doors opened behind him. When he looked back, the Africans who had been covering them were already wandering off.

Duernberg invited them into the house and they gathered around a heavy kitchen table by the light of a kerosene lamp. "We have to make all our own electricity out here," he explained. "So we shut everything down at night. The generators make an awful racket."

He pulled a few bottles of beer from a cupboard and passed them out. They were warm but Smith popped the cap gratefully.

"Where are you headed?" Duernberg asked, settling onto a hand-hewn bench near the window.

"Here," Smith said.

"Here? You mean this area? What—"

"I mean this farm."

The man was obviously confused, so Smith continued. "Is it safe to assume that Dr. Lukas Duernberg is your father?"

He nodded. "Was. He's been dead for years."

"I'm sorry to hear that."

"We didn't really think we'd find anyone still living here," Sarie said. "We couldn't find any information on you and were just hoping to get something from the local people about where your family ended up."

"My father saved one of Idi Amin's children and he gave us this land. I think we've pretty much been forgotten—a few white people running a farm in the hinterland is the least of the government's worries these days."

"It must be hard with Bahame gaining power in the region," Howell said.

The farmer nodded sadly. "My father built this house. We have a life here, friends, people who count on us for the bread on their table. But right now my wife and son are living in Kampala trying to find a country that will take us. It's just too dangerous here now."

"I understand what you're going through," Sarie said. "I grew up on a farm in Namibia and had to leave. I still think about it every day."

Duernberg took a long pull from his beer. "Enough about things that are in God's hands. What's your interest in my family?"

Smith pulled out the document Star found mentioning his father's suspicion about a parasitic infection. Duernberg's eyes ran across it for a moment before he stood and went to the cupboard for another beer.

"You must have been pretty young when he was working on this," Smith said.

"I was twelve."

Smith's brow furrowed. There was no date on the document. "You remember him talking about the parasite?"

"No," Duernberg said, sitting again. "But I remember him contracting the disease and attacking my sister Leyna. And I remember using the rifle he'd given me for my birthday to kill him."

Silence descended and Duernberg focused on a window turned into a mirror by the darkness outside.

"I'm sorry to come here and dredge this up," Smith said finally.

"Our field hands burned his body and wanted to kill Leyna—they said the demons were growing inside her. We had to run for one of the outbuildings and barricade ourselves inside. They surrounded us and just sat there. After a while, Leyna started getting confused, irrational. Then she got angry. Eventually, I shot her too."

Smith crossed his arms in front of his chest and leaned against the wall behind him. There was still no hard physical evidence, but this was enough. It wasn't mass hypnosis or drugs. It was biological and it was as dangerous as hell.

"I know this must be horrible for you, but is there anything else you can tell us about this illness?" Sarie said. "Did your father do any kind of experiments? Do you have any idea how he contracted the infection?"

Duernberg shook his head. "I was too young. But I have some things that might help you."

CHAPTER FORTY-ONE

Northern Uganda
November 25—0209 Hours GMT+3

Jon Smith reached into the trunk and dug out an antique doll, complete with prairie dress and yellowing lace bonnet. He laid it carefully next to a pile of black-and-white photos, disintegrating clothing, and leather-bound books.

The temperature in Duernberg's attic was well over a hundred and the heat was combining with lack of sleep to make his head feel like it was full of gauze. Howell had staged a strategic retreat an hour ago and was now snoring comfortably on a hammock stretched across the front porch.

"Anything?" he said, wiping the sweat from his face before it dripped on Lukas Duernberg's medical school diploma.

Sarie, stripped down to a tank top and pair of shorts, was planted in the middle of the cramped space surrounded by the loose papers and notebooks they'd found.

"It's hard not to get bogged down," she said, tapping the bound volume in her hand. "This is a diary from the mid-thirties talking about his experience with persecution under the Nazis and his plan for getting his family out. I wonder if Noah's planning on taking it with him when he leaves. Our library would go crazy for this stuff."

"Yeah," he said, digging another stack of papers from the bottom of the trunk and dropping them next to her. "But if I'm up here much longer, I'm gonna melt."

"Americans . . . ," she said, setting aside the diary and opening a notebook filled with Lukas's distinctive script. "All that air-conditioning has made you soft."

Smith smirked and leaned over her, looking at the detailed drawings of local flora and struggling to read the caption. Having grown up in a former German colony, Sarie was faster and flipped the page.

He felt for Noah Duernberg. This part of Uganda was stunning, and to be forced to leave everything you knew, to have to try to build a new life in an unfamiliar place, was hard to imagine.

What made it so much more tragic, though, was how unnecessary it was. The farmland was fertile, the country was wall-to-wall with natural resources, and people seemed anxious to work. There was no reason that everyone in Uganda shouldn't be living a safe, rewarding life.

No reason but the inherent darkness of human nature—something that was particularly easy to remember when sitting in Bahame country surrounded by Nazi memorabilia.

"Wait a minute …"

Smith slid in next to Sarie. "Do you have something?"

"I don't know," she said, spreading the papers out across the wood floor and pawing through them. "Yes! Right here—a parasite that causes a violent rage and bleeding from the hair. It says that the locals are familiar with it and think it's a form of demonic possession. It flared up in a village forty kilometers away and appears to have had a one hundred percent mortality rate. None of the locals would go anywhere near the place because they believed they could be tainted by the evil. But Duernberg managed to find it on his own. He describes it as looking like a war zone. Burned-out huts, decaying bodies lying where they fell …"

She went silent for a moment, searching for the next relevant entry. "Okay, this is dated a week later. He corrects himself and says that mortality from the infection wasn't a hundred percent—not even close."

"So some of the villagers survived?"

"I said the *infection* didn't get them. Apparently, the ones who got away were killed and burned by the surrounding tribes."

"Like Noah's family."

190

"Exactly. It says there are stories of this phenomenon going back for hundreds of years—maybe thousands. It's likely that the traditions of isolating, killing, and burning people you suspected could be possessed arose over time because they worked."

"A primitive quarantine procedure," Smith agreed.

She continued her search through the papers, finally snatching one from a pile to her right. "Jon! Look at this."

He leaned closer and examined a neatly drawn map with the house they were in at one corner.

"He talks about a cave system and the fact that he thinks the parasite is dormant in an animal that lives in it. He did some exploring and took samples of some of the insects, reptiles, and mammals there."

"Did he find what he was looking for?"

She flipped over the next page and then another and another. They were all blank. "Apparently so."

Smith descended the stairs and went out on the front porch, passing Howell and walking another fifty yards before digging out his sat phone. Fred Klein picked up on the first ring.

"Jon. Are you all right?"

"I'm fine. We've got something."

"Go ahead."

"We're at Duernberg's farm going through his diaries and it turns out he believed the infection was centered on a series of caves about twenty miles northeast of here. We're going to head over there at first light to see if we can get some samples."

"Is that safe?"

Smith laughed quietly, mindful of the people sleeping around him. "Other than Bahame's guerrillas, an unexplored and probably unstable cave network, lions, hippos, and the infection itself, it should be a piece of cake."

Klein ignored his comment. "So you think Duernberg could be right?"

"It makes sense based on what little we know. Years could

go by with no flare-up; then someone wanders into one of those caves for whatever reason and comes into contact with a carrier. Look, you need to call Billy Rendell at CDC and get him started thinking about this. If the infection does get out, we need a containment plan and he's the best in the business."

"Rendell," Klein repeated. "Can he be trusted?"

"Billy knows how to keep things quiet. You don't have to worry about that."

"I just have to worry about you."

"Yeah. Look, Fred. If you don't hear from us in a couple days, we've had problems and you're going to have to consider escalating this thing—sending a military force to create a perimeter and a fully equipped team to go into those caves."

"I understand, Jon. But we're in a delicate position—not only with the Iranians and Africans, but with Covert-One itself. It's safe to say that the CIA suspects there's a new player in town and we have to be very careful about tipping our hand."

"If this thing gets out, Fred, that's going to be the least of our problems."

"I'm meeting with the president tomorrow. I'll fill him in and give him your recommendation. But American credibility isn't that great when it comes to Middle East intel right now—at home or abroad. If we want to come down on the Iranians or send a significant force into Africa, we need something concrete. And then there's the time it's going to take to ramp up that kind of operation ..."

"I know, Fred. But I can't stop thinking about that video and extrapolating it out to somewhere like New York or London."

"Yeah," he responded quietly. "Me too."

CHAPTER FORTY-TWO

Tehran, Iran
November 25—1055 Hours GMT+3:30

Ayatollah Amjad Khamenei sat cross-legged on the cushion listening to a wiretap recording provided by the men hovering around him. He closed his eyes, trying to remain serene, trying to put his faith in God as the details of the plot against him unfolded. Rahim Nikahd's daughter-in-law had died of the injuries she'd suffered at the hands of Omidi's men and it was more than the politician could forgive.

No, that wasn't true—as Mehrak would have undoubtedly pointed out if he weren't so far away. The treasonous conversation between Nikahd and a number of his colleagues in parliament hadn't sprung up due to just that mistake. It was too intricate, too elaborate. Much more likely they had been planning for months. Perhaps even years.

"Leave me," he said, waving a hand.

The men in the room had been handpicked by him, but still he didn't trust them. In these dangerous times, he was certain only of his immediate family and of Omidi, who was as much a son to him as the ones his wife had given birth to.

Khamenei listened to the details of the plan to assassinate him, of the transformation of Iran into a "modern" country, of the olive branch that would be offered to Farrokh.

When the recording ended, he took off the earphones and laid them on the floor. He had made so many errors during his long life. First and foremost, though, was underestimating the power of money. International sanctions had caused Iran's economy to falter and prevented its citizens from getting the useless baubles they saw on the Internet and in Western advertisements. The things they now put above God.

He had also badly misjudged the reaction of the country's youth to America's occupation of Iraq and Afghanistan. He'd seen it as a harbinger of things to come—the rise of a new imperialism that would annihilate them if they didn't have weapons to defend themselves. Now, years after the utter failure of the American military to control those countries and the uncertain financial future of the U.S. government, many Iranians naïvely believed that the chance of invasion was remote. Particularly if no concrete provocation was offered.

And so the Iran he had helped build was being rotted from the inside by people who cared only about feeding their own appetites. The dream of the Islamic Republic would be smothered in expensive cars, lurid clothing, and uncontrolled media.

He picked up a large manila envelope and pulled a photo from it, once again examining the faces of the people it depicted. Jon Smith was a microbiologist at the U.S. Army's bioweapons center in Maryland. Sarie van Keuren was the world's leading expert on parasites. And Peter Howell was former MI6 and SAS. The Americans knew something. And that meant time was short.

Omidi no longer had sufficient control of the Iranian security forces to fire into the protesters plaguing the country. Leaders in parliament were plotting his death. And there were whispers that Farrokh was seeking military capability.

Khamenei knew that he had already waited too long, allowing his power to erode to the point that he could no longer be certain of anything. The only answer was to gouge directly at the root of the evil casting its shadow over the republic.

He looked at the clock. Less than a minute.

When the phone finally rang, he immediately reached for it. "God be with you, Mehrak."

"And with you, Excellency."

"It is good to hear your voice. I have few friends here. Fewer, I think, than even you imagine."

"I heard about the meeting between Nikahd and the others. We'll deal with them when I return, but we have to move cautiously."

"It's too late for that, old friend. I should have listened to your warnings. Sometimes I think I am becoming old and foolish."

"You see piety in men who have none, Excellency. That isn't foolishness. It's what it means to be a man of God."

"You always know how to comfort me, Mehrak. And I thank you for it. Now tell me what you've learned."

"Bahame's weapon is nearly perfect. I saw it used and his descriptions were entirely accurate. It is truly the wrath of the Almighty."

Khamenei closed his eyes again, picturing America collapsing into chaos, broken bodies littering the streets, survivors cowering and begging their false God for salvation that would never come.

"You said *nearly* perfect. Why nearly?"

"It's impractical to wield and will have to be weaponized."

"The anniversary of the victory of the revolution is in eleven weeks. We will release it in America then."

"Excellency, that's impossible. We don't have people with the necessary expertise. It will—"

"Have faith, Omidi. God will provide."

"Of course, Excellency. But we have to be realistic. The difficulties of—"

"What Bahame wants is waiting on the Sudanese border. I will authorize the transfer immediately."

CHAPTER FORTY-THREE

Northern Uganda
November 25—1207 Hours GMT+3

Jon Smith checked the hand-drawn map again as they crawled along a barely discernible jeep track cutting through the rolling terrain.

They'd left the farm after downing an elaborate breakfast Duernberg insisted on making, and now the sun was directly overhead. Temperatures had risen to a level that was taxing even the overbuilt cooling system of Janani's truck, and the wind was churning up thick clouds of dust in the distance.

"Won't work," Sarie said from the backseat when Smith leaned out the window to dry his sweat-soaked face. She was right—the air felt like it was blowing out of a wet convection oven.

He pulled back again, adjusting the assault rifle sticking up between the front seats so he could lean forward and get his back off the leather. "The map shows an intersection with a better-defined road ahead. We turn left on it and then it's not much more than a mile to the cave area."

"If the intersection is still there," Howell said. "That's not exactly a new map."

"All we've got. How are we looking behind, Sarie?"

"Nothing. I think our friends must have abandoned us."

The soldiers tracking them hadn't made an appearance since the prior afternoon. They'd probably broken an axle or been washed away in a stream crossing like they themselves had nearly been no less than twenty times since leaving Kampala. Or maybe they'd just turned back.

Bahame wouldn't be particularly accepting of Ugandan soldiers wandering around in his backyard.

The road leveled out and Howell used the opportunity to accelerate as they came around a sweeping curve. The heat and empty landscape had dulled his normally razor-sharp reflexes and he slammed on the brakes just a fraction too late. The vehicle fishtailed in the loose dirt, sliding forward until the brush guard rammed the side of the military truck parked in their path.

Howell immediately went for the assault rifle, but Smith grabbed his wrist. The cab of the truck was empty, but there were three armed men in the back, their elevated position perfect for shooting down into the Land Cruiser's windshield. Camouflage-clad men appeared out of the tall grass and approached cautiously with weapons at the ready.

"Get out of the car!" one demanded in heavily accented English.

"You're the ones who have been following us since Kampala," Smith said as they stepped cautiously from the vehicle. "We have permission to be here."

Six guns were trained on them, and out of the corner of his eye Smith could see Howell sizing up the men holding them. They appeared to be a few notches above the poorly trained part-timers so common in this part of the world.

It suddenly struck him just how alone they were. Had Sembutu decided that they were more trouble than they were worth—that it would be better if they just disappeared? It would be so easy. No one would ever find the bodies, and their disappearance could be credibly blamed on Bahame or any of the hundreds of other things that killed people every day in that part of the world.

"You must turn back," the man said. "Go home."

"We're scientists," Sarie added. "We're here studying some of your local animals."

"You study ants, yes?"

"That's right, we—"

"You want to die for ants?"

"We don't just study ants," Smith said. "We study diseases

and the way they're spread. The work we do saves lives."

"Not yours if Bahame finds you."

"That's a risk we're willing to take."

The man just stood there for a few moments, scowling silently at what he undoubtedly saw as soul-crushing stupidity. Finally, he pulled a sat phone from his pocket and began speaking unintelligibly into it. When he hung up, he looked even less happy.

"If you refuse to go back, my men and I have been ordered to protect you."

"We appreciate that, but it's really not necessary. We don't want to put you in danger. It—"

"Then go back to Kampala."

"I'm afraid we can't do that."

The man let out a frustrated breath and started back to his truck.

"How are you holding up?" Smith said, scrambling over a pile of jagged boulders as he jogged toward Sarie. The terrain had opened up into rocky grassland punctuated by occasional stands of trees that looked like enormous parasols. She was standing in the shade of one of those, and he pulled out a canteen, taking a sip before holding it out to her.

"Just another day at the office." The edges of her eyes crinkled as she squinted through her sunglasses at the shapes the wind was creating in the grass. "But I'm starting to wonder if this is the right place. It seems like with this many people we'd have found something by now."

They had pressed Sembutu's soldiers into service, and they, along with Peter Howell, were walking across the field at twenty-five-yard intervals, searching for a cave entrance.

"This is what the map said."

"For his patients' sake, I hope Duernberg was a better doctor than he was a cartographer."

Smith pulled off his straw cowboy hat, holding it up to block the sun as he looked out over the endless landscape.

"These are hard conditions," Sarie said. "You're doing a lot better than I would have expected."

Smith grinned. "I can't figure out if that's a compliment or an insult."

"It's an observation," she said, her expression turning probing. "You and Peter don't seem very bothered by the terrain or the sun or people pointing guns at you. I understand that he was in the SAS, but what's your excuse?"

"I may not be SAS, Sarie, but I've worked on the front lines in MASH units attached to special forces units."

"Uh-huh," she said, clearly unconvinced. "I get around, Jon. I've known military doctors. Some have had some interesting adventures. But in the end, they're city strong."

"City strong?"

"They go to the gym religiously three days a week. They do their little midlife-crisis triathlons. It's different in the bush. But then, you know that, don't you?"

Smith wasn't happy with the direction the conversation was going and was almost relieved when he heard a frightened cry from one of the soldiers searching to the north. He pulled his pistol from its holster and ran over the uneven ground toward the voice with Sarie a few feet behind.

Sembutu's other men had dropped to their knees and were sweeping their rifles back and forth while Howell called for calm.

Finally, Smith spotted the cause of the commotion. One of the soldiers he thought was crouching had actually fallen chest-deep into a hole. His arms, spread out flat on the ground, were the only things keeping him from plunging the rest of the way through.

Smith and Sarie grabbed him by the shoulders and pulled him out while the others gathered around.

"Are you all right?"

He didn't seem to understand, and Smith pointed to the blood beginning to soak through the right leg of his fatigues. "Just sit back and relax for a minute. I'm a doctor."

Someone translated, and Smith took out a knife, cutting through the fabric and looking at the gash made by a sharp outcropping the man had hit on his way down.

"I have a first-aid kit," Howell said, digging through his

pack and handing over a well-stocked plastic organizer that he'd obviously created himself. Smith cleaned the wound with alcohol and then pulled out a hooked needle and some thread.

"Tell him this is going to sting a bit."

The man lay back but, to his credit, didn't flinch or make a sound while Smith stitched up the wound.

"I think Dr. Duernberg has redeemed himself," Sarie said, lying flat on the ground and peering into the hole. "It's about fifteen meters to the bottom. Can't see how far it goes in either direction, but it looks pretty big."

"What about the rock he hit?" Smith said.

"Clean and dry."

Smith nodded. There was a good chance they'd found the parasite's hiding place. The cave's entrance was hidden by a tangle of grass and vines, making it easy for anyone walking through the area to tumble in. Had the soldier gone all the way down and gotten his cut contaminated with water or bat guano, things could have gotten complicated. They'd been lucky.

Smith bandaged the wound while Sarie unpacked her equipment and Howell enlisted the remaining soldiers to clear the foliage from around the hole.

When he was done, Smith grabbed a flashlight and leaned in, shining the beam in a slow circle. There was no way to climb down—the entrance was in the middle of a vaulted roof that he couldn't see the edges of. The floor was strewn with rocks from millennia of miniature cave-ins, and he could hear dripping echoing somewhere beyond the hazy ring of illumination.

"What do you think?" he said, sliding back out.

"I say we take a look," Sarie responded, uncoiling a rope next to a box of surgical gloves.

He frowned and looked around them. Beyond the gloves and a few basic surgical masks, they had no bio-hazard equipment. And beyond the rope, they had no climbing equipment. Not exactly ideal. Then again, these weren't exactly normal circumstances.

"You sure you got me?"

There was nowhere to anchor the rope, leaving no choice but to have Howell and the soldiers dig in like a tug-of-war team on one end. The result was less than confidence inspiring.

"You'll be the first to know, mate."

"Great," Smith muttered, weighting the rope enough to test their grip as he slid into the hole. It gave a good foot, and he soon found himself in the same position as the soldier who had fallen, unwilling to completely abandon terra firma.

"Off you go, then," Howell said, repositioning his boots in the soil for maximum traction.

Smith closed his eyes, trying to clear his mind of the fifty feet of air beneath him and the effect of the parasite whose lair they were bumbling into.

Finally, he took a deep breath and let go, wrapping his legs around the rope and gripping the knots Howell had tied into it with white-knuckle intensity. He heard the worried shouts of the Africans as they skidded toward the hole and winced as the rope dropped another couple of feet.

"Faster would be better than slower," Howell called, the strain audible in his voice.

Smith descended quickly but found little comfort in the sensation of solid ground once it was beneath his feet. He checked again to make sure his pants were tucked tightly into his boots and his sleeves into the surgical gloves. "I'm off, Sarie. Go ahead and come down."

She slid down awkwardly, struggling to find the knots with her feet and grunting audibly. When she got within reach, Smith grabbed her legs and eased her to the ground.

"You made it look easier than it was," she commented, flexing her right hand painfully.

"Are you all right?"

"I'm fantastic, thank you for asking. Have you noticed how lovely it is down here?"

He hadn't, but now that she mentioned it, he noticed the

temperature had dropped a good thirty degrees and there was a slight stirring of air. Every cloud had a silver lining. Sometimes you just had to look really, really hard.

She helped him off with his pack, accidentally dropped it, and then began fumbling around with the top flap.

"Scared?" he said, gently pushing her hand away and unfastening the plastic clips himself.

"A little. The truth is, I don't much care for confined spaces. And most of the parasites I work with don't ..." Her voice trailed off for a moment. "You?"

"Scared? Yes. Afraid of confined places? No. I love them. In particular a nice hazmat suit."

She smiled, her teeth flashing in the bright sunlight coming from above. "I can see how maybe that wouldn't be so bad."

A shadow passed across her and Smith looked up to see Howell peering down at them.

"You all right down there?"

"Can't complain. It's air-conditioned."

The Brit shook his head. "I reckon I'd rather be up here in the sun."

Smith knew that Peter Howell wouldn't think twice about facing down twenty armed men with nothing but a ballpoint pen and a damp tea bag, but he'd never been a fan of microscopic creepy crawlies. Not a fair fight in his mind.

"I'm going to see if I can find somewhere to hang a net," Sarie said. "I'd love to get a bat spec—"

The unmistakable crack of a gunshot floated down to them, followed by the just-as-unmistakable thud and grunt of a man stopping a bullet. A moment later their rope dropped down on top of them.

"Peter!" Smith shouted, but Howell had disappeared and the only response was multiple bursts of machine-gun fire from at least three separate weapons.

"Peter!" Sarie called. "What's happening? Are you all right?"

Another wet thud sounded above and everything went briefly dark. Realizing what was happening, Smith grabbed

202

Sarie and yanked her out of the way before she could be crushed by the soldier falling through the cave entrance.

Smith dropped to his knees next to the man and checked for a pulse.

"Is he …," Sarie started.

"The bullet hit him in the chest. He was dead before he hit the ground."

Smith gave the man's rifle to Sarie and checked his pockets for anything else they could use. Nothing but a few Ugandan shillings and a hot-pink rabbit's foot that was apparently defective.

"We can't get out the way we came in. It's too loose and too overhanging," Smith said, grabbing her arm and leading her down the slope into the darkness. "Sarie? Are you listening?"

Her breath was coming in short gasps and she seemed unwilling to take her eyes off the spotlit corpse lying only a few yards away. Smith positioned himself to block her view and put his hands on her shoulders. "Are you all right?"

"Just give me a second, okay?"

Her breathing began to slow and she closed her eyes for a moment. When they opened again, some of the fear had dissipated. "What about Peter?"

"There's nothing we can do for him right now. We have to concentrate on ourselves. On getting out of here."

"How exactly are we going to do that? I've never been pinned down in a cave by people with guns before. How about you?"

"Actually, I have."

"You've got to be kidding."

"Nope. Do you feel the breeze?"

She nodded.

"Let's go find out where it's coming from."

The broken rocks made travel slower than he would have liked, but at least the ground was flat and not sloping endlessly toward the center of the earth. They stopped every few minutes to listen for anyone following, but everything

203

had gone silent except for the occasional crack of stone dislodging from the roof.

The passage narrowed and finally dead-ended into a wall with a three-foot-wide hole in it. Sarie shined her flashlight inside but it just glinted off a crystal-encrusted wall where the tube jogged right.

"You're going to tell me we have to go in there, aren't you?"

Smith held out a hand to test the air blowing from the passage. "If you've got any better ideas, I'm listening."

She just stood there, chewing her lip miserably.

"Ladies first," he prompted.

"You want me to go in front? You can't be serious."

"No offense, Sarie, but if you freak out, I'd rather have you in front of me than behind me. Just take it slow and watch for drop-offs. I'll be right with you the whole way."

She stood there for a lot longer than he would have liked, staring into the darkness while he listened for any sign that they were being followed. Peter would hold off the attackers as long as he could, but with no way to know how many there were or what kind of firepower they were packing, it was impossible to estimate how much time they had.

Finally, she picked up the rifle they'd taken off the dead soldier and slithered inside.

Time ceased to exist in the tiny passage, and Smith had to keep checking the glowing hands of his watch to confirm that minutes and not hours had passed. Sarie stopped a few times for brief hyperventilation breaks but then soldiered on, never uttering so much as a single complaint.

They went on like that for another fifteen minutes before she stopped—a little more abruptly than she had before. "Jon? I think we might have a problem."

"That's okay. I'm right here with you. Are you all right?"

"*Ja.* But I'm on a ledge and the flashlight doesn't go far enough to see the bottom."

"Is there a loose rock? Toss it down and count until you hear it hit."

"Okay. Hold on."

Her answer didn't come as soon as he'd hoped.

"Six seconds."

"That's going to be a little longer than our rope. Does the ledge lead anywhere?"

"It goes right."

"How wide is it?"

"Half a meter."

"Can you get out on it?"

"Without falling, you mean?"

"That would be best."

He heard her sigh and then the scrape of the rifle as she pushed it farther out in front of her.

"Damn!" she said, her shout echoing off the stone walls. He was about to ask what had happened but then heard the metallic clatter of the rifle hitting the ground far below.

Great.

"It's okay, Sarie. No problem. Focus on what you're doing."

He gripped her ankle as she turned the corner, though he doubted he could stop her if she fell. More likely they'd both go over.

"All right," she said, struggling to keep her breathing under control. "I'm out. I'm on the ledge. But it stops in front of me. There's a meter gap before it starts again."

"Can you stand up?"

"No way in hell."

"The only way you're going to make it across a gap that wide is by jumping it."

"You think I don't know that?" she snapped. When she spoke again, her voice was calmer. "I'm sorry, Jon. I know you're just trying to help. But the ledge I'm on is narrow enough that my left side is hanging in the air and the wall above me just feels like a bunch of dirt and mud. There's no way I could keep my balance."

"I understand," he said calmly. "Here's what you're going to do: you're going to slide straight back until your hips are even with the hole I'm in. Understand?"

"Yeah. Okay. Back. Back is good."

The illumination from the flashlight in her hand played off the cave walls as she carefully reversed herself.

"That's far enough. You're doing great."

He slid a hand down the back of her cargo pants, getting a solid grip on the heavy cotton waistband.

"I'd like to get to know you better, too, Jon. But do you really think this is the time?"

They both laughed, longer and harder than the joke probably warranted, but it helped drain off a little of the tension.

"Okay, Sarie. I've got myself wedged in here like a tick. I'm not coming out and I'm not letting go. So just stand up and don't worry about falling."

"That's easy for you to say."

"It was pretty easy, actually."

They laughed again and he dug harder into the contours of the wall as her hips rose. When her shoulders came even with the top of the hole he was in, he started pulling, causing her back to scrape against the rock as she straightened.

"Move right and look around on the wall for something solid to hold on to."

"Yeah … Okay, I found something. It feels pretty solid."

"Your turn to help me, then."

Less than a minute later he was on his feet, spine pressed into the wall and toes hanging over a pit as black as outer space. They eased right and he took one of her hands, steadying her as she crossed the gap.

They circumnavigated the chamber carefully, the breeze strengthening the farther they went. When it turned into a wind powerful enough to affect their already precarious balance, they stopped.

"Turn off your light a second, Sarie."

"What? Why?"

"Just humor me."

She flicked the switch and he waited for his eyes to adjust. As they did, the blackness turned gray with the dim glow of sunlight.

CHAPTER FORTY-FOUR

Northern Uganda
November 25—1549 Hours GMT+3

"Give me your hand."

Smith never thought he'd actually be happy to have the Ugandan sun pounding down on him, but he was having a hard time remembering anything feeling so good. The hole he was hovering over was about the same size as the one they'd entered but had the benefit of opening over a pile of shattered boulders that reached to within six feet of it.

He grabbed Sarie's hand and pulled her through, making sure neither of them rose higher than the top of the grass. She lay on her back for a few moments, staring into the sky and gulping at the humid air.

"Thank you, Jon."

"It was a team effort."

A single shot sounded in the distance and he peeked over the grass in the direction it had come from.

"They're still shooting," Sarie said. "It never stops …"

"Yeah, but that's exactly what we wanted to hear."

"What do you mean?"

"If someone's still shooting, it means there's still someone to shoot at. At least one of the good guys is still alive."

"What are we going to do about it?"

"*We're* not going to do anything. You're going to wait here. I'm going to see if I can get to them."

"No way. We stay together. When it comes to Caleb Bahame, you're better off going down fighting than sitting around waiting to get caught."

It was hard to fault her logic. Leaving her in the middle of guerrilla-controlled territory wasn't exactly an act of chivalry.

"Fine," Smith said, starting to drag himself through the grass with his elbows. "Stay right behind me. Remember: low and slow."

Their luck held and no more shots were fired in the hour and a half it took them to cover what he calculated was no more than a quarter mile.

Cover became more sparse as they approached the cave entrance, forcing him to signal Sarie to stop and continue on without her. He flattened himself on the ground, timing his advance with the movement of the wind over the grass. After another fifteen minutes, the ground cover thinned to the point that going any farther would be guaranteed to expose him. Fortunately, it was far enough. He could see Peter Howell sitting with his back against a low boulder next to the man who had so wisely tried to convince them to go back to Kampala.

The brief flash of pride Smith felt at having managed to sneak up on his friend was short-lived. Howell's head suddenly swiveled in his direction, the concern visible in his eyes as he reached for his rifle.

Maybe next time.

"Don't shoot," Smith said in a loud whisper. "It's me."

Howell turned as far toward him as he could without breaking cover. Behind, the African held up a hand in greeting and then began dialing his sat phone—undoubtedly to inform Sembutu that Smith was still alive.

"Is Sarie all right?" Howell said.

"A little beat-up, but nothing serious."

"I was starting to think you'd buggered off back to Cape Town."

"Stopped for lunch. What's the situation?"

"Not good, mate. We've lost two men and we're pretty well pinned down. Every once in a while they fire off a round to remind us they're still there, and I reckon they're either sending men around to try to flank us or waiting for reinforcements." He thumbed toward the African speaking urgently into his phone. "Okot and I figure our only chance is to wait until dark and try to get out to the east. But I doubt they're going to let the sun go down without throwing something at us we're not going to like."

Okot stuffed the phone back in the pocket of his fatigues and picked up his weapon. Howell never saw the rifle butt that smashed into the back of his head and sent him pitching face-first into the dirt.

Smith tried to raise his pistol, but the African was already lined up on his head. He called back to his men, and a moment later one of them was waving a dirty white handkerchief above the grass.

CHAPTER FORTY-FIVE

Outside Washington, DC, USA
November 25—1159 Hours GMT–5

Randi Russell drifted up behind a slightly listing Honda and waited for a place to pass while NPR faded to static. When the winding rural road straightened, she slammed the Chevy Aveo's accelerator to the floor and tapped the wheel impatiently as it limped up to seventy.

She'd sold her Porsche along with her house a few years ago, finally fed up with dealing with them from halfway across the world. Now, on the rare occasion she was stateside, she stayed in a tiny farmhouse her college roommate had renovated but never found the time to use. The property was perfect—two hours from DC in traffic, quiet, and built around a huge fireplace that was the ideal place to unwind before her next assignment.

All Things Considered finally completely died, and she flipped off the radio, turning her attention fully to Jon Smith. He still hadn't responded to the message she'd left, and a more insistent call to USAMRIID had once again gotten her nothing but the party line—Colonel Smith had taken personal leave and was unreachable at this time.

Her friend at TSA had come through, tracking Jon to Cape Town, South Africa. Interestingly, just the continent the late Brandon Gazenga had built his career around.

She had a plane reservation for tomorrow, made under an alias the CIA knew nothing about. A girl could never be too safe.

The road turned steep and she pressed the accelerator to

the floor again, barely maintaining forty miles an hour as patches of snow began to appear in the trees. Honestly, a quick trip to the Cape wouldn't be a bad change of pace. She despised being cold and most likely she'd find Jon lying on his surfboard catching rays. Heck, maybe she'd pack a bikini and stay on a few days.

Or maybe not.

Their relationship was one of the few things in life she couldn't quite wrap her mind around. Fate constantly threw them together, usually along with a few near-death experiences and a soul-wrenching personal disaster or two. As close as they'd become, she wasn't sure how many more meetings they were both going to survive.

As Randi crested the hill, the engine began to lose power, lurching weakly and finally cutting out as she rolled the tiny Chevrolet onto the shoulder. A few twists of the ignition key produced precisely nothing. Not even dash lights.

The stupid thing had less than ten thousand miles on it and not so much as a scratch in the paint or a chip in the windshield. After spending the last year on a camel that spit on her every time she got within ten feet, was a little reliable transportation too much to ask?

Knowing from experience that there was no cell reception, Randi got out and looked down at the hood for a moment before reaching into the back for her gym bag. It was four rolling miles to the house, with temperatures just below freezing under a partly cloudy sky. A nice jog, a cup of tea, and a quick call to AAA or an hour digging around in an engine that was probably suffering from an unfathomable computer glitch? Not a terribly hard decision.

She was searching for her shoes when the Honda she'd passed earlier pulled in behind her.

"Car trouble?" a man in his early thirties said, throwing his door open and leaping out with a level of enthusiasm that suggested former Boy Scout.

"Yeah, but I'm okay. I just live up the way."

"We'd be happy to give you a lift."

"I appreciate it, but honestly I could use some exercise."

The very pregnant woman in the passenger seat struggled through her door and waddled around in front of the bumper. "We can't just leave you out here in the cold."

"Really, I'm fine. I—"

Neither of their movements was fast or coordinated enough to cause alarm, but suddenly both were holding pistols aimed at her chest.

"If you could hand over your Glock, I'd be grateful, Ms. Russell."

She didn't move, examining both of them carefully. Their position was perfect—far enough from each other that she couldn't engage both at the same time and lined up in a way that they had her in a cross fire without putting themselves in danger of hitting each other. The woman was now standing in the slightly crouched position of an expert marksman, apparently no longer affected by her "pregnancy".

Whoever they were, they were good—even by her standards. Also, they were well connected. Not only did they know the brand of firearm she carried, but it seemed likely that they'd used the OnStar System to shut down the Chevy. Those codes weren't given out to every carjacker with an e-mail address.

Randi slowly pulled the gun from the holster at her back, silently cursing her stupidity. Being in the States with most of her long list of enemies half a world away had dulled her edge. Not a lot, but apparently enough to get her killed.

"Move away from the car, please."

As she did, a woman she hadn't seen emerged from the backseat of the Honda and started toward her. They were about the same size, with exactly the same clothes and hair. Randi watched as she got behind the wheel of the Chevy and turned the key. It started right up and she immediately sped away.

Based on that, it seemed unlikely they were just going to execute her. And every moment she was still breathing was a moment she could escape. If they put her in the car, they'd be close enough for her to use the knife she still had. It was a slim chance, but it was all she had.

212

"Looks like you could use a lift," the man said. "But first, why don't you give me the blade you keep strapped to your thigh."

CHAPTER FORTY-SIX

Northern Uganda
November 25—2018 Hours GMT+3

Mehrak Omidi awoke to the sound of cheering and exited Bahame's command tent, where he had retreated to escape the jungle's insidious biting bugs. Young soldiers had crowded around an old pickup, and he was forced to climb onto Bahame's podium in order to see the two unconscious white men in the back.

The mob kicked and spit on them as they were dragged toward captivity and, soon, death. Charles Sembutu, for all his fearsome reputation, had proven to be an old woman where the Americans were concerned. He had ignored every opportunity to get rid of Smith's team, and when they'd finally gotten too close, he'd continued to refuse to act—instead calling Omidi with their position and washing his hands of the matter.

The lights of the pickup flickered off, revealing a dim glow approaching through the trees. A moment later, an extravagant four-wheel-drive vehicle came skidding into camp. Caleb Bahame leapt out, ignoring the adulation of his soldiers as he pulled a woman across the front seats and out the driver's door.

Omidi stepped forward, his gaze moving from the tangle of blond hair to the face so unconvincingly trying to portray courage. The Ayatollah's continued insistence that they release the parasite on the anniversary of the victory of the revolution had seemed impossible—even with their top biologists working around the clock. And his unwavering belief that God would provide a solution had seemed dangerously naïve. But Omidi once again found himself humbled by the aging cleric's wisdom and faith.

He leapt from the podium and retreated to the blackness at the edge of the jungle, unable to take his eyes off the woman. The doubts he'd had about their plans and his fears regarding the American intelligence agencies were suddenly gone. God had made his presence known, and now the success of what lay ahead seemed almost preordained. Sarie van Keuren, the person most qualified to stabilize and weaponize the parasite, had been delivered to him.

Jon Smith opened his eyes, watching the vague shapes around him slowly coalesce into a stone ceiling, rusted bars, and primitive lab beyond. He still didn't have the strength to get up, and he let his head loll toward the motionless body of Peter Howell next to him.

"Peter. Are you all right?"

The blow to the back of the old soldier's head had been vicious enough that Smith suspected he might never wake up.

"Peter. Can you—"

A low moan came from the man and then something that may have been words.

"What? Did you say something?"

When he spoke again, his voice had gained strength. "The easiest fifty grand you ever made ..."

Smith hadn't quite managed to sit fully upright when a piercing scream sounded. The jolt of adrenaline didn't do much more than amplify the pounding in his head, and he scooted instinctively away from the bars, scanning for the source of the terrible sound.

About ten feet away, a woman was imprisoned in a similar cell built into the opposite wall of the cave. Smith watched through a curtain of blood-smeared plastic as she stretched her arm through the bars, looking like she'd be willing to break every bone in her body to get to them.

"You're awake."

Smith turned sluggishly toward the voice, struggling to focus on an old man wearing a canvas apron that looked like it had spent the last fifty years in a slaughterhouse.

"Where's Sarie?"

"Who?" the man said.

Smith used the depressingly solid-feeling bars to pull himself to his feet while Howell assessed the damage that had been done to the back of his head.

"Sarie van Keuren. She was with us."

"I don't know."

The man clearly wasn't one of Bahame's henchmen—he was too white, too old, and, based on his speech, too well educated.

"Who are you?"

"Me?" he said, looking a bit startled by the question. "Thomas De Vries. I'm a retired doctor who was kidnapped to keep a man alive so Bahame could kill him. Then I was put in here and told to find a way to keep a brain parasite alive outside the body so it could be transported."

"Did you succeed?"

He shook his head. "I'm not a scientist. And even if I was, I wouldn't do it." He pointed to the infected woman, who had tired a bit, but not so much that she'd completely given up trying to get through the bars. "Bahame keeps the infection alive by passing it on to successive victims. You're in the holding tank now. When she starts to die, you'll be put in with her. And when you start to die, your friend will be. I'm sorry."

"That's just outstanding," Howell said as Smith grabbed him under the arm and helped him to his feet. "Tell me, mate. Is there any way—"

He fell silent at the sound of approaching footsteps, and De Vries ran to a plywood-and-cinderblock table, where he tried to look busy.

The man who entered a few moments later wasn't the one Smith expected. He was clearly Middle Eastern, and despite filthy, sweat-stained clothing, he had a strange air of meticulousness. When Smith mentally cleaned him up, there was

216

something familiar. He'd seen the face before.

"Colonel Smith, Mr. Howell. I have to say I'm surprised you were captured so easily."

The Persian accent was the final piece he'd needed. "Slumming a bit, aren't you, Omidi?"

The man smiled. "Well done, Colonel. Of course, my presence wouldn't be difficult to predict. Someone has to stop America's bioweapons division from getting hold of this parasite and using it against the Muslim people."

"You and Bahame make an excellent team," Howell commented. "What's the old saying? Two peas in a pod?"

Omidi ignored the insult, secure in the knowledge that he had the upper hand. "How much does the American government know about what's happening here?"

"It's not going to be that easy," Smith said.

"No, I suppose not. But it doesn't really matter. You've run out of time."

Footsteps again echoed through the chamber, and Smith counted them, trying to add an estimate of their distance from the cave entrance to the things he'd put together about their surroundings: The bars were solid despite some surface rust, and the lock was modern. Much of the equipment in the lab could be used to cut flesh, but there seemed to be nothing that could be used effectively on steel. The old doctor was certainly an asset but had neither the temperament nor the physical ability to do anything heroic. In the end, Omidi was probably right. Their time had run out.

Sarie appeared first, stumbling into the chamber in a way that suggested she'd been pushed. One of her sleeves was soaked through with blood and her eyes were red and swollen, but beyond that she seemed unharmed.

Caleb Bahame came in behind her and, with the exception of some graying at the temples, looked exactly like the twenty-five-year-old photos Star had included in the dossier she'd prepared.

Howell moved suddenly to the bars, wrapping his fingers around them and glaring at the African as he walked casually to the center of the chamber.

"Peter Howell," he said. "It's been many years. You look sick and weak."

Bahame saw the surprise on Smith's face and smiled. "Did Peter not tell you? We are old acquaintances. He killed many of my men. Many of my flock."

"You had a lot to cower behind," the Brit responded.

"They love me. They understand who I am. What I am."

"And what is that, exactly?" Smith said, but Bahame ignored him.

"You know, I hired a man in America to come for you, Peter. It's unprecedented. You should be flattered to command the attention of a man like myself."

"I remember," Howell said. "If you'd ever like to visit him, he's buried out by my shed."

Bahame's smile widened. "You must be very anxious to hear what happened to Yakobo. He was a very fine boy and became a very fine soldier. You'll be happy to know that I eventually found some of his family. An aunt, I believe. I told him to rape her and then burn her alive, though he certainly didn't need my encouragement. He enjoyed himself very much."

Howell yanked powerfully enough on the bars to cause dirt to shower down on them.

Bahame laughed. "But now God has delivered you to me. Just as he promised he would. I will very much enjoy dealing with you."

"Do it now," Omidi said, speaking for the first time since the African entered.

"In good time."

"Not in good time. Now. They're of no use to us. Keeping them alive is an unnecessary risk."

The African waved a hand dismissively, obviously wanting to savor the sensation of having Howell completely at his mercy. "I said in good time. I'll use the whites to keep the spirits alive. To show my people that no one can stand against my magic."

"We have an agreement. We—"

"An agreement? How do prisoners that *I* captured enter into our agreement?"

"I'm the one who gave you their location. It was my source in the American—"

"*God* told me their location. You were just a convenient messenger."

He grabbed Sarie by the hair and pulled her to him. She was smart enough not to fight but drew the line at hiding her hatred.

"And now I have the woman. Maybe I don't need you anymore, eh, Mehrak?"

It was clear that Omidi understood the weakness of his position. Bahame was a mystic and a psychopath, but he had enough of an understanding of biology to know how useful Sarie could be in making the parasite a more practical weapon.

"Perhaps we could strike a bargain for her," Omidi said.

Bahame looked vaguely insulted. "She isn't part of our deal and I can make use of her myself."

"Of course you are right," Omidi said, his tone softening into something that approached subservience. "But we have the facilities to put her skills fully to use. Certainly there is room for negotiation."

The African nodded. "There's always room for negotiation between good friends. Come, let's drink and we can talk of this more."

CHAPTER FORTY-SEVEN

Outside Washington, DC, USA
November 25—1244 Hours GMT–5

The crunch of icy gravel sounded impossibly loud as Randi walked toward a small cabin tucked into the woods about ten miles from the nearest asphalt. The drive there had offered no opportunity for escape, and the situation wasn't getting any better. Her captors were a good ten feet behind her, one thirty degrees left and the other thirty degrees right, staying close to the tree line.

The chances of her making a break and getting to cover without catching a bullet seemed to be hovering somewhere between slim and none. It would have been an easy shot for someone half as good as the people covering her. But even if by some miracle they did miss, that left her running unarmed through the snow in heels and a skirt.

Randi stopped at the front door and glanced back, unsure what to do. The woman, who looked much more sleek after shedding the elaborate foam belly, motioned her inside.

The trees were tantalizingly close, and Randi focused longingly on them in her peripheral vision before reaching for the knob. At this point she just had to keep breathing long enough for someone to make a mistake. Not a great strategy, but the only one currently available.

There was a green-wood fire crackling to her right as she entered, and she couldn't help reveling for a moment in the heat coming off it. The galley kitchen at the back of the cabin was separated from the main living area by a granite-topped island, and there was a man standing next to the sink working on something she couldn't see. He was a little less than six feet tall, with thinning hair and a suit that apparently had a healthy fear of irons.

"Randi," he said, glancing up at her. "I'll be right with you. Pour us some wine."

There was a carafe on a coffee table near the fireplace, and she examined the odd way the light played off it and the two glasses next to it. Plastic. A quick sweep of the room confirmed that any object more dangerous than a soft cushion had been removed.

The man came around the counter and slid a plate of cheese and fruit onto the table before settling into one of the sofas surrounding it. "Please. Sit."

He didn't look even mildly athletic, but behind his glasses his eyes were sharp—a little sharper than she would have liked. The intelligence didn't just reflect there; it glowed.

Still devoid of options, she took a seat across from him and poured. He reached for a glass and took a careful sip, nodding approvingly. "I was afraid it might be a little past its prime, but I'm happy to say I was wrong. Please don't let it go to waste. If I wanted you dead or unconscious, you already would be."

It was hard to argue with his logic, and she put the plastic glass to her lips. Credit where credit was due. The man knew wine.

"First let me apologize for the melodrama. You're being watched by a surprising number of people, and not all of them are from my organization. We had to make the switch quickly enough that no one would notice."

"Your organization?" Randi said.

The man frowned. "I'm sorry. I'm being rude. My name is Fred Klein."

Randi took another sip of wine, processing the name impassively.

"Can I assume you've heard of me?"

"There was a Fred Klein who worked for a while at the CIA and then spent years at the NSA. After leaving there, though, I don't know what happened to him."

"Oh, he did a bit of this and that—finally culminating in our meeting."

"I see," she said, not bothering to hide her skepticism. She'd never met Fred Klein personally, and there was no way to confirm this was him. It was an intriguing claim, though. He had a serious reputation in the intel community, and the suddenness of his resignation from the government had led to more than a little speculation in the circles she ran in.

"You left Jon Smith a message a few days ago," he said. "I mentioned it to him and he was concerned."

Smith. Still popping up in the oddest places.

"It was nice of him to be worried, but it was just a personal call about my sister. Do you know where he is? I'd like to connect with him."

"Unfortunately, he and I recently lost touch."

"That's a shame. Well, I'll try to catch up with him when he gets back. Thanks for the wine. Any chance I could get a ride home?"

Klein smiled and stabbed at a piece of cheese with a toothpick. "Do you know where Jon is?"

"No idea."

"So I should just chalk it up to coincidence that you booked a ticket to Cape Town for tomorrow?"

"My compliments. You're extraordinarily well-informed."

"I have to admit to a little luck on that one. I've had occasion to do business with the same Czech forger you used to have that passport made. But, unfortunately, Jon's no longer in South Africa."

"No?" Randi said, unwilling to reveal anything herself, but perfectly happy to let Klein—or whoever he was—talk.

"He caught an internal flight to Uganda four days ago."

"Really?" she said noncommittally. "How interesting."

Klein sank back into the sofa.

"Perhaps we should change the subject for a moment. The reason I knew about the message you left Jon isn't because we're watching *him*. It's because we're watching you."

"Me? Why?"

"Because there are people high up in our government who have been interested in you joining our little family for some time now."

"Exactly what people and what family is that?"

Klein studiously ignored the first part of her question. "I work for an organization called Covert-One."

"Never heard of it."

"And neither has anyone else. We were formed as a fast-response team—small, agile, and outside the normal bureaucracy. I think you're familiar with one of our top operatives …"

"Jon."

He nodded.

"I can't tell you how much that explains …," she said before catching herself and falling silent again.

"And I can't tell you how far beyond top secret the things I'm telling you are."

There was no question of that. If it came out that there were forces in the U.S. government running a black ops group that circumvented oversight, there would be hell to pay. Having said that, she'd worked with the conventional intel community long enough to be sympathetic to the need for such a group.

"Do you know a man named Brandon Gazenga, Randi?"

"Never heard of him," she lied smoothly.

Klein smiled. "You're not going to make this easy on me, are you? I wonder why it is, then, that you called your friend at the FBI and asked him to send someone to Gazenga's house."

This time, Randi didn't bother to hide her surprise and Klein didn't bother to hide his satisfaction at finally getting a reaction out of her.

"Okay, Fred. I'm officially impressed. But what are we really talking about here? Why pick this moment to recruit me? Could it be that you sent Jon on an errand to Africa and something went wrong? That you need me to bail him—and you—out?"

He frowned and reached for another piece of cheese. "It's

a little more complicated than that, but I wouldn't say your assessment is *entirely* inaccurate."

"Then let's cut to the chase. Why is Jon in Africa?"

Klein didn't react immediately, thinking for a few seconds before using a remote control to start a video on the cabin's television. "This was taken in northern Uganda two weeks ago. The men are from our top blacks ops unit. I'm afraid none of them are still alive."

CHAPTER FORTY-EIGHT

Northern Uganda
November 27—1904 Hours GMT+3

Caleb Bahame paced back and forth across the clearing, his gait becoming faster and stiffer as time passed. Most of his men had retreated to the safety of the jungle, but a few novices remained, unwittingly standing far too close.

Omidi glanced at his watch. Two hours late.

There was no way to contact the men bringing the weapons shipment in. The transfer to Bahame's team had been successfully made, but there had been no communication from them since.

Even without the delay, it was a very delicate situation. Sembutu had agreed to allow Omidi to move freely around Uganda without informing the Western intelligence agencies and to allow the Iranian weapons delivery to go through, though now it appeared that he may have once again panicked. If he'd stupidly decided that arming Bahame was too much of a risk for the reward he'd been promised, then the situation was going to deteriorate very quickly and very dangerously.

A young soldier suddenly burst from the jungle at a full run, skidding awkwardly and losing his balance when Bahame raised a machete and started screaming. The boy held up a hand protectively, unintelligible words tumbling from his mouth. The violent rage burning in the cult leader's eyes cooled so suddenly that it was hard to believe it had ever existed, and instead of dismembering the child, he cheerfully helped him to his feet.

It wasn't necessary to speak the local language to understand what had happened. The shipment had been spotted.

It was another fifteen minutes before the first truck appeared, lumbering along the poorly maintained road used for transporting parasite victims to and from the villages Bahame overran. It was painted with the logo of one of the many aid agencies operating in the country, and when the first boxes were thrown from the back, emergency rations spilled out.

Despite their obvious malnourishment, the young soldiers emerging from the trees showed little interest in the food. It wasn't until a box full of mortars was crowbarred open that their enthusiasm flared.

Bahame took personal control of the unloading, directing the crates of guns, mines, rifles, and ammunition to various storage areas at the edges of the camp, watching each one with glassy-eyed obsession.

When the second truck pulled up, he lost interest in traffic control and stepped back to examine the single enormous crate strapped to the flatbed. Omidi smiled imperceptibly. He hadn't been sure if this one would actually arrive, but once again, God had provided.

"It is a gift," the Iranian said. "From His Excellency the Ayatollah Khamenei to you."

Bahame leapt onto the back of the truck and shouted for help as Omidi pressed two boys into service pulling down the ramps on the trailer. The front of the box was pried open and Bahame disappeared inside, his excited shouts audible as he kicked out the remaining sides.

When it was done, something that looked like a small tank sat amid the splintered wood. It was squat and angular, with thick Plexiglas windows and a single seat.

"It's made by an American company for police bomb-disposal units," Omidi explained. "I'm told it can take a direct hit from an RPG and travel more than sixty kilometers per hour."

Bahame leapt to the ground and snatched the machine gun from around the neck of one of his soldiers. What was going to happen next seemed obvious, and Omidi threw himself to the ground as the sound of automatic fire ricocheting off steel filled his ears.

By the time he stood again, the African was already back on the truck, stepping over the body of a girl who hadn't fled fast enough and reaching out to caress the undamaged skin of the vehicle. He opened the door and squeezed into the confined space, searching for the ignition. A moment later, the engine roared to life in a cloud of black diesel smoke.

Omidi retreated to the makeshift podium set up at the edge of the jungle and dialed a number into his sat phone. The line clicked a few times and then a familiar voice came on.

"Yes?"

"The first two trucks have arrived."

Bahame managed to get the vehicle down the ramps and started chasing his terrified men around the clearing.

"Then should we begin our final preparations?"

"Immediately."

"We will wait for your signal."

Bahame skidded a hundred and eighty degrees and began roaring in his direction, but Omidi didn't bother to move. If there was one thing he was absolutely sure of, it was that the African would never risk damaging the stage he used to display his godhood.

CHAPTER FORTY-NINE

Langley, Virginia, USA
November 27—1129 Hours GMT–5

Dave Collen looked haggard as he fell into one of the chairs facing Drake's desk. The redness of his eyes suggested that he'd been up for at least twenty-four hours straight, and his expression implied that the time hadn't been as productive as it needed to be.

"We still don't have any details on what happened to Smith and his people during their arrest beyond the fact that they were taken to an old military base and released eight hours later. It could be nothing more than some soldiers happening to witness Smith pulling a knife on Sabastiaan Bastock—"

"Quite a coincidence," Drake said. "And it doesn't explain why Bastock seems to have ended up dead."

"I'm not buying it either, but the people we have watching them don't have access to that base. We have no way of knowing what happened there."

"And after they were released?"

"They picked up a vehicle at the black market and drove north followed by some of Sembutu's men. No stops to speak of until they got to a farm owned by Noah Duernberg. They spent the night there and then headed deeper into Bahame country. That's where we lost them."

"Is there any link between Duernberg and the parasite?"

"None that we know of. He's the second generation in that house. His father was a doctor by training and was loosely connected to Idi Amin."

"A doctor? Is it possible he had experience with the infection?"

Collen shrugged helplessly. "He's been dead a long time, and record keeping in that part of the world isn't exactly state-of-the-art."

"There's a lot you don't know, isn't there?" Drake said, starting to lose control of his frustration.

"I told you before we got rid of Brandon that it was going to partially blind us in Uganda."

"Do we at least have someone we can send to Duernberg's farm to look around?"

Collen shook his head. "That's where the news gets worse. After Smith and his people left, the farm was burned to the ground with Duernberg in it. His wife and child were in an apartment in Kampala trying to work out a way to emigrate. We sent people there …"

"And?"

"They found them in the bathtub with their throats slit."

Drake ran a hand over his mouth and it came away slick with sweat. Duernberg knew something, and someone wanted to keep it quiet. But who? Bahame was the obvious answer, but was it the correct one? The fact that Smith and his team had been taken to a military base and were now being followed pointed in another direction—Charles Sembutu. Could there be a connection between him and the Iranians?

Collen seemed to read his mind. "Larry, we're losing control here. This started as an exercise in spinning data. Now we've got an American team lost somewhere in the jungle, an old doctor's family murdered, and one of our most dangerous operatives sniffing around to the point that she has to be dealt with. I think it's time we consider going to the president with what we've got."

"Are you getting cold feet?" Drake said, the volume of his voice rising in the soundproof room. "Were you only in this as long as there was no personal risk? As long as—"

"Bullshit, Larry! I've been with you from the very beginning, and I've been the only one getting his hands dirty.

You're not stuck trying to find reliable people to track Smith through the damn jungle. And you sure as hell weren't in Brandon's bedroom when he died. But we've lost track of one of our top microbiologists and the world authority on parasitic infections. What if Bahame has them? Jesus, what if Omidi has them? Then we may not be looking at an unsophisticated infection that would be relatively easy to control. We could be looking at something that's been weaponized."

Drake opened his mouth to reply but instead took a deep breath. "I'm sorry, Dave. I didn't mean to question your commitment."

"I guess tempers are running high," he said, forcing a smile.

Drake nodded. "I agree that the risks—to us and to the country—are higher than we hoped. But I disagree that pulling the plug will change that. What would Castilla be able to do? Go after Bahame? He already took out our best team. Make our suspicions public? That will just turn into a bunch of political posturing that'll give the Iranians even more time to work on this thing and cover their tracks. Khamenei's losing his grip—he knows that better than we do. He's going all-in on this. He doesn't have any choice."

Drake paused to let Collen respond, but the man just stared at the ground.

"Here's what I propose, Dave. We initiate another shake-up of our bioterror response system—throw a bunch of new scenarios at them, including one that quietly approximates a worst-case scenario for this parasite being weaponized. That way we'll have something that can be implemented quickly if the Iranians manage to refine the parasite before they release it. Casualties will be worse than our estimates but should stay within the three quarters of a million that we considered the high side of acceptable. In the end, though, I doubt we're going to see that kind of sophistication. My hunch is that Smith and his team are dead."

His assistant nodded silently.

"Do you agree?" Drake prompted.

Collen finally met his eye. "Yeah. I'm sorry, Larry. You're right. We always knew that taking down the Iranians wouldn't be easy, but ..."

"We hoped it would be easier than this," Drake said, finishing his thought.

"Yeah."

"Okay, then. Randi Russell. Where do we stand with her?"

"The news is better there. She's locked down tight—physically and electronically—and she doesn't seem to have done anything at all since contacting the TSA."

"No more follow-up on Brandon's death with her FBI contact?"

"Nothing."

"Has she made any more attempts to get in touch with Smith?"

"Not after the second call to Fort Detrick."

"So you're confident she's gotten nowhere?"

"All I can say is that I'm fairly confident she doesn't know anything more than whatever was written on the piece of paper Brandon put in her pocket."

"Do you think she's given up? Should we step back from our plans to deal with her?"

Collen shook his head. "If it was anybody else, I'd say we should reassess. But Randi Russell never gives up. Once she gets her teeth into something, she doesn't let go until she's satisfied. My take is that she's hit a dead end and this is just a pause while she figures out her next move."

"I agree. Now's the time to do this—before she gets hold of some loose end we missed. Have you contacted Gohlam?"

"Everything's set. We've given him all her details and he's waiting for the go-ahead."

Drake drummed his fingers on his desk, fixing for a moment on the closed door to his office. Padshah Gohlam was an Afghan mole living in Maryland on a student visa. The CIA had known about him since the beginning and let him into the United States to try to ferret out his contacts. They'd managed to crack his communications system, which allowed Collen to impersonate his Afghan handler while circumventing the agency's surveillance. As far as Gohlam knew, he was being activated to take out an American operative responsible for the deaths of countless jihadists across the globe.

It was a seemingly perfect scenario. Not only would there be no reason for anyone at the agency to be suspicious of Gohlam's motives; they would be very anxious to sweep their failure to control him under the rug. Randi Russell would disappear and the details of her death would be swallowed by a black hole of administrative ass covering.

"Do it."

"To be clear," Collen said carefully, "you're telling me to give him the signal to take out Russell."

Drake nodded. "Do it now before she figures out a way to bring all this down on top of us."

CHAPTER FIFTY

Northern Uganda
November 27—2105 Hours GMT+3

"Can you hold it out a little more, Sarie?"

She pressed herself tighter to the bars and twisted the padlock in her hands, giving Smith a better angle to attack it with the rusted saw. They'd been at it for hours and he guessed they weren't much more than a sixteenth of an inch through the hardened steel. But what was the alternative? Sit and wait for death?

His arms felt like they were on fire and the sweat streaming down his nose occasionally choked him as he gulped the blood-scented air. When he nearly fumbled the blade, he finally staggered back and let Howell take over.

Dr. De Vries was standing lookout at the edge of the only passage into the chamber but was too old and decrepit to be counted on for much else. The infected woman imprisoned next to them was weakening fast, lying in mud created by her own blood. She saw him looking at her and lunged feebly at the bars with twisted, shattered hands. It wouldn't be long now before she was too far gone to do even that. And then Bahame would be back.

Smith pressed his back to the cave wall and slid down into the dirt, trying futilely to find something he'd missed. Some way to get out of there.

"How do you know Bahame?" Sarie said.

Her face and Howell's were only a few inches apart, and she seemed to be searching his eyes for the answer.

"There was a time we ran in the same social circles," he said, starting in on the lock.

"It's a little late to be mysterious, isn't it? We're going to die here."

Howell stopped sawing for a moment. "Dead is dead and almost dead is alive. Very different things."

He went back to work, and Smith turned his attention to the equipment in the lab. There had to be something there. Something they could use.

He was examining the broken generator against the wall for what must have been the twentieth time when Howell started talking again.

"I did some work in Angola years ago. After it was finished, I decided to travel around the continent a bit. See the sights. I ended up in a village not far from here where an aid agency was working on an irrigation project. They were a man down and I had some knowledge from growing up in farm country, so I threw in for a bit ... A tad higher, dear."

Sarie adjusted the position of the lock and he continued. "Bahame wasn't the man you see today. He was leading a group of former drug runners and cutthroats on a bit of a pillaging-and-raping spree. I suppose this was before he found God." Howell smiled bitterly. "In any event, I'd been at the village for about six months when he and his men showed up."

"What happened?"

"Oh, they overran us quite quickly—the people living there were a peaceful lot. No weapons beyond the tools they used for farming."

"But you got away."

"You'd be surprised how effective certain farm tools can be in the right hands. I killed six or seven of Bahame's men before I was forced into the jungle. I tried to get back, but I'd been shot and couldn't move very quickly. I'm afraid by the time I managed to stop the bleeding, it was over."

"Who is Yakobo?"

Howell didn't answer immediately, focusing his full attention on the lock. "He was a boy whose parents had died and whose aunt and uncle weren't particularly interested in his upbringing. I helped him out here and there. More trouble than he was worth, really."

The heaviness in his voice suggested that Yakobo had, in fact, been very much worth the trouble.

"I'm so sorry, Peter."

Howell stopped and took a step back, signaling that he needed a break.

Before Smith could push himself fully to his feet, though, De Vries turned toward them. "I hear footsteps!" he said in a harsh whisper. "They're coming!"

Smith put an arm around Sarie's shoulder, and they moved to the back of the tiny enclosure. She reached up and squeezed his hand, a simple act that magnified the guilt gnawing at him. What had he been thinking when he'd agreed to let her come with them? He'd known damn well that it could turn out this way.

Bahame entered with the same young boy and three guards that he'd used to put Sarie in the cage with them. The system the African had devised was simple, but also all but foolproof: the boy, unarmed and too small to use for cover, unlocked the cage while the guards set themselves up well out of reach with guns at the ready. Undoubtedly, there were additional men strategically posted in the passageway, turning it into a hopelessly constricted shooting gallery.

Smith supposed it was to be expected. No one was going to be happy about being put in a cage with one of the victims of the parasite—particularly after sitting a few feet away watching what it was going to do to them. Even the gentlest soul could be counted on to risk the most suicidal opportunity to escape.

"What now, Caleb?" Howell said, approaching the bars.

The African smiled and stepped aside as Mehrak Omidi and a tall man in a spotless white turban and galabiya entered. His skin gleamed like obsidian, as did his eyes as they scanned the room. Definitely not one of Bahame's followers. Almost certainly from Sudan.

"Who's he?" Smith said.

Omidi didn't acknowledge the question, instead watching as the man rolled out the prayer rug he was holding and knelt.

Bahame seemed barely able to contain his impatience, fidgeting like a child in church as the man prayed.

"I'd like to show you why you will never win," Omidi said when the man stood again and swept aside the plastic in front of the woman's cage. The bars clanged dully when she stretched an arm through.

The Sudanese used a bejeweled dagger to put a long cut in his forearm and then held the wound out to the woman.

He wasn't expecting her sudden burst of strength and was pulled hard into the bars as she clawed at him. Blood spattered his arm and he was forced to grab her hair with his free hand to prevent her from biting him. They fought like that for a full thirty seconds before he finally managed to pull away, his weight and the slickness of sweat and blood finally trumping her superior strength.

He was clearly shaken by his experience and kept his eyes on the woman as he retreated to the sound of her frustrated screams.

Omidi pointed at De Vries. "Tend to Dahab's wound."

The old doctor looked to be on the verge of collapsing from fear, but he managed to pull on a pair of surgical gloves and keep his hand from shaking too much to suture.

Bahame grunted and pointed to their cage, prompting the boy with the key to approach and release the lock.

"Dr. van Keuren," Omidi said. "Please come out."

She pressed her sweat-soaked body a little tighter to Smith's. "I think I'll stay here if it's all the same to you."

"You know what will happen to you if you stay. I'm offering you a way out of here. I'm offering you freedom."

She just shook her head.

Howell had the tip of the saw blade between his fingers, and he turned his hand subtly so that Smith could see the rest of it running up his forearm. A burst of adrenaline throbbed in Smith's head, further clouding it. The Brit wasn't suggesting an escape attempt—that was pointless. He was offering to put a quick and painless end to Sarie van Keuren.

"No …," Smith stammered. Suddenly, it was impossible to separate her from Sophia. Impossible to separate this day from the one he'd watched the woman he loved die.

Omidi let out a frustrated breath and pointed to De Vries, who was winding a bandage around Dahab's arm. "Kill the old man."

One of the guards redirected his aim, and Sarie jumped toward the open door to their cell. "*Stop!*"

The Iranian just smiled and held a hand out to her.

The Sudanese shoved Sarie and De Vries into the back of a canvas-covered military transport as Omidi looked on. Her companions were still alive—a loose end that infuriated him, but one that he would have to tolerate for the moment. They were formidable men, but the chance that they could escape their prison and stay ahead of Bahame's men in unfamiliar terrain was unlikely in the extreme. Particularly with time running out so much more quickly than they imagined.

"You remember our agreement?" Bahame said as Omidi started toward the cab of the truck. "You will give me whatever the woman discovers."

"Of course, my good friend. We fight for the same thing. The freedom of our countries."

That seemed to please the African, and Omidi accepted his hand, counting on the darkness to hide his disgust. Bahame put his own desires before those of God—something he would be made to pay dearly for.

The Iranian climbed into the truck and started the engine, putting a hand through the open window in a respectful salute as he pulled away.

Bahame glowed red in the taillights and Omidi waited until his image disappeared from the side mirror before pulling out a small GPS unit and switching it on. The signal would transmit the coordinates of Bahame's camp to a Ugandan military force waiting some two hundred kilometers to the southeast.

In a way, it was regrettable. Smith and Howell didn't deserve the quick death that he was giving them. No, they deserved to die like their countrymen soon would: insane and bleeding.

CHAPTER FIFTY-ONE

Northern Uganda
November 27—2153 Hours GMT+3

Jon Smith had taken over holding the lock and Howell was sawing again, though they both knew their time had run out. The infected woman hardly moved anymore, even when their eyes met through the spattered plastic. She'd be dead soon, and that meant the parasite killing her would need a new host.

Footsteps became audible in the passageway and Howell shoved the blade down the back of his pants as they moved away from the bars. A moment later, Bahame and the team he'd so meticulously trained to shuttle people in and out of the cells appeared.

"I'll allow you to choose who goes in with her first, Doctor. You or your good friend Peter?"

Howell just shrugged. There was no way he was going to spend the last few hours of his life lying in a muddy cage losing his mind. He would undoubtedly choose to go down in a futile last charge. The question in Smith's mind was, would he do the same? The thought of a few quick rounds to the chest had become strangely comforting over the time they'd been imprisoned there, but he was a survivor by both nature and training. Could he knowingly run straight at the barrel of a loaded AK-47?

"I'm sorry," he said, clapping Howell on the shoulder. "I think this may have been one adventure too many."

The Brit smiled. "I told you men like us don't get old. We just—"

The unmistakable *whup* of a bomb detonating was followed quickly by three more, shaking the ground violently enough that Smith had to put a hand against the rock wall to keep his balance. Muffled automatic-rifle fire started a moment later, along with a string of shouted orders from Bahame as he tried to get to the passageway leading outside.

Another explosion sounded and Smith threw his arm in front of his face as part of the ceiling collapsed, kicking up a choking cloud of dust that temporarily obscured everything around them. He lunged for the bars, hoping they'd been loosened by the blast, but Howell yanked him back just as the woman who had been imprisoned next to them collided with the rusted steel.

"Watch your eyes and any cuts!" Smith yelled as they pressed against the back of the cell in an attempt to stay clear of the blood running down her outstretched arm.

It took only a few seconds for her to determine that they were out of reach, and she turned, rushing through the haze toward the other men in the chamber. Bahame had fallen and was just getting back to his feet when he saw her coming. One of the guards and the boy were already gone, and the last man was going for the passageway when Bahame grabbed his arm and spun him into the woman. A joyful screech erupted from her when they collided—the sound of endless, unbearable frustration finally being released.

The young guard cried out to Bahame as she flailed at him with crushed hands, but the man he revered as a god was already disappearing up the passageway.

The rumble of the fighting outside was suddenly lost in the deafening static of a rifle on full automatic and bullets ricocheting off stone. Smith and Howell both dove to the ground as the guard finally managed to get control of his weapon and press the barrel to the woman's chest. She jerked wildly as he pulled the trigger, finally going limp and sliding to the ground.

Smith jumped to his feet and rammed his full weight against the bars. Despite the considerable damage to the cave, they didn't budge.

"Hey!" he called to the blood-spattered guard staring down at the woman's body. The desperation in his eyes was powerful enough to be visible even through the swirling dust. Powerful enough to use.

"Hey!" Smith shouted again, trying to get his voice to rise above the sound of the escalating battle outside. "Do you speak English?"

The young man looked at the passageway leading out and then back at Smith. He gave a short nod but otherwise seemed paralyzed.

"I'm a doctor. You heard Bahame say it himself. This isn't magic. It's just an infection. I can cure you."

"You … You can help me?" came his heavily accented reply.

"Yes," Smith lied. "You just need to let me out."

The man looked up the passageway again, unsure what to do.

"Bahame ran like a woman. You saw the fear in him. He has no power over this. I do."

Western medicine commanded a substantial amount of respect with most Africans, and fortunately for him this man was no exception.

"Get back," he said, aiming his rifle at the lock and firing a controlled burst. Smith kicked the door and took a deep breath of the thick air. They were out. Probably only to die in the fighting outside, but at least they'd go down swinging beneath an open sky.

The guard trained his gun on him and nodded toward the medical instruments strewn across the ground. "You do it. You cure me."

"I need—"

"No more talk!" he shouted, aiming his weapon directly between Smith's eyes. "You cure me now. I want to go home. To my village. To my family."

A blast came a little too close, and Smith ducked involuntarily, looking up at a wide crack opening above them. They didn't have time for this.

He dropped to his knees and rummaged around, finally

241

turning up a syringe. When he stood again, he saw that the man was so preoccupied by the thought of ending up like the woman at his feet that he hadn't noticed Howell slipping silently up behind him. The Brit had decided to minimize any bloodletting by opting for a softball-sized rock in place of the saw blade. Smith fussed with the syringe, keeping the attention of the young man as Howell closed in.

Then it was over. The guard, who had undoubtedly been kidnapped by Bahame as a child, would never go back to his village. He would never again see his family.

Smith scooped up the dead man's gun and followed Howell into the passageway. It took only a few seconds to reach the mouth, and they pressed themselves to opposite sides, trying to make sense of the chaos beyond.

Three helicopters were visible, lit by the flash of their cannons as they mowed down everything in their path—trees, fleeing soldiers, children. The fighter planes that had carried out the initial rocket attacks were retreating south, but Smith wasn't convinced they'd seen the last of them.

Broken, burning bodies were everywhere, and, suddenly leaderless, the surviving soldiers scrambled for open crates of weapons that they seemed unclear how to use.

Smith crossed to Howell and shouted over the din. "We need to find our truck. Omidi's got enough of a head start that it's the only thing fast enough to catch him."

The Brit didn't seem to hear, instead scanning the destruction in front of them.

"Peter! Are you—"

"There!" the Brit said, pointing to the west side of the clearing. A small group of soldiers were gathered in a tight formation, moving awkwardly along the edge of the jungle. Smith focused on them and immediately spotted what his companion found so interesting: the graying hair of Caleb Bahame glowing in the firelight as he tried to escape the inevitable result of making deals with the Iranians.

Howell took off across the clearing without a thought, dodging through bodies and confused soldiers before scooping up a machete lying across a stump. Smith cursed under his breath and followed, holding the gun he'd taken at the ready despite the fact that he didn't know if there was any ammunition left in the clip.

Fortunately, the people around him were more interested in survival than in two running white men, and Smith crashed into the jungle a few seconds behind Howell and Bahame.

When he came to the edge of a much smaller clearing than the one they'd just abandoned, he stopped to look for unfriendlies and was shocked when Howell just charged into the open without breaking stride. On the western rim of the glade, a vague outline of three young soldiers was visible in front of what looked like a carport constructed of vines and leaves. Beneath it, the truck they'd bought in Kampala suddenly lit up.

Bahame was already behind the wheel, and the familiar whine of the starter was audible as he tried to get the engine to turn over. Smith wasn't paying attention, though, instead focusing on the muzzle flashes from the frightened boys trying to line up on the crazed white man bearing down on them with a machete.

Smith squeezed off a short burst just over their heads, relieved that the clip wasn't empty.

"Run!" he shouted, waving them off.

They didn't, though, instead continuing to fire wildly in Howell's direction. None of the shots seemed to be getting within twenty feet of him, but there was no telling when someone would get lucky.

Smith switched the gun to semiautomatic and winced when he put a round into the chest of a kid who, in America, would have just started high school. The two surviving boys decided they'd had enough, and one ran east along the edge of the trees, finally disappearing into them on what was hopefully his way home. The other took a less advantageous route behind the Land Cruiser that Bahame was slamming into reverse.

The rear bumper caught him in the legs, pulling him under the tires as Bahame tried to get to a narrow dirt track leading into the jungle. Smith squeezed off a careful shot just as the cult found first gear. The round shattered the driver's-side window a split second before Howell collided with the door and punched through what was left of the glass.

There was a muzzle flash from inside the car, and the Brit fell away, landing on his back in the dirt. Smith got off another shot, but it passed harmlessly by Bahame and punched a hole in the right side of the windshield. The African looked in his direction, realizing that the next shot was going to kill him. He ducked down and threw the passenger door open, sliding out and vanishing into the darkness.

"Peter! Are you all right?"

The SAS man was just making it back to his feet when Smith came up alongside. Miraculously, he hadn't been hit, but there were powder burns on his face, and his eyes were tearing badly.

"Can you see?" Smith said, checking the sky for attack choppers before pulling open one of Howell's lids to look for damage.

"Yeah, I can see," he said, jerking away. "I'm fine."

There was no time to argue, so Smith pulled open the Land Cruiser's door and slid behind the wheel. "Keys are still in it and it's got a full tank. Get in. I'll drive."

Instead, Howell backed away and picked up the machete he'd dropped. "Why don't you go on ahead? I'll catch up."

"What the hell are you talking about, Peter? Get in the damn car."

"I'm sorry, Jon."

"You're sorry? I didn't bring you here to settle a personal vendetta. Omidi's got the parasite and someone with the expertise to weaponize—"

"Don't lecture me about personal, Jon. I'd have hated like hell doing it, but we both know you should have let me take care of Sarie back in that cage. You're on your own, mate."

CHAPTER FIFTY-TWO

Northern Uganda
November 27—2226 Hours GMT+3

Peter Howell jumped over a rotting log and then slowed when a group of Bahame's soldiers darted in front of him. None took a shot, instead scattering and disappearing in a chorus of panicked shouts.

Their deity-driven command structure had collapsed, and the forces attacking them weren't the unarmed villagers they were used to. As near as he could tell, the entire Ugandan air force was overhead, unloading the country's stockpile of rockets and machine-gun rounds. Behind him, the jungle was on fire, sending an impenetrable wall of flame nearly a hundred feet into the hazy, chemical-scented air.

Most of Bahame's followers would be running east toward the river. It was the easiest terrain, and the water would act as a firebreak, but it was also a fatal error. They were clearly being flushed, and the Ugandans would have troops dug in on the far shore—something those terrified children wouldn't discover until the water was over their heads.

Howell spotted a streak of blood on a leaf and angled left, picking up speed again. The wind was with him for now, but if it shifted he could find himself wandering aimlessly in a cloud of choking, opaque smoke. He was too close to let that happen.

The sound of helicopter rotors became audible behind him, and he ignored it until he could feel the thump of them in his chest. The people he'd seen a few moments ago were being targeted, and he was forced to throw himself to the ground as the nose gun opened up.

Rounds arced over his head, bringing branches as thick as two inches down on top of him as the gunner refined his aim. The cries of children sounded for a moment and Howell found himself wishing them a quick death—not out of sympathy, but expedience. He didn't have time to be pinned down here. Bahame was on the move.

His wish was answered, and he ignored a pang of guilt as the screams went silent and the helicopter moved off. The trail continued—Bahame was obviously bleeding badly from the cut he'd suffered when Smith shattered his window. Still, the farther he got from the firelight, the harder he would be to track. Howell knew that it would be only a matter of minutes before the trail disintegrated into the deepening gloom.

The ground rose on either side as he ran, funneling him into an inky canyon with vine-covered walls. Despite the obvious terrain trap, he continued, savoring the burning in his legs, the stench of the battlefield, the intermittent gleam of Bahame's blood. Finally, he forced himself to stop. As much as he didn't want the intoxicating sensation of hunting Bahame to end, he also didn't want to be dead. Not yet.

Howell grabbed a sturdy vine and went hand over hand up the slope, turning to move parallel to the deep furrow when he reached the top. Progress was slower than he hoped, but finally he spotted movement.

Unfortunately, the unreliable light made it impossible to discern what was causing it. He got to his knees and crawled forward, trying to clear his mind of the possibility that he was creeping up on an aardvark while Bahame disappeared into a thousand miles of jungle. It didn't work, though, and he found himself going too fast, the sound of leaves brushing past him carrying into the air.

The crack of the gunshot was quickly followed by a searing pain in his shoulder. He dove behind a tree, his training demanding a strategic retreat to assess Bahame's position and check the severity of his wound.

Instead, he broke cover, sprinting full bore in the direction the shot had come from. Another sounded but went wide as the person firing tried to run and shoot at the same time. A moment later the outline of his attacker became visible. Not another child. A full-grown man in fatigues. Bahame.

Howell barely noticed the bullets hissing past, a dangerous illusion of invincibility overtaking him as everything else faded away—the jungle, the explosions, the helicopters. And when it was all gone and only Bahame remained, he did seem strangely godlike. The last thing on earth.

They collided near the edge of the shallow ravine and fell into it, locked together as they tumbled through the vines. Bahame swung a knife and Howell was forced to drop his machete in order to deflect the blow. He went for the African's eyes with his thumbs, but they hit the ground hard and were thrown apart.

Caught up in the emotions of finally having Bahame so close, Howell hadn't pushed the air from his lungs before the impact and was now completely unable to breathe. Bahame had fared better and managed to stagger to his feet, but instead of finishing off his opponent, he went to the vines and started trying to climb out.

Howell was grateful that the men who had trained him weren't there to see this pathetic display—the dazed African repeatedly climbing a few feet before sliding back to the ground, and him lying there gulping at the air like a dying fish.

He was getting a little more oxygen in with every breath, though, and his head finally cleared enough for him to crawl to the machete he'd dropped.

"Too … late, Caleb."

Bahame looked back, losing his grip and slipping to the ground again. He didn't try to run, instead just standing there dumbfounded that this could be happening to him— to a living god.

He ripped open his camouflage shirt and used one of the bones hanging around his neck to put a gash across his chest. His eyes rolled back in his head, the whites gleaming in the flickering light as he chanted in his native language.

"Are you summoning demons to strike me down?" Howell said, feeling his balance and strength return. He tested his right shoulder by lifting the machete over his head. Fully functional. Bahame's bullet had only grazed him.

"I think I'm a little old to be afraid of the dark, Caleb."

CHAPTER FIFTY-THREE

Washington, DC, USA
November 27—1706 Hours GMT–5

President Sam Adams Castilla pushed his titanium glasses up and swiped at his exhausted eyes. "I don't even under-stand what you're saying to me, Fred. That Larry Drake—who I've known for years—had one of his analysts killed?"

"Sam, we—"

"Wait, I'm not done. He had one of his analysts killed so that he can help Iran get hold of a horrifying biological weapon that they would then use against America?"

"That's a little oversimplified," Klein said.

He hated coming to his old friend with something this speculative— the president of the United States had more than enough concrete disasters to deal with on any given day. At this point, though, the situation was too dangerous to ignore and impossible to pursue without Castilla's direct involvement.

"What do you want me to do with this, Fred? Call the FBI director and tell him that a man who spent his entire life serving this country is actually some kind of radical Muslim mole? And then when he asks me for evidence—a murder weapon—I could pull out a spare rib that's a week past its sell-by date?"

Castilla stood suddenly and began pacing back and forth across the Oval Office.

"Sam, are you all right?"

"Hell no, I'm not all right. If anyone but you came to me with this, I'd fire them and then have them committed. But you're not just anyone and that means I actually have to take this seriously—I have to start worrying about the loyalty of the man running our intelligence network."

"If it makes any difference, I doubt Larry's a radical—at least not a Muslim one. And in his own way, I think he believes he's still serving the country."

"What in God's name are you talking about, Fred? By letting what killed those soldiers loose in the streets?"

"He could be trying to force your hand on Iran."

"I don't understand."

"What would you do if this did get out and he could prove the Iranian government was behind it?"

"I'd knock down everything in their country taller than a fire hydrant," Castilla replied, slowing and finally coming to a stop. "You're saying Drake is trying to manipulate me? Trying to get me to authorize a military strike?"

"Based on his feelings about the threat Iran poses, I think it's worth considering."

Still unable to bring himself to sit, Castilla went back to pacing, muttering unintelligibly.

"Sam?"

"Okay," the president said. "Let's say this is true—and I'm not convinced it is by a long shot—what do you propose we do about it? Drake has a lot of allies—hell, I'm one of them. And taking down a man who's familiar with every skeleton America has in its closet isn't exactly trivial."

Klein nodded and reached for the steaming cup of tea on the table in front of him. "Not trivial at all. But we have someone I trust on the inside—"

"Randi Russell took you up on your offer."

"Honestly, I'm not entirely sure. But I can tell you that she isn't buying into Gazenga's food poisoning and she's never going to turn her back on Jon Smith."

"Any word from him?"

Klein shook his head. "And I'm not hopeful there will be. The farm he visited has been burned to the ground and the Ugandan government seems to be bombing the area around his last known position. Reports are that they found Caleb Bahame's camp."

"If Bahame's gone ..."

"The threat from the parasite could be too," Klein said. "But I wouldn't count on it. It's a little suspicious that after decades of searching, the Ugandans finally manage to find him this week. More likely the Iranians got what they were after and betrayed him."

The strength seemed to drain from Castilla and he collapsed into a chair. "I assume you have a recommendation?"

"If Randi will agree to help, I think we have a chance of controlling Drake."

"If you think he's guilty, why not just take him down?"

"Because, frankly, I'm not sure I'm right. And because our problems with Drake—if they exist at all—are secondary."

"The Iranians," Castilla said, and Klein nodded.

"I'm in the process of inserting a backup team into Uganda, and I'm working through our contacts in Iran to see what we can find out there."

Castilla leaned his head back and stared at the ceiling. "So to sum up: you're sending a second-string team to deal with something that most likely killed your top operative and you're trying to learn about a beyond top secret bioweapons program in a country where we can barely figure out what day they pick up the garbage."

The image of Smith and Howell flashed across Klein's mind, but he pushed it away. There would be time to mourn later. "And that's what we need to talk about, Sam. Covert-One's resources are limited, but yours aren't. I need your authorization to bring more personnel in on this—CDC, USAMRIID, and some university people. Also, I think it's time you start considering what we're going to do in the very likely event that my people fail."

"You're talking about a military option."

Again, Klein nodded. "We have to start preparing for that eventuality, and you need to decide what threshold of intel you need in order to head down that road."

CHAPTER FIFTY-FOUR

Northern Uganda
November 28—0143 Hours GMT+3

Jon Smith's foot hovered over the brake for a moment and then slammed back down on the accelerator as he approached a washed-out section in the dirt road. It was a good ten feet wide, but the Land Cruiser lofted obediently into the air and landed on its reinforced suspension without so much as a creak.

It was impossible to know for certain which way Omidi had gone, but a good bet was toward Kampala, where he would find the modern airstrips necessary to bring in a jet. Another benefit of chasing in the direction of the city was that the wind was with him, carrying enough smoke to make the Land Cruiser invisible from the air for the first twenty miles. By the time Smith had broken out of the haze, he'd been well away from the area Sembutu's forces were concentrating on.

He came around a bend, the halogen-loaded light bar making it possible to creep up to ninety on the straight-away that followed. Where was that Iranian bastard? Had he guessed wrong? Was there an airstrip to the north? Was Omidi planning on escaping by another means?

Thoughts of Sarie encroached on his mind, and he tried to limit them to the ramifications of letting her fall into Omidi's hands. Soon, though, he found himself sinking into vague fantasies of a teaching job at the University of Cape Town. About Saturdays working on her old farmhouse followed by grilled kudu and beer with the neighbors. But most

252

of all, about never again picking up the phone and hearing Fred Klein's voice on the other end.

He shook his head violently. Where the hell had that come from? Concentrate!

He drifted the vehicle around another corner and leaned forward over the steering wheel, squinting at two pinpricks of red light barely visible ahead. When he made it to within two hundred yards of the beat-up military truck, its gentle sway turned violent and confirmed that it was the vehicle he was looking for. Omidi had spotted him and was making a run for it.

The road was far too narrow to pass, leaving few options. Ramming the back of the heavy vehicle seemed pointless —most likely it would just destroy the front of the Land Cruiser. Hanging a gun out the window and trying to aim with one hand seemed equally low percentage. And that left him with one last possibility that was only marginally better.

He selected the best maintained of the AK-47s he'd found on his way out of the jungle, set the cruise control, and stood up through the open sunroof.

Before he could line up on the left rear tire, though, the flap on the back of the truck was thrown open. His position wedged into the sunroof was surprisingly stable, and he swung the barrel in the direction of the movement, filling his sights with the battered, dirty form of Sarie van Keuren. She was on her knees and Dahab was behind her, a bandaged arm around her throat and a machine gun resting on a crate next to her.

The motion of the vehicles made it pointless to try anything more ambitious than going for Sarie's center of mass and hoping the bullet passed through into the man holding her.

Smith hesitated for only a fraction of a second before tightening his finger on the trigger, but it was all the jihadist needed. He opened up on full automatic, punching through the Land Cruiser's grille and then moving up to shatter the windshield.

Smith dropped back inside, letting the AK skitter across

the roof and land in the road behind him. Rounds continued to hiss past as he grabbed the wheel, trying to get control. The tires on the passenger side dropped into a ditch, and he felt himself being thrown around the interior as the vehicle rolled.

A tree finally stopped it on its roof, Dahab's bullets pummeling the underside in an attempt to ignite the gas tank. Fortunately, they bounced harmlessly off the protective plating that Sarie had been so impressed with, and soon the gun went silent.

Dazed, Smith managed to crawl through the broken passenger window and stagger into the road with one of the remaining AKs, but by that time, the truck had disappeared into the darkness.

CHAPTER FIFTY-FIVE

Langley, Virginia, USA
November 27—1902 Hours GMT–5

Randi Russell slid a half-eaten sandwich into the trash can next to her desk and looked around at the temporary office she'd been assigned. The only other things in it were a computer, the chair she was sitting in, and a framed poster by the door. It depicted four rowers in a boat, and the caption read "Teamwork". Someone's idea of a joke, no doubt.

What she really wanted at this moment was to be back in Afghanistan. To hear the wind against the cliffs, to see the shocking color of the poppy fields, to get swallowed up by the emptiness. She longed for the simplicity of knowing the Taliban would do everything in their power to kill her and that her men would do everything in their power to make sure that didn't happen.

In many ways she'd spent her life trying to prolong the game of cops and robbers that she'd abandoned her dolls for as a child. Black hats. White hats. And a whole lot of guns.

But those days were gone. The grown-ups were playing now.

She'd spent the last two days using both legal and illegal means to dig into every aspect of Nathaniel Frederick Klein's life. His work record was sterling, respect for him was almost universal, and even his enemies begrudgingly used words like "brilliant" and "patriot" to describe him. Still more interesting was that her vague memory of his personal relationship with President Castilla turned out to be right—they'd been friends since college.

The obvious implication was that Castilla was the "people high up in our government" Klein had referred to and the White House was behind Covert-One's funding and power. But implications weren't proof.

She'd contacted Marty Zellerbach because he was the first person she'd have gone to if someone had given her a copy of that Uganda video. The hunch had paid off and he'd shown her his analysis after making her swear that she wouldn't tell anyone he'd kept a copy.

So everything Klein had said checked out. But did that mean he was on the up-and-up or just that he was as smart as everyone said he was? Could he be working as a private contractor? His modest lifestyle didn't suggest a highest-bidder scenario, but that didn't prove anything either. Even if he was raking in serious cash, he wouldn't be stupid enough to make it obvious.

And finally, there was the irritatingly enigmatic Jon Smith. Klein knew the name would be a powerful motivator—both because of her desire to make sure he didn't end up dead and because she would tend to give the benefit of the doubt to anyone he'd already vetted. But how could she be sure that Jon actually worked for Covert-One? Hell, for all she knew, he was working *against* the organization and Klein wanted to use her to track him down and get him to lower his guard.

The bottom line, though, was that Klein's story wasn't something she could turn her back on. If he was on the level and she didn't help, countless people could die. On the other hand, if she let herself be played, even more people could die.

Randi sat in silence for a few more minutes, finally reaching for the phone and dialing Charles Mayfield, the CIA's deputy director.

"Don't tell me you're backing out of lunch tomorrow," he said by way of greeting.

They'd been friends for a long time and Mayfield had always watched her back—even when it wasn't in the best interest of his career. But how far was he willing to go?

"We need to talk, Chuck. Now."

"I don't like the sound of that. About what?"

She propped an elbow on the desk and rested her head in her hand. Good question.

CHAPTER FIFTY-SIX

Northern Uganda
November 28—0402 Hours GMT+3

Peter Howell skidded the stolen jeep to a stop and jumped out, running through the dust cloud he'd created to the Land Cruiser resting on its roof. The front and side, dimly lit by his one working headlight, were full of bullet holes and he hesitated before looking inside.

No blood to speak of and, thank God, no body. Just a couple of rusting AK-47s with missing clips.

He'd lost friends on ops before—in fact, Jon Smith was one of his last comrades in arms still aboveground. But the circumstances of the others' deaths had been very different.

Now that the fog of vengeance had lifted, he could see clearly what he'd done. He'd jeopardized a mission that he'd given his word to carry out, he'd turned his back on the millions of people who could be victimized by the parasite, and, worst of all, he'd abandoned a man who wouldn't have done the same to him.

Howell pulled back and searched for tracks, finally finding footprints in the dust at the edge of the road. He followed them for a few feet, seeing the stride lengthen. Smith was not only alive but in good enough condition to run. No thanks to him.

He jumped back into the idling jeep and floored it up the road. Its top speed wasn't much more than forty—something he couldn't confirm with any precision because there were only loose wires where the speedometer had once been. Fortunately, the one piece of electronics the vehicle's late owner hadn't pawned was the temperature gauge, and Howell managed his speed to keep it just below redline.

Almost a half an hour passed without a breakdown but also with no sign of Smith. Frequent stops confirmed that the footprints were still there but also that the stride was beginning to wander. Despite the darkness, the temperature was still hovering around one hundred degrees. Even Jon Smith couldn't run for long in that kind of heat. No one could.

The jeep's headlight continued to dim, and he concentrated on the tiny swath of illumination it provided, covering the brake with his left foot in case of a sudden obstacle.

It was a strategy that worked well for keeping him from snapping an axle but one that made it impossible to see the man aiming an AK-47 at him until it was almost too late.

Howell slammed on the brakes and spun the wheel, sending him into an uncontrolled fishtail as the figure dove back into the jungle to avoid being hit. When the jeep finally skidded to a stop, the Brit jumped out, not bothering to reach for one of the weapons in the back. "Janani's not going to be happy about what you did to his car."

Smith didn't acknowledge his attempt at a joke, instead dusting himself off and shouldering his rifle. His clothes were soaked through with sweat and his face still carried sooty streaks from the fires started by Sembutu's air force.

"Jon, I—"

When he got within range, Smith slammed a fist into Howell's midsection hard enough to lift him off the ground. The Brit sank to his knees and then rolled onto his side in the dirt, trying desperately not to throw up.

"Okay," he said when he could breathe again. "I had that coming. But it worked out, eh, mate? It'd be a long walk to Kampala."

"And that's the only reason I didn't shoot your ass," Smith said, holding out a hand and helping him to his feet.

"Water in the jeep," Howell said, and Smith limped over to it, reaching greedily for one of the bottles before jerking his hand back and retreating a step.

"What the hell is that?"

Howell came alongside and picked up Caleb Bahame's severed head, looking into the half-closed eyes while Smith used his sleeve to clean the blood off a liter container.

"Just a little souvenir."

"I think it could make keeping a low profile a little hard," Smith said, pouring the water over his face and into his open mouth.

Howell frowned. "I suppose you're right. But you have to admit it would have made a handsome ashtray."

CHAPTER FIFTY-SEVEN

Near Entebbe, Uganda
November 28—0806 Hours GMT+3

The sun had escaped the horizon and was now pounding down on the chaotic morning traffic outside of Entebbe. Mehrak Omidi swerved to prevent someone in a seventies-era pickup from passing him on the shoulder but then mentally reprimanded himself. Now wasn't the time to let his frustration get the better of him.

A quick glance through the broken back window confirmed that the situation was still under control. Van Keuren and De Vries were bound and gagged in the truck's canvas-covered bed, and Dahab was at the back flap watching for anyone following. Much of the power and grace the Sudanese had demonstrated in Bahame's camp was gone, though. He was struggling to keep his balance in the swaying truck, and his immaculate robe was damp with sweat.

It was to be expected. Soon his usefulness as a host for the parasite would be over and he would have to die—a fate known to him since the beginning. He would be delivered into the hands of God a martyr.

"I see them!" Dahab shouted suddenly.

"What are you talking about?" Omidi responded, looking into one of the side-view mirrors at the traffic behind them.

The African's English was limited and he jabbed a finger at the now closed canvas flap. "I see the white men!"

Omidi kept his eyes on the mirror but put a hand on the pistol next to him. There had been no outward signs of confusion. Had he simply not noticed their onset? Was the Sudanese becoming delusional?

Then he saw it: an open army jeep ten cars back swerving dangerously into oncoming traffic in an attempt to pass. Omidi wiped the dust from the mirror and concentrated on the image of the two men. It was impossible to make out individual features, but he felt a dull jolt of adrenaline when he cataloged their general builds, clothing, and hair color. It couldn't be, but it was. Jon Smith and Peter Howell.

They tried to pass again, this time on the left, and were forced to veer back into the line of traffic by a gap in the shoulder that fell away into a ditch.

Omidi took a deep breath and let it out slowly, trying to quell the panic building inside him. He couldn't fail now. Not when he was this close.

Ahead, he could see a plane rising into the air and arcing out over Lake Victoria. Entebbe was no more than twenty kilometers away, but his ultimate destination—a private airstrip where a jet was waiting for him—was well beyond that. Eventually, the men chasing him would leapfrog the cars in front of them—a maneuver he wouldn't be able to match in the lumbering truck.

Omidi took his hand off the pistol and picked up a phone, dialing Charles Sembutu's personal number. It was picked up almost immediately.

"Mr. President. I'm on the Entebbe road nearing Kisubi. Smith and Howell are behind me. I—"

"How is this my problem, Mehrak?"

Omidi tried to keep his voice calm and respectful. "I need you to intervene. They are driving dangerously in an open jeep. Have your police pull them over. Fifteen minutes is all I need."

"I arrested and questioned Smith and Howell for you. But that wasn't enough. I delivered them into your hands in the north country. But still this wasn't enough. The fact that you failed to deal with them is—"

"And *I* delivered Bahame and his people, which allowed

you to put an end to an insurgency that would have destroyed you."

"Then we have both honorably lived up to our agreements. I wish you good fortune."

The phone went dead, and Omidi slammed it down on the seat. Coward.

A quick check of his mirror confirmed that the ailing jeep still hadn't managed to pass and now there was steam rolling from under the hood. They were still moving, though, and the military truck would be easy to track.

"Dahab!"

The African lurched through the back of the truck and came to the window.

"There's been a change of plans," Omidi said, enunciating carefully so the African would understand. "Do it now."

Dahab grabbed De Vries and rolled him onto his stomach, ignoring his muffled screams as he carved a deep gash in his back. Van Keuren tried to kick out as the African put a similar cut in his own thumb and then ground it into the aging physician's wound.

It didn't take De Vries long to comprehend what had happened— that there was nothing left to fight against. His body convulsed gently as he began to sob through his gag.

Satisfied, Omidi turned his full attention back to the road. "Dahab, you're getting out at the Entebbe airport. Do you understand?"

"I understand. What are my instructions?"

CHAPTER FIFTY-EIGHT

Entebbe, Uganda
November 28—0828 Hours GMT+3

"Stop here," Smith said, standing so that he could see over the steam coming from the jeep's radiator. The truck Omidi was driving had turned off for the airport, but then they'd lost sight of him while they were stuck crawling along the congested road.

"Is he up there?" Howell said as he let the vehicle coast to a halt close enough to see the terminal and parking area but not so close as to draw the attention of security. Two beat-up white men driving around in an old army jeep coated in dried blood was bound to generate unwanted attention.

"No," Smith said, falling back into his seat.

"Then what's the plan, boss?"

He thought about it for a few moments, but no brilliant ideas presented themselves. Just desperate ones.

"We go into the airport," he said, using water from their last bottle to try to clean the dirt, soot, and blood from his face and hands.

"You think Omidi's going to try to get Sarie on a commercial flight?"

Smith passed the bottle. "No, but they may handle private planes here. And even if they don't, you should be able to find someone who's familiar with the private airstrips in the area."

"And what will you be doing while I'm playing detective?"

"Making a phone call."

Howell frowned at the cryptic answer. "Might I suggest the cavalry?"

They strolled into the airport wearing matching T-shirts silk-screened with the Ugandan flag—the only thing the souvenir vender outside stocked in their size. Smith immediately split off toward a bank of pay phones, smiling casually and smoothing his wet hair as he passed a mildly curious, but extremely well-armed guard. When he reached the phones, he immediately picked one up and pressed it to his ear. No dial tone. Same with the second one he tried. And the third.

"They don't work."

The woman was wearing a neatly pressed airport uniform and spoke with a light African accent. "I'm sorry. We had a fire recently and they haven't been fixed. Apparently, it's not a priority because so many people carry their own phones now."

He managed a polite smile. "I really need to contact my family. Are there any phones that do work?"

"I'm afraid not."

"Do you have a phone I could use? I'd be happy to pay you."

"I do, but it isn't capable of making international calls. I think your only option would be to buy a cell phone and—"

"Buy a phone," he interjected. "There's somewhere I can do that here?"

"Of course. Just follow this corridor to the end and turn left. You can't miss it."

The store was right where she said it was, but there was only one person working and five customers in line. Based on the impatient tone of the man in front of the counter and the bored expression of the woman behind it, progress could be stalled for hours.

"Jon?"

He spun and saw Howell at the entrance to the shop, waving him over. They retreated to the terminal's far wall, out of earshot of the people flowing back and forth.

"We've got a problem, mate."

"What? Are there other airstrips?"

"No. But I found that tall bloke from the cave."

"The one who infected himself?"

Howell nodded.

"Where?"

"Going through security. He's getting on a direct flight to Brussels and he doesn't look like he's feeling all that well."

Smith blinked hard, calculating how long the man had been infected and adding the time it would take to fly to Belgium.

"Even using De Vries's most optimistic estimate, he's going to go fully symptomatic on that plane," Smith said. "When he starts attacking the other passengers, they'll most likely think he's a terrorist. There's no telling how many people he'll infect before they get control of him."

"Boarding has already started," Howell prompted. "We don't have much time. Can you get in touch with someone who can bring that plane down somewhere safe?"

"He's a decoy, Peter. Omidi infected someone else and left Dahab here as a diversion."

"No question. But you have to admit, it's one hell of a *good* diversion."

He was right. Omidi could be anywhere—waiting for his jet to arrive in a private lounge a hundred yards away, on his way to a remote airstrip in a hired helicopter, or heading for the border in an unmarked car full of Iranian security personnel. Their chances of finding him at this point were hovering around zero.

Smith looked at the man still arguing about his phone and the mild interest they were getting from yet another machine-gun-toting guard. Trying to cut in line would be pointless—it wouldn't get him the phone any faster and would certainly bring airport security down on them. Explaining to the guard that the Sudanese had to be prevented from getting on that flight would likely accomplish nothing but involving an ever-increasing number of supervisors and setting into motion the glacial African bureaucracy.

"Boss?" Howell prompted.

"I'm entertaining suggestions."

"If we can get into the boarding area fast enough, we may be able to find a way to take him."

Smith shook his head. "Too much possibility of blood getting thrown around. We'd be killed or arrested, and someone infected could get on that plane or out into Kampala. Are there seats left on the flight?"

"Probably, but I seem to have misplaced my travel documents."

Smith pulled his, Howell's, and Sarie's passports from his pocket. "They were still in the glove box. The one thing a child soldier living in the jungle would have no use for."

"So we're going to let him get on a plane to Europe?"

"You see a plane; I see an airtight quarantine with a good international communication system and only a couple hundred people at risk."

Howell shrugged, not bothering to hide his skepticism. "It's your party. I just hope you know what you're doing."

"Me too," Smith said, starting for the Brussels Airlines counter.

CHAPTER FIFTY-NINE

Outside Washington, DC, USA
November 28—0257 GMT–5

Padshah Gohlam looked down at his watch, but the hands had ceased glowing. The movement of the stars suggested that it was past two a.m. and the aches beginning in his young body supported that estimate.

His training for this mission had begun almost the day he was born in a remote part of central Afghanistan. The mountains of the Hindu Kush were more barren but had the same penetrating cold, the same overwhelming solitude. His father, a great and pious man, had taught him to move silently and invisibly through the desolation, avoiding the Americans' technology and ambushing their special forces as they tried to claim his country for Christendom.

When his father died, the Americans, who still believed the fiction that he was a supporter of the infidel invasion, had given the young Padshah a visa to study in Maryland. And he had suffered through it—the arrogant professors, the women sitting unashamed next to him in his classes, the curriculum devoid of God. In truth, though, he'd only been waiting to be called upon. Waiting for this night.

He reached up and gently folded back a branch of the tree he was sitting in, examining the tiny farmhouse a hundred meters away. Much of it was obscured by foliage, but there was a natural hole that revealed the driveway and part of the icy path to the front door. Once again, God had provided.

The snow started again, and he had to admit to himself that the Western hunting clothing he'd purchased was far superior to what he grew up with. So many of his enemies were still alive because of a slight cold-induced tremor in his hands. But not tonight.

He saw headlights for the first time in hours and lifted his rifle, sighting through the scope at the vehicle turning into the driveway. The door was thrown open and a shock of blond hair gleamed in the dome light as the woman pulled herself unsteadily from the car.

Probably drunk, he thought. Without the supervision of a father or husband, who knew what she might have been doing? This was what the Americans wanted to do to his people—strip them of their identity and turn their daughters into whores. How could a country that was unable to control its women ever hope to control Afghanistan?

She moved awkwardly along the slick ground, turning up the collar of her long coat as she picked her way toward the door. This was the great Randi Russell? The woman who had killed so many of his Taliban brothers? It was almost impossible to believe the stories now that he saw her in person.

She was initially in profile, and he waited until she turned toward the door, unwittingly squaring her back in his crosshairs. Gohlam took a breath and held it, quelling his excitement and concentrating on not subconsciously anticipating the rifle's recoil.

The crack of it seemed impossibly loud amid the falling snow, echoing through the forest for a moment before fading into the ringing in his ears. Russell pitched forward, bouncing off the door before collapsing into the snow piled at the edge of the walkway.

Gohlam chambered another round before sweeping the scope across her blood-spattered back, finally letting the crosshairs stop on the back of her head. A silent prayer for the men who had fallen to her was on his lips as his finger began to tense again on the trigger.

The sound of the shot was all wrong, and instead of the satisfying impact of the butt against his shoulder, he felt the hot sting of wood shards penetrating his cheek.

It took him only a moment to understand what was happening, and he threw himself to the right, narrowly avoiding a second bullet that exploded against the tree trunk he'd been leaning against. Branches buffeted him as he fell, slowing his descent enough that when he hit the ground, he was able to immediately roll to his feet and start running. Another shot sounded and he waited for it to carry him to God, but instead it hissed harmlessly past.

Randi Russell tried to move, instinct telling her to get to cover when virtually every other system had shut down. She could hear shouting and gunshots but couldn't feel her arms or legs. The flair of pain in her back had disappeared into numbness, and she found it impossible to discern whether or not she was breathing. The snow next to her had turned red and she tried to grasp what that meant.

"Randi!"

A sense of weightlessness came over her as she was dragged away from the house.

"Hold on, Randi!"

But she couldn't. Not this time. She closed her eyes and the sense of weightlessness grew. They'd planned this so carefully. How the hell had she ended up being the one lying facedown in the snow?

Eric Ivers had Randi's collar in one hand and his gun in the other, firing it in the general direction of the woods as the man he'd set up on the roof took much more careful shots.

"Almost there, Randi! Hold on!" he said, leaving a crimson trail as he dragged her behind her car. His partner sprinted across the street and disappeared into the woods as the voice of his sniper came over the radio. "I no longer have line of sight. The shooter is uninjured."

Ivers swore under his breath as he eased Randi onto the driveway, unsure what else to do. He was a combat specialist, not a medic. In the end, he just rolled her onto her stomach so that if she vomited her passageway would remain clear, and then set off after his partner.

"Karen, do you have anything?" he said into his throat mike.

"Easy tracking because of the fresh snow. But I could use some backup."

"On my way."

Ivers entered the trees twenty-five yards south of where she had and ran hard, risking the use of open ground to make time.

He saw a muzzle flash ahead and adjusted his trajectory to take him into the darkness just behind it.

"I got him!" he heard Karen say over the radio. "The shooter is down. I repeat, the shooter is down."

Ivers came in from the side, spotting her creeping toward a man lying across an icy log. He was on his back, struggling to sit up while she screamed at him to stay down.

The man released the rifle he no longer had the strength to wield and rolled far enough left that Karen wouldn't be able to see his hands. From the opposite angle, though, Ivers saw him pull a metallic tube from the pocket of his camouflage parka.

"Bomb!" Ivers shouted. "Karen, get dow—"

He covered his eyes to protect them from the flash, dropping into the snow as a hot gale washed over him.

When he looked up, his partner was on the ground, clearly injured but not so badly that she couldn't give him a shaky thumbs-up. Satisfied that she was all right, Ivers switched his radio to a separate encrypted channel.

"Mr. Klein. Are you there?"

"I'm here. Go ahead."

"Randi's down—she took a bullet dead between the shoulder blades. The shooter was booby-trapped and there's not much left of him."

"How did he get close enough to the cabin to take a shot?"

"I don't know, sir. But I take full responsibility. The rest of the team was flawless."

"This isn't the time to start allocating blame, Eric. Is your situation stable?"

"We've got the start of a forest fire up here, Mr. Klein. I'm not sure the snow's going to stop it."

"Understood. An extraction helicopter is four minutes out. Burn the cabin and Randi's car, then get out. The better we can obscure what happened there, the more time it buys us."

CHAPTER SIXTY

Over Central Uganda
November 28—0953 Hours GMT+3

The plane leveled out and the seat belt sign went off, prompting Jon Smith to slip from his seat and walk to the back of the first-class cabin. Dahab was easy to spot through a small gap in the curtain, his height and turban making him tower over the other passengers. He was in a window seat, looking around him with paranoid jerks of his head and dabbing at his face with a handkerchief.

Smith brought his eye closer to the gap, looking for blood on the white cloth. Nothing, thank God. There would be soon, though. Too soon.

"More champagne?"

Smith glanced back at the flight attendant putting a cup onto Howell's tray.

"Looks like it's almost empty," the Brit said, tapping the bottle in her hand. "Perhaps you could just leave it?"

She cheerfully complied and then headed back to the galley for a fresh one. Howell brought it to his mouth and drained it under the disapproving stare of a woman who clearly wasn't pleased to be stuck across the aisle from two men who smelled like sweaty camels.

As always, Howell was thinking ahead. The bottle would be a useful weapon—heavy enough to do serious damage to any skull it came into contact with, but blunt enough not to generate much blood.

The flight attendant reappeared, this time with a cheese tray, and headed straight for Smith. "Antsy already? We've barely been in the air fifteen minutes. Would some Brie help?"

"I don't think so," he said and then lowered his voice. "I'm Colonel Jon Smith with the U.S. Army. There's a situation on the plane that I need to speak to the pilot about."

"A situation? What kind of situation?"

"I've been tracking a terrorist for the past few weeks and I finally caught up with him at the Entebbe airport. But I wasn't able to keep him from getting on the plane."

Her eyes widened a bit, but she was clearly not convinced. "Do you have any identification?"

"Just a passport. For obvious reasons, I don't have anything on me that could connect me to the U.S. government."

She examined his face for a moment and, finding nothing to suggest that he was joking or a crazy, turned toward the cockpit. "I'll speak to the pilot."

When he looked through the curtain again, Dahab was in a heated exchange with the man sitting next to him. Smith tensed, preparing to signal Howell to move, but the Sudanese seemed to lose his train of thought and the argument was suddenly over.

"Sir?" the flight attendant said, reappearing behind him. "If you could follow me, please?"

She led him to the galley, where a short, fastidious-looking man in uniform was waiting.

"I'm Christof Maes, the captain of this flight," he said, extending his hand hesitantly. "I'm told you believe we have a problem?"

"I'm afraid so, Captain. A Sudanese terrorist I've been tracking managed to get on board—"

"Is he armed? Did he get a weapon through security?"

"Not in the normal sense," Smith said, deviating into the story he'd invented during takeoff. "What he does have, though, is an extremely serious form of drug-resistant tuberculosis. His plan is to get into Europe and spread it."

"And it's my understanding you have no identification or proof of this."

"If you let me use your radio, I think I could get you con-firmation."

"Perhaps it would be better if I notify the authorities in Brussels myself. They can—"

"It may be too late for that, Captain. He's also extremely violent and borderline psychotic. He knows that my part-ner and I are on board, and it's likely that he isn't going to go quietly. Also, there's the matter of quarantining the passengers."

"Quarantine? You think that will be necessary?"

"Unfortunately, yes. Now, if you could please let me use your radio to contact my people, they can get in touch with your government and we can try to deal with this thing as efficiently as possible."

"I'm afraid it's against regulations to allow you access to the cockpit," he said, pulling a satellite phone from his pocket. "I can offer you this, though. In the meantime, I'll notify ground control—"

"The phone will work just fine," Smith said, having to suppress the impulse to snatch it from the man's hand. "But could you hold off contacting ground control? It might be more appropriate to let our respective governments handle that."

Maes frowned as Smith dialed. "I'll wait for a short time, Colonel. But then I'm going to expect to be satisfied as to who you are."

Smith nodded and turned away when Maggie Templeton came on the line. He never thought he could be so happy to hear someone's voice.

"Creative Party Supplies. How can I direct your call?"

"Hi, this is Jon on an open line. Is Fred around?"

"He's been anxious to talk with you," she said with prac-ticed ease. "Hold, please."

Klein came on a moment later. "Hi, Jon. It's good to hear from you. We were disappointed when we lost touch."

"Sorry, Fred. I wasn't able to get to a phone. But now Peter and I are on a Brussels Air flight heading for Europe."

"Should I have one of our salespeople meet you at the airport?"

"I don't think that'll be necessary. There's an ill man on the plane and Mehrak and Sarie decided they didn't want to fly back with us. I'm not sure how they're getting home."

There was a brief pause before Klein responded. "Understood. How ill is the man on the flight?"

"I think in the next couple of hours he's going to need attention."

"And are there facilities on the plane to give him the help he needs?"

"I hope so."

"Let me see if I can make some arrangements, Jon. I'll get back in touch as soon as possible."

The line went dead and Smith handed back the phone.

"That was a very cryptic conversation," the pilot observed coolly. "Perhaps your British friend has some sort of identification?"

He did, but an Argentine passport in the name of Peter Jourgan wasn't going to carry a lot of weight.

"Just hold off a little longer, Captain. My people are working on this. You should get confirmation of my identity soon."

"And in the meantime?"

"I'd like your permission to subdue the man."

The pilot shook his head. "Impossible. Until I know exactly who you are and have some kind of authorization, you *will not* take action against any passenger on this flight. Is that understood?"

Smith wasn't happy about the response, but there was very little he could do about it at this point. He headed back into the first-class cabin and crossed over to where Peter Howell was standing at the curtain.

"Were you convincing, mate?"

"Apparently not. I talked to my CO. He's going to contact the Europeans and try to get us some cooperation."

"I hope your CO is very fast and very persuasive," he said, pointing through the gap in the curtain. "Take a look."

A flight attendant was offering Dahab a drink, but he didn't react at all, just sat there banging his knuckles into the window at an alarmingly precise six-second interval.

"We can go anytime, Peter, but at best we're on our own."

"And at worst?"

"The crew fights us."

Howell sighed quietly. "Too many passengers and too little space, Jon. This is a cock-up waiting to happen."

They had been watching the Sudanese for an excruciating two hours when the flight attendant came up behind Smith and tapped him on the shoulder. He followed her back to the cockpit, saying a silent prayer that Klein had been able to work his magic. A thin ring of red was visible at the edge of Dahab's turban and he seemed to have completely lost touch with the world around him. The only good news was that the passenger sitting next to him had retreated to a vacant seat at the back of the plane. One problem down, a thousand to go.

"I'm still not entirely certain who you are," the pilot said as Smith stepped into the cockpit and closed the door. "But I'll grant that you have a great deal of influence. We've been diverted to a military base on an island near the Maldives. It also appears that we'll be acquiring a fighter escort from a nearby American carrier."

His expression suggested that he wasn't happy about the assist from the U.S. Navy. Maes was smart enough to know that there was nothing a fighter could do to help them. The only reason for its presence was to make sure that if things went seriously south, the plane never made it to land.

"I've also been told in no uncertain terms that you are now in full command of this flight and that we are to follow your orders without question."

Smith nodded, not bothering to hide his relief. Fred Klein once again had come through.

Jon Smith strolled casually down the aisle in the copilot's uniform, sunglasses on and hat pulled low over his forehead.

He smiled and nodded at the passengers as he passed but stayed focused on the Sudanese in his peripheral vision.

The flight attendants had been fending off an increasing number of complaints about the African, and as Smith got closer, he could understand why. The edges of Dahab's turban were wet enough that the blood would soon be running down his face. He didn't seem to notice, though, and continued to rap split knuckles against the window.

As bad as viruses like Ebola and Marburg were, Sarie was right—they were just mindless biological machines. The creatures infesting this man seemed almost sentient. It was as if they understood that their host was dying and were consciously trying to find a way to escape.

Dahab's stare remained fixed as Smith approached carrying a canvas mailbag containing a heavy wrench and a roll of duct tape—the most sophisticated weapon and hazmat equipment the plane had to offer.

He stopped at the rear bathrooms, watching a terrified flight attendant come down the aisle and lean her impressive bosom into the row behind the Sudanese.

"You look like two very fit gentlemen," she said, following the script they'd concocted. "A drink cart tipped over up front. Would it be possible for you to help me?"

Smith retrieved the tape from his bag and used it to secure the sunglasses to his face while the men followed her up the aisle. A pair of surgical gloves completed his protective clothing, and he ran a latex-covered hand over a gash in his cheek sealed with Krazy Glue.

Showtime.

He tried to keep his gait relaxed as he slipped into the empty seats behind Dahab, removed the wrench from the bag, and double-checked the cord threaded through the grommets around the opening.

His actions had attracted a fair amount of attention, and he grinned at a toddler staring at him three rows forward. The gloves were easy to hide, and most of the duct tape was obscured by his hat, so after a few minutes the passengers went back to their books and movies.

He rose casually and gave the child still staring at him another quick smile before ramming the canvas bag down over Dahab's head. The African immediately tried to jump from his seat but discovered that his seat belt was fastened—something Smith had confirmed when he'd walked past.

By the time he thought to reach for the clasp, Howell had vaulted the people trying to escape the seats directly in front, going headfirst over them and clamping a hand around the buckle mechanism. Smith used the cord to tighten the bag around Dahab's neck with one hand and arced the wrench toward his head with the other, ignoring the rocking of the plane as the passengers shifted en masse.

It was only inches from impact when the Sudanese jerked forward. The power of his movement felt utterly inhuman, and the wrench missed its target as Smith was pulled helplessly over the seats.

With three grown men now thrashing around in the confined space of two economy seats, there was no way to cock the wrench back far enough to build any real momentum. Smith abandoned it, concentrating on trying to keep the bag in place as Dahab reached back and found his throat.

His grip felt more like a five-fingered vise than anything human. Air and blood flow suddenly cut off, all Smith could do was grab weakly for the man's wrist. He tried to use the wall for leverage, but his vision began to swim and he became confused as to where the wall was. The sound of a snapping bone that initially seemed to be signaling the collapse of his spine instead eased the pressure suffocating him. Another quiet crack and his vision cleared enough to see Howell digging beneath Dahab's fingers, breaking them one by one.

When the third one went, Smith pulled back, falling into the aisle gasping for air. He was free.

But so was the Sudanese. The seat belt had released and he was now staggering into the aisle with Howell hanging like a rag doll over one of his shoulders. Smith stayed low and wrapped his arms around Dahab's legs, unintentionally bringing him down on top of Howell. The bag slipped, but the Brit managed to shove it back down despite the fact that he was absorbing a steady stream of blows that reverberated with the same sickening thud as a butcher pounding meat.

Smith released the African's legs and grabbed for the wrench, bringing it down full force on the back of his head.

Instead of falling over dead, though, Dahab just kept beating the increasingly defenseless Howell. The protection provided by the bag and turban had combined with the infection to allow him to completely ignore the impact.

Smith brought the wrench down again and again, grunting and huffing like a madman. The African's skull turned soft on the left side and he focused on that spot, gritting his teeth and throwing his entire weight behind each swing.

Finally, the man went limp and Smith fell back against the seat behind him, gasping for breath. The sunglasses he'd taped to his head were still in place and he ripped them off, checking to make sure the cut on his face was still glued together. It was, but that didn't mean much.

Howell finally managed to get out from under Dahab's lifeless body and tried to get to his feet like any self-respecting SAS officer would. His legs couldn't support him, though, and after a few valiant attempts, he just sank back to the ground, coughing uncontrollably.

CHAPTER SIXTY-ONE

Over Northern Ethiopia
November 28—1312 Hours GMT+3

Jon Smith stepped over Dahab's garbage bag–cocooned body and peered into the open door to the bathroom. "You okay, Peter?"

Howell was leaning over the sink, supporting himself with palms planted on either side. When he spoke, the water in his mouth ran out red.

"Just cricket, thank you for asking."

"Do you think any of his blood got in your cuts?"

"How the hell should I know, Jon? There isn't a square inch of me that isn't torn or broken."

"Yeah ..."

"What about you?"

"The same."

"Well, I guess we'll know soon enough, then."

The pilot had done the best he could to calm the passengers, telling them that Dahab was a drug runner wanted for murder and that they were from Interpol, but not everyone was convinced. Cautious whispers had evolved into loud, multilingual discussions, and then into a constant, panicky drone. Ten rows up, two men were standing in the aisle jabbing at each other in one of a number of arguments that seemed almost certain to get out of hand. When one got shoved into the lap of the woman behind him, Smith stepped through the curtain and banged loudly on the wall.

"Hello! Can I have your attention, please?"

Silence immediately descended on the plane, and everyone turned toward him.

"My name is Jon Smith and I'm a doctor with the U.S. Army. If you'll give me a minute, I'd like to tell you what's going on."

His voice didn't quite achieve the calm authority he'd hoped for, but in truth, he was lucky he could talk at all. The sensation of Dahab's grip on his throat was still palpable beneath the finger-shaped contusions.

"The man who was killed was a terrorist."

The volume went up again as people shouted a barrage of questions: Could he have accomplices on the plane? Was there a bomb? Why had he been allowed to board?

Smith waited for the cacophony to die down before starting to flesh out the story told to the flight crew.

"He wasn't armed and there are no explosives. He had a drug-resistant form of tuberculosis that he planned on trying to spread throughout Europe."

More shouted questions as the level of fear notched noticeably higher.

"Please! Let me finish. I want to stress that this strain of TB can be cured with special antibiotics. However, those antibiotics are expensive and we only have a few thousand doses stockpiled. Obviously, that would be a serious problem in a pandemic, but it's *not* a serious problem for the people on this plane. We're currently being diverted to a naval base where we'll be met by American medical specialists. In the *extremely* unlikely event you've contracted this illness, you'll be given medication that will take care of it."

Jon Smith stood at the back of the cockpit, looking through the windscreen at the scene below. There were three C-5 transport planes on the ground, and medical tents were in the process of being set up. Various military vehicles were lined up along the runway, and green-clad figures rushed through the glare of portable spotlights. This wasn't going to do much for the passengers' peace of mind, but the time for subtlety was long past.

They touched down and bounced around a bit before rolling to a stop in front of a steel barricade. Armed men in biohazard gear immediately surrounded the plane, and blocks were put around the wheels to make certain the plane couldn't take off again. The frightened voices of the passengers rose to a volume that almost obscured the ringing of the pilot's sat phone.

Smith picked up. "Go ahead."

"What's your situation?" Fred Klein asked.

"Unfortunately, the patient didn't make it. We've wrapped up the body and put it in the back."

"Possibility of spread?"

"To the passengers and crew, I'd say minimal. To me and Peter, medium to high."

"I'm going to get you two off the plane. We have a situation that needs your attention. Everyone else stays put until we finish setting up. Go to the door closest to the cockpit. We're bringing up a ladder."

"Two minutes," Smith said. "I need to brief the passengers."

"Two minutes."

He went back out and found Peter trying to make his way to the front of the plane as people grabbed at him and pointed out the windows at the soldiers.

"Hello! Can I have your attention again, please?"

They all looked to him, and Howell used the diversion to limp to the front of the plane.

"Peter and I are getting off," Smith started before once again being drowned out.

"Everybody calm down and listen to me! We came into direct contact with the infected man, so we're the most likely people here to have contracted the illness. We're being taken to quarantine so there's no chance of us passing it on to any of you. More medical personnel and equipment are being flown in and you'll be let off when they get set up."

"When do we get the antibiotics?" someone shouted.

"Most likely you won't need them, because I doubt any of you are going to get ill—this strain isn't particularly contagious. Look, I know a lot of the doctors out there and they're the best in the world. You're in good hands."

Someone outside banged on the door and he twisted the handle. By the time he got it open, the man on the ladder was already on the ground and retreating to a sandbagged machine-gun placement.

A few of the passengers surged toward the door, but Howell blocked them. "Please stay back," he said, retreating toward the ladder. "I could be infected."

That slowed them enough to allow Smith to climb onto the ladder and quickly descend, trying not to think about the battery of guns trained on his back.

CHAPTER SIXTY-TWO

Diego Garcia
November 28—2300 Hours GMT+6

"Keep moving, sirs."

Smith glanced back at the soldier coaxing them forward and then at the armed men in hazmat suits falling in around them. The private jet he and Howell were walking toward seemed to have just come off the assembly line, with nothing that would betray the identity of its owner or suggest any connection with the United States. Smith dutifully climbed the steps to an open hatch, pausing at the threshold before committing to enter.

A thick wall of plastic had been erected to his left, sealing off the front third of the plane. To the right, all the seats had been removed with the exception of the rearmost two, and portable filters had been installed to keep the air supplies separate. A bottle of single-malt scotch gleamed on one of the cushions, and the other contained two glasses and two pairs of handcuffs. The incredibly thorough hand of Fred Klein.

Howell followed him down the aisle and fell into one of the seats, examining the bottle and reclining in the soft leather with a satisfied groan. Smith held out the glasses and the Brit filled them, raising his in salute. "To the fleeting pleasures of the here and now."

It was as good a sentiment as any, and Smith tipped the glass up, reveling in the smoky sensation of the liquor burning its way down his raw throat. When he leaned back, he spotted a shoebox-sized device set up near the plastic wall. It was topped with a line of green LEDs and, unless he missed his guess, was filled with enough plastique to completely disintegrate the plane should it become necessary.

"How are you gentlemen feeling?"

Smith leaned forward and squinted, trying to put the man emerging from the cockpit with the voice that unmistakably belonged to Fred Klein. His normally medium-length hair was cropped close to his skull, and his glasses had been replaced with blue contacts. The rumpled suit that he seemed to have been born in was gone, too, in favor of a heavily starched U.S. Army uniform that clung to a waist so narrow that it suggested some kind of girdle. An expedient disguise that would shield him from undue attention and prevent Peter Howell from recognizing the old spook.

"Better now, Brigadier," Howell said, using the scotch bottle to effect an improbably respectful salute.

Klein took a seat facing them through the plastic. "Based on the reports I've read, I thought you boys could use a drink."

"Thank you, sir," Smith said, playing along.

He gave a short jerk of a nod and then moved on. "It's my understanding that if you're infected, you'll start showing symptoms between seven and fifteen hours from exposure."

"Yes, sir," Smith said, calculating for the hundredth time how long it had been since their fight with Dahab: seven hours, thirty-nine minutes. "It appears to start with general disorientation, followed by the bleeding you're familiar with and then violent insanity."

The plane started taxiing and Klein pointed in their general direction. "Buckle up."

The implication was clear, and after fastening their seat belts they each secured one wrist to their seat with the provided handcuffs.

"I also understand, Colonel, that if you start showing symptoms, there's nothing I can do to help you."

"That's correct, sir. But I think I speak for both myself and Peter when I say we'd appreciate it if you didn't let us die like that."

"If it becomes necessary, we're equipped to take care of the situation."

"Thank you, sir."

Another curt nod from Klein. "The two of you have left us in a bad way. We've talked to a few top people, and they all believe that van Keuren is going to be able to weaponize the parasite and that it's not going to take her long. Apparently, she wrote the book on transporting live parasites. And I mean that literally—she wrote a text on getting parasites from the field to the lab."

Smith took a swig of his drink, swishing it painfully over the cuts in his cheek. Again, it was his failure. He'd had multiple opportunities to do what was necessary with regard to Sarie and he'd hesitated. Now it wasn't just her blood on his hands; it could be the blood of millions.

"I've spoken at length with the president," Klein continued, "and we don't have many alternatives. Let's start with the bad news. Diplomacy is a dead end—there's no point in even starting. The Iranians will deny involvement and we've got no cards to play other than the testimony of two men who—and I regret saying this—will probably be dead in a few hours."

"What about military options?" Howell said.

"Complicated. We don't have anything convincing enough to get our allies on board, and the Russians and Chinese aren't going to stand by while we go in with guns blazing. And that's assuming we even had the troops available. A more surgical strike would be feasible, but we have no idea where Omidi is or where he's taken the parasite."

"I already know I screwed up," Smith snapped. "Do we really have to dwell on the point?"

Klein's eyebrows rose perceptibly, and Smith went into self-examination mode. Was his outburst the product of frustration and exhaustion or something more?

"I didn't intend that as some kind of backhanded reprimand, Colonel. Everyone involved knows that you did everything you could. Now, where was I?"

"I hope getting around to the good news, Brigadier," Howell said.

"The good news. Yes. The CIA has a number of contingency plans for dealing with bioterror attacks, and one of them was easily adapted to this scenario. We've put together a team of experts to refine the plan and we're quietly rolling out equipment and procedures across the U.S., as well as pulling back some military from abroad to handle implementation."

"Are there casualty projections?" Smith asked.

"Three hundred thousand is a best-case scenario from the infection. Another twenty to thirty thousand in the general chaos. A more likely number would be in the million range."

"That's the good news?" Smith said. "That over a million people could die?"

"Our hope, obviously, is to keep it under that number, and with the body of the infected man you killed on the plane, we might be able to learn something useful. At the very least, though, it'll help us refine our containment plan."

"A containment plan? That's it? The Iranians are creating a weapon that could make people look back fondly on the atomic bomb and we're working on a *containment plan*?"

"No, there's more. We've been talking to the Iranian resistance."

"The resistance? You have a line to Farrokh?"

"*Line* might be an overstatement. We have tentative communication with people who say they're linked to him. This is about as back-channel as you can get, Colonel. You can imagine what would happen if word got out that we're involved with the leader of the Iranian resistance."

Howell had abandoned his glass and was now drinking directly from the bottle. "All due respect, sir, but it sounds as though you're not sure if you are."

"That's not entirely unfair. Look, we took the leap of being more or less honest with them about the situation and we asked them to help us get a special forces team into Iran to track down the facility where Omidi's working on the parasite."

"What did they say?"

"They flatly refused. However, they may be amenable to a visit from the investigating doctor and his British escort."

"*May* be amenable?"

"It's the best I can do. They're a very suspicious bunch."

"So, assuming we don't die en route, you're sending us into Iran?"

"I'm afraid so. You're going to be inserted from Turkey and link up with a resistance force. Get them to trust you and help you find van Keuren. Then contact us with what you've learned and stand by."

Smith just stared at his boss. "Is that all?"

"I know it's a tall order, Jon. And to be honest, I don't expect you to succeed. In the unlikely event you actually make contact, there's a good chance Farrokh will just decide you're spies and kill you."

"And then a million people die," Smith said.

Klein shook his head. "A million *Americans*. We've drawn up plans for a retaliation, and I can tell you that it won't be pretty."

"What are you estimating Iranian casualties at?"

"After we take out their entire military capability, we're looking at destroying all their major cities and annihilating their power grid and freshwater systems. It's not possible to accurately estimate casualties because there's honestly no historical precedent. What I can tell you, though, is that the deaths from disease, starvation, and thirst in the aftermath could be more than ten times what they are in the initial assault. If we can't use the scalpel, Jon, it's been made clear that we'll use the hammer."

CHAPTER SIXTY-THREE

Above Central Iran
November 28—2234 Hours GMT+3:30

Sarie van Keuren could feel Omidi's eyes on her as she walked to the back of the plane holding a cup of water.

"Thomas? Are you thirsty? Would you like something to drink?"

The white-haired doctor was belted tightly into his seat, further restrained by a straitjacket and ankle shackles. It was an incredibly dissonant image—the frail, elderly man trussed up like some kind of psychopath or mass murderer.

Despite everything she'd seen in her years researching parasites, all this still seemed impossible. Intellectually, she knew that humans weren't special in the animal kingdom, but somewhere deeper she had always harbored a belief in the soul. To see it so easily stolen, to be forced to watch this gentle man turn into a monster, was terrifying.

"Thomas?"

He was staring blankly at the seat in front of him, and she was ashamed at the fear she felt when his head finally turned toward her. There seemed to be no recognition in his eyes at all, no acknowledgment of the fact that another human was close.

As it always did when she was depressed or lonely or scared, Sarie's mind retreated into science. How did the parasite work? What places in the brain did it target? How fast did it multiply? Was the detachment she was seeing the first step in creating a creature with no compassion or mercy?

"We're nearly there," Omidi said. "Sit."

She glared back at him but his face remained a mask—not much different from poor Thomas's. Some men didn't need a parasite. They became monsters all on their own.

The landing strip was well camouflaged and they were probably less than a hundred meters from the ground when two dim strips of light appeared to mark its boundary. Beyond that, all she could make out was a few rocky outcrops and a distant wall of cliffs outlined by moonlight.

"Your new home," Omidi responded. "The place where you will make the parasite transportable and more virulent."

"What? Why in God's name would you want to do that? Bahame's insane, but you're not. How could someone who understands what this does to people—innocent people—want to use it as a weapon?"

The Iranian smiled easily. "The West has created a moral framework for the world that is unwaveringly in their favor, Dr. van Keuren. If an American missile hits a primary school or market in an effort to kill a single man whose ideology they don't agree with, the casualties are considered collateral damage—an unfortunate by-product of a war that doesn't exist. If, on the other hand, a plane flies into an American office building, it's an earth-shattering act of terrorism. Why do you think that is?"

"I don't even know what the hell you're talking about."

"The West tells the world that it is right and just to kill only if you use the weapons they consider honorable. And then they do everything they can to prevent others from acquiring those weapons. They can stockpile thousands of nuclear weapons and threaten my country with them, but we cannot do the same. They can kill countless women and children with sophisticated bombs built by Lockheed Martin and General Dynamics, but it would be unthinkable for a Muslim to do the same with an explosive built in his basement. The Americans have brainwashed the world—constantly changing the rules of the game in their favor. But that time is over. *Their* time is over. The order of things is about to change."

CHAPTER SIXTY-FOUR

Eastern Turkey
November 29—0820 Hours GMT+2

"A train sounds higher pitched as it approaches and lower when it moves away. What is that phenomenon known as?"

Jon Smith snapped out of a half doze and blinked a few times. "Uh ... the Doppler effect?"

The man behind the wheel grinned at him in the rear-view mirror and pushed the station wagon's accelerator to the floor, punching through a snowdrift as he piloted the station wagon up the steep mountain road.

It had been more than nineteen hours since they'd killed Dahab, but Klein had decided to err on the side of caution. He'd provided their escort with a lengthy list of questions designed to ferret out signs of disorientation and clear instructions on how to proceed if they should display any.

It was a bit like being a contestant on hell's top-rated game show. Miss a question, get two in the head and a gasoline-fueled roadside cremation.

The vehicle lurched right and high-centered on a drift, prompting their driver—Nazim was the name he'd given—to throw up his hands in frustration. "What is it you say? End of the line?"

He shoved his door open and stepped outside, grimacing at the fat snowflakes suspended in the wind. Smith knew nothing about him beyond the fact that he was one of the many talented free agents that Klein maintained contact with all across the globe.

Howell leapt out after the Turk, throwing an arm around

his shoulders as they made their way to the rear of the vehicle. It was good to see him back to normal. Bahame was dead and they were well past the time symptoms would have presented if they'd been infected. In the context of the lives they'd chosen, things were more or less back to normal.

Their skis and packs were already lying in the snow next to the car when Smith eased himself out into the cold. He felt like he'd been run over by a semi. No serious injuries, but at least two lifetimes' worth of bruises, strains, and abrasions. Combined with the fact that he'd spent most of the flight to Turkey monitoring every angry impulse and moment of confusion while Howell snored into his scotch bottle, he wasn't sure how much he had left.

"This is the best I could do without making it look like camouflage," Nazim said, handing them each a stack of used backcountry clothing in tones of light gray and white. Smith stripped, letting the cold attack the swelling in his lower back and elbow for a few moments before getting dressed.

"I checked over the skis personally and they're in perfect condition," Nazim said. "One of the pairs of boots is less so, but I'm told that this isn't a problem."

When he saw them, Smith managed a smile at Klein's—or more likely Maggie Templeton's—otherworldly efficiency. They were his. Taken from his garage and flown to Turkey in time for their arrival.

"You're going there," the Turk said, pointing toward a steep canyon sandwiched between two wind-scoured mountains. Smith tried to look up it, but between the snow and the gray clouds hanging from the edges of the rock walls, it was impossible to penetrate more than a quarter mile.

"The Iranian border is about ten kilometers, and while there are no fixed defensive structures, there *are* patrols. Your passports and other papers are in your packs and the cover story of two adventurers getting turned around in bad weather is solid but less than original. Better to just avoid contact."

"What about Farrokh's people?" Smith said, settling onto the bumper and pulling his boots on. Despite the ungodly pounding he'd taken only a few hours ago, Howell was already busy attaching climbing skins to his skis in order to give them the traction necessary to carry him up canyon.

"They know you're coming and by what route."

"How will we identify them?"

Nazim thought about it for a moment. "They probably won't kill you right away."

"No code word?"

"Our communication with them isn't that good. It's channeled through too many intermediaries to be reliable."

"Great."

The Turk slammed the back hatch closed as soon as Smith stood, obviously anxious to get out of there.

"Do you know anything about the snowpack, Nazim? Is it stable?"

"I'm afraid I'm from a small village on the Mediterranean," he said, climbing behind the wheel. "To me, snow is snow."

The motor roared back to life and he began rocking the car out of the hole his wheels had sunk into. When he was free, he rolled down the window and motioned Smith over.

"Mr. Klein says you have many enemies. Perhaps even in your own intelligence agencies. Be careful who you trust."

With that, he started backing down the way they'd come. After a few yards, though, he slammed on the brakes and leaned out the window again. "Peter! The Battle of Gaugamela in 382 BC. Who had the larger army?"

"Darius. And it was 331."

Another thumbs-up from Nazim and he disappeared into the fog, guiding the car in a controlled skid down the slope.

Smith clicked into his bindings, then checked to make sure the batteries in his avalanche beacon were fully charged. "You ready?"

"Absolutely."

Smith nodded in the direction of the canyon. "Age before beauty."

CHAPTER SIXTY-FIVE

Central Iran
November 29—1044 Hours GMT+3:30

Sarie van Keuren followed along obediently. There was no other option.

She'd spent the last eleven hours locked in a dormitory-style room, unable to sleep. De Vries, the Iranians, Smith, and the parasite were enough to keep her awake for the rest of her life.

Mehrak Omidi opened a heavy steel door that looked like every other door they'd passed and motioned her inside. When she started to back away, he shoved her through.

It turned out to be nothing more than a simple conference room. There weren't enough chairs around the large table and some of the people were standing against the walls, expressions ranging from stony resolve to barely controlled panic.

Sarie barely saw them, though, instead focusing on a Plexiglas wall that displayed a white cube of a room and its lone occupant: Thomas De Vries.

He rushed at the glass when he saw her enter, slamming into it, mouth twisted in a silent scream. Blood washed across his face as he tried to get through, adding fresh streaks to the dried ones already there.

She looked away, telling herself that the thing in that room wasn't the person she'd known in Uganda. De Vries was gone—destroyed by Mehrak Omidi and the indifferent cruelty of nature.

"I'd like to introduce your team," Omidi said, closing the door behind him with a metal clang that carried a strange finality.

"My team?"

"The men who are going to help you alter the parasite. Make it more controllable."

She had a hard time tracking on the names as he went around the room introducing biologists, chemists, and lab techs. Instead she looked each one in the eye, trying to find something meaningful. Why had they been chosen and not someone else? Were they the best minds Iran had to offer or were they just believers?

When the introductions were complete, Omidi pointed to a stack of folders centered on the table. "They've all read my report on what I've observed about the parasite, and everyone is aware of your background and reputation."

"My background and reputation?" she said, though it almost sounded as if someone else were speaking. "What are you talking about? What are you people doing here?" She pointed at De Vries, who had exhausted himself and was now on his knees in front of the glass. "Do you see him? They want you to turn this into a weapon. To use it against other human beings."

"Your moral outrage is commendable," Omidi said. "But weren't you part of a team that included a microbiologist from America's bioweapons research program and a former employee of the British Secret Service?"

"The U.S. doesn't *have* a bioweapons program," she responded.

"You're being a bit naïve now, aren't you, Doctor? The Americans spend more on their military than the rest of the world combined. They are the only country to have ever used a nuclear device during war— against primarily civilian targets." He looked at the people in the room as he spoke and it became obvious his words were meant more for them than for her. "They invade and bomb any non-Christian country at the slightest provocation—sometimes at no provocation at all. Do you really believe that they've drawn some sort of line that prevents them from doing this kind of research?"

"Even if that's true, why would you want to do the same?"

"What we develop here will never be used, Doctor. It will be held up as a deterrent—a safeguard against America trying to take away our freedom again."

"What makes you think you can control it? That no one else will ever get hold of it? That it won't get out of this facility by accident? We have to destroy it. We have to let it disappear."

"It can never disappear again. You know that."

"It doesn't have to—"

"Enough!" Omidi said, clearly finished using her as a foil for his lecture. He pressed a button on the room's intercom and said something that Sarie couldn't understand. Everyone else did, though, and the sound of rustling fabric filled the room as everyone shifted uncomfortably and shot nervous glances at one another.

A moment later, a door at the back of the room holding De Vries slid open, revealing a tiny elevator and its lone occupant. He was tall and dark skinned, with a thick build and matching beard. There was no fear in him at all, only defiance.

De Vries heard the door and turned, leaping to his feet and charging the man, who, unable to retreat, stepped forward and raised his fists.

He had the look of someone who had seen, and probably perpetrated, a great deal of violence in his life. It was understandable that he didn't see the pudgy, bleeding old man as much of a threat.

The shock was clearly visible in his eyes when he was lifted into the air and slammed into the wall behind him. De Vries clawed at his face, going for his eyes as the man threw a forearm up and used the leverage of the wall to push his attacker back.

The gap opened between them was wide enough for the man to lift a booted foot and deliver a kick that caused De Vries to slide back on the slick floor. He stayed on his feet, though, and ran at the man again, this time bringing him down.

The battle became impossible to follow after that—De Vries's arms blurring as he broke down the man's pathetic attempts to defend himself. They stayed locked together like that for what seemed like an eternity before the elevator door slid open again, revealing an armed man in a hazmat suit.

De Vries abandoned his barely conscious victim and charged to within a few meters before a muzzle flash glinted off the glass. He went down hard, thrashing wildly but unable to get back to his feet.

A uniform gasp rose when the gun sounded again, sending a round into the center of the old man's chest. It was impossible to know if it was the act of shooting the helpless man that affected them or the fact that De Vries didn't stop trying to get up until the gun was empty.

Smoke swirled around the room as De Vries's body was dragged into the elevator and the man on the floor crawled toward the glass. His right cheek was split from the edge of his mouth almost to his ear, and bare cartilage was visible on the bridge of his nose. Both eyes were still intact, but one no longer tracked straight as he silently pleaded with the people watching from the safety of the conference room.

Sarie swallowed hard, fighting the urge to throw up as Omidi looked on.

"We got him from a rural prison where he was awaiting execution for rape and murder. To pity him would be a waste of time you would be well-advised to use more productively."

She'd been in danger all her life—in the backcountry, on her father's farm, in her home outside of Cape Town. But it was danger she had grown up with, that had become part of her.

This was different. There was no sky above her, no beat-up rifle in her hand—nothing familiar at all. It wouldn't be malaria or a snake or even a gang of violent men. No, she'd lose who she was a thousand feet underground, finally bleeding to death while Omidi's people jotted notes.

She took slow, even breaths like the psychologist had taught her as a child and felt a little of her calm returning. She wouldn't let Omidi use fear and empty promises to break down her resistance. There would be no reward for helping him—no safety, no flight home, no rescue. Her life was coming to an end. The question was, what was she going to do with the time she had left?

Sarie let the fear and uncertainty remain etched deep into her face, though she felt only anger and hate. It would be those emotions that would get her through this. Anger and hate.

"All diseases spread quickly in Africa," she said, beginning the speech she'd worked out during the hours she'd spent locked away. "AIDS is a perfect example of that. But it's different in the West. They have sophisticated medical response systems, reliable media, and an educated population."

Out of the corner of her eye, she could see the man in the glass cage staring at her, and it caused her to lose her train of thought.

"Go on," Omidi prompted.

"The initial symptom of the infection is obvious disorientation. Warnings will be all over the news about this, and since nearly everyone in America has a house, a gun, and a phone, they'll have a lot of options. They could barricade themselves somewhere, shoot the infected person, call the police or an ambulance ..."

Of course, she was talking nonsense. The disorientation phase wasn't serious or lengthy enough to ensure that it would be noticed. Even a married person with a family might become sick while their spouse went to work and go fully symptomatic while alone. Or, even more likely, the disorientation phase could occur at night when the victim was asleep. Hospitals, unable to provide a cure and handle thousands of violent patients, would shut down. Family members would try to protect loved ones from authorities, who would have no choice but to euthanize victims in an effort to contain the pandemic. And to the degree that people in America had guns, did it really help? Many would find it impossible to shoot family and friends, while others would panic and shoot everything that moved.

Omidi nodded thoughtfully. His own arrogance and misogyny would work against him. Despite not having a background in biology or disease control, he would never believe that anyone could outsmart him—particularly a woman.

"I agree," he said finally. "Along with making the parasite easily transportable, we'll have to make the onset faster and more violent. We can't leave time for people to react."

CHAPTER SIXTY-SIX

Langley, Virginia, USA
November 29—1607 Hours GMT–5

"So we're still not completely certain," Lawrence Drake said, leafing through the stack of police and fire reports.

Dave Collen slid another folder onto the desk. "We don't have a body, if that's what you mean. But the local investigation is still ongoing and I wouldn't expect to at this point. What we know is that Russell's car was there and that she hasn't been seen since. The cops believe she was in the house when it went up."

"And what do you believe?"

"I don't know. It was too risky to have surveillance there when it went down. We're still not sure how the fire started or what happened to Gohlam. It's possible that instead of using a gun, he decided to use some kind of incendiary device and he blew himself up in the process of getting Russell—either by accident or by design."

"That's a lot of speculation, Dave."

"I know, but at this point there isn't anything we can do about it. It's possible that Russell escaped and went to ground, but I doubt it. With an Afghan coming after her, it's more likely that she'd want to use our resources to find out where the orders came from."

"Unless Brandon's message spooked her."

Collen nodded. "Unfortunately, it gets worse. I think we have to assume at this point that the Iranians have van Keuren."

"Do we have updated casualty estimates?"

"Even with the response plan we've put together under the cover of upgrading our biological attack readiness program, adding her into the equation could push it to a million."

Drake let out a long breath and pointed to the file Collen had placed on his desk. "Smith and Howell?"

His assistant nodded. "They were on the plane to Brussels that got diverted to the military base on Diego Garcia. The public story is that the plane had a problem with its navigation system and made a safe emergency landing. Based on what little I've been able to get out of Army Intelligence, the real story is that there was a Sudanese man with an unknown infection aboard and that he's been killed. The passengers all look clean and will be released soon."

"What about Smith and Howell?"

"They got on a private jet that we don't know anything about. Every avenue I've tried to get information on it turns into a dead end."

Castilla, Drake thought. It had to be. "Do we know where it went?"

Collen flipped open the folder, paging to a satellite photo of a small jet landing on a remote airstrip. "Turkey. They got immediately into a car and started toward the Iranian border. The satellite lost them in the cloud cover when they started into the mountains. By the time I got a man up there, the tracks were already covered. He estimates that they couldn't have gotten their vehicle any closer than seven or eight miles from the border before the snow got too deep."

"To what end?"

Collen jabbed a finger onto a topographical map of eastern Turkey. "In all likelihood, Smith and Howell went up this canyon on foot."

"So we have the enigmatic Dr. Smith and a former MI6 operative headed into Iranian territory under orders from what can only be the White House. The Iranians may have van Keuren, and no one has actually seen Randi Russell's body. Jesus Christ, Dave. Is there anything *left* to blow up in our faces?"

"It's not all bad news. Even if it is Castilla, I think we can be pretty confident that he's grasping at straws by sending two lone men across the border like this. How are they going to find the facility Omidi's taken the parasite to? And even if they do find it, how are they going to stop him?"

Both interesting questions, but by no means the ones foremost in Drake's mind. Clearly, the CIA was being purposefully kept out of the loop. Given the fact that Castilla wouldn't want to reveal that he was operating an extralegal team, it wasn't entirely surprising. But it was still extremely worrying.

"Do we have anyone we can use in that part of Iran?"

Collen nodded. "Sepehr Mouradipour. He's a former Iranian special forces man who grew up not far from where Smith and Howell were inserted."

"Reliable?"

"If the money's right, he and his men never fail."

Drake leaned forward, resting his elbows on his knees and staring down at the carpet. There were two paths laid out in front of him. He could walk away and explain the CIA's ignorance of the situation as just another intelligence failure. Or he could stay the course and do everything he could to bring about a permanent end to a threat that was potentially greater than even the Third Reich or Soviet Union. Germany would have never been able to mount a viable invasion of North America, and the members of the politburo had never been anxious to destroy their world of Crimean dachas and young Czech models.

But the Muslims were different. They were acquiring first-strike technology that Hitler could only dream of, and they didn't share the Soviets' aversion to self-annihilation. In many ways, they courted it.

Finally, he looked up at Collen. "Pay the man what he wants and get rid of them."

CHAPTER SIXTY-SEVEN

Western Iran
November 30—0802 Hours GMT+3:30

Jon Smith unzipped the tent and crawled out, leaving Howell to roll up their sleeping bags. The rising sun was still obscured by clouds, but the gust seemed to be dying down. For most of the night, it had sounded like they were camped in a train station—the wind would build in the north, the roar of it slowly approaching until it got hold of their nylon shelter and tried to tear it apart.

He waded through three feet of new snow, skirting along a stone wall that probably dated back a couple of thousand years. At its end was a six-foot sculpture of a face topped by an elaborate headdress. It had once watched over the entrance to a thriving city but was now relegated to the less lofty job of securing one of their tent's guylines.

This was the beginning of their second day skiing from the-middle-of-nowhere Turkey to the-middle-of-nowhere Iran, and he could feel the stress building in his stomach. Sarie was out there somewhere, as was the parasite. Had she agreed to use her expertise to modify it and doom millions to death? Or had she refused and doomed herself?

It was becoming increasingly difficult to keep himself in check, to think things through and give their situation the respect it deserved. All he wanted to do was throw his skis on and go until his lungs burst. But to where?

Howell's head appeared from inside the tent and he examined the sky with a smile. "Doesn't look so bad."

"See if you still feel that way after ten hours of breaking trail."

"Every day aboveground is a good day," he said, dragging their packs into the snow. "What's on the agenda for today?"

Smith pointed down a steep slope that started thirty feet from their camp and then started dismantling their tent. At one time, the grade had probably given the city's archers an advantage over invading armies, but now it just screamed "terrain trap" to any backcountry skier or military man worth a damn.

Howell clicked into his skis and eased up to the edge, frowning down at the cliff bands and cornices that overhung the shadowed canyon. He thumbed back at the silent heads watching them. "One well-placed grenade and we'll be joining our friends here as permanent residents."

Smith stuffed the tent in his pack and skied up next to the Brit. "You're forgetting one thing—we're actually *trying* to get ambushed."

Howell shrugged. "I guess we should look on the bright side, then."

"Which is?"

"We'll probably get killed skiing down."

With that he kicked off and arced gracefully down the slope. Normally, the British weren't known for their skiing prowess, but Howell's time in the California mountains had obviously overcome the challenges of his birth. Fresh powder curled over his head as he dodged a rock outcropping and picked up speed.

Smith tensed when a large slab of snow around his friend began to move, pacing him as gravity dragged it into the gap ahead. The avalanche he thought was coming didn't materialize, though, and a few moments later, Howell was waving a pole enthusiastically up at him.

He put his AvaLung in his mouth but then spit it out. The device was designed to help a buried skier breathe long enough to be rescued, but if he kicked off a slide, they would both be buried. And with no help forthcoming, it would only serve to prolong his suffering.

The cornice he was standing on was about five feet high, and he jumped off, hip checking in the deep snow before springing upright and hurtling down the slope. Under other circumstances, it would have been a perfect day, and he tried to enjoy the roller-coaster sensation as he dove in and out of the powder, occasionally looking back to see if the snowpack was holding.

It did, and he pulled up to Howell, who was grinning through the ice clinging to his stubble. "I don't suppose we have time for one more?"

Smith actually laughed, managing for a brief moment to forget why they were there.

"Maybe we'll hit it again on our way out," he said, taking off his skis and reaching for his skins before realizing that Howell wasn't listening. Instead, he was completely focused on the canyon wall ahead of them.

"You got something, Peter?"

"Movement at the top."

"Nothing we can do. Skin up and let's get moving."

He did but clearly wasn't happy about it. Walking into an obvious trap was embarrassing enough for an SAS man, but not fighting his way out of it would be downright mortifying.

"Anything behind us?" Howell said.

Smith tried not to be obvious scanning the ridge. "I don't see anything. But that—"

A puff of snow erupted ten feet to their right and they dove away from it as the muffled sound of the gunshot filtered down the cliff. Smith immediately rolled upright and tried to get to their skis, but more rounds rained down on them, spraying him with ice and snow.

"We're in a cross fire!" Howell shouted, reaching instinctively into his jacket for the gun that wasn't there. Lost backcountry skiers tended not to be armed.

The intensity of fire increased, closing in on them as the snipers found their range. Howell started wading toward a small rock outcropping at the base of one of the canyon walls, making comically slow progress through the deep powder. Shots were striking within two feet of him, one every second or so, from what Smith calculated to be at least three separate guns. He wasn't going to make it.

Then everything went silent.

Howell slowed and finally stopped a few yards short of cover. A hole in the clouds had opened up, and he raised a hand to shade his face as he scanned the ridge again.

"Stay where you are! Do not move!"

The accented voice echoed through the gap, making its source impossible to pinpoint. A moment later, ropes appeared above them, tumbling gracefully through the air. Before the ends had even hit the ground, men appeared on both sides of the canyon, rappelling quickly as a few more shots kicked up the snow between Smith and Howell. A reminder that any aggressive move on their part could be easily dealt with.

CHAPTER SIXTY-EIGHT

Western Iran
November 30—1449 Hours GMT+3:30

After they were relieved of their backpacks, it was made crystal clear that if they fell behind, they would be left to die. And the threat wasn't an idle one. With the wind picking up again and a high-pressure system pushing temperatures into the single digits, they wouldn't last long with only their skis and the clothes on their backs.

For now, though, it appeared to Smith that they were safe. The nine men who had ambushed them were dispersed in an ever-lengthening line across the open plain. He glanced back to check on the man charged with guarding him and saw that he was stopped more than a hundred yards back, leaning weakly on his poles as someone helped him off with his oversized pack and slipped it over his own shoulders. Smith smiled when he realized that the young soldier's benefactor was none other than Peter Howell.

Beyond the initial barked orders and threats, none of their captors had said much of anything. In fact, Smith still wasn't dead sure who these men were. Had they been sent by Farrokh? Were they an Iranian military patrol taking them to prison for violating the border? Were they bandits or drug runners interested in a ransom? All questions had thus far gone unanswered.

What he did know was that it was a fairly ragtag unit. Their fitness and skiing ability were all over the place, and their equipment was dated at best and on the verge of falling apart at worst.

Smith picked up his pace, feeling the cold air penetrate his lungs as he closed in on the unfortunate man who had been stuck taking possession of his seventy-pound pack. One of the soldier's hands was stuffed in his jacket, and he held both poles in the other as he shuffled awkwardly forward, the cold and monotonous grade starting to take their toll.

He was startled when Smith came alongside and yanked down one of the pack's side zippers but was too tired to do anything to protect himself against the weapon he assumed his American prisoner was retrieving.

Instead, Smith pulled out a pair of state-of-the-art ice-climbing gloves that he'd been carrying as spares. The young man looked at him over wire-rimmed glasses caked with ice and gave a short nod of thanks.

Smith sped up again, passing one exhausted captor after another until he settled in behind the man on point.

"Your team needs a break."

The man tensed and twisted around, apparently surprised that his prisoner had been able to close the gap between them so quickly and silently.

"Perhaps it's you who needs the rest?"

By way of response, Smith just thumbed behind him.

The man looked out over the line of stragglers, his irritated frown turning to an expression of disgust when he saw Howell, now carrying both a pack *and* a rifle, giving an impromptu seminar on efficient snow travel.

"Academics and intellectuals," the man said in lightly accented English. "They're loyal to the movement, but even with training so many are … What's the word I'm looking for?"

"Unathletic?" Smith offered.

The man shook his head, sending a cascade of snow from his hat to his neatly trimmed beard. "Wimps. That's it. Not like you Americans and British. In the West a doctor and an old man can penetrate the jungles of Uganda, escape one of the cruelest terrorists in the world, and then travel forty miles into the mountains of Iran. You're killers. Born and bred for it."

He skied away and Smith just let him go.

"Making a new friend?" Howell said, coming up behind him. The next closest man was more than fifty yards back, struggling to incorporate the Brit's advice into his skiing technique.

"Actually, I'm getting the distinct impression he doesn't like us. Based on what he just said, though, I think we found the people we were looking for."

"And that means we're supposed to trust them?"

"Don't have much choice."

"I used to have a mate who liked to say, 'What's the worst that could happen?'"

"*Used* to have?"

"IED. We never managed to scrape up enough of him to put in a box. I guess he finally answered his own question, though."

Smith didn't respond, taking off up the canyon at a pace that once again brought him up behind the man breaking trail. "I think we need to remember that we're on the same side here."

"Are we?" he said without looking back. "Like we were in 1953 when the CIA deposed our democratically elected leader and replaced him with a dictator?"

Smith knew he should just remain silent—this man was their only chance to find Farrokh. On the other hand, it wasn't in his nature to just roll over when his country was insulted.

"Am I mistaken, or was that in response to him nationalizing British Petroleum's holdings in Iran?"

"Ah, yes. Your oil. The most important thing in the world—more important than the lives of innocents. More important than the democracy you want to force on everyone. That is, everyone but the Saudis, where women aren't even allowed to operate a car."

"All we ask is that you send us a relatively stable supply of fuel and don't harm our citizens. In return, we agree to keep a gigantic money hose aimed at the entire region."

"And if we don't want your money? If we want to pursue a

nuclear deterrent against your government, which has publicly threatened us with annihilation?"

"That was never our government's position—it was just a few congressmen shooting their mouths off."

"But regimes and circumstances change, do they not?"

"I don't think we're going to resolve the world's problems today," Smith said as the sun dipped behind the mountains. "So why don't we just say that both of our countries have been very naughty and focus on what's ahead instead of what's behind?"

CHAPTER SIXTY-NINE

Central Iran
December 1—2206 Hours GMT+3:30

Sarie van Keuren moved carefully in her hazmat suit, constantly glancing back at the poorly maintained tubes supplying her with fresh air. The lab had the look of something slapped together over the course of a few weeks, with containment protocols that were well below one hundred percent functionality. And anything less than one hundred percent might as well be zero.

She could credit Omidi with one thing, though. He'd been incredibly diligent in making certain that the lab—and virtually every other room she used—shared a glass wall with the cell where he kept his parasite victim. A constant reminder of where she would end up if she didn't behave.

The man Omidi had called a rapist and murderer was fully symptomatic now but hadn't yet started to weaken. Every move she or the people working in adjacent rooms made attracted him, and he went back and forth in a mindless frenzy, slamming into the glass barrier over and over in a desperate attempt to find the parasite a new host.

She tried to forget about him, but it didn't do much to calm her. A few feet away, De Vries's corpse was lying on a table with the top of his head missing and an expression of rage frozen into his face. Blood had pooled on the floor beneath him due to a backed-up drain that probably just emptied untreated into the ground. Overall, better than Bahame's cave, but only just.

The slide in her microscope contained one of many cross

312

sections of his brain, which combined with a heavily moni-tored Internet connection, had been useful in confirming some of her guesses about the infection and providing some surprising refutations of others.

The initial targets of the parasite were the frontal lobe and anterior cingulate cortex, virtually shutting off any com-plex reasoning that would allow the victim to control base emotions such as rage or to understand the potential conse-quences of their actions.

Even more interesting was the damage to mirror neurons that had a hand in giving humans empathy and a connection to others. The pattern of damage was very specific, though, and she wasn't sure why. A compelling hypothesis was that it destroyed victims' ability to identify with uninfected humans while allowing them to continue to identify with infected humans—thus explaining why they didn't attack each other.

Most interesting, though, was the bleeding. The capil-laries in the head burst due to high concentrations of the parasite in that area and not necessarily because the infec-tion was targeting them specifically. It was similar to sneez-ing or coughing or diarrhea—a symptom that evolution selected because it allowed for the spread and survival of the pathogen. In the end, though, the bleeding from the hair was nowhere near as bad as it appeared. Victims did *not* die of blood loss as everyone assumed. They died as a result of brain damage.

The parasite multiplied unchecked and seemed to have a frighteningly slippery genetic code that adapted quickly. As crowding in the targeted areas got worse, parasites with a mutated taste for other parts of the brain became increas-ingly successful. Eventually, they began going after areas controlling autonomic functions such as heart rate, thermo-regulation, and respiration.

The good news was that it was far more than she'd expected to learn in such a short time. The bad news was that she wasn't sure what she was going to do with the information.

CHAPTER SEVENTY

Central Iran
December 2—0755 Hours GMT+3:30

The only empty seat remaining was at the head of the table next to Omidi. Along each side sat what could be described as her department heads—highly educated scientists with different specialties and backgrounds. While none had degrees specific to parasitology and some were less impressive than others, each was perfectly competent. And that made them dangerous.

"Dr. van Keuren," Omidi said as she sat. "You've had an opportunity to do the initial autopsy on Thomas De Vries. What did you discover?"

She'd never been a good liar, but it was time to learn or die. There would be no white knight or last-minute rescues. She was on her own.

"The parasite has a very fast breeding cycle and is as adaptable as any I've seen. That should make it relatively easy to modify. Getting a quicker onset of full symptoms will just be a matter of using lab animals to artificially select the fastest-acting parasites over the course of successive generations."

She wasn't telling Omidi anything a second-year biology student couldn't figure out, but he didn't seem aware of it. Maybe this was going to be easier than she'd thought.

"Would that also have the potential of decreasing the time to death, Doctor? And if that's true, wouldn't the parasite's ability to spread be compromised as its hosts die off more rapidly?"

The glimmer of hope she'd felt a moment before faded.

It was a question that she'd wanted to avoid as long as possible—one that demanded lies that could expose her. Once again, Omidi had demonstrated that while he was as evil a son of a bitch as she'd ever met, he was by no means stupid.

"Attacks on the frontal lobe and related areas of the brain are correlated with blood loss, but only loosely. What I'm talking about here isn't increasing parasitic load; it's making it more targeted. It's actually possible that this would *slow* the time to fatal blood loss, because bleeding is just a secondary effect."

"Are you certain that death is from blood loss?"

His question sent a jolt of adrenaline through her that she struggled to hide. Did he know something?

"Injury and exhaustion are probably the number one killers," she equivocated.

"But barring that?" he said.

"I . . . I think blood loss is the obvious answer, but I haven't looked directly into it. I'm not a neurologist."

"Ah," he said, gesturing toward the man directly to his right. "Fortunately for us, Yousef here is."

Dr. Yousef Zarin was the only person on her team that she hadn't been able to fit into the categories she'd developed. The men she now thought of as the *softies* were generally clean shaven and round faced— academics and research scientists who appeared to have been plucked from their cushy university jobs by Omidi right before she arrived. Many seemed as frightened as she was and were prone to dropping things if you walked up behind them too quietly.

The second category was the *believers*. They were men with wiry builds and full beards who had less intellectual horsepower than their softy counterparts. They, too, seemed to fear Omidi, but more in the sense of being awestruck by him. When he talked about the rise of Iranian power and the decline of the West, they tended to get a faraway stare that recalled Soviet paintings of farmers.

Then there was Zarin. He was wiry and wore a rather grand beard, putting himself firmly in the category of believer. On

315

the other hand, he was quite brilliant and, when he thought no one was looking, seemed worried. Clearly softy traits. The final test—his reaction to Omidi—was impossibly enigmatic. He seemed almost dismissive of the man.

"I'd be interested to hear what Dr. Zarin's found," Sarie said.

He nodded, fixing dark, controlled eyes on her. "I believe that the victims' blood loss is exaggerated by their profuse sweating and constant motion. Dr. van Keuren is correct that injury or exhaustion is the most likely cause of death, but if we ignore those factors, it will be damage to autonomic brain functions, and not blood loss, that kills them."

Sarie realized that her polite smile had been frozen long enough that it was probably starting to look painted on. She tried to relax, but inside she was cursing like her father used to when one of the cows knocked down a fence. If Zarin had already figured that out, what else did he know? What else had he told Omidi?

"And the issue of making it transportable?" a believer whose name she couldn't remember said. "Faster onset makes using a human host even more difficult."

"I don't think it should be much of an issue," Sarie responded. "I've never found a parasite that couldn't be transported with much more primitive equipment than you have access to. But trying to work out a way to do that now isn't a good use of our time. There's no telling what sympathetic changes will occur when we start the selective-breeding process, so any transportation procedure we come up with now may not work later."

In truth, the likelihood of the modifications they were talking about having any effect on transportability was about zero. But the longer she could keep them from being able to deliver their weapon, the more time she had to carry out her plan to sabotage it.

CHAPTER SEVENTY-ONE

Western Iran
December 3—1051 Hours GMT+3:30

Sepehr Mouradipour peered through his scope at the line of men partially obscured by blowing snow. The shallow draw they were traveling along was nearly flat, and the easier terrain had, as anticipated, allowed their formation to tighten.

He was wearing a white hooded jumpsuit and was partially buried, lying on an inflatable mattress to keep him insulated from the cold. Even his face was streaked with greasy white paint, breaking up its outline and transforming it into just another exposed area of earth and rock.

The group he was tracking appeared to consist primarily of his own countrymen—followers of Farrokh, according to his information. Traitors and atheists. It would be a pleasure to kill them, but that was just an unplanned bonus.

He finally found the men he was being paid to take out near the middle of the column. Both were wearing light gray Western ski clothing, the one in front broad shouldered and dark complected, with black hair poking out from beneath a wool hat. His companion was thinner and had fair skin burned red behind ski goggles.

Mouradipour pressed a button on the side of his rifle, sending a signal that the targets were two hundred meters out. An LED built into his sunglasses flashed seven times in response. His men were ready.

It took a little longer than expected for the column to cover the distance, but speed was notoriously hard to predict in this kind of terrain and he was confident that his team would make any necessary adjustments without his involvement. He demanded nothing less than perfect discipline from his men and had dug many graves for those who didn't live up to that standard. The group he was working with now had completed nine missions of this type without a single material error.

Mouradipour waited until the middle of the column was even with a cliff band that he was using for perspective, then sent out three clicks in quick succession.

It was over almost before it started.

His men burst from their buried positions and snipers appeared along the ridge across from him. A few of Farrokh's men made awkward grabs for their weapons, but most were hung on packs out of reach or were incompatible with the bulky gloves they seemed to favor. In less than five seconds, everyone in the column was on their knees with hands laced on top of their heads.

Mouradipour snowshoed down the slope and approached the first of the Westerners, ripping his hat off and comparing his face to the photo he'd burned into his memory. The coloring was right, as were the high cheekbones, but the eyes were not the intense blue he'd been expecting. A trick of light? Contacts?

When he dragged the broad goggles off the second man's face, Mouradipour was horrified to find the unlined skin of someone in his early thirties.

"Trap!" he screamed in Persian, clawing for the rifle on his shoulder.

The intermittent crack of controlled gunfire sounded and his men began crumpling around him. Their prisoners, who had seemed so awkward and exhausted a moment before, dove to the icy ground so as not to block their hidden compatriots' line of fire and pulled weapons from beneath their jackets.

Mouradipour had barely managed to get a hand around his rifle when his feet were swept from under him. Before he'd even landed, a thin strand of wire was looped over his head, cutting through the insulated collar of his jumpsuit and tightening around his neck. Every move he made now caused the icy metal to dig a little deeper.

A lone skier became visible down canyon, moving stiffly through his dead and dying men. The outline was inexplicable—strangely curvaceous and willowy despite heavy clothing. He squinted upward, his confusion growing when the figure stopped in front of him and pushed back a thick hood, revealing the short blond hair and perfect skin of a young woman.

"Make your phone call," Randi Russell said, gritting her teeth and adjusting her rifle into a slightly less excruciating position on her shoulder.

The flight from America crammed into the cargo hold of a C-141B Starlifter, the clandestine crossing of the Iranian border, and nineteen hours tracking these bastards hadn't done much for her mood.

Fred Klein had been so enamored with the body armor he'd provided her—waxing rhapsodic about how the genetically modified silk was four times stronger than Kevlar and how it tipped the scales at only ninety-eight pounds including the fake blood packs duct-taped to it.

In the end, though, her reluctance to stand in front of an Afghan assassin's bullet wearing something made of the same thing as her lingerie had been entirely justified. The bruise across her back was almost a foot in diameter and radiated over her spine in roughly the color scheme of a Miami sunset.

"Phone?" Mouradipour said. "I don't know what you're talking about."

Randi retrieved a bottle of ibuprofen and shook five into her mouth, swallowing hard before speaking again. "You don't want to screw with me today, Sepehr. I swear you don't."

He didn't answer immediately, instead watching the bodies of his men sink into snow melted by the heat of their blood. "And what if I agree to make your call?"

"Then we're going to hold you long enough to make sure

you didn't do anything stupid like use some sort of code word to indicate you'd been caught. Then, if everything works out, we'll let you go."

"What assurances do I have?"

"How's this: I *assure* you that if you don't get on that damn phone in the next five seconds, I'm going to have my friend here cut your head off."

The wire around his neck tightened, and after a brief hesitation, he reached slowly for his pocket.

Randi took a step back and squinted into the distance. All the maps, satellite photos, and coordinates Mouradipour had been working with were elaborate fakes—carefully altered to hide the fact that Jon and Peter were actually a hundred miles to the north. That is, if they hadn't frozen to death, run into an Iranian border patrol, or been shot in the back of the head by the notoriously unpredictable Farrokh.

She pulled out her own sat phone and sent Covert-One a notification that Mouradipour's call was about to go through so they could begin tracking it. Unknown to Klein, Charles Mayfield would be doing the same thing at CIA headquarters—a little independent verification to help her sleep at night.

Randi turned and skied slowly away, feeling the anger building inside her but also an unfamiliar sense of despair that wasn't as easy to deal with. Only when the voices of her men had been swallowed up by the wind did she stop and reflect on how much she'd hoped to find nothing out here but snow. How much she'd wanted Klein to be wrong.

But there was no way to nurse that illusion anymore. In her gut, she knew that call was going to go exactly where he said it would: to a man whose orders she'd risked her life countless times to carry out. To a man she'd respected and admired.

To Lawrence Drake.

CHAPTER SEVENTY-TWO

Western Iran
December 3—1503 Hours GMT+3:30

They were nearly on top of it, but the village was still virtually invisible. Cone-shaped rock formations jutted a hundred feet in the air, many with windows and doors built into them. The more modern buildings looked a thousand years old—crooked one-room dwellings constructed of stone blocks and surrounded by ancient fences designed to corral livestock.

They skied in from the east, Smith taking a route too steep for the Iranians, most of whom had given up all pretense of guarding him. His momentum took him to the base of a packed-down track that acted as Main Street, and he skated along it. Faces appeared in icy windows and then just as quickly disappeared at the realization that he was a stranger.

He felt a poke in the small of his back and turned to see that it had come from the man who'd led their seemingly endless expedition through the mountains. They stopped near a set of rough-hewn steps and removed their skis before climbing up to a door that led directly into the cliff. The man went through a complex series of knocks, and a moment later he was being embraced by a bear of a man carrying an AK-47.

The sensation of heat against his skin was incredibly seductive, and Smith stepped inside, crossing a mishmash of traditional rugs to the fireplace.

"Is Farrokh here?" he said, pulling off his gloves and

holding his hands to the flames. The journey had taken three days—far longer than he'd anticipated—and there was no telling what progress Omidi was making with weaponizing the parasite. Or if he was even bothering. By now, it was possible that he'd smuggled a victim over the U.S. border and the infection had wiped out half the population.

"Have something to eat."

A beautiful young woman in a head scarf appeared a moment later with a plate of Middle Eastern meze and two steaming cups of tea.

"Look, I don't have any more time to screw around. I want to see Farrokh. Now."

The Iranian took off his outer clothing and flopped onto a pile of colorful pillows by the fire. "Farrokh is a busy man."

Without his hat and sunglasses, he looked quite a bit younger than Smith had originally estimated. His eyes reflected not only unusual intelligence, but also a calm sense of power and confidence. Not a man you'd waste on an errand like the one he'd just performed.

"It's you, isn't it?" Smith said, silently cursing his own stupidity. "You're Farrokh."

His only reaction was to point to the pillows next to him. "Please, Dr. Smith. It's been a long journey. Rest."

He did as he was told, pulling off his ski clothes and trying to keep his impatience in check. The pace in this part of the world was different, and trying to fight millennia of cultural norms was going to get him nowhere.

"Our organization must be diffuse so that it will live on if any individual dies. But, to answer your question, yes. I am the one they call Farrokh."

Despite his best effort to play the diplomat, Smith couldn't hide his anger. "Then what the hell have we been doing? I was told you'd been briefed on what's happening."

"Rash action is never advisable," Farrokh said. "And taking the measure of a man who wants to be my ally is never a waste of time. In fact, it's why I'm still alive."

When Smith spoke again, he'd managed to calm down a bit. "What's the verdict?"

"You appear to be a man who should be taken seriously."

"So you trust me now?"

Farrokh laughed and reached for one of the cups of tea, offering it to Smith. "I can count the number of people I trust on one hand, and I don't anticipate needing an additional finger because of our acquaintanceship."

"But you believe that the parasite exists and that your government has it."

"Yes, though I fail to see why this is my problem."

Despite his attempt at nonchalance, it was clear that he knew exactly why it was his problem.

"I understand that you don't much like the U.S., but you have to admit that we've been leaving you and your country alone. Do you think that'll continue if Omidi succeeds in releasing a biological weapon inside our borders?"

Farrokh shrugged. "America is directly or indirectly responsible for millions of Iranians dead, the reign of a brutal dictator, and frankly the repressive and backward Islamic system we live under now. Perhaps this is simply a balancing of the scales."

"No," Smith said. "You're smarter than that. It doesn't matter how many Americans you kill; there will still be one of us left to push a button. And then there won't be an Iran for you to liberalize."

Farrokh nodded thoughtfully. "The ayatollah has become senile and Omidi is insane. They believe that God has delivered this weapon to them and that he will guide their hand as they use it to destroy the enemies of Islam."

"I'm not sure it's going to work out that way."

"No. I have come to understand that God rarely takes sides in such matters. The righteous and innocent are as likely—perhaps more likely—to suffer as the wicked. To rely on his intervention is the height of arrogance and stupidity. America has both the power and the will to butcher anyone who shows even mild defiance."

Smith tried to shut out the quiet tick of the ancient clock

323

on the wall. It seemed to get louder and louder as their pointless geopolitical debate dragged on.

"America is a massive stabilizing force in the world, and you know it as well as I do. How many countries with our military and economic power would have shown the same restraint? What would *your* country do with our arsenal? Hell, what would the Germans do with it?"

Farrokh sipped his tea for a few moments before taking a step away from philosophy and toward something more concrete. "Do you know where Dr. van Keuren has been taken?"

"No. Our intelligence-gathering capabilities inside Iran are pretty much a joke."

"Ah, so this is to be left up to me too?"

"It's your country, and I'm guessing you keep up with these kinds of things."

Another shrug. "I hear whispers."

The words were enigmatic, but the tone wasn't. Farrokh's network had undoubtedly been digging into this from the moment Klein's people first contacted him.

"Where? Where is she?"

Farrokh browsed the food on the tray between them, crinkling his nose and finally smearing something unidentifiable on a piece of flatbread. "There has been recent activity at an abandoned research facility in the central part of the country. Also, a number of academics have been called away on government business and have been out of touch with their families ever since. The timing seems more than coincidental."

"How heavily protected is it?"

"It's underground and the entrance is well guarded."

"I don't know if I can get us air support, but I can sure as hell try."

Farrokh frowned and lay back in the pillows. "Do you really think I would coordinate a foreign attack on my own country? I am a reformer, not a traitor."

"But—"

The Iranian held up a hand, and a moment later the man

who had let them in appeared in the doorway. This time he looked less cheerful and his weapon was no longer safely shouldered.

"Teymore here will take you to your quarters. I hope we have an opportunity to speak again soon."

CHAPTER SEVENTY-THREE

Central Iran
December 3—1912 Hours GMT+3:30

Sarie van Keuren guided the scalpel carefully as she cut a cross section from the brain on the table in front of her. Its small size made it more difficult to work with, but she was grateful she'd been able to convince Omidi that working with animals would be more productive. The glassed-in room bordering her lab was now full of a bizarre variety of caged monkeys—some lab animals but others appearing to have been snatched from zoos and private owners.

Each individual cage was covered with cloth draping, something she'd accurately said was necessary to prevent them from dying of injuries sustained trying to get to the people on the other side of the glass. The real reason, though, wasn't to keep them from seeing her new colleagues, but to keep them from seeing each other—a subtle distinction easily missed by Omidi and his scientific lapdogs.

Sarie glanced up and noticed that the canvas covering a number of the cages in the middle section of animals had blood on it. She jotted down the time on a pad next to her and went back to working on the brain.

There were a number of potential strategies for making the parasite less dangerous, but almost all fell apart under the weight of any serious thought. The most obvious was to nurture the mutation that attacked the victim's corneas in order to cause blindness. Biologically straightforward, but it was a bit far-fetched to believe that a bunch of infected animals wandering around bumping into things would escape notice. Omidi's toadies weren't world-class, but they weren't *complete* idiots.

Improving attention span had been her second plan. At first it had seemed perfect in a somewhat horrifying way. If she could reduce the infected's ability to be distracted during an attack, she would increase the probability that they would kill their victims and stop the chain of infection. Unfortunately, though, the areas of the brain responsible for that type of focus were too diffuse to target. The parasite had been working on the problem for millions of years. Her time was somewhat shorter.

The answer, surprisingly, had been lurking in the mirror neurons. The pattern of damage was easy to change, and she'd already managed to affect the way that parasite victims identified with each other—creating the first seeds of reciprocal animosity. While the plan had many obvious weaknesses, if she could get them interested in attacking each other, she estimated that she could reduce the rate of spread by as much as forty percent.

Even more important, she'd discovered that the parasite had a significant exposure–response relationship—the higher the initial parasitic load, the faster the onset of symptoms. She'd used that to convince Omidi that she was actually making progress in reducing the time to full symptoms when, in actuality, she was just giving progressively larger doses of infected blood to the test animals.

What he wasn't happy about, though, was that this was creating a corresponding effect on the time to death. The fact that the believers were starting to slowly disappear seemed to indicate that Omidi was setting up an alternate group somewhere else in the facility to review her research and work on the time-to-death problem. She also had to assume that they would be testing her "modifications" on humans and that it wouldn't be long before they figured out that they didn't actually work.

That's why it was so important that phase two of her plan be enacted quickly and decisively. Unfortunately, she hadn't yet been able to come up with a phase two.

Sarie finished with the brain and went through the primitive decontamination procedures before entering the large room next to the lab. Five softies manning somewhat-dated computers watched her as she took a seat in front of the only terminal with an English operating system.

She was just starting to enter her notes when Yousef Zarin slid his chair up next to her.

"I know what you're doing," he said, leaning close and keeping his voice barely above a whisper.

"Excuse me?" she responded, continuing to enter numbers into a matrix of bogus mortality rates.

"I've been looking at your data and examined some of your samples myself."

She smiled weakly through clenched teeth, refusing to let her growing fear affect her ability to think.

"Mirror neuron damage is evolving very quickly."

"I have to apologize for my ignorance of neurology, Dr. Zarin. What are mirror neurons again?"

It was his turn to smile. "You might be surprised to know that I actually read your paper on the effects of toxoplasmosis on human behavior. Your intellectual gifts and grasp of brain function were very much on display."

"I appreciate the compliment," she said, sounding a little too cheerful for a woman in her position but finding it impossible to get the right balance. "It's just that I'm not sure what—"

His voice lowered even more. "I believe that if these changes continue, victims of the parasite will no longer be able to differentiate between infected and healthy people."

She stopped typing, but her fingers seemed frozen to the keyboard.

"It's very clever," Zarin continued. "I would have thought you'd simply try to reduce aggressive impulses, but of course that would have been too obvious, wouldn't it? How do you say ... I take my hat off to you."

"I think you're misinterpreting—"

"I don't pretend to be your equal, Doctor, but I am not an uneducated man."

"You …," she stammered, trying to come up with something credible to say. "Maybe it's a side effect of decreasing onset times that I missed. We could—"

He shook his head and she fell silent.

"No, the more I think about it, the more I see the brilliance of it. Given time, it could have a significant effect on the spread of the infection. Unfortunately, time is something we don't have."

"What?"

"We are not all fundamentalists and fanatics, Sarie. The time for more and more horrifying weapons is done. It must be. Technology has put too much power into men's hands—the power to destroy everything that God has created."

Was it a trick? Was he just trying to find out the details of what she had done in order to reverse the damage? How the hell was she supposed to know? The bottom line was, she'd been caught. There was no point to further scheming or protests. If Yousef Zarin was truly with her, he could potentially help her save millions of lives. If he was against her, she was already dead.

"You're not going to tell Omidi?" she said, mindful of the ever-present cameras bolted to the ceiling above them.

"Omidi is a pig. This is an act of desperation—an evil perpetrated by politicians trying to cling to power and disguising it as piety. I will help you. But I'm afraid the path you've taken is of no use."

He was right, of course. It had been her own act of desperation. In the unlikely event that she was given the time necessary to perfect the genetic modifications, they wouldn't last. The parasite was too adaptable—if it were released in a place that didn't have Africa's geographic isolation, it would evolve with devastating speed, hiding its symptoms, modifying the way it spread, extending the contagion period in the people it infected.

In the back of her mind, she knew she should be cautious, but she so desperately needed someone to stand with her. To not be alone anymore.

"Is there a way out, Yousef? Or a way to communicate

with the outside world? I have friends who might be able to help."

The Iranian shook his head. "We are a hundred meters underground and all messages leaving the facility have to be approved by Omidi personally."

"Then we have to think of something else."

He nodded. "And quickly. I suspect that the scientists who are no longer with us—the ones loyal to Omidi—are working on a way to transport the parasite outside the human body."

"What? Are you sure?"

"He came to me and asked if I agreed that work on transportation should wait until the final genetic sequence was done and I supported you, but he asked questions that were too technical for him to have devised on his own. It was clear that his people were advising him that the modifications wouldn't affect transportation modalities."

"Then we have to get out of here, Yousef. We have to get help."

"I'm afraid that's impossible. However, we are not powerless."

"What do you mean?"

"I was brought here years ago when this was a secret bioweapons lab and asked to write a report on safety issues. There were many problems—systems that are archaic or nonfunctional, poorly thought-out procedures, unrepaired cracks in the walls and ceiling. The government counted on the facility's isolation. The closest population center is a village two hours' drive from here."

"As near as I can tell, they didn't listen to you. This place is a disaster waiting to happen."

He nodded. "Shortly after my inspection, America attacked Iraq because of the WMD program they believed was going on there. My government feared the same fate could befall Iran and shut the facility down."

"So you still understand the weaknesses in the systems here?"

"Better than anyone, I imagine."

She leaned back in her chair and stared past him, watching the other people in the room doing their best not to call attention to themselves. She wondered what they'd say if they knew what she and Yousef were about to doom them to.

CHAPTER SEVENTY-FOUR

Above Central Iran
December 4—1014 Hours GMT+3:30

The ancient Russian helicopter felt like it was going to rattle apart as it skimmed across the top of the ridge. Smith gripped the rusted instrument panel as the ground fell away and Farrokh dove hard toward the valley below.

He hadn't been given access to his phone or any other method of communication, and all questions—about the search for Omidi and the parasite, about where Peter Howell had disappeared to, about when the hell they were going to *do* something—had been politely deflected.

"There," Farrokh shouted over the sound of the rotors. He pointed toward a group of fifty or so people who were still at the very edge of visibility, some in formations that were obviously military, others moving quickly over what may have been an obstacle course.

"Our newest training ground," the Iranian explained, tracing a sweeping arc over the men and then setting down in the shadow of a towering cliff. "Before this, we were focused on purely peaceful protest techniques enhanced with technology. But the more successful we are, the more desperate and violent the government becomes."

"So you're developing a military arm?"

The Iranian shut down the engine and jumped out with Smith close behind. "It isn't intended as an offensive force. I believe that if we're patient, we can win without blood on our hands. Trying to depose the old men entrenched in our government would be a poor strategy."

"Better to just wait for them to die and quietly replace them."

"Just so," Farrokh said. "Overt violence against the government would be a publicity disaster for us. I suspect it's no different in the United States. No matter how despised the government, any attempt by a group to physically overthrow it would be wildly unpopular. On the other hand, having no capability to protect my followers seemed irresponsible."

"Hope for the best but prepare for the worst," Smith said. "It's a policy that's always worked for me."

He shaded his eyes from the sun and watched two men fail to climb a ten-foot obstacle course wall, then scanned right to a line of prone men having mixed success shooting targets at fifty yards. An instructor paced impatiently behind them, occasionally stopping to adjust a poor position or give a piece of advice. His face was shaded by a broad straw hat, but the athletic grace and pent-up energy were unmistakable.

"Will you excuse me for a moment?" Farrokh said, breaking off and heading toward a knot of men studying something rolled out on a collapsible table.

Smith nodded and kept walking, cupping his hands around his mouth as he neared the range. "Peter!"

Howell turned and then barked something at the men on the ground. A moment later, they were running in formation toward a scaffold hung with climbing ropes.

"I was starting to worry about you, old boy," he said, taking Smith's hand and shaking it warmly.

"I could say the same. But you don't look any worse for the wear."

"A cot and three squares a day. What more can men like us ask for?"

It was an interesting philosophical question, but one better dealt with later. "What have we got?"

"Forty-eight men with a few months of combat training and nine army veterans, two of whom have a special forces background. They're like me, though—a little long in the tooth."

"What about the forty-eight? Can they fight?"

Howell frowned. "They're dedicated and smart as hell. But I'll bet at least half of them are carrying inhalers, if you take my meaning."

"You go into battle with the army you have, not the army you wish you had."

"Indeed. Just make sure you're behind them when they start shooting."

CHAPTER SEVENTY-FIVE

Central Iran
December 5—0201 Hours GMT+3:30

Jon Smith adjusted his stiff legs into a slightly less uncomfortable position on the hard ground. They were 180 miles northeast of Farrokh's training camp, and the last quarter of the trip had been done on horseback. Quiet and efficient in the torturous terrain, granted, but a mode of transportation he'd last employed at his fifth-birthday party.

He swept the tripod-mounted night-vision scope slowly, taking in the double chain-link fence, the guard towers, the machine-gun placements. Worse, though, was what he didn't see: a building. The entire bioweapons lab was underground—deep underground if Farrokh's intelligence was right.

There was a stone outcropping at the center of the heavily defended perimeter, and he could see a smooth gray section set into it. Steel doors about twenty feet square and of unknown thickness. It was hard to imagine a worse scenario that didn't actually involve giant alien robots.

"You still haven't been able to get a schematic of the facility?" he said quietly. They were lying in the rock-strewn sand a mile east of the fence. Getting any closer would demand military skills his companion lacked.

"I'm afraid not," Farrokh replied.

"Old building permits? Architectural plans? Inspection reports?"

"The information blackout is absolute. In some ways, too absolute. It was the sudden disappearance of all information relating to this place that first led us here."

The towers and the outer fence looked new and haphazardly constructed of local materials. The apparent shoddiness, though, was an illusion—the result of the Iranians' trying not to erect structures that would create a pattern that could be identified from above.

Smith adjusted the scope again, focusing on the base of the easternmost of two towers protecting the entrance. Even though he knew exactly where to look, it was an impressive thirty seconds before his eye picked up movement.

Peter Howell and an even older retired Iranian special forces operator had spent the last five hours beneath a dirty piece of canvas, inching their way toward the facility's outer defenses. They'd finally made it to the top of the low berm that was their objective and Smith heard the vibration of the phone on Farrokh's hip. The Iranian looked down at it for a moment and then held it out so Smith could read the text on the screen.

Ditch. 2Ms deep 4Ms wide. bridge booB trapped.

He'd suspected as much but had been hoping for a little luck. Any assault that attempted to breach anywhere but the main entrance would get trapped and cut to pieces by the machine guns in the towers.

"So it's through the front door or not at all," Farrokh said.

Smith nodded in the darkness but couldn't help thinking that the most likely scenario was not at all. There was no way for an adequate force to approach without being seen for miles and no way to avoid stopping on the bridge, which was apparently rigged to blow at the first sign of trouble.

Farrokh punched in a brief response and then returned to his spotting scope as Smith rolled onto his back and looked up at a sky full of stars. He wondered if Sarie was still alive. If she was in that bunker.

"What can you bring to the party, Farrokh?"

"Fifty good men willing to die for what they believe in."

And that was exactly what his green troops would do if they went up against battle-tested soldiers in an entrenched position.

"Artillery?"

"No. We have some explosives, but no way to deliver them other than by hand."

"What about technology? Can we cut communications to the facility?"

"No, they're using satellite and there's no practical way for us to jam the signal."

"What about power?"

"There are no lines in, so it must be generated on-site."

Smith let out a long breath. This wasn't an operation that could be done by half measures. Breaching the security and then not finishing things created the possibility of the parasite escaping. If they got in, the place had to be sterilized. And Sarie van Keuren had to be either retrieved or eliminated.

"You need to let me talk to my people, Farrokh. We might have enough information to convince them to enter Iranian airspace. We have bunker busters that—"

"Out of the question. I will not use the American military against my country."

"I *am* the American military."

"A bit different, wouldn't you say?"

"Millions of lives are at stake, Farrokh. This isn't a—"

"What if you had known for a fact that the Iraqis didn't have weapons of mass destruction? Would you have helped the Iraqi air force cross your border and destroy your military bases in order to stop an invasion that has spread death and misery throughout the region? We have fifty men willing to die at my order, Colonel. Nothing more."

Smith rolled onto his stomach again, fantasizing about slamming a rock into the back of the Iranian's head and taking his phone. Unfortunately, he'd noticed him entering a PIN to unlock it with every use and he hadn't been able to determine what that PIN was.

"You're the boss, Farrokh. Call Howell and your man back. I want to be well clear of here before the sun comes up."

The Iranian punched in another text and a few moments later the phone vibrated with a response.

nt yt. got idea. gnteed fun 4 all.

CHAPTER SEVENTY-SIX

Central Iran
December 5—0654 Hours GMT+3:30

The horrible screeches and metallic rattle of cages were nearly unbearable as Sarie entered the room containing the test monkeys. She fought the urge to strip off her stifling hazmat suit and run out, instead calmly setting down her clipboard and slipping a thumb through the ring at the back of an oversized syringe.

It was full of blood from an animal in the final stages of infection, and she knew that the sensitive parasites suspended inside would soon begin to die. There was no more time for reflection. No more time to second-guess or try to devise a less horrifying end to this. No more time for anything.

As she passed the first of the canvas-draped cages, the monkeys inside keyed on the sound of her footsteps and attacked the bars imprisoning them, trying desperately to get to her. The next section contained animals infected only a few hours ago, and they didn't react at all, trapped in a dazed, silent stupor. It was the third section she was interested in, though—the one containing the group that hadn't yet been exposed.

Each animal was connected to an IV that led to a central system for introducing drugs and pathogens. Sarie filled it from the syringe and tapped a command into a plastic-covered laptop. The parasitic load sent was an order of magnitude greater than they would have ever been exposed to in an attack. Based on the formula she'd come up with, groups of two and three would reach full symptoms around the same time. By then, group one would be dying but still in possession of around thirty percent of their peak strength and mobility. More than enough to be deadly.

The procedures for disposing of the syringe and shedding her protective clothing were pointless now, but she went through the motions with the same deliberate resolve as she had every other day. Even with time so short, she couldn't risk the security cameras picking up anything out of the ordinary.

By the time she entered the outer office, the clock on the wall read seven thirty a.m. Yousef Zarin was the only person there, working on a computer terminal surrounded by files and loose papers.

She sat next to him, keeping her back to the surveillance camera as she looked at the schematic filling his monitor. In a monumental stroke of luck, the facility had been shut down so soon after flunking his inspection that no one had bothered to delete the passwords he'd been given. Zarin had full access to the system and enough knowledge of programming to put that access to use.

"Is everything ready?"

He nodded. "When we signal an emergency, all doors leading to the outside world will automatically seal, as they were designed to do. However, I've made two subtle changes. The first is to the interior doors. The original programming caused them to close and lock in order to section off the building and contain any leak in as small an area as possible. I left the locking subroutine intact but introduced an error into the subroutine that causes them to shut."

"So they'll still be open when the deadbolt extends," Sarie said. "It'll block them open."

"Exactly. The other change was more difficult because I had to create the code from scratch, but I just ran a simulation and it is fully functional."

"The monkey cages?"

"Yes. The locks on the cages will retract and then be permanently frozen in that position."

She nodded slowly, trying to will her heart to slow. For all intents and purposes, they were turning the facility into a tomb. One that would descend into unimaginable violence and chaos before going silent forever.

"Are you all right?" Zarin said, concern visible in his dark eyes.

"Yes."

"It's not a pleasant prospect, is it?"

"No. But I'm coming to terms with it."

"As am I," he said. "But I would like to have seen my family again. There is so much left unsaid when you think you have time."

She smiled weakly, a bit queasy at the realization that there was no one she needed to see. The university would have a tasteful memorial when it became clear that she was never going to reappear. Her colleagues would shake their heads and say that they'd warned her about spending so much time alone in the bush. And then life would go on.

"If you'll excuse me," Zarin said, standing. "I'm going to pray."

She watched him leave, wishing she'd inherited her father's devotion to the Bible. A little comfort from above would be welcome in light of the facility's complete lack of alcohol.

The coffee machine still had some dregs in it from last night, and she'd have to settle for that. It seemed a bit surreal to have reached the point in her life that there was no longer time to brew a fresh cup.

She wondered what the people who found them would think of what they saw: the blood, the demolished makeshift barricades, the human and animal corpses still tangled together.

The important thing, though, was that by then, the parasite would be long dead.

CHAPTER SEVENTY-SEVEN

Central Iran
December 5—0902 Hours GMT+3:30

Sarie van Keuren sat in front of Zarin's terminal listening to the endless drone of the monkeys and watching the clock march inevitably forward. She'd hoped he would come back—that she wouldn't be left to do this alone. But she respected his desire for solitude.

It was hard to recognize herself in the reflection on the sleeping computer screen. The drawn features, dark-rimmed eyes, and dead expression seemed to belong to someone else. Someone who had wandered too far from home.

She wiped away a tear and touched the keyboard, bringing the monitor back to life. A few clicks of the mouse brought up the emergency lockdown button, and she hovered the cursor over it, thinking of Zarin and the family he was leaving behind. Of the family she would never have.

An insignificant twitch of her finger activated the alarm, overpowering the screams of the monkeys. She held her breath, resisting the urge to run. Better for it to be over quick.

But nothing happened.

Sarie turned in her chair and examined the closed door leading to the hallway. It should have automatically opened and the deadbolt should have extended. Confused, she clicked the button again. The alarm kept droning, but the door stayed closed and the monkeys remained safely in their cages.

The screen flickered and went blank for a moment, finally

reverting to the log-in page. She typed in Zarin's password and was trying to access the facility's schematic when the door behind her finally opened.

The computer wasn't responsible, though, and she jumped to her feet as three men with machine guns burst in. Omidi followed a moment later, dragging Yousef Zarin along behind him. The academic's right leg was broken and it gave way when Omidi let go, leaving him bleeding and confused on the tile floor.

"Do you think I wasn't watching you?" Omidi screamed. "Do you think I didn't read the report Zarin wrote about this place?"

"I . . .," Sarie stammered. "I thought one of the cage locks was defective. That—"

The Iranian rushed her, slamming an open hand into the side of her face hard enough to knock her to the ground. "We have people monitoring the computers! We saw him rewriting the security subroutines. Now tell me what *you've* done!"

Sarie shook her head violently, trying to clear it. Zarin hadn't talked. He'd managed to hold out despite the torture he'd endured.

"I . . . I infected the rest of the lab animals," she said, sticking to the obvious. "We—"

"I know that," Omidi said, aiming his pistol at Zarin. "You've been working day and night with the parasite. Tell me what you've done to it!"

"Nothing!"

Omidi pressed the barrel of his gun into the back of the injured scientist's head. "Tell me or he dies!"

"That's what I did—nothing!" Sarie said, being careful not to give away anything his believers couldn't easily figure out on their own. "I haven't really sped up the time to full symptoms; I've just been infecting the animals with larger and larger loads."

"The great Sarie van Keuren could think of nothing better than that?" he said, curling a finger around the pistol's trigger. "Give me the truth! Now!"

It was over. One last diversion that might save a tiny handful of lives was all that she had left. "Okay! Don't hurt him. I was selecting for parasites that attack the corneas to add blindness to the symptomatology."

She jerked at the sound of the gun, raising a hand to shield her eyes from the blood and brain matter splashing across her.

"You will show our scientist *exactly* how you have sabotaged the parasite and how to repair the damage," Omidi said, redirecting his aim to her.

Sarie stared down at the scientist's body, no longer feeling fear. No longer feeling anything. Finally, she just raised her hand and extended her middle finger.

CHAPTER SEVENTY-EIGHT

Central Iran
December 5—0930 Hours GMT+3:30

The truck fishtailed in a bog of deep sand, causing the canvas at the back to flutter open. Through it, Peter Howell could see a similar vehicle close behind, straining to keep up. It'd be a miracle if it made it. Or, perhaps more accurately, it would be a miracle if any of them made it.

He pulled the canvas closed again and scanned the faces of the men crammed in among the sandbags used to make the truck heavier. The stoicism and laser-like focus he'd found so comforting in the SAS were completely absent. Every expression told a different story: hatred—for him, for the British in general, for the Iranian government. Fear. Self-doubt.

A rousing pep talk was probably in order, but since only a few of the men spoke English, it probably wouldn't have much impact. Instead, he peered out a small hole cut in the canopy, squinting into the sun at the approaching guard towers. There was one on either side of the entry gate, each armed with a well-placed machine gun and manned by soldiers he suspected were far more seasoned than any of his boys—many of whom were now enjoying what would be the last few minutes of their short lives.

Their driver, a rock-solid former special ops man named Hakim, began to brake. They'd done no fewer than fifty live-fire simulations, and Howell was pleased to see the young men around him begin to check their rifles as they'd been taught.

When the truck bumped up onto the concrete bridge, he returned to the peephole. One of the two soldiers in the guardhouse cautiously approached the driver's door while the other made his way to the back. Howell had no idea what Hakim was saying, but the bored irritation in his voice sounded spot-on over the grinding gears of the truck rolling up behind.

Howell pulled out a silenced .22 pistol, frowning down at it as he listened to the approaching footsteps of the guard. A knife would have been more appropriate for the situation, but Smith, who was in the other truck with Farrokh, had been concerned that it could end up being messy enough to spook their green troops.

The canvas rustled as the guard untied it, and Howell carefully raised the pistol. No need to rush—it would take a moment for the man's eyes to adjust, and if Hakim was as convincing as he sounded, there would be no reason for anyone to expect trouble.

Howell waited until the flap was fully thrown back, reaching out casually with one hand while using the other to put a round neatly through the man's eye.

The low-caliber and elaborate silencer combined to produce almost no sound at all, and Howell guided the limp body over the gate. After an inexcusable second-and-a-half pause, two of his men pulled the corpse inside.

The driver of the second vehicle gave a subtle nod through the windshield to indicate that no one yet realized what was happening. The trade-off to putting the machine-gun towers in an ideal position to create a cross fire on the bridge was that their line of sight was blocked by the trucks' canopies.

Howell wiped a streak of blood from the gate and helped one of his men to the ground. They'd taken photos of the soldiers in the guard shack and had reasonably convincing doubles for both of them, right down to uniforms hand-sewn by the women in Farrokh's training camp.

The young man did himself proud, walking casually to the window of the driver behind them as Howell climbed out and unloaded a few more of his people. Smith would be doing the same, getting his team into position by the rear wheels.

Howell gave the frightened men next to him the thumbs-up, then calmly stepped out into the open and began firing on the west machine-gun placement. The surviving guard clawed for his sidearm, but Hakim dropped him with a pistol shot before slamming the accelerator to the floor and leaving Howell and his men completely exposed.

As expected, the first volley from the tower guns went wide as the soldiers manning them tried to make the adjustment from boredom to combat. It was obviously not the first time they'd been under fire, though, and it didn't take them long to realize what Howell already knew: the design and construction of the towers made them completely impervious to the small arms that Farrokh's fledgling army had access to.

In his peripheral vision he saw Smith and his team concentrating their fire on the other tower and Hakim ramming the gate. The truck managed to get through but then went up on two wheels and teetered for a few moments before tipping on its side. The Iranian tried to crawl through the window but made it only halfway before a sniper from a tower along the facility's western perimeter blew most of his neck away.

The young man a few feet to Howell's right was caught in the side by a round from the machine gun, and the Brit dove toward the truck still stopped on the bridge, a loud grinding coming from the transmission as the driver tried to force it into gear.

The gunners in the towers were gaining confidence, and with it came accuracy. Another man went down, and Howell saw Smith running, barely staying ahead of a steady stream of bullets knocking loose chunks of concrete behind his heels.

Inside the shattered gate, men were pouring out of the back of the capsized truck, ducking behind it to stay out of the sniper's sights but leaving them defenseless if the tower gunners should decide to turn on them.

The sound of the truck behind him going into gear rose above the drone of the machine guns, and he rolled out of the way as it started forward, taking heavy fire.

"Blow the bridge, you bloody idiots!" Howell said to himself as he fell in behind the vehicle.

As if they'd heard him, a sudden, searing blast knocked him to the still-intact concrete.

Dazed, he did his best to focus on the east tower, watching it sway for a moment before tipping toward the one on the other side of the bridge.

"Hakim, you beautiful bastard," Howell said when the structures collided and the machine guns went silent.

During their reconnaissance, they'd moved the charges meant to take out the bridge to the base of the tower. Hakim had spent most of his career attached to an elite demolition unit and personally guaranteed that the tower would fall exactly like it had. Of course, Howell hadn't believed it. How often did things actually go to plan once the shooting started?

The second truck was inside the perimeter now, picking up speed as it closed on an enormous steel door set into a rock outcropping. Howell ran to the east edge of the bridge and fell into a prone position above Smith, who was dug in at the lip of the protective moat.

The vehicle was up to at least forty when it hit, the impact setting off charges hidden beneath the floorboards. It was impossible to tell if the door had been breached, but Howell silently saluted the dead driver's courage as he flipped the lens cover off his scope.

"What am I looking for?" he shouted.

"Towers at nine o'clock and three o'clock are active," Smith yelled back. "There are men coming in from the north trying to get an angle on our guys in the overturned truck."

Howell peered through the scope, finally catching a glimpse of movement along the west fence line. He squeezed off a round and winged the first of six men running for the cover of a boulder about 150 yards away.

"Oh, and Peter?" he heard Smith say as he searched for another viable target. "It's good to see you still breathing."

CHAPTER SEVENTY-NINE

Central Iran
December 5—0946 Hours GMT+3:30

Sarie van Keuren struck uselessly at the man dragging her down the corridor, losing her footing and nearly falling as the deafening alarm finally went silent.

She had no idea what was going on, but there was no way to miss the change in her captors' demeanor when the sound of a muffled explosion had drifted down to them a few minutes before. Omidi's casual superiority and smug smile immediately disintegrated, and he'd run ahead, barking orders at the frightened people occupying the offices and labs lining the hallway.

She swung another pointless fist into the side of the man holding her as they passed through a set of blast doors she'd never seen open. Inside, the scientists who had slowly been going missing—Omidi's believers—were scurrying around with arms full of files, samples, and computer drives.

The guard released her, jabbing a finger in her direction and saying something that clearly meant that she wasn't to move.

He ran off to help the others pile everything that wasn't bolted down into a chute that led to the incinerator, while she turned her attention to the glass wall to her left. There were three infected men imprisoned behind it, pounding their broken and bleeding hands against the barrier as the chaos in the lab continued to intensify. They didn't display any animosity toward each other—or even seem aware of the others' presence. Were they not infected with her latest version of the parasite? Were her modifications not effective in humans? Perhaps the alterations weren't yet powerful enough. It was possible that they still had a strong preference for uninfected victims and wouldn't turn on each other unless they were isolated from that temptation.

Mehrak Omidi was desperately punching commands into a computer terminal as he looked at two monitors near the ceiling. She took a few hesitant steps toward them, squinting at the tiny images of the exterior of the facility.

Sarie felt a wave of elation at the sight of men with guns engaging the guards but then felt some of it fade when she saw that it wasn't the Americans. They appeared to be Iranians, and even she could pick out their lack of cohesiveness. Some didn't even seem to be looking in the direction they were shooting.

Omidi was on the move again, running to a refrigerated safe and entering a lengthy code into the keypad on the front. It opened with a puff of frosty air, and he retrieved a rack of glass vials, carefully transferring them to a foam-lined briefcase.

Less and less attention was being paid to her, and she edged over to a desk a few meters away. She felt around behind her for the scissors lying on it and was in the process of slipping them down the back of her pants when Omidi closed the briefcase and ran at her with three guards in tow.

He grabbed her arm and pulled her toward the hall, pausing in the doorway to shout a few last orders at the two remaining security men in the room. They slid the guns from their shoulders and she watched in horror as they opened up on the scientists still working to destroy the evidence of their work.

It was over in a few brief seconds. Smoke hung in the room and the stench of gunpowder filled her nostrils as she looked down at the dead researchers, at the men who had murdered them, and at the three parasite victims still trying to get through the glass.

When Omidi began pulling again, she no longer had any strength to resist.

They came to the end of the corridor amid the echo of continuing gunfire behind them. One of Omidi's men punched a code into a pad mounted to the wall, and a steel door slid open to reveal an enormous cave hung with lights and reinforced with concrete pillars. She was shoved into the cab of a military truck, followed by Omidi, who was cradling his briefcase as though it contained the cure for cancer.

He noticed her staring at it and smiled humorlessly. "My people have kept the parasite alive outside the body for almost forty-eight hours. Plenty of time to get it to Mexico and smuggle it over the U.S. border."

One of the guards slipped into the driver's seat carrying a laptop that she recognized as belonging to Yousef Zarin. Omidi started the computer as another of his men jumped into the back of the vehicle to take control of a machine gun mounted to the bed.

"Ironic, isn't it?" Omidi said. "That the program you created to destroy us will be the thing that saves us?"

The engine started and a moment later they were reversing out of the parking space. There was no more time. She had to do something.

The scissors were still in her waistband and she grabbed them, swinging the blade into the driver's ribs with one hand while using the other to take hold of the wheel. He shouted in surprise and pain, but the scissors penetrated only a few millimeters and left him with the strength to slam on the brakes.

They were thrown forward, and she instinctively reached for the handle of Omidi's door. It flew open and she pushed off, sending them both through it. They hit the ground hard, but she'd been ready for it and managed to tuck into a roll, while Omidi landed square on his back.

The impact knocked the briefcase from his grip and sent it skittering across the dirt. She made a grab for it, catching the handle and letting her momentum carry her back to her feet.

There was no point in looking back, and instead she sprinted toward the door they'd come through. Shouts rose behind her, followed by the static of the gun mounted on the bed of the truck, but the rounds went wide.

It didn't take as long as she had hoped for the guard to swing the gun into position, and she was forced to dive behind a support pillar as he zeroed in. The powerful rounds hammered it for a few moments, tearing away enough concrete to expose the rebar inside. Then suddenly everything went quiet.

"Dr. van Keuren," Omidi called, breaking the silence. "Listen to me. There's nowhere for you to go. Come out and I will guarantee your safety. Do you hear me?"

She poked her head from behind the column and then pulled it immediately back. The man she'd stabbed was working his way right with a pistol in his hand and a bloodstain spreading across his shirt. Omidi was on the ground typing on the laptop, which apparently hadn't been smashed into the million pieces she'd counted on.

His offer of safety was complete bull—he'd called off his gunner only because he was afraid of damaging the briefcase. Given the chance, Omidi would either kill her and unleash the parasite on America or take her prisoner again and set her back to weaponizing it. Neither was a particularly attractive scenario.

She heard a creak behind her and saw the door leading back into the facility begin to close. He was running Zarin's program—trying to seal in the force attacking them and set the infected animals loose.

With no other choice, she ran for the closing door, gripping the briefcase tightly to her chest as she broke into the open. She ignored the sound of gunshots behind her, focusing entirely on getting to the door before the gap became too small to pass through.

A searing pain flared in her leg and she went down, sliding uncontrollably forward as the briefcase flew from her hand. She came to a stop halfway across the threshold and made a move back toward the case but was forced to stop when a bullet exploded against the rock wall next to her.

The door hit her in the shoulder and she shoved uselessly

back against the powerful motor closing it. The man she'd stabbed was running hard in her direction, and the barrel of the mounted machine gun was aimed directly at her. There was nothing she could do. They were going to get the brief-case. But hell if they were going to get her.

She dragged herself the rest of the way through the door, barely managing to clear her feet before it sealed, and then just lay there trying to get control of her breathing.

The wound in her leg was only a graze, and she tore off one of her sleeves to use as a bandage. There was no way to know who was attacking the facility, but whoever they were, they were her best—only—hope.

Sarie pushed herself to her knees and was trying to get to her feet when she froze, straining to decipher a faint buzz just beginning to rise above the ringing in her ears.

It was the monkeys. They were free.

CHAPTER EIGHTY

Central Iran
December 5—1015 Hours GMT+3:30

Jon Smith looked over the edge of the dry moat and studied the tower on the northeastern edge of the fence line, searching for the sniper ensconced there. Hakim's truck tipping over had been a complete disaster, pinning down Farrokh's team and potentially turning the entire operation into an unwinnable war of attrition.

Howell was prone on the bridge above, using his freakish marksmanship to cover the men huddled behind the capsized truck. Farrokh was crawling back and forth among them, patting shoulders and delivering words of encouragement, but most still looked like they were about thirty seconds from melting down.

The distance between them and the remaining towers had neutralized the advantage of elevated machine guns, and the men in them had switched to rifles. They were good, but not particularly great shots—with one exception. There was a sniper in the northeastern tower who was a damn prodigy. He'd already taken out three of their men and was throwing an extremely large wrench into what little was left of their machine.

His bearded face appeared over the rim of the tower, and Smith was unable to adjust his aim before the muzzle flash. The round ricocheted off the bridge and he turned to see that it had knocked loose a chunk of concrete near Howell's shoulder. The Brit remained completely still, eye glued to his scope.

"I'd be much obliged if you'd *kill* that son of a bitch, Jon."

"Working on it."

A bullet kicked up some sand two feet from Smith's head, and Howell fired off a few rounds in the general direction it had come from. Sitting there waiting for the Iranians to find their range and call in reinforcements wasn't an option. If they broke cover, though, the sniper to the northeast would have a field day.

And so it was a guessing game. On what part of the tower would he appear next? In order to have time to get off an accurate shot, Smith would have to anticipate his position within about a foot.

"I think I'm starting to get a sunburn," Howell said, making the point that he hadn't come there to get involved in a deadly stalemate.

"South, east, or west?"

"What?" Howell said.

"Choose one."

"South."

"Pick a number between one and ten."

"Six."

Smith aimed at the south side of the tower, about six feet from the left, and waited. Five seconds. Ten. Fifteen. When the dark face appeared again it was almost exactly where Howell had unknowingly predicted.

Smith held his breath and squeezed off a round, waiting the split second it took to travel across the compound before seeing the head jerk back in an explosion of blood.

"You have the luck of the Irish, Peter. Go!"

Farrokh's men laid down suppressing fire at the line of men Howell had been keeping in check, but their position made it impossible to do anything about the remaining snipers in the towers.

Smith heard the bullets hissing by as he tried to coax a little more speed from his legs in the heavy sand. "Break right!"

Howell did as he was told, diving behind the sandbags that had torn through the truck's canopy when it tipped. He fired controlled rounds at the towers as Smith jumped over the body of one of their people and slid up next to Farrokh, who was trying to keep his surviving nine-man force from completely depleting their ammunition in one panicked burst.

"We're safe! Pull back!"

Farrokh shouted for his men to retreat fully behind the truck again. Smith grabbed the youngest of them, swatting away the phone he was inexplicably using to film the battle, and dragging him toward Howell.

"The tower at three o'clock!" Smith said, throwing him down next to the Brit. "Do you understand? Cover the tower at three o'clock!"

He cried out when a round struck a few feet away, but then rolled dutifully onto his stomach and propped his rifle on a sandbag. It was his first time in combat, but he'd grown up hunting with his father and was a better-than-average shot.

Howell reached over and patted him on the back. "That's a good lad. You're going to do fine."

Farrokh and the others had crammed themselves into the now empty bed of the truck while Omidi's men blasted away at its underside, undoubtedly trying to penetrate the armor protecting the fuel tank.

Finally afforded an unobstructed view, Smith looked toward the rock outcropping that held the entrance to the facility. The heavy doors were blackened and dented, but the breach wasn't what he'd hoped—no more than a two-foot-by-five-foot gap where the steel plates had been pushed apart. It would be enough, though. That is, if they could get to it. The truck was the only thing keeping them from a cross fire no one could survive. And since there was no way they could abandon it, they'd just have to take it with them.

"Come on!" Smith shouted, digging his fingers into the sand beneath the top of the cab. "Let's get this thing on its wheels!"

Farrokh and his men came to his aid, and with all ten of them working together, it began to rise.

"Keep going!" Smith yelled over the sound of Howell and his new protégé trading fire with the towers. The man to Smith's left was hit in the shoulder blade and went down, causing the truck to lurch back toward the sand. "Harder!"

They managed to get it on the edge of its tires, and he walked his hands up the windshield pillar as the load lightened. When gravity finally took over, he dove through the open window, shoving Hakim's body out of the way and jamming the clutch down with his elbow.

He twisted the ignition key and was surprised to hear the engine fire almost immediately. Maybe their luck was finally changing.

Still stuffed up under the dash, he used his knee to move the shift lever and eased off the clutch, propelling the truck toward the facility's entrance as bullets rang off the armored door.

After what seemed like an hour but was probably less than a minute, the truck slammed into something and came to a stop. The motor stalled and Smith kicked the door open, sliding out to see that Howell and his companion had already repositioned themselves and were once again lining up on the towers.

In the distance, he could see a cloud of dust coming toward them and knew it was the convoy of men they'd held back so that they wouldn't arrive on the bridge looking like the invading army they were. It would be another fifteen minutes before they arrived, though, so no help there.

Keeping tight to the truck, Smith approached the blackened steel doors. He could feel cold air blowing through the gap and see the shimmer of fluorescent light inside. But that was all. There was no sound and nothing that would indicate movement.

He stood motionless for a moment, hearing a round shatter the windshield of the truck behind him. Howell was doing everything humanly possible, but it was just a matter of time before the snipers picked them off.

"What now?" Farrokh said, slipping up next to him. Smith shouldered his rifle and pulled out the .45 he'd been given. It felt heavy and clumsy compared to the one Janani had made, but it would have to do.

He eased forward, but when the gun came even with the gap in the doors, a shot sounded and the pistol was ripped from his hand.

"Damn it!" he said, jerking back and making a quick count of his fingers. All still there.

A few more shots followed, scattering Farrokh's confused men as Smith tried to decipher what he was hearing. Three, maybe four, separate guns, all trained on the narrow gap that they needed to pass through.

"Do we have any explosives left?"

Farrokh shook his head. "The men coming have a few grenades, but we put everything else we had in the truck."

"You've got to be kidding. You didn't hold any back?"

"If we didn't get through the door, what would we have done with them?"

It was a valid point, but not what he wanted to hear. They still had the truck. How could they use it? Ramming the doors was unlikely to get them anywhere—they still looked solid. Maybe attach chains and pull?

Great idea, if they *had* chains. And a few hours. And no one trying to kill them.

More shots sounded from inside, and Smith backed away from the opening before he realized that the bullets weren't coming through. Panicked shouts became audible a moment later, followed by an eerie, echoing screech that sounded strangely like monkeys.

He picked up the charred remains of a fender and waved it in front of the breach. The shooting and shouts continued inside, but none of it seemed to be directed at the fender.

As much as he hated leaping in blind, an opportunity had presented itself and it was impossible to know if there would ever be another.

"Peter!" he shouted. "We're going!"

Howell slapped the young man next to him on the back and then ran toward Smith, who was barking orders while Farrokh translated.

"You. Take Peter's place and cover those towers as best you can. You three, use the truck and whatever else you can find to block this entrance after we go in. Nothing comes out. You understand what we're dealing with, right?"

They all nodded. "All right. Hold tight. Reinforcements are on their way. The rest of you are with us."

Smith pulled his assault rifle in front of him and took a deep breath before leaping through the gap. He immediately fell to the floor, staying as close to the wall as he could and yelling for anyone following to do the same.

He had been right about there being three men covering the entrance, but now they had so little interest in it, they hadn't even noticed him come in. They were firing wildly at two small, blood-soaked monkeys darting from wall to ceiling to floor so quickly it was hard to believe they didn't have wings. Ricochets filled the air as the rounds bounced off stone and steel in search of something more forgiving.

Farrokh came through next and Smith grabbed him, making sure he stayed low as his men followed.

"Hold your—," he started, but it was too late. The second man through let loose a series of uncontrolled bursts at the red blurs streaking around them, filling the air with even more lead.

"Peter! The monkeys!" he yelled as the Brit came through.

The benefit of Omidi's guards' being completely preoccupied with the animals on the ceiling was that it made them easy targets. They crumpled unceremoniously to the floor when Smith put a single round into each of their chests.

"Stop shooting!" Smith yelled as Howell crammed himself into a corner and began tracking a monkey darting across an oblong light fixture hanging on cables. No one seemed to hear, so he threw himself over Farrokh, grabbing the closest man's rifle and giving it a hard jerk. "Stop!"

A series of bulbs exploded as Smith went for the next man firing out of turn. In the dark, their chances against these little demons went to precisely zero. He managed to yank the gun from him and was trying to get to the last man shooting when one of the monkeys dropped down and did his job for him.

The young man screamed and dropped his rifle, clawing at the animal sinking its fangs into the back of his neck.

It was just the opportunity Howell needed. His bullet shattered the right half of the monkey's skull and passed through, severing the desperate man's spinal cord. A quick and humane end for both.

The last monkey was smaller and faster but obviously confused by the shadows created by the swinging of the last light fixture. Farrokh and his men tracked it with their guns but to their credit managed to control their fear and not fire.

The animal leapt for the wall and missed the hole in the concrete it was going for, causing it to somersault to the floor. The impact dazed it, slowing its chaotic movements enough to make it a viable target. Howell's first shot spun it around and his second tore away most of its chest.

Suddenly, all that was audible in the room was their ragged breathing and the creaking of the light. Smith was the first to stand, feeling a little disoriented in the stillness. He pulled Farrokh to his feet and then held a hand out to the other three men. They just stared blankly at him as Howell started toward a steep ramp leading into the earth.

"Look on the bright side," the Brit said as he disappeared around the corner. "How much worse could it possibly get?"

By the time they reached the main level, Smith's heart had slowed to what still felt like twice its normal rate. He was on point as he came around a blind corner, rifle thrust out in front of him.

Nothing.

"Clear!" he said, aware of the cameras looking down at them but unable to do much about it.

Halfway down the passage they came upon three corpses wearing lab coats, each with a neat bullet hole in the back of the head.

"Nobody touch anything."

When he got no response, he turned back to Farrokh. "Are you going to translate?"

The Iranian gave him a quizzical look and thumbed back at his men. "Do you really think it's necessary?"

He was right. They were clearly petrified. It was unlikely that there was enough money in the world to get them to come into contact with those bodies.

They continued on, clearing every room in sequence, finding some empty and others strewn with corpses. None had been attacked by the animals they'd run into when they entered, though. They'd been executed.

Smith backed out of a room containing two people slumped over their desks, once again feeling a sense of relief at not finding Sarie. In truth, though, it would be better if he had. His problems were bad enough without her in the hands of Iranian Intelligence.

A dull whine started in the distance, and he froze, listening to it separate into a chorus of shrieks as it closed on them.

"Are you hearing that?" Howell said. "It's not going to be two of them this time."

He was right. It was impossible to pick out individual voices in the screams of the approaching animals. If his team got caught in the confined space of the hallway, they wouldn't last thirty seconds.

"Inside!" Smith said, leaping back into the room with the others close behind. He slammed the door behind them only to find that the dead-bolt was extended far enough to prevent it from fully closing.

"Farrokh. The lock. Can you get it to retract?"

The Iranian knelt to examine it. "No. It's electronic. Controlled centrally, probably."

"Incoming!" Howell shouted, grabbing a rifle and slipping the barrel through the narrow gap between the door and the jamb.

There were at least ten of them, coats so wet with blood that they were leaving streaks on the floor and walls as they charged. Smith dropped beneath the Brit, aiming his .45

362

into the corridor and trying futilely to track individual targets.

"Farrokh! Hold the door."

The Iranian shoved his back against it and waved his men over to help him. Their prayers were just barely audible over the howls.

CHAPTER EIGHTY-ONE

Central Iran
December 5—1102 Hours GMT+3:30

The arm appeared again, flicking around the crack in the door and grasping desperately at darkness. Sarie jerked back, tangling herself in the coats hanging in the crowded closet but keeping a death grip on the leather belt looped over the knob.

She stabbed at the arm with the sharp end of a broken broom handle, connecting with the blood-soaked biceps on her fifth try. The man gave no indication that he even noticed, adjusting his strategy from groping blindly for her to trying to pry open the door.

All she wanted to do was cover her ears to block out his enraged screams. And maybe she should. There was no way out of the facility, and she would eventually get tired, while he would just keep coming until his heart failed. If she let him in, it would be over in a minute. Maybe less.

He managed to get a shoulder through, and she could see his face in the dim light—the saliva hanging in long, pink strands across his beard, the wide eyes trying to catch a glimpse of his prey.

She swung the broom handle at his face, and it tore a deep gash beneath his eye. Other than making him even more grotesque, though, it accomplished nothing. Dropping her useless weapon, she put a foot against the wall and gripped the belt with both hands, trying to use her superior leverage to trap him between the door and the jamb.

Her forearms felt like they were on fire and her palms

were slick with sweat, causing the leather to slip slowly but irretrievably through her fingers. The door opened another few centimeters, and the man's head intruded a little farther, the gash in his face flowing with parasite-infested blood. She felt the heat of it splash across her hands, but it didn't matter. In a few seconds she wouldn't be able to fight any-more—she'd lose her grip, the door would fly open …

And then he was gone.

The extended deadbolt clanged loudly as she pulled it into the metal jamb, her mind unable to process the mean-ing of the muffled shouts and gunfire outside.

A few moments later, fingers curled around the edge of the door and began trying to pry it open again.

"Get away from me!" she screamed, grabbing the broom handle and narrowly missing the hand when it was jerked away at the last moment.

"Sarie! Is that you?"

The hand reappeared and she slashed at it again.

"Let go of the door, Sarie! And for God's sake, stop trying to stab me!"

The accent wasn't Iranian. It was American. And there was something familiar about it.

"Sarie. Listen to me. Open the door, okay?"

The belt fell from her hands and she squinted into the light as Jon Smith lifted her from the closet.

"Are you all right?" he said, looking her over for cuts that the parasite could have invaded, finally settling on her leg. "What happened? Is it from an attack? Did it—"

She shook her head and threw her arms around him, sob-bing uncontrollably. The man who had been trying to get to her was lying on the floor fifteen meters away with most of the top of his head missing. Peter Howell was standing next to the body, keeping watch over the empty hallway with three armed Iranians.

"I'm sorry, but there's not much time," Smith said, gently pushing her away.

"Less than you think," Sarie said, wiping at her eyes. "Omidi's people made the parasite transportable. I tried to stop him, but he's gone. And he took it with him."

Smith looked up the hallway as the howls of monkeys started echoing along it. Luck had played a significant role in their surviving their last encounter—the fact that none of the animals had been small enough to get through the crack in the door or large enough to push it open, combined with a one-in-a-thousand shot that he still couldn't believe he'd made. The gods wouldn't be as kind the next time around.

"What do you mean *gone*, Sarie?"

"I mean he got in a truck and drove away."

CHAPTER EIGHTY-TWO

Central Iran
December 5—1123 Hours GMT+3:30

Mehrak Omidi squinted through the dusty windshield at the road disappearing into the horizon. The rutted surface and the insecure position of the guard manning the machine gun in back was limiting them to eighty kilometers per hour—a speed that seemed impossibly slow.

"How far are you from Avass?"

Omidi held the satellite phone with his shoulder and scrolled on a handheld GPS. The village, a crumbling rural outpost with fewer than three thousand residents, was too small to be noted on it, but based on the topography he could make a reasonable estimate.

"Less than an hour, Excellency."

"And the facility?" Ayatollah Khamenei said. "What is the situation there?"

"The infection is loose inside and the main door has been breached."

"Was it the Americans?"

"Iranians. Members of the resistance, I suspect. But there can be little doubt that the Americans have a hand in it."

"Then they know a great deal."

"Too much, Excellency."

The alien sensation of fear was slowly working its way to his belly. There was no way to go back—they had burned every bridge behind them. Bahame was almost certainly dead, and according to the international press his guerrilla army had been all but wiped out. Whatever Jon Smith's fate, it was certain that he had told his superiors everything he'd learned and the Americans would act on that information—with allies if possible, alone if necessary.

"Excellency, I'm sorry. I—"

"You don't have anything to be sorry for, Mehrak. You have been nothing but a loyal and tireless soldier in the service of God."

The years seemed to have drained from his voice, which resonated with the certainty and confidence that Omidi remembered from decades before.

"Continue to Avass," Khamenei said. "I have contacted the police there, and they are gathering others who are loyal to God and the revolution. They will offer protection until the military can reach you."

"How long?"

"The first transport plane should arrive in less than four hours."

"Four hours," he repeated quietly. It seemed like an eternity. The forces that had breached their defenses would almost certainly know by now that he had escaped and would be coming for him.

"Excellency, I—"

The window next to him exploded, showering him with glass as the truck swerved violently. Omidi dropped the phone and slid to the floorboards, protecting the briefcase with his body as bullets pounded the door next to him.

His driver was bleeding from a deep cut in his forehead but managed to regain control of the vehicle. The man in back had been slammed into the cab and was struggling to swing the machine gun in the direction of the riflemen who had appeared on a ridge bordering the east side of the road.

A moment later, the satisfying roar of the mounted gun replaced the ring of bullets on the door, and Omidi rose enough to see over the dashboard while the driver wrung all the speed he could from the engine.

A rusting compact car appeared from behind a low rise in front of them, entering a narrow section of road bordered by a deep ditch on one side and a cliff face on the other. It continued to pick up speed, and Omidi saw unwavering resolve in the hunched position of the man behind the wheel. He was going to ram them.

The sound of the machine gun grew in volume as it turned on the approaching vehicle, ripping through the grille, pockmarking its hood, and finally tearing away most of the roof.

The car skidded left and then careened right, its driver's head now held on by nothing more than a thin ribbon of skin. The truck's right fender took most of the impact, slamming the much smaller vehicle into the rock wall and grinding along its length.

The machine gunner's back was pressed against the cab again, and he was laying down suppressing fire, moving smoothly between the intermittent muzzle flashes fading behind them.

"Mehrak! Are you there? Mehrak!"

Khamenei's tinny voice was audible again, drifting out from beneath the truck's seat. Omidi remained on the floorboards, reaching around blindly for a few moments before laying his hand on the phone.

"Yes, Excellency. I'm here."

"What happened?"

"We were attacked. The resistance is obviously aware that this is the only road leading away from the facility."

"Are you injured?"

"No. I'm fine."

"And the parasite?"

Omidi tapped a code into the briefcase's keypad and popped it open, revealing nine separate vials.

"Intact."

"Praise be to God."

"If there are terrorists on the road, Excellency, there may be more in the village."

"I'll contact our people in Avass and warn them. They will be waiting to escort you in."

"Thank you, Excellency."

"Mehrak, I know I don't have to impress upon you how

important it is that those vials reach Tehran intact. We have seven men with U.S. visas standing by. We must strike quickly and fatally before the Americans can move against us."

CHAPTER EIGHTY-THREE

Central Iran
December 5—1141 Hours GMT+3:30

"This is all we have?" Smith said, staring down at a single grenade that looked like World War II surplus.

The young man standing in front of him nodded weakly, bending at the waist and trying to slow his ragged breathing.

"How hard would it be to get back to the main entrance?"

"There were four of us when we entered," he replied in thickly accented English. "I'm the only one left."

"Jesus, Sarie. How many of those monkeys are there?"

"Thirty-one. And two people not counting the one you killed."

"Everybody back!" Howell shouted as the clatter of claws became audible down the hallway.

They'd erected floor-to-ceiling barricades on both sides of the corridor, but the available materials—mostly office furniture—made for a fairly porous barrier. Howell and Smith stood in the middle of the floor with their pistols at eye level as the others retreated behind them. The animal was approaching fast, brief flashes of crimson through the gaps.

Despite its less-than-impressive construction, the barrier did what it was designed to do. The monkey hit hard and immediately went for an obvious hole they'd made sure was large enough to be enticing but not so large that it would be easy to fully pass through. The macaque got its head in but then was stalled when its shoulder got caught. Smith held his fire and let Howell use his superior marksmanship to put a round through the top of the animal's skull.

"It worked!" Farrokh said, coming up behind them. "I have to admit I had my doubts."

"We were lucky," Howell responded, checking his clip. "One is easy to handle. Maybe even two. More than that and they're going to get through."

He was right. As bad as infected humans were, they were relatively large, slow targets compared to these little horrors. And according to Sarie, there were six full-grown chimps that wouldn't be drawn in by the gap left in the barricade. They'd make their own.

"What now?" Farrokh said. He was holding a walkie-talkie in his hand, but after his initial success in getting the grenade brought down to them, all attempts to raise his men had failed. Beyond knowing that their reinforcements had arrived, they were completely in the dark as to what was happening outside the hallway they'd barricaded themselves in.

"Sarie, you're sure this is the door Omidi went out?" Smith said.

"Positive. The fact that it's locked means it leads outside," she said and then pointed to a smear of blood on the floor. "And that's mine."

"Then we have to get through."

"The steel's too thick," Farrokh said. "That grenade won't penetrate."

He was right. Putting the explosive directly against the door would probably just bend the metal—making it even harder to open.

"Perhaps...," Farrokh continued hesitantly.

"What? If you have an idea, speak up."

"I've never worked on this type of mechanism specifically, but I used to be an engineer. If you were designing this, how would you make it lock?"

"Sure ...," Smith said, focusing on the wall to the left of the door. "Why make things any more complicated than you have to? All you need is a simple actuator that moves something to block it."

They worked quickly, tearing down the rear barricade

and using the pieces to create a structure that would help direct the blast against the wall next to the door. It left them unprotected, but at this point, there was no choice but to go all-in.

When they were finished, Smith pulled the rusty pin on the grenade. "Everyone back!"

They ducked around the corner and flattened themselves against the wall as the explosive detonated, filling the air with a haze of shattered concrete.

It worked. The mechanism was exposed, but also twisted and charred. Smith used his hands to clear away the debris while Farrokh examined the design.

"This is it," he said, pointing to a simple steel rod lodged against the main gear.

Smith picked up a piece of concrete and swung it repeatedly at the bar, bending it back while Farrokh and his men pulled on the door. It moved a couple of inches and then stopped.

"Harder! Come on!" Smith said.

They put everything they had into it, but it didn't budge. "Again!"

"Jon," Sarie said, coming up behind him. "What's that at the top of the hole you made?"

He wasn't sure how he'd missed it, but there was a blackened wiring harness tangled in the top rail, blocking the door's movement. He reached up and yanked it out as Farrokh and his men curled their fingers through the small gap they'd made.

It happened a painfully slow quarter-inch at a time, but the door ground its way back. When they'd opened it a little more than a foot, the young man who had brought them the grenade stepped in front of it. "I think it's large enough!" he said. "I can get through."

"Stop!" Smith shouted, but it was too late.

The man had barely entered the gap when a gunshot sounded and he went limp, his body suspended between the door and the jamb—a victim of the same trap they'd set for the monkeys.

Farrokh dove for cover, but Smith moved up behind the man. There was no time for regret or respect for the fallen. Omidi was getting farther away with every minute and they couldn't afford to get pinned down here.

More shots rang out, thudding dully into the dead man's flesh as Smith grabbed him by the back of the jacket and lifted him fully upright. It sounded like a single gun, semi-automatic, with rounds designed for impact, not penetration.

"Peter! You're with me!"

The Brit fell in behind as Smith shoved the bleeding corpse through the hole, using it as a shield as he entered a cavernous, intermittently lit parking garage.

The shots kept coming, absorbed by the dead weight of the body, which was getting increasingly awkward to maneuver. He could feel Howell pressed up against him as they moved right, taking cover behind a concrete pillar that looked to be on the verge of collapse.

Howell returned fire, getting close enough to the prone man to spray sand and broken rock into his eyes. He leapt to his feet and ran stumbling toward a van twenty yards behind him, but instead of taking cover behind it, he just kept going.

"I believe he's had about enough of this day," Howell said. "Hard to blame him."

Smith turned back toward the door. "It's clear. Come on through."

After Sarie, Farrokh, and his surviving men were safely out, Smith ducked back into the facility and worked a table into the cavern so that he could use it to block the gap.

"You three stay here," he said, pointing to Farrokh's men. "Nothing comes out—even if it's someone you know. Do you understand? If they want out, tell them to go back to the main entrance, where we've got people trained to check them for wounds that could indicate infection."

They nodded and he ran toward a group of vehicles parked on the other side of the cavern with Farrokh in tow. A quick search didn't turn up any keys, and Smith jabbed a finger in the Iranian's direction. "You said you're an engineer, right? Can you hot-wire a car?"

"An engineer is different from a thief, Colonel."

"Great," Smith muttered as Howell kept watch in case the guard they'd chased off rediscovered his courage. Sarie, though, had disappeared.

He was about to call to her when the sound of an engine firing up echoed through the enormous chamber. A few moments later, a pickup full of maintenance equipment skidded to a stop in front of him.

"Need a ride?" Sarie said, leaning out the open window.

"Peter! We're rolling!"

She slid over and let him take the wheel as Farrokh jumped through the passenger door. They were already pulling away when Howell threw himself into the bed, tossing out toolboxes and shovels to make room as they accelerated toward what Smith prayed was an exit.

The cavern was much larger and more complex than he expected, but they followed a set of fresh tire tracks until they passed through the mouth of a meticulously camouflaged cave entrance.

Farrokh immediately got on his phone and Smith squinted into the blinding sunlight, heading toward the road leading north. They were a good half mile outside the facility's perimeter fence and probably two hundred feet higher in elevation. It looked like all the fighting was inside the building now, and trucks had been used to block the bridge, with supporting gun placements being constructed out of sandbags.

Farrokh spoke urgently into the phone in Persian and then looked over at him. "My men engaged a vehicle with a mounted machine gun on the road to Avass."

"That's it," Sarie said. "That's the truck Omidi was in. Did they stop him?"

The Iranian shook his head. "We have people in the village, though. They've been told what to look for."

"Can they stop a vehicle like that?" Smith said.

"Given a free hand, yes. But Avass is a conservative place, and the government will have many friends there."

"What about the lab?"

"We are gaining control. The two remaining infected men are dead, though there are still some animals loose."

"How many of your men have been exposed?"

"Many more than we anticipated. But that problem is being handled with the procedures you put in place. Everyone understood the risks of volunteering for this. And the consequences."

Sarie leaned forward and put her head in her hands. "It's my fault. I infected them—we were going to lock down the facility and set them loose. If I just hadn't done anything, you'd have only had a few half-dead animals to deal with. Your men would be okay."

"There was no way for you to know," Farrokh said. "You had to act. It was my own stupidity for not anticipating the possibility that Omidi would release lab animals to cover his escape."

"*Our* stupidity," Smith corrected. "Any word on the Iranian military?"

"I'm afraid so. An elite force is in the air."

CHAPTER EIGHTY-FOUR

Near Avass, Iran
December 5—1204 Hours GMT+3:30

Avass came into view as they crested a small rise, and Mehrak Omidi examined the ancient buildings lining a maze of poorly maintained streets. The terrain steepened precipitously at the edges of the village, asphalt giving way to cobblestones worn down by a thousand years of foot traffic.

"There!" he said, tapping his driver on the shoulder and pointing to four cars idling by the side of the road. A police vehicle and a pickup full of armed men pulled out in front of them, accelerating to match their speed. Omidi looked in the side mirror as they passed the remaining two vehicles, watching them fall in to protect their flank. According to Khamenei, they were to be escorted to the city center and deposited at the police station, a building that had been heavily fortified over the last few hours.

It was another ten minutes before they penetrated Avass, and Omidi held the briefcase tightly to his chest as his eyes shifted from the buildings hanging over them to the pedestrians rushing to get out of their way. Farrokh's traitors were everywhere—watching, waiting, plotting. No one was above suspicion. Not anymore.

They passed a crowded market with vendors lined up in front of a stone building hung with antique rugs. Through the windows he could see booths selling jewelry and spices, as well as the Western conveniences that his people had become so addicted to.

At the northern edge of the market, two men dressed in slacks and wool sweaters were struggling to get a large wooden crate to the curb while a woman on a cell phone watched disinterestedly.

As the motorcade closed, the men gave up and started toward an alley, their gait slightly unnatural, as though they were struggling to hold themselves back from running. The woman broke off, too, threading herself through the people on the street and into the market building.

"Stop!" Omidi shouted, and his driver slammed on the truck's brakes, locking up the wheels just before they were hit by one of their chase cars. The sound of the impact, though, was completely obscured by the roar of an explosion.

The device in the crate had been surrounded by nails, and the pickup in front of them was enveloped in a deadly cloud of fire and shrapnel. The police car swerved right, running down a group of fleeing shoppers before crashing into the stone archways of a pharmacy.

Gunfire erupted a moment later, seemingly from every-where—the narrow alleys leading off the main road, the rooftops, the open windows of shops and private homes.

"Go!" he yelled, sliding to the floorboards. "Get us out of here!"

When the truck just idled slowly forward, he looked up and saw his driver slumped over the wheel. The machine gun in back started but went silent again when the gunner's body bounced off the rear window and toppled into the street.

Bullets hissing overhead kept him pinned down, and steam billowing from the radiator surrounded him in a hot, blinding cloud. He wouldn't last much longer—one lucky shot or well-placed grenade and he would die along with Iran's only hope of survival.

The door was jerked open and he shrank back, trying to push the briefcase behind him for protection.

Instead of shooting, though, the man held out a hand. "Come! Hurry!"

Omidi followed, running crouched toward the pharmacy building as others loyal to the republic closed around him, firing wildly in every direction.

The man in front of him and the one to his right fell in rapid succession, causing the cohesiveness of his human shield to fail. Omidi abandoned them, sprinting toward the arches protecting the front of the pharmacy. He was only a few meters away when something impacted his back and threw him toward a table stacked with oil lamps. He toppled over it, hitting the ground before a powerful hand lifted him and dragged him through the pharmacy's doors.

He managed to keep hold of the case, but it was becoming slick with his own blood. The man released him and went to one of the broken windows, pressing his back against the wall as bullets streamed through, pulverizing the items neatly lining the store's shelves.

Omidi managed to get to his knees, crawling unsteadily toward the shoppers huddled beneath a row of tables. When he got within a few meters, two men came out and pulled him to safety.

"Are you all right?" one said. "I think you're shot!"

He tried to examine the wound, but Omidi slapped his hand away. The sensation in his legs was already beginning to fade, as was the sharpness of his mind. Farrokh's force was too large and well prepared for the men Khamenei had recruited. They would gain access to the pharmacy before the military could arrive.

"Do you work here?" he said to the woman next to him, trying to give his weakening voice authority.

She shook her head and pointed to a white-haired man cowering in the corner. Omidi struggled over to him, dragging the briefcase with numb fingers.

"You! Are you the pharmacist?"

"Yes," he said, eyes wide as he watched splinters fly off a wooden display case that two policemen were pushing against a shattered window. "I am Muhammad Vahdat."

"I am Mehrak Omidi, the director of the Ministry of Intelligence."

The man's face went blank for a moment, but then registered recognition. "Yes … Yes, of course. I have seen you—"

"Listen to me now," Omidi said, but then lost his train of thought as blood loss starved his mind. What needed to be done? The parasite! He had to concentrate. To think clearly for just a little longer.

"The men outside are Farrokh's soldiers. They've developed a biological weapon and we received reports that they were going to test it on your city."

The man went from looking terrified to looking as though he was going to pass out. "Here? But we're just a—"

"You're perfect. Small, isolated, and devout," Omidi said, patting his case with a hand dripping blood. "I have the antidote here—I brought it personally the moment we learned of his target. I need syringes. Enough for everyone. Do you have them?"

"Yes. Of course. Behind the counter."

"You have to get them so I can begin inoculations."

"But they're all the way—"

"You would rather die slowly of a disease that eats you from the inside?"

The pharmacist considered the question for a moment and then dropped to his stomach, slithering across the floor toward the back of the building.

Omidi watched him go, falling against the wall and fighting to remain conscious.

They had experimented extensively with the dose–response relationship and found it to be extremely strong. He had enough in his case to give everyone in the building a parasitic load many times greater than they would get from the normal mode of transmission. Based on the tables his scientists had developed, full symptoms would occur in less than two hours.

It was the only way. The fate of the parasite and the fate of Iran were now one and the same. He could not allow them to be destroyed or to fall into the hands of traitors. They had to survive.

CHAPTER EIGHTY-FIVE

Avass, Iran
December 5—1410 Hours GMT+3:30

"Another stalemate," Peter Howell said, easing around a building constructed of indigenous rock.

He was right. They'd come into Avass on foot and were now about five blocks from the city center, wandering along a narrow, twisting alleyway. The sound of gunfire had slowed to a shot every thirty seconds or so, and in this kind of closed-in urban terrain, that generally meant the two forces had dug in.

Farrokh was bringing up the rear, talking urgently on his phone as he navigated a patch of snow protected from the sun by a broad awning.

"Omidi is trapped in a pharmacy with what we believe to be four armed men and as many as twenty hostages," he reported. "He has the briefcase and my people say he's badly injured."

"Can they get to him?" Smith said.

"The street in front of the pharmacy is impassable, and there are no rear or side entrances."

"Do you have an ETA on the Iranian forces?"

"About an hour," Farrokh said. "Two C-130s carrying Takavar paratroopers. Seven more to follow, but my people haven't been able to determine when."

"Do you know how many are targeting Avass and how many are going to the lab?"

"No. But my men have sealed the facility and are in a good defensive position. They'll hold until the parasite there dies out."

Smith wasn't so sure—nine planes could transport upward of six hundred men, and Takavar troops were the best the Iranian military had to offer.

The gunshots were close now, and he followed Howell onto a muddy slope that terminated in a low wall. From their elevated position, it was clear that the situation was an absolute worst-case scenario. There were men everywhere—behind cars, on rooftops, peering around the edges of alleyways—but it was impossible to sort out who was who. The remains of a pickup were still burning in front of what looked like a market building, causing smoke to further obscure the situation. The pharmacy that Farrokh's people were talking about had stone arches across the front that looked like they could stop a tank, and there was at least one man stationed at each partially barricaded window.

"Maybe if we could get to the truck in the middle of the—," Howell started but then fell silent when a man darted from cover and ran for an overturned cart that would give him a better angle on the pharmacy windows. The silence was immediately broken by a barrage of gunfire, and he was cut down before he made it five feet.

"Never mind," Howell said.

Smith slid down with his back against the wall, swearing under his breath. The Takavar were going to be raining down on them like the wrath of God in less than an hour. It wouldn't take them long to wipe out Farrokh's forces and put Omidi on a plane to Tehran.

"Do your people have anything heavier than assault rifles?"

"One rocket-propelled grenade." Farrokh pointed at a rooftop to the north. "It's up there."

Smith dared a quick look, spotting a launcher hanging over the shoulder of a man holding a camera phone around the edge of a chimney. The angle wasn't great, but with a little luck it might be possible to thread the archways and get the charge through a window.

"We have to use it," Howell said. "No choice."

"What?" the Iranian said. "No. There are hostages. Women and children."

Smith peered over the wall again. "If Omidi's injured and it's bad enough, maybe we can offer him a deal. He gives us the case and we let him walk."

"No way," Sarie said. "I know him better than anyone here. If you want that case, you're going to have to pry it out of his dead fingers."

"I tend to agree," Farrokh said. "Omidi is not a man of compromises."

Smith sat silently for a moment, trying to focus on the tactical situation and not imagine the faces of the frightened people inside that building.

"Then Peter's right. Ask your man if he can make the shot."

Farrokh stared angrily back at him. "I can't help wondering if you would be so perfunctory if those were American hostages and the weapon was a threat to Iran."

Smith raised his head over the wall a few inches again and examined the pharmacy, trying to determine the strength of the barricades and catch a glimpse of the men behind them. When he got to the last one, his eye picked up movement. The shelving pushed up against the window began to rock violently, causing the few products remaining on it to cascade to the floor.

"No ...," he muttered when the cop who had been manning the position came partially through the window, breaking free the last shards of glass. He twisted around, throwing wild punches at something just out of sight as gunfire hammered the walls around him. He was hit in the shoulder, but kept fighting until two more rounds penetrated his back and left him hanging unnaturally on the sill. A moment later, the blood-streaked face of a woman appeared. She fell on the lifeless man, tearing at him, her mouth working in silent rage as bullet after bullet impacted her thin body.

"He's infected them!" Smith shouted. "Blow it! Blow it now!"

Farrokh still had his phone line open and began screaming into it. A moment later a contrail appeared from the rooftop and the grenade glanced off one of the pharmacy's archways, exploding in front of the heavy doors with a lot of smoke and noise, but little damage.

Smith yanked his rifle over his head and shoved it into Sarie's hands before pulling his .45 from its holster. "Kill everything that moves. Do you understand me? Kill *everything*."

Omidi's victims came out of the smoke, moving fast as Farrokh continued to shout orders into the phone. Howell fired calmly, hitting everything he aimed at like he always did. Sarie, despite her exceptional skill, was finding shooting people very different from shooting animals and targets. The men on the rooftops and in the streets hesitated, and by the time they understood what was happening, it was too late.

CHAPTER EIGHTY-SIX

Central Iran
December 5—1439 Hours GMT+3:30

General Asadi Daei stood in the C-130's cockpit door looking through the windscreen as the plane rose from the air force base and banked right. The most recent reports were that as many as fifty resistance traitors were digging in at the lab and that another twenty-five or so were fighting in the streets of Avass. Fortunately, the local police had managed to get Mehrak Omidi to a defensible building and he was there awaiting the first wave of paratroopers to drop.

Daei was about to ask for an updated ETA now that they were in the air, but the pilot turned and tapped his earphones, indicating that a communiqué was coming through.

The general grabbed a spare headset and leaned over the copilot to toggle the switch isolating the line. "This is Daei."

He straightened slightly when the static-ridden voice of Ayatollah Khamenei came on. "Security has been fully breached, General."

Despite having been wounded three separate times in the war with Iraq, Daei felt a trickle of fear. "Breach" meant that the disease he'd been briefed on had escaped containment. "Full breach" meant the infected were loose in the streets.

"I understand, Excellency."

"God be with you."

The channel went dead, and Daei opened a separate line to the commanders of the other transports. "We are moving to plan Theta. I repeat. Plan Theta."

After getting acknowledgments from the entire force, he

hung the headset back on the wall and stood motionless for a moment, feeling slightly dazed. In the other planes, envelopes would be opened and his officers would be describing the nature of the expected resistance to their teams: people with the strength of three men, drenched in blood and attacking everything that moved like a pack of rabid dogs. It seemed impossible—a paranoid fantasy. But the intelligence had come directly from Omidi and he was not a man prone to fits of hysteria.

Daei walked to the back of the plane, where a well-equipped medical team was strapped into utilitarian seats. "We have a full breach."

They immediately released their harnesses and began rushing around, opening crates filled with protective clothing, digging through stacks of medical equipment, and talking in loud, frightened tones.

He would now be forced to concentrate the vast majority of his troops on Avass. His biohazard team would unload at a nearby airstrip while paratroopers secured the streets. Their only mission now was to get a live victim of the parasite back to the plane. When they were in the air, he would be told where the deadly organism was to be taken.

Somewhere south of their current location, bombers with instructions to turn Avass into a burning hole in the ground were waiting for the green light. Even the Takavar soldiers would not be allowed to survive—the risk that they could spread the infection or relate details that didn't support the official story was too great.

CHAPTER EIGHTY-SEVEN

Langley, Virginia, USA
December 5—0619 Hours GMT–5

"What you're looking at was recorded about six hours ago," Dave Collen said.

The DCI took a seat in front of a laptop displaying a series of satellite images. They were hazy and the resolution had been degraded by magnification, but there was still no doubt about the ferocity of the fighting. A military truck had exploded after slamming into what looked like a rock outcropping, and its burning parts were strewn out among the bodies lying in the sand.

"An underground facility?" Drake said as the images were replaced with ones of a group of men flipping a similar truck back onto its wheels and pushing it forward as moving cover.

Collen nodded. "We had no idea it was there, and as near as I can tell neither did any of the other intelligence agencies. We're going back over our satellite data from the last few months and finding evidence of increased activity, but whatever the Iranians are doing there, they've pulled out all the stops to hide it."

"And we think this is related to the parasite?"

"No way to know for sure, but I'd bet good money on it. We have photos of a private jet landing on an abandoned strip not far from there a week ago."

"Omidi?"

"Again, there's no way to be certain. But when you combine the jet with the fact that Smith and Howell saw fit to try to get into Iran on foot and the noise we're getting about

biologists being pulled off their jobs by the secret police ..."
His voice faded for a moment. "I'm pretty confident that
Omidi got his parasite and that he's weaponizing it in this
facility. Maybe with the help of Sarie van Keuren."

Drake leaned back and watched the battle unfold until it
looped to the beginning. "I assume we're not the only ones
with access to this data."

"You assume right. Those images came from the National
Reconnaissance Office."

None of this was completely unexpected, but that
didn't make it any less dangerous. Smith and Howell hadn't
gone into Iran to try to stop Khamenei's forces on their
own. No, they'd contacted the resistance and despite their
deaths at the hands of Sepehr Mouradipour, Farrokh had
used the information he'd been provided to track down
Omidi's facility. The question was, what should they do
about it?

"There's more," Collen said. "We have reports of heavy
fighting in the streets of a village a hundred miles north of
that facility, and the Iranians are airlifting special forces
there as well as scrambling a squadron of bombers."

"ETA?"

"By now, they could have soldiers on the ground. I don't
have current information on the bombers."

"Is it possible that the parasite has escaped the facility?"

"We don't have any assets in the area and the satellite's
gone out of range. We won't have another overhead for six
hours."

Drake let out a frustrated sigh. "I have—"

The phone on his desk rang and he fell silent when he saw
the incoming number. The Oval Office.

Castilla tended to be a predictable man wed to his sched-
ules and formal briefings. Impromptu predawn calls were
very much not part of his management style.

Collen took a step back and watched him pick up the
receiver. "Hello, Mr. President."

"What the hell is going on in Iran, Larry? Have you
looked at these satellite images?"

"I'm just going through them now, sir. We're still gathering data at—"

"We've got a war going on between two unknown factions at a facility that we didn't know anything about and you're gathering *data*?"

"We should know more soon. The—"

"I'm at Camp David, Larry, and you're going to be in front of me in one hour with everything we've got on this. I want to know what the hell the Iranians are doing with an underground bunker in the middle of nowhere and I want to know who just crashed their party. Do you understand me?"

"Sir, that's not going to be enough time. It's a complicated—"

"Let me repeat myself, Larry. You are going to be standing in front of me in one hour."

Drake swallowed hard, fighting back a wave of nausea as the sweat broke across his forehead. "Yes, sir."

The line went dead and he slowly replaced the receiver. "Get together everything we have on the parasite and the Iranians."

"Everything?" Collen said, obviously alarmed.

"We're getting on a helicopter for Camp David. We'll strategize on the flight and sanitize what we have to. I'm not going to let this fall apart now. Not when we're this close."

CHAPTER EIGHTY-EIGHT

Avass, Iran
December 5—1505 Hours GMT+3:30

Jon Smith forced himself to slow, glancing over his shoulder at the people strung out behind him. Sarie wasn't having any trouble keeping up—her life in the African bush had combined with a healthy dose of terror to keep her injured leg turning over. Farrokh was lagging a bit, struggling for breath as he shouted for everyone to stay inside their homes and barricade the doors and windows. Howell was bringing up the rear, running in an awkward sideways lope as he covered their flank.

Satisfied that everyone was all right, Smith faced forward again and leapt over a hastily abandoned basket of vegetables. A burning pain suddenly flared in his head, and he went down on the jagged cobbles, rolling as the sound of the shot bounced off the stone buildings.

His balance was gone and his vision was spinning, making it pointless to attempt to get to his feet. Instead, he stayed as flat as possible, trying to clear his mind. A familiar voice reached him and he crawled toward it, still confused when Sarie grabbed him and dragged him behind a parked car.

"Hold still!" he heard her say as she tore off a piece of the jacket they'd found for her and pressed it to his scalp. "Jon? Are you okay? How many fingers am I holding up?"

He blinked hard and watched her hand come slowly into focus. "Uh ... two?"

She helped him to his feet and then carefully let go, making sure he could stay upright on his own.

"I'm fine. It's just … It's just a graze."

"It's more than a graze, Jon. It looks pretty deep."

"Don't worry. It's not my first."

"You still with us, mate?"

Howell had broken out the driver's window of a vaguely Soviet-looking flatbed, and he and Farrokh were pushing it into a position that blocked the street behind them.

"Not dead yet."

"Well, if we get pinned down here, you will be soon."

He was right. They didn't know how many infected were headed in their direction or the positions and strength of the Iranians fighting against them.

"Omidi gave it to them," Sarie said, sounding a little dazed. "He infected a bunch of innocent people to keep it alive."

"We'll worry about that later," Smith said. "If the guy who just shot me calls in our position or can hop enough rooftops to get above us again, we're going to have serious problems. We need to keep moving."

"How? He can—"

"Incoming!" Howell shouted, and they both spun to see a man sprinting around the corner. He let out something between a scream and a choking growl when he saw them, the blood that had run into his mouth spraying down the front of his shirt. Howell rested the butt of his pistol on the hood of the truck while Farrokh fired wildly, managing to hit the man in the stomach and left thigh. Howell did better, catching him just below the sternum and dropping him to the ground. The Brit stayed lined up on the man as he tried desperately to get up, not lowering his weapon until he went completely still.

"Keep our flank covered!" Smith said, pulling Sarie to the wall and tapping the rifle hanging around her neck. "I need you to do something for me."

"What?" she said.

He pointed to the roofline. "I need you to shoot the guy up there."

"Me? Why me?"

"Because I can't see straight, Farrokh can't shoot straight, and we need Peter behind us."

"It would be nice if we could get out of here," Howell called back. "Sooner would be better than later."

"Working on it!" Smith responded and then turned his attention back to Sarie. "Listen to me. I'm going to run out into the open again. When I do, lean around the corner and sight along the rooftop."

"Are you crazy? He almost killed you last time and now he'll be ready."

"Then you're going to have to hit him."

"I'm not a soldier, Jon. I—"

"You are today," he said, backing away. When he had a good ten yards to get a running start, he took a deep breath and charged forward, passing Sarie as she flattened herself against the building.

He heard a shot and saw the round impact a wall a few feet away. When the second sounded, he tensed, certain it would be the one that got him. He remained upright, though, and a moment later he was safely around the next corner.

A series of bright flashes threw shadows across the building next to him, and he eased back the way he had come, listening to a strange crackling that was impossible to decipher.

A careful peek around the corner revealed the shooter. He'd fallen into a tangle of power lines and was hanging upside down from them as sparks showered the ground.

Sarie, Howell, and Farrokh appeared a moment later, running hard in his direction. He ignored them, instead focusing his attention on a growing drone from above. Two C-130s were coming overhead, flying low enough that he could make out their open doors.

"I don't suppose you have any antiaircraft capability you've been keeping from me?" he said as Farrokh stopped next to him.

The Iranian just shook his head as the first parachutes opened against the deepening blue of the sky.

CHAPTER EIGHTY-NINE

Over Frederick County, Maryland, USA
December 5—0701 Hours GMT–5

They'd left the glare of the DC suburbs behind, and Larry Drake looked down into the darkness before turning his attention back to Dave Collen, who was sitting next to him in the back of the helicopter.

"Even with everything there is on the Iran–Uganda connection, it's still plausible that we thought it was too soft to pursue," Collen said through a headset isolated from the pilot.

"What are we going to say changed our minds and made us collect all this data?"

"This is where Brandon's death finally benefits us. We'll say he told us that he had unconfirmed reports of Iranian operatives meeting with President Sembutu and that he was in the process of following up when he died. We've been trying to look into it but losing him caused us to go temporarily blind in Kampala."

The best lies were the ones only a few degrees off the truth, and this very much qualified.

"Do we have anything at all that points to the fact that the attack on the facility is a resistance operation?"

"Nothing."

"Can we fabricate something?"

"Farrokh keeps his organization locked down tight and the president knows we don't have eyes there. It would be risky."

"Then we'll have to rely on the fact that it's the only

plausible guerrilla force that could attack a fixed position like that in Iran. The trick is going to be playing up the danger—that the parasite exists, that the Iranians have it, and that the facility is in play. We have the possibility that the infection Castilla saw on that video is loose in Iran, we have the possibility that the Iranian government has weaponized it and is planning on using it against us, and we have the possibility that Farrokh wants to get his hands on it to strengthen his position."

"The last one is a stretch."

"Is it? To date, we've considered the resistance to be a relatively peaceful, grassroots effort, and now we see evidence of a hierarchical organization with paramilitary capability. We have enough to make Castilla question everything he thinks he knows about Farrokh. If we're careful and don't miss anything, we still have a good chance of getting him to authorize a unilateral attack befo—"

A loud buzz drowned him out and suddenly the cabin was filled with the dull red pulse of a warning light. Drake flipped the switch reconnecting him to the pilot's headset just as the terrifying sound of the engine cutting in and out began.

"What the hell's going on? What's the problem?"

"I think it's a blockage in the fuel line!" the pilot said as the chopper dropped sickeningly and then struggled to regain altitude. "I've got to put it down. Now!"

Collen slammed himself back in his seat and tightened the harness around his shoulders, chest heaving with rapid, staccato breaths.

"What the hell are you talking about? We're over a forest!" Drake shouted into the microphone hovering in front of his mouth.

"There!" the pilot responded. "There's a clearing to the east."

The nose dipped and they dove for it, engine sputtering and choking, threatening to go silent at any moment.

Drake could feel the blood pounding in his temples and he slapped off his headset, fighting back the bile coming up in his throat. A long, formless shout rose above the alarm buzzer, and it was only when the skids slammed into the ground that he realized it was coming from him.

The harness tightened painfully across his chest and the screech of tearing metal filled his ears.

Then everything went silent. The pilot shut down power, killing the instrument lights and letting the momentum of the blades die. Blood was flowing from the side of Drake's head where it had hit the window, but otherwise he was unharmed. He'd made it.

The pilot didn't speak, instead kicking open his door and jumping out into the darkness. His footfalls echoed through the clearing for a moment and then faded as he retreated into the early morning gloom.

"Hey! Where are you going?"

No answer.

He turned to Collen and grabbed his shoulder. "Dave. Are you all right?"

He was still gasping for breath but managed to nod.

"The papers," Drake said, pointing to the sheets of highly classified material strewn around the tiny space. "Pick them up and get them back into your briefcase."

He sat there long enough to confirm that Collen understood and then shoved his way through the damaged door. His jaw tightened when he saw that the pilot, a decorated former Coast Guard man, had completely disappeared.

Drake pulled out his cell phone and looked down at it, swearing quietly when he saw that there was no signal. Had they called in a Mayday? He couldn't remember. The president's people would contact Langley when he didn't arrive, but how long would that take? He was wearing nothing but a suit jacket and it was below freezing.

"Son of a bitch!" he shouted, fear and frustration finally breaking down the calm facade it had taken a lifetime to build. He slammed the phone repeatedly into the side of the chopper, not stopping until parts of it were strewn out in the dirt around him. This was all supposed to have gone so smoothly. But then Castilla sent that damn black ops team and Gazenga decided to grow a spine. Now he was standing in the middle of nowhere with the president of the United States waiting to rake him over the coals. One mistake—one moment of confusion in the maze of lies he'd created—and it could all come crashing down on top of him.

He took a few deep, controlled breaths and watched the fog roll from his mouth in the dull light of dawn. "Dave! What the hell are you—," he started, but then fell silent. There was something at the edge of the clearing, something with an outline distinct from the trees.

They weren't alone.

CHAPTER NINETY

Outside Avass, Iran
December 5—1540 Hours GMT+3:30

Jon Smith shaded his eyes and watched as more canopies popped into existence above. Frightened voices rose from the fifty or so Avass residents they'd fallen in with and the pace of the group increased perceptibly, sweeping past the edge of town and into the open desert. Twenty yards ahead, Sarie's blond hair was visible as she and Farrokh pushed their way toward him.

"Seven injured people we could find," she said when she got within earshot.

"Did you talk to them? Did they have contact with anyone infected?"

Farrokh nodded. "One fell down a set of stairs and another was wounded by a bullet. But the others were attacked."

"And all five of them have open wounds," Sarie added. "I'm not sure how the higher parasitic loads are going to affect things, but I think we have to be ready for a faster than normal reaction."

"How long?"

"A guess would be seven hours before full symptoms. Eight if we're lucky."

"Is there any way we can separate them from the group?"

"An American, a Brit, and a South African trying to get families to abandon their injured?" Farrokh said. "I think not."

"What about you? You're Iranian and people know you."

"My position is even weaker, Jon. This is a very conserva-

397

tive, poorly educated part of the country. If these people knew who I was, they would probably kill me. And even if we keep my identity from them, they will still see me as a liberal, urban outsider."

Smith slowed and finally stopped, watching the haggard refugees flow past. Scared and unsure what was happening, they would do the same thing they had for a thousand years—disappear into terrain that no foreigner had any hope of navigating.

"What is it?" Howell said, making a subtle move for the pistol in his waistband. "What's wrong?"

What was wrong was that Smith had no idea what they were doing or where they were going. Groups like this, some probably with even more victims, were undoubtedly spreading out in every direction, surrounded by friends and family who had no way of understanding or dealing with what was going to happen. He'd completely lost control of the situation, and the idea that the Iranian military could regain that control might just turn out to be the most deadly delusion in history.

"Farrokh," Smith said. "Give me your phone."

The Iranian took a hesitant step back. "To do what? Order your military to destroy my country? To insert another dictator?"

"You want me to be honest?" Smith said, the anger obvious enough in his voice that people passing by began giving them a wider berth. "I don't know what Castilla will do. But this is going to spread—first through Iran, then through the region. At this point, a new dictator might be your best-case scenario."

"No!" Farrokh said, but his voice quickly lost its force. "We can ..."

"You can do what? Because as near as I can tell, we're just wandering around in the desert. You want to walk into that line of paratroopers? You want to go into those canyons with a bunch of infected people and wait for it to get dark?"

"No. I—"

"Then what's our next move, boss?"

A woman wearing a coat soaked with blood collapsed twenty feet away, unable to go any farther. The people around her rushed to her aid, and Sarie immediately began shoving her way toward them. "Stop! Don't touch her!"

No one spoke English and all she managed was to garner a few startled looks before being completely ignored.

Farrokh watched in silence for a moment, and then entered the PIN into his phone and held it out.

Smith dialed quickly, moving to the edge of the crowd with Howell scanning the faces around them for any hint of threat.

"Hello?"

There was definitely a sense of relief at the sound of Fred Klein's voice, but not as much as he'd hoped.

"We have a few problems here."

"Jon? Jesus! Are you all right? Where are you?"

"About a mile outside a town called Avass."

"Then it *was* you who attacked the underground facility south of there."

"You know about that?"

"We have a few satellite photos but that's about all. We've been trying to get U-2s overhead but there's a lot of Iranian air force activity in the area already and more on the way. What's your situation?"

"It's bad, Fred. The parasite was loose in that facility and I'm not sure what the status is there. What I do know is that there are infected people in Avass and people injured by them running for the canyons."

"This isn't a perfect connection, Jon, and there can't be any miscommunications between us. Are you telling me that there are infected, symptomatic people loose in Avass and that it's spreading into the countryside?"

"That's correct. Can I assume you've planned for this?"

"We've spent the last week moving biowarfare equipment and teams to Iran's borders with Iraq and Afghanistan. Your friends at USAMRIID and the CDC aren't confident it's going to be enough, though."

A well-justified lack of confidence, as far as Smith was

concerned. Containment plans generally assumed that victims got sick, lost mobility, and sought help. Contagion vectors were well understood, and some level of treatment was available even for pathogens as devastating as smallpox. None of those things were true in this case.

"We've been working more or less blind," Klein continued. "And I don't mind telling you that it's causing some panic. Right now the president is in with the Joint Chiefs and representatives from Europe, China, and Russia. We have a submarine armed with nuclear warheads off the coast and the idea of using it hasn't been taken off the table. Do you understand what I'm saying?"

Smith didn't respond, instead watching Sarie and Farrokh trying to physically pull people away from the injured woman. He thought of the town and of the residents caring for victims of similar attacks. He thought of the recently infected people who were already losing themselves in the canyons and of the ones who had made it to vehicles that were now carrying them to friends and relatives in surrounding villages.

"Jon? Are you still there?"

"Do it, Fred. Nuke everything. The entire area."

There was a long silence over the phone. "Again, I want to make sure that I'm not misunderstanding you. As an infectious disease specialist familiar with this particular illness, you are recommending the use of tactical nuclear weapons centered on your position."

"That's my recommendation."

"Is there anyone else there with you? Van Keuren? Peter?"

Smith held the phone out to Howell. He looked a bit confused but accepted it. "Hello? Yes, Brigadier. I recognize your voice."

Smith bent at the waist and concentrated on not throwing up. In all likelihood, he'd just doomed himself, his friends, and thousands of innocent people to death.

"A grazing shot to the head," he heard Howell say. "But he seems fine to me. Yes, unfortunately, I think that seems reasonable given the situation on the ground."

Smith felt a tap on his shoulder and Howell handed back the phone.

"Jon?" Klein said.

"I'm here."

"Can you give us your current position? I can call our people. There's a possibility that we could get a helicopter through and—"

"We both know that's not going to happen, Fred. Just do it, okay?"

Another long pause. "I'm going to pass along your recommendation to the president with my support. Thank you for everything you've done, Jon. And good luck to you."

The line went dead and he slid the phone weakly into his pocket.

"You all right, mate?" Howell said, putting a hand under his arm and helping him upright.

"Not my best day, Peter."

"I suppose things could have turned out better," he said, extending his hand. "But even so, I want you to know that it's been a privilege."

CHAPTER NINETY-ONE

Frederick County, Maryland, USA
December 5—0722 Hours GMT–5

"Hello?"

Lawrence Drake took a hesitant step forward, the sound of frozen leaves beneath his feet shockingly loud in the silence of the clearing. "Is someone out there?"

"Larry, who are—," Dave Collen said from inside the helicopter, but Drake cut him off.

"Shut up and secure those papers!"

The dense clouds to the east glowed dully with dawn, transforming the vague shapes into the outline of an SUV and a large panel van. Four human figures—three men and a woman—stood motionless in front of the vehicles.

The cold morning air caught in Drake's chest and he stopped, looking around him at the black wall of trees surrounding the clearing.

It was obvious now that the helicopter's mechanical failure had been staged—that the pilot had been paid to put down there. But by whom? Terrorists? Foreign agents? Were they here to kill him?

A few years ago, this would have been impossible. But the Muslims didn't play by the rules that had been set out during the cold war. No one was off-limits. Death was something to be courted, not avoided.

"What do you want?" he said through a bone-dry mouth.

Dawn's glow continued to intensify, adding detail to the scene in front of him. The woman was tall and athletic, with blond hair that gleamed in the semidarkness. Despite the fact that her face was still in shadow, there was something familiar about her, about the strength and grace that projected even when she was motionless.

He began to back away but then stopped short at the sound of her voice.

"Where do you think you're going, Larry?"

"Russell?" he responded. "Randi Russell? What the hell is this? What are you doing here?"

"I found the team you sent after Jon and Peter."

He tried to keep the shock and fear from his face but in the end could only hope that the gloom hid it. "What are you talking about?"

"It was all fake," she said. "Everything you saw about them crossing into Iran came directly from me and Chuck Mayfield: their plane's flight path from Diego Garcia, the satellite photos of the car taking them into the mountains. Everything. They were a hundred miles away the whole time."

For a moment, Drake found it hard to draw air into his lungs, but then he forced himself to relax. There was a way out of this. He just had to think.

If what she said was true and he had been working with disinformation, Smith was almost certainly still alive and involved with what was happening in Avass. That meant the call from Sepehr Mouradipour had been a setup and undoubtedly recorded.

He didn't dare look back at Collen, but the papers he was collecting consumed his mind. It was all there—everything they'd done, everything they'd kept from Castilla.

Calm down!

If Russell got her hands on those documents, it would be extremely complicated, but perhaps not the ruinous disaster it seemed on the surface. Politics could be a very messy business.

"I want to talk to the president."

Russell shook her head slowly. "I don't think he wants to talk to you."

Drake grunted in pain as a blow to the back of his legs

drove him to the ground. His arms were wrenched behind his back and he heard the metallic clack of handcuffs over the shouts of Dave Collen being dragged from the damaged helicopter.

When Drake was pulled to his feet again, Russell was walking across the clearing toward him.

"What are you going to do, Randi? Prosecute me? Do you know how much of this country's dirty laundry I have locked up in my head? The black ops, the renditions, the backroom deals? And what about you and Smith? Who exactly is it you work for? Could it be that the president has put together a group that exists outside the law? Because that could turn out to be very uncomfortable for him if it goes public."

She stopped a few feet away, her head tilted slightly as she examined him. "The docs told me that if the shooter you sent to my house had aimed an inch more to the left, the body armor wouldn't have saved me. At best I'd be paralyzed."

"You're a hell of an operator, Randi. I'll give you that. But you're out of your depth now."

"And *you're* a man who swore to protect this country and the people who live in it!" she shouted. "You owe them your loyalty, and you sure as hell owe your loyalty to the operatives out there risking their lives for you every day."

"Do you have any idea how naïve you sound, Randi? Now, get these damn handcuffs off me. And tell Castilla I'll be willing to offer my resignation for personal reasons. But that offer isn't going to last forever."

"Then off to a lucrative private-sector job, huh, Larry? No need to get bogged down in all this nonsense about you covering up a bioweapon that could kill millions of Americans. And what about all those innocent people in Uganda? Or the ones dying right now in Iran? What about Jon and Peter, who won't ever be coming home? We'll just forget all that too, right?"

Her reputation, combined with the very real fury in her voice, was admittedly enough to make him sweat. But it was all bluster. Randi Russell was just another soldier—an expendable cog in a machine that she didn't even have the capacity to fully understand.

"You can rant all you want, Randi, but Castilla isn't going to put me on the stand with what I know. And after the Lazarus fiasco, the CIA can't afford another black eye."

She laughed and started back toward the vehicles parked at the edge of the clearing. "Who sounds naïve now, Larry?"

Drake felt a gun against the back of his head and he was forced to follow. Collen came alongside, similarly motivated by a man carrying the briefcase containing their papers.

Ahead, the back of the panel van was open and Russell's men were pulling out three large sacks. Confused, Drake watched as they began dragging them toward the helicopter. It was only when they passed that he was able to identify what was inside the black plastic.

Corpses.

"Wait!" he said, stopping short. "What—"

The man behind Drake pushed him forward hard enough that he barely managed to keep from pitching onto the icy ground. Randi grabbed him by the back of the neck, pulling him upright, and shoved him into the back of the van. "Like you said, Larry, the CIA can't afford another black eye."

"*No!*" he shouted as Collen was thrown in after him.

The door slid down, leaving them in blackness as the engine came to life and the vehicle began lurching forward. A moment later, he heard a sound that he'd been dreading— the explosion that would incinerate the helicopter and the three bodies inside.

The entire world would believe he died in the crash.

There would be a state funeral, a eulogy praising his selflessness and service to the country. His wife would accept the flag from a coffin containing the body of a stranger, never knowing that her husband was lying in an unmarked grave carved from the country he'd betrayed.

CHAPTER NINETY-TWO

Near Avass, Iran
December 5—1839 Hours GMT+3:30

"Arfa! Do you copy? Respond!"

General Asadi Daei watched angrily as his men brought an armored SUV down the C-130's ramp with almost comic slowness. The biomedical team was already suited up and had been standing by the side of the dark road for almost five minutes.

The condition of their primary landing site had been far worse than the deskbound academics at Omidi's intelligence ministry reported, forcing them to fly over the road to Avass and search for a place wide and smooth enough to set down. It was an unforgivable error that had put them twenty minutes behind schedule and farther from the village than planned.

"Arfa! Respond!"

The radio sputtered to life and the barely intelligible voice of the man in charge of the containment troops became audible through the static. Daei stalked up the road, putting distance between him and the nervous scientists double- and triple-checking their equipment.

"General? Do you read me?"

"Barely. What's your situation? Have you secured the town center?"

A burst of gunfire came over the radio followed by indecipherable shouts from Arfa.

"Major! Are you there?"

"I'm here, sir. No, we haven't been able to fully secure the

406

area. It's difficult to tell the police from resistance, particularly now that we've lost the light. And there are civilians—"

"I don't care who's who!" Daei shouted. "You're to eliminate anyone who isn't actively helping you. Was that not clear?"

"It was, sir, but—"

"There are no excuses, Major! Follow your orders."

"Yes, sir."

His commander's reticence was understandable under the circumstances. What he didn't know, though, was that heavy bombers were on their way and that, upon Daei's orders, Avass would be obliterated with Arfa and his forces still in it. The remaining paratroopers would create a wide perimeter, cutting off any fleeing residents, and, in the end, forfeiting their lives, too. The area would be completely sterilized.

"Have you captured a parasite victim yet, Major?"

"We've made two attempts, but they're much faster and stronger than we anticipated. One was killed in a fall and we were forced to shoot the other."

Daei slammed a fist angrily against the C-130's fuselage as he continued up the road. The sound of approaching air cover became audible behind him, but he didn't bother to look back.

"I want to be perfectly clear, Major. If I arrive in Avass and you haven't secured a specimen, not only you but your family will pay the price. Am I being clear?"

Arfa responded, but between the static and the approaching jets, his words were impossible to understand. Daei spun angrily, looking into the sky at a tight formation of fighters barely visible in the moonlight. What in the name of Allah were they doing?

"Repeat your last transmission, Major. I—"

He fell silent when one of the fighters broke formation and began to climb, displaying an unmistakable profile against the black sky.

Daei dropped his radio and ran for the open desert. "Get away from the plane!" he shouted at the startled scientists watching him sprint across the loose sand. "Find cover!"

The blow seemed to come out of nowhere, lifting Smith off his feet and knocking the gun he'd been so carefully aiming from his hand. He tried to twist himself out from beneath the man who had jumped him but realized there wasn't time and instead braced for the impact with the rocky ground.

He ignored the soft crunch of at least one of his ribs and threw a hand out for the loose weapon. It was pointless, though. The man on top of him had both superior position and a fifty-pound weight advantage. He was going to get to it first.

"Peter! The g—"

There was a brief flash of blond hair in the darkness and suddenly the weight was gone. Smith rolled and grabbed the pistol, ignoring the excruciating pain in his side as Sarie began losing her wrestling match with the man she'd tackled. The scales swung back in her direction, though, when Smith pressed the gun against the back of the man's head.

He pulled her away, examining the moonlit faces around them over the sights of the pistol. The group of refugees they'd joined during their escape from Avass had dwindled to about twenty-five individuals, four of whom were definitely infected. Three were still in the confusion stage, but the other had just turned on two boys helping him walk.

Farrokh had immediately waded in, shouting in Persian and waving his machine gun, but the scene quickly turned to chaos. Some people fled, pushing and tripping over each other, while others tried to control the screaming, bleeding man and protect the boys from what Smith assumed was their father.

Howell had taken over the attempt to put the man down but was facing the same problem of a shifting crowd and dim light that Smith had been contending with. Finally, the infected man escaped the person trying to hold him and presented his chest for a split second before he could turn again on his fallen sons.

It was a stunning shot—barely missing no fewer than

four people before impacting center of mass. The man went down on his back, thrashing wildly and howling like a wounded animal.

By the time he went still, all eyes were on Howell and the gun still smoking in his hand. None of the people fully understood what was happening or why there were three Westerners with them, but they'd tolerated their presence. Now, though, a British stranger had just shot an unarmed man they'd known all their lives.

Farrokh tried to take advantage of the ominous silence to offer an explanation, but no one seemed to be listening. He hadn't been lying about his credibility in this part of Iran—it wasn't much better than theirs.

The boy whose life Howell had saved jumped to his feet and shouted at them, his accusations falling on what appeared to be sympathetic ears.

"I think we've worn out our welcome here," Smith said. "Time to go."

Farrokh ignored him, continuing his pointless explanation and barely managing to sidestep a much older man's lunge. More and more people approached, hurling epithets and insults that even Smith's nearly nonexistent Persian could decipher.

Finally, Farrokh faced reality and squeezed off a quick burst over the crowd's head before joining their retreat. They kept their weapons trained on the mob, dodging hurled rocks and not stopping until they'd put a good five hundred yards between them.

"The other three are going to go fully symptomatic in less than an hour," Sarie said. "We can't just leave those people. We're the only ones who're armed."

"The guns don't matter," Smith said. "They've turned against us. There's nothing more we can do."

"Nothing more we can do?" she responded, the fear and despair twisting her voice into something very different than what he remembered from their first meeting. "The Iranians aren't going to be able to control this. These people have no idea what they're facing."

"She's right," Farrokh said. "You said the Americans were going to help us, Jon. Where are they?"

"I don't know."

"What do you mean you don't know? You spoke with them."

"Yeah. I did."

"And?"

He looked at Howell, but there was no help there.

"I told them to wipe out the entire area."

"What do you mean 'wipe out'?" Sarie said.

"We have a nuclear submarine off the coast. I told them to use it."

There was a brief silence before Farrokh spoke. "I don't understand. By nuclear submarine, you mean a nuclear-powered submarine armed with conventional weapons—"

"I mean a submarine armed with nuclear missiles."

Smith saw it coming but didn't bother to defend himself, instead taking a rifle butt to the center of the chest and falling painfully to the ground. Howell's hand hovered over the gun in his waistband, but beyond that he didn't seem to want to get involved. Sarie just stood in dumbfounded silence.

"You told your people to attack my country with nuclear weapons?" Farrokh shouted, aiming his rifle at Smith's head. "I trusted you. My men died for you!"

"Farrokh...," he started. It was hard to get the words out with his cracked ribs and the weight of what he had done trying to suffocate him. "What choice did I have? I couldn't risk—"

An explosion flashed to the west, followed a moment later by a deep rumble that shook the ground. They all turned and saw a wall of flame at least a hundred feet high spring up from the main road about fifteen miles south of Avass.

The planes over it broke formation and began spreading out, their outlines gaining detail in the glow of the fire until Smith could positively ID them. American F-16s.

It took him longer than it should have to process what was happening. The prospect of certain death had dulled his sense of the here and now, bogging him down in past regrets.

"Castilla's not going to do it," he said finally. "He's not going to use the nukes! Farrokh, give me your phone again. If I can call in our position, there's a chance I can get us the hell out of here."

EPILOGUE

Central Iran
December 9—1618 Hours GMT+3:30

Smith steadied himself on a bracket supporting the Humvee's computer system as Randi Russell launched the vehicle across a washed-out section of road. They'd run into each other the day before at a UN-staffed mobile hospital where he was giving a briefing on the effects of the infection. She was part of a CIA team charged with preventing grassroots insurgencies from popping up and interfering with efforts to head off a pandemic.

"Are you sure you know where you're going, Randi? All I see out here is rocks and sand."

"Farrokh's a man who likes his solitude and anonymity," she shouted over the roar of the engine. "But now that we know who he is, you can count on the fact that we'll be keeping close track of him."

Sarie leaned up between the seats. "Is he all right?"

"Oh, he's fine. I think he's just milking a last little bit of peace and quiet before he has to jump into the middle of the chaos he's created."

Farrokh's people had uploaded hours of raw video depicting what had happened at the lab facility and Avass, effectively turning the entire world against Iran. The Russians and Chinese had finally seen the light and committed to heavy sanctions, Al Jazeera had turned into a twenty-four-hour-a-day anti-Iranian rant, and the United States was being publicly criticized by the Arab League for not just flattening the entire country.

412

"Is our position still that we're not going to jump in after him?" Peter Howell asked from the back.

"That's the agreement the politicians made," Randi replied. "Though it feels more like a Mexican standoff at this point."

She slammed on the brakes and skidded to a stop, pointing to what looked like a goat trail winding its way up a boulder-strewn slope. "That's where you'll find him."

"It looks really steep," Sarie said apprehensively. "And it's dead in the sun."

Her leg was mildly infected, and between the antibiotics, the fever, and the twenty-hour workdays, she was a little less spry than normal. Despite that, though, she let Howell help her to the ground and then came alongside the open driver's window. "It was good meeting you, Randi."

"Likewise. Now, are you sure you want to walk all the way up there? I'd be happy to drop you with a patrol on my way out."

"No, I want to say good-bye."

"Your call. I'll have someone here in two hours to pick you all up."

Sarie smiled and tapped the windowsill before limping off after Howell, who had already made it to the trail's first switchback.

"Don't want to join us?" Smith said.

She shook her head. "I think I'd rather keep a little anonymity where Farrokh is concerned. He's the West's darling today, but things have a way of changing. And when they do, a lot of times I'm the one who gets the call."

"Still the insufferable cynic."

Her lips curled into an enigmatic grin. "Be nice, Jon. You owe me."

"What—for the ride? It was only a few miles, and, as near as I can tell, you stole the Hummer."

She gazed thoughtfully into the desert. "Ever hear of Sepehr Mouradipour?"

"Iranian mercenary, right? Last I heard, he was operating in the Balkans or something."

"Your information is out of date. He was operating in Iran on Larry Drake's dime. If it hadn't been for me, you'd have walked right into his ambush."

Smith's expression went blank. He'd been given a sketchy briefing on Drake's betrayal and the suspiciously timed helicopter crash that he'd died in, but it was made clear that no questions on the subject would be entertained. This was a Covert-One operation—how the hell would Randi have learned about it, let alone gotten personally involved?

She seemed to be enjoying his distress and let the silence drag on for a while before speaking again. "Fred Klein says 'Hi', by the way."

Smith let out a breath that he hadn't realized he'd been holding, surprised at the intensity of the relief he felt. "I'm glad you're finally in, Randi. It's been hard keeping this from you."

She scowled. "Keeping what from me? I mean, you're just a simple country doctor, right?"

He opened his mouth to speak but she held up a hand. "You'll have plenty of time to grovel when you get back to the States and take me out to an incredibly expensive dinner."

"Can we split the wine bill?"

"Absolutely not," she said sternly and then pointed through the windshield at Sarie lurching up the steep slope. "Looks like your little girlfriend could use some help."

It was clearly a dismissal and Smith threw the door open. Before he slid out, though, he grabbed Randi's hand and gave it an exaggerated kiss. "You're a goddess among women. A pillar of virtue and beauty—"

"Good start," she said, shoving him through the door and leaving him laughing to himself in a cloud of dust and gravel. Dinner would probably run the better part of a paycheck, but it would be worth it. She was the best in the business, and with both her and Peter Howell watching his back, he might just live long enough to see his next birthday.

It took him longer than he expected to overtake Sarie, and he wrapped an arm around her waist, more because he

414

liked being close to her than because of any illusion he could help. In truth, he wasn't in much better shape than she was. Army doctors had taken an embarrassingly wide swath from his hair, and white gauze covered the thirty-five stitches it had taken to close the bullet graze on his scalp. Much worse, though, were the three cracked ribs that wouldn't allow him to take in more than a half breath before the pain became overwhelming.

Sarie pointed at Howell, who was picking his way nimbly through the boulders above them. "Why is it that we both look like we were run over by a truck and he looks like he just got back from golf?"

Smith smiled through a split lip. "Believe me, you're not the first person to ask that question. How are you feeling? Are you okay?"

"I'll live. But I don't think I'd want to do this kind of thing every day."

They finished the climb in silence and found Farrokh sitting cross-legged on the edge of a tall cliff. Howell was a few feet away, gazing into the valley at its base.

"I have to hand it to you," the Brit remarked as Smith came up behind him. "It's a hell of an operation."

Another example of Howell's gift for understatement. What it was, was nothing less than a miracle.

Below, the sun reflected off the greatest concentration of military and medical technology ever assembled: three mobile level-four labs, a temporary airstrip that had been built in less than seven hours, and a constant flow of transport planes dropping off supplies and equipment. Overhead, attack choppers from no fewer than twelve countries patrolled the desert floor. Farther up, spy satellites and surveillance planes from Russia, Europe, and the United States were using heat imagery to track every warm-blooded animal within a two-hundred-mile radius.

To the east was a massive city of tents emblazoned with red crosses and surrounded by temporary fencing—a holding area for anyone who'd been in contact with victims of the parasite but hadn't yet been cleared.

Machine-gun placements and razor wire had been set up at every known entrance to the canyons, along with thousands of buried mines. Every surrounding town and village had a contingent of coalition forces and their coordinates were locked into the navigational computers of redundant missile batteries. If an outbreak was reported and ground troops couldn't quickly gain control, even the most remote population centers could be completely incinerated in a matter of minutes.

"I normally object to politicians overriding the recommendations of men in the field," Howell continued. "But in this case ..."

Smith frowned perceptibly. He agreed that any day aboveground was a good day, but it had been a reckless decision on Castilla's part. The consequences of guessing wrong would have been almost too devastating to imagine.

But it appeared that the president hadn't guessed wrong. The last contact with a parasite victim had been forty-eight hours ago when an infected man charged a Belgian special forces team clearing a cave system to the north. Fortunately, he'd had a broken femur and the injury slowed him down enough to allow the soldiers to take him out before he got within fifty feet.

"I suppose you think I should thank the American people for not irradiating a third of my country," Farrokh said.

"Don't be too hard on Jon," Sarie replied. "If I'd been the one on the phone to the Americans, I might have told them the same thing."

The Iranian continued to look down at the coalition forces occupying his land. "And what is he telling them now? Why is it that we haven't received even the level of assistance given to the Libyans?"

Smith considered lying but knew that Farrokh would see right through it.

The video his people had posted to the Internet hadn't just shocked the outside world; it had created a massive backlash in Iran—allowing the formation of an unlikely alliance among secular liberals, moderates, and even conservative followers of a few imams who had pronounced bioweapons un-Islamic. The size and dynamism of the demonstrations erupting across Iran were so far beyond what had come before, the government was forced to immediately enlist the military in a last-ditch effort to cling to power.

"It was a complicated situation, Farrokh. We—"

"Can I assume those complications are the reason that over three thousand of my people have died at the hands of the Iranian army in the last forty-eight hours?"

Smith sighed quietly. "Nobody wanted this. But you have to understand what we're dealing with here: more foreign militaries and UN forces than even I can keep track of, press, international observers, and organizations like WHO and the CDC. Khamenei has access to modern missiles, and if even one or two made it through our defenses, the whole operation might have fallen apart. Then you could have seen this infection in Riyadh, or Cairo, or Damascus. There was no way we could take that chance."

"So you made a bargain with the devil."

"We told Khamenei that if he left us alone, we'd do the same. But we also made it clear that if so much as a fire-cracker goes off within a hundred miles of one of our people, we'll take out his entire military and impose a no-fly zone until we get color eight-by-tens of him dangling from a rope."

"So we're on our own," Farrokh said.

"You never miss an opportunity to tell me that you want the West to stay out of your business. Well, we have a saying in America: Be careful what you wish for."

"And the parasite?"

"Not my sphere of influence anymore," Smith said. "President Castilla's put a certain South African you know in charge of that part of the operation."

Farrokh twisted around and looked up at Sarie. "Is this true?"

"One hundred percent," she said, jabbing Smith in the shoulder. "From now on, the colonel here will be calling me ma'am."

Smith grinned and considered a salute, but he wasn't sure he could lift his arm that far.

"Have you been able to cure the people who have contracted it?" Farrokh asked.

She shook her head sadly. "Most of the victims we've tried to treat were already fully symptomatic. At that point, the brain damage is irreversible and there isn't really anything we can do for them. I think that if we can catch the infection within an hour or so of transmission, a cocktail of existing antiparasitics might work. But so far we haven't been able to find the right combination."

"It's still spreading, then?"

"I'm cautiously optimistic that it's not," Sarie said. "We don't understand exactly how the parasite affects different animals, though, so we're still running tests. The good news is that it's too arid out here to have much wildlife, and the livestock is fairly easy to keep track of. I think we're going to be okay."

"And if you're wrong?"

She put a hand on the Iranian's shoulder. "Maybe you should try focusing on the bright side for a change. At least you're not an ashy outline on some wall."

AUTHOR'S NOTE

It all started for me when I was one year old.

My father came in and announced that he'd quit his job and joined the FBI—something my mother didn't even know he was interested in. We were shipped off to her parents while he trained in Quantico and then quickly found ourselves in Salt Lake City, one of our many homes over the years.

As it turns out, this wasn't as impulsive as it first seemed. My father grew up in a small cotton-farming town in southeast Missouri, and on a visit to his family when I was a teenager, my grandmother told me the story of his first encounter with the Bureau. It was 1953 and there had been a bank robbery in the area, prompting an FBI agent to interview the owner of the local general store. My father, then twelve years old, wandered in for supplies and hid behind a shelf to listen. When he got home, he told his mother about the experience—that the man had been "dressed real fine and talked real good". And that one day he, too, would be a G-man. She just smiled.

Growing up in a Bureau family is about as interesting as it gets, but also a bit challenging. Of course, there are the constant moves that can be tough on a kid trying to fit in. Even stranger, though, is the sense of secrecy. It may be that my early training as a novelist came from filling in imaginary details to circumspect conversations I overheard. The need-to-know attitude is oddly pervasive, as anyone who has watched my father and me move a ladder will attest. It's always teetering upright with him yelling "Left! Right! Not that far right, for Christ's sake!" Now that he's retired, I aspire to get him to just tell me the ladder's final destination before we pick it up. I'm not hopeful, though.

Whatever the negatives, it was all worth it. How many kids get to have dinner with a man who, by law, cannot be photographed? Or drink a beer with the SAS? Or discuss Northern Ireland with the head of the Royal Ulster Constabulary? And then there was the time I came home from my summer job and was told that we were having dinner with an insurance salesman who needed help with the FBI-related sections of his third novel. He was nice enough to bring us a copy of his first effort. It had been published by the Naval Institute Press under the title *The Hunt for Red October*.

And how many people get to read about their college graduation dinner in history books? It was 1988 and my family was at a restaurant in London where my father was the legal attaché. About halfway through the hors d'oeuvres, someone from the embassy came in and told us that a Pan Am flight had gone down in a little town called Lockerbie. That was the last I saw of my father for months.

With all this cloak and dagger, it was hard not to be a huge fan of thriller novels. The first I can remember reading was *Shogun*, still vivid in my mind because I was supposed to do my seventh-grade book report on it and was a little shocked to find out there was a second volume. I wasn't only a fan, though, I was also a critic. Authors who made factual errors or failed to faithfully capture the operatives they wrote about drove me crazy. And that led me to focus on the masters of the genre— people like Jack Higgins, John le Carré, and Robert Ludlum.

So it's a great honor for my eleventh novel to be part of the Covert-One series. Hopefully, you enjoyed reading it as much as I enjoyed writing it.

Kyle Mills
May 12, 2011

If you have enjoyed

The Ares Decision

Don't miss

Robert Ludlum's ™
THE JANSON COMMAND

Written by Paul Garrison

Available now in Orion hardback

ISBN: 978-1-4091-1647-9

PROLOGUE
THE RESCUE

Three Years Ago
41°13′ N, 111°57′ W
Ogden, Utah

"Ogden's a great town if you like hiking and mountain biking and skiing." Doug Case gripped the broken armrests of his secondhand wheelchair and pretended they were ski poles. "That's what I'm doing here, since you ask. How'd you happen to track me down? I wiped my names from the VA computers."

Paul Janson said, "When it all goes to hell, people go home."

"The place where they have to take you in? Not me. I'm not asking any favors."

"I don't see you getting any either."

Case's home was the mouth of an abandoned railroad tunnel with a view of a garbage-littered empty lot, a burned-out Kentucky Fried Chicken, and the snowy Wasatch Mountains. He hunched in his chair with a frayed backpack on his lap, stringy hair down to his shoulders, and a week of beard on his face. His dull gaze flickered occasionally toward four muscular teenage gangbangers who were eyeing them from a Honda parked beside the KFC.

Paul Janson sat on an upended grocery cart. He wore lightweight assault boots and wool trousers, a sweater, and a loose black ski shell.

"Kill me and get it over with," Case told him. "I don't feel like playing games."

3

"I'm not here to kill you."

"Just do it! Don't worry, I won't defend myself." He shifted the pack on his lap.

Janson said, "You are assuming that I still work for Consular Operations."

"Nobody quits Cons Ops."

"We have an arrangement. I went private. Corporate security consulting. Cons Ops calls me now and then. Now and then I call back."

"You never were one to burn bridges," Case conceded. "You work alone?"

"I have someone to bring along if I need a sniper."

"Good?"

"As good as I've ever seen."

"Where from?" Case asked, wondering who of that caliber Janson had recruited.

"Top of the talent pool," was all Janson would reveal.

"Why'd you quit Cons Ops?"

"I woke up one morning remembering all the people I killed for the wrong reasons."

Case laughed. "For Christ's sake, Paul! The State Department can't have covert operators *deciding* who to kill. When you have to kill somebody to do the job, you kill him. That's why they're called sanctioned in-field killings."

"Sanctioned *serial* killings was more like the truth. I lay in bed counting them up. Those I should have. Those I shouldn't have."

"How many in total? Shoulds and shouldn'ts."

"Forty-six."

"I'll be damned. I edged you out."

"Forty-six *confirmed*," Janson shot back.

Case smiled. "I see your testosterone hasn't passed its sell-by date."

He looked Janson up and down. The son of a bitch hadn't aged. Paul Janson still looked thirty-something, forty-something, fifty. Who knew with his close-cropped hair a neutral iron-gray color? And he still looked like somebody you wouldn't look at twice. Unless you were another profes-

4

sional and then if you were really, really good, you'd look twice and see the shoulders under the jacket and the watchful eyes and by then it might be too late.

Janson said, "We have company."

The gangbangers were strutting toward them.

"I've got 'em," said Case. "You got lunch." The empty Sonic burger bags were neatly folded under one of his wheels. Doug Case let them get within ten meters before he said, "Gentlemen, I'm offering one free lesson in survival. A survivor never gets in the wrong fight. Turn around and go away."

Three of them puffed up. But their leader, the smallest, shot an appraising glance at Case and another at Janson, and said, "We're outta here."

"The guy's in a fuckin' wheelchair."

The leader punched the dissenter hard in the ear and herded them away. "Hey, kid!" Case shouted after him. "You got what it takes. Join the army. They'll teach you what to do with it." He grinned at Janson. "Don't you love raw talent?"

"I do," said Janson and called in a voice accustomed to obedience, "Come here!" The kid came, light on his feet, wary as a stray. Janson gave him a business card. "Join the army. Call me when you make buck sergeant."

"What's that?"

"A rung up the ladder that says you're going places."

Janson waited until the Honda squealed away on smoking tires. "I remembered something else. I remembered every idea I used to believe that I turned my back on."

"You could use a dose of amnesia."

"There's none available."

Case laughed again. "Remember when that happened to an operator? Forgot everything. Woke up beating the crap out of people. Couldn't remember how he learned close combat. What the hell was his name? … I can't remember. Neither could he. Unlike you; you remember everything. Okay Paul, if you're not here to kill me, what are you doing in fucking Ogden?"

5

"Telling the truth about what I did is pointless if I don't atone."

"Atone? What? Like an AA drunk apologizing to people he was mean to?"

"I can't change what I did, but I can pay back the next guy."

"Why not just buy a pardon from the pope?"

The sarcasm button didn't work. Janson was deaf to it. He said, "You take the skills of observation we learned and turn them into yourself, it's not a pretty sight."

"Saul on the road to Damascus discovers his moral compass and changes his name to Paul? But you already are Paul. What are you going to change? The world?"

"I am going to do my best to save every covert government operator whose life was wrecked by his covert service. Guys like you and me."

"Leave me out of this."

"Can't."

"What do you mean?"

"You're my first project."

"A million people hold top secret clearances. If one in a hundred work undercover that's ten thousand covert agents you could save. Why me?"

"Some people say you were the worst."

Case returned a bitter smile. "Some said I was the *best*."

"Fact is, *we* were the worst."

"I don't need saving."

"You're living outdoors. Winter is coming. You're hooked on Percocet and the docs have cut you off. When this month's prescription runs out you'll be scrambling to find it on the street."

"Paul Janson's famously accurate research?"

"You'll be dead by Valentine's Day."

"Janson's renowned discerning analytic tradecraft?"

"You need saving."

"I don't want saving. Get out of here. Leave me alone."

"I've got a van with a ramp."

Doug Case's pale, grizzled cheeks flamed angry red. "You

6

got a van with a ramp? *You got a van with a ramp?* You got shooters in the van going to help you wrestle me up your fucking ramp?"

An awkward smile tightened Janson's face. For the first time since appearing at the mouth of Doug Case's railroad tunnel, he looked unsure. The man they called "The Machine" was suddenly vulnerable, and Doug Case pressed his attack.

"You're falling down on the planning end, fella. No assaulters in the van. No rehearsal. No quick-reaction force backup. No contingency. You're kind of, sort of, fumbling on impulse. Should have gone about this the way you'd plan a Cons Ops job. Tortured soul muddles toward atonement? And you're going to get *me* straightened out?"

"More than straightened out. We're going to put you back together with a life."

"With a *life*? So first you'll get me off the Perc? Then you'll have shrinks fix my head? And when the docs get through you'll find me a career that will employ my considerable talents? Go to hell."

"You will be made whole."

"Maybe even find me a girl?"

"If you want one, you'll be whole enough to find one on your own."

"Jesus, Paul, you're as wired and freaked out as I am. Who in your mental wilderness do you imagine would pay for this fantasy?"

Janson said, "On my last job someone deposited a ton of money in my overseas accounts to make it seem I turned traitor. That someone no longer exists. Money will not be an issue."

"If you ever do rope some poor fool into your pipe dream, you'll need more than money. You'll need help. Lots of it. You'll need a staff. Hell, you'll need an entire company."

Again Janson looked unsure. "I don't know about that. I've had it with companies. I've had it with institutions. I've stopped trusting any more than two people in one room."

"Poor, tormented Paul. Trying to make everything right

7

by saving the worst guy you know, singlehanded? What are you going to call this outfit? The Paul Janson Institute for Raising Fucked-up Former Field Agents Out of Deep Shit? No, keep it simple: the Phoenix Foundation."

Janson stood up. "Let's go, my friend."

"This guy ain't going anywhere. And I'm not your friend."

"Maybe not," Janson agreed. "But we've worked together and I could be sitting where you are, so we are brothers."

"Brothers? Is your halo pinching?" Doug Case shook his head, scratched an armpit, and covered his face with his dirty hands. After a while, he lowered his left hand and spoke through the fingers of his right. "They called you 'The Machine'. Remember? Some operators they call an animal. Some a machine. A machine usually beats an animal. But not always."

In a blur of coordinated movement drilled ten thousand times, Case's left hand flashed from his knapsack pinching the barrel of a Glock 34 9mm automatic between thumb and forefinger. His right hand closed around the butt, forefinger curling into the trigger guard and his left pulled back the slide, loading a round into the chamber and cocking the pistol with the speed of liquid flame.

Janson kicked it from his hand.

"*Fuck!*"

Doug Case rubbed his wrist where Janson's boot had connected. Should have remembered that Cons Ops combat instructors, the best in the world, had a saying: Lightning-fast; nano-fast; Janson-fast.

Janson scooped up the gun. He was suddenly grinning ear to ear, optimistic, full of hope, and absolutely convinced he could fix what was broken. "I see you're not completely screwed up."

"What gives you that idea?"

Janson tapped the Glock. "You replaced the crappy factory sights with ghost rings."

He removed the magazine and pocketed it, removed the round from the chamber, snapped the knapsack off Case's lap, removed two spare magazines from a side pocket, pulled a third from the waistband of his sweatpants, and handed the empty gun back to Doug Case.

"When do I get the rest of it?"

"Graduation day."

PART ONE

THE MOTHER OF ALL RESERVES

ONE

Now
1°19´N, 7°43´E
Gulf of Guinea, 260 Miles South of Nigeria, 180 Miles West of Gabon

"Vegas Rules," said Janet Hatfield, captain of the *Amber Dawn*. Her three-thousand-ton offshore service vessel was running up the Gulf of Guinea on a black night, pitching and rolling in following seas. Her voice rang with quiet authority in the near silence of the darkened pilothouse. "What you saw on *Amber Dawn* stays on *Amber Dawn*."

"You already swore me to Vegas Rules when we sailed from Nigeria."

"I'm not kidding, Terry. If the company finds out I snuck you aboard, they'll fire my ass."

"And a lovely ass it is," said Terrence Flannigan, MD, nomadic corporate physician, globetrotting womanizer, world-class snake. He raised his right hand and gave Janet Hatfield a sleepy-eyed grin. "Okay. I swear, again, to keep my mouth shut about *Amber Dawn*, about oil in general and deep-water petroleum exploration in particular, cross my heart and hope to die."

The captain, a solidly built blonde of thirty-five, turned her back on the snake and ran an uneasy eye over her radar. For the past several minutes the screen had been throwing out a ghost target. The mystery pinprick of light fading and reappearing was too dull to be another ship, yet bright enough to make her wonder what the heck was out there. The radar was a reliable unit, a late-model Furuno. But she

13

had the lives of twelve people in her care: five Filipino crew, six American petroleum scientists, and one stowaway. Thirteen, if she counted herself, which she tended not to.

Was the hot spot only sea clutter? Or an empty oil drum bobbing in the heavy seas, topping crests, hiding in troughs? Or was it something bigger, like an unreported, half-sunken hulk that she did not want to run into at fifteen knots?

It glowed again, closer, as if it were not merely drifting, but moving toward her. She fiddled with the radar, adjusting range and resolution. Otherwise, the sea looked empty, except for some large oil tankers a safe twenty miles to the west. A single land target at the top of the screen marked the summit of Pico Clarence, the six-thousand-foot volcanic mountain at the center of Isle de Foree, tonight's destination. "Foree rhymes with moray," she told visiting company brass new to the Gulf of Guinea oil patch. "Like the eel with the teeth."

She glanced at her other instruments. Compass, autopilot, and a wide panel of gauges monitoring the diesel generators that powered the twin three-thousand-horsepower electric Z-drive thrusters all gave her standard readings. She stared intently at the night-blackened bridge windows. She grabbed her night-vision monocular, shouldered open a heavy, watertight door, and stepped out onto the stubby bridge wing into equatorial heat, humidity she could slice with a knife, and the brain-numbing roar of the generators.

The southwest monsoon was blowing from behind, swirling diesel smoke around the house. The following seas had gathered ponderous momentum rolling three thousand miles up the African coast from Cape Town. They lifted the ship's stern and plunged its bow nearly to the foredeck. The heat and humidity had the captain sweating in seconds.

Her night-vision device was an eighteen-hundred-dollar birthday splurge to herself to help spot navigation buoys and small craft. It did not magnify, but it pierced the dark dramatically. She glassed the sea ahead. The 2G image intensifier displayed everything green. Nothing but whitecaps swirling like lime chiffon. Probably just a barrel. She retreated back into the cool quiet of the air-conditioning. The red glow of the instruments reflected in Flannigan's come-here smile.

"Don't even think about it," she warned him.

"I am merely offering to express my gratitude."

"In four hours you can express your gratitude to the ladies of Porto Clarence's massage parlors."

Low-rent Eastern European and Chinese cruise ships had discovered the capital city. A mix of poverty, an embattled dictator desperate for cash, and the legendary beauty of Isle de Foreens' West African and Portuguese bloodlines had sex tourism booming in the old colonial deepwater port.

Terry paced the pilothouse. "I've been company physician on enough oil jobs to know to keep my trap shut. But this voyage is the most secret I've ever seen."

"Stop saying that."

"You spent the week towing hydrophone streamers and air guns. When was the last time your OSV was Rube Goldberg-ed into a seismic vessel?"

"Last month." Janet Hatfield kicked herself the instant she admitted it.

Terry laughed. "The 'captain's curse'. You love your boat too much to keep a secret. This isn't the first time? Are you kidding? She's an offshore service vessel, not an oil hunter. What is going on?"

"Forget I said that. I shouldn't have—So it's weird. So what? When the company makes me vice president of marine services, I'll ask why. Till then, I'll drive the boat. Now shut up about it. Jesus, I should have left you in Nigeria."

"I'd be dead."

"Roger that," Janet Hatfield agreed. It was easier than ever to die in the oil-soaked Niger Delta. Militants kidnapped petroleum workers right off their rigs, drunken soldiers strafed their own checkpoints, and fanatics rampaged in the name of Jesus and Muhammad. But catnip-to-women Dr. Terry Flannigan had come close to getting killed the old-fashioned way: a jealous husband with a machete; a rich chief, no less, with the political connections to get away with hacking up the wife-poacher.

"Janet, where did we go wrong?" Terry asked with another soulful smile.

"Our relationship collapsed under its own lack of weight."

He made a better friend than lover. As a boyfriend he was treacherous, head over heels in love with himself. But as a friend-friend, there was something steady deep inside Terry that said he would take a bullet for you. Which was why Janet Hatfield had not hesitated to bundle him aboard before the angry husband killed him. For ten days she had hidden him from the crew in her cabin, "airing" him when it was her watch.

The bridge and her attached cabin stood in splendid isolation atop a four-story deckhouse near the front of the ship. Under it were crew cabins, mess and galley, and the lounge that the petrologists had taken over as their computer and radio room. The scientists had declared it off-limits to the crew. They even told her that the captain had to ask permission to enter. Janet had informed them that she had no plan to enter unless it caught fire, in which case she would not knock first.

"You know what the petrologists are doing now?"

Terry was staring out the back windows, which looked down on the hundred-foot-long, low and flat cargo deck, empty tonight but for the OSV's towing windlass, deck crane, and capstans.

"Get away from the window before they see you."

"They're throwing stuff overboard."

"What they're doing is their business."

"One of them is crawling around with a flashlight— Oh, he dropped something."

"What are they throwing?" she asked in spite of herself.

"Computers."

Belowdecks, jubilant petrologists peeled off their sweat-soaked shirts and did a victory dance in the now empty computer room. They had worked twenty-four hours a day for ten days, trapped on a boat where possession of booze or drugs or even a bottle of beer would get you banned from

16

the oil business for life. Now they were headed for a well-earned party in the brothels of Porto Clarence, having successfully uploaded multiple terabytes of the hottest 3-D seismic data on the planet.

The data acquisition was done, the client's seismic model refined, the success of what oilmen called an elephant hunt confirmed beyond any doubt. The client had acknowledged receipt of the densely encrypted satellite transmissions and ordered them to throw the computers into the sea. Every laptop, desktop, even the fifty-thousand-dollar subsurface-modeling workstation that took two men to lift over the side of the ship. The monitors went, too, so no one would see them and ask what they were for, as did the hydrophones and air guns and their mil-spec satellite transmitter.

In a few more hours the petrologists would celebrate the discovery of the "mother of all reserves"—billions and billions of barrels of oil and trillions upon trillions of cubic feet of natural gas that would transform Isle de Foree from a remote plantation island trickling oil through a neglected infrastructure into a West African Saudi Arabia.

"Hey, Janet. How many dinosaurs died to make the oil patch?"

"Algae. Not dinosaurs."

Terry Flannigan stared at the dark ahead of the boat. The big secret could only be about oil. The water was miles deep here, but if you took the long view in eons, eras and epochs, the seabed was actually an extension of the shallow African coast. For more years than there were stars in the sky, the Niger River had been dumping sediment into the Atlantic Ocean. This slurry of mud, sand, and dead plants and animals had filled the troughs, rifts, and clefts of the Atlantic, and had kept spilling across the continental slope into the deep and continued seaward, drifting, filling. A lady petrologist once told him that the compacted fill was eight miles deep.

"What did dinosaurs make? Coal?"

"Trees made coal," Janet answered distractedly, her eyes

locking on the radar. She switched on the powerful docking lamps. They lit a brilliant hundred-yard circle around the OSV. "Oh, shit!"

"What?"

An eighteen-foot rigid inflatable boat driven by enormous Mercury outboards swooped out of the dark bristling with assault rifles and rocket launchers. Janet Hatfield reacted quickly, grabbing the helm to override the autopilot. The RIB was struggling in the heavy seas. Maybe she could outrun them. She turned *Amber Dawn*'s heels to it, locked the new course, rammed her throttles full ahead, and yanked her radio microphone down from the ceiling.

"Mayday, Mayday, Mayday. This is *Amber Dawn, Amber Dawn, Amber Dawn*. One degree, nineteen minutes north. Seven degrees, forty-three minutes east.

"One degree, nineteen minutes north. Seven, forty-three east. One degree, nineteen minutes north," she said, repeating her position. "Seven degrees, forty-three minutes east." They couldn't help if they couldn't find her.

"Pirates boarding *Amber Dawn*. Pirates boarding *Amber Dawn*. One degree, nineteen minutes north. Seven degrees, forty-three minutes east."

There was never a guarantee that anyone was listening. But the 406 MHz satellite EPIRB, which was out on the bridge wing in its float-free bracket, would broadcast her position continuously in case of sinking. She pushed through the door again to switch it on manually.

The inflatable was so close she could see eight soldiers dressed in camouflage. *Jungle camouflage on a boat?*

They had to be from Isle de Foree, she thought, the only land within the inflatable's range. But they couldn't be government troops in that little commando boat. Free Foree Movement rebels? Pirates or rebels, what did they want? The only thing valuable on an offshore service vessel was the crew. To hold hostage or for ransom. So they wouldn't kill her people. At least not yet.

Muzzle flashes lit the inflatable like a Christmas tree and all the windows in *Amber Dawn*'s bridge shattered at once.

Janet Hatfield felt something tug hard in her belly. Her legs skidded out from under her. She pitched backward into Terry's arms and she almost laughed and said, "You never stop trying, do you?" except she couldn't speak and was suddenly afraid.

A cargo net edged with grappling hooks cleared the low side of *Amber Dawn*'s main deck, clanged onto steel fittings, and held fast. Seven FFM insurgents scrambled aboard with their assault rifles, leaving their rocket launchers with one man in their boat. They were lean, fit, hard-faced fighters with the distinctive café-au-lait coloring of Isle de Foreens. But they took their orders from a broad-shouldered South African mercenary named Hadrian Van Pelt.

Van Pelt carried a copy of *Amber Dawn*'s crew list.

He sent two men to the engine room. Bursts of automatic fire echoed up from below and the generators fell silent, but for one powering the lights. The men stayed below, opening sea cocks. Seawater poured in.

Two others kicked open the door to the improvised computer room. Van Pelt followed with the crew list. "Over there! Against the wall."

The petrologists, shirtless and terrified, backed against the wall, exchanging looks of disbelief.

Van Pelt counted heads. "Five!" he shouted. "Who's missing?"

Eyes flickered toward a closet. Van Pelt nodded at one of his men who triggered a short burst, shredding the door. The ship rolled and the body of the scientist hiding there tumbled out. Van Pelt nodded again and his men executed the rest.

A burst of gunfire from the quarters on the levels above spoke the end of *Amber Dawn*'s Filipino crew. Eleven down. Only the captain to go. Van Pelt drew his pistol and climbed the stairs to the bridge. The door was locked and made of steel. He signaled a soldier, who duct-taped a chunk of C-4 onto it. They sheltered halfway down the steps and covered their ears. The plastic explosive blew the door open with a

19

loud bang and Van Pelt vaulted through it.

To the mercenary's surprise, the captain was not alone. She was sprawled on the deck, a pretty blonde in blood-soaked slacks and blouse. A man was kneeling over her, working with the sure-handed economy of a battlefield medic.

Van Pelt raised his pistol. "Are you a doctor?"

Terry Flannigan was holding death in his hands, and when he looked up from Janet's riddled chest to the gunman standing in the door, he was staring death in the face.

"What kind of doctor?" the gunman demanded.

"Trauma surgeon, you asshole. What does it look like?"

"Come with me."

"I can't leave her. She's dying."

Van Pelt stepped closer and shot Janet Hatfield in the head. "Not anymore. Get in the boat."